BEACON

BEACON

NATHAN STONE

This is for you, Dad.
I'm sorry you never got to read it.

1 /   A BLINKING RED LIGHT

A blinking red light. She just didn't see it, not straight away, not with sufficient time, and that's how it began.

Her gaze was on the data, and her thoughts on the calculations. No, that wasn't true; she'd been focussing on that cream-cheese breakfast bagel, its cinnamon aroma and dense raisin filled flesh filling her mouth with saliva and bringing a sympathetic ache to her jaw.

Not now, though. Now that light, blinking or otherwise, was the most important object in the lab.

Kim licked her fingers and blew the remaining crumbs off her nice, expensive top. It wasn't special, no gold thread woven into the fabric or high-end designer label in the back. Normal people doing normal jobs would wear this top. Human beings with friends that could cope with too much noise or light. That was why she liked it, and she didn't want to ruin it, so she didn't stop brushing or blowing until she felt that the one small blob of sauce that remained on her just-too-big stomach bulge wouldn't stain. Then she turned her attention back to the monitor. She didn't like what she saw.

There was supposed to be a single line, instead several traced across the screen, which meant the calibration was still wrong.

"Son-of-a.."

Her voice cut some much needed punctuation through the silence and then outstayed its welcome by reverberating around the open plan workspace, the price of high ceilings and hard surfaces.

Reflex curled the corners of her mouth upwards into a rictus of bared teeth and creased skin, which she aimed at the project lead desk. Years of workplace bullying had honed this instinct, along with the constant need to hide the disrespect she had for her colleagues.

Fortunately, she had the entire floor to herself, so allowed her face to relax back into its default mix of snarled anxiety with a hint of constipation, and her eyes returned to the pair of lines traversing the screen.

They were getting further apart.

"Oh, come on, seriously!"

Four years, that's how long she'd been working on this technology. Worse, she was an unpaid intern, so the dangerous conditions and extreme hours didn't come with any money. During that time, she'd made no friends and had some of her best ideas stolen.

Then a few months ago, Paul squeezed out a huge metaphorical turd all over her worn through life by hurdling one of the biggest roadblocks they'd encountered. Just to rub her nose in it, he'd used one of those stolen ideas and taken full credit for it.

She could have taken the high ground and just been happy with the project. Or maybe put laxatives in his coffee. Instead, she would show everyone how indispensable she was by putting the entire system together on her own, and she would do it as soon as she could get the place to herself that following Tuesday. Four years ago, she'd started on a Tuesday, so the choice had a nice symmetry, but mostly no one worked Tuesday mornings. That meant no one would see her fail if nothing happened, which was handy.

Only she couldn't wait, so she'd come in late Monday night instead. Like Tuesday mornings, no one would be there since social etiquette demanded a post weekend early night and whatnot, but there was a disadvantage which she hadn't been aware of. The lab had its own power source, separate from the mains grid and in theory uninterruptible. They occasionally tested it for fail-safes, disabling and then re-enabling, to be sure that experiments reliant on vast amounts of power wouldn't render the surrounding county of Hampshire uninhabitable if an emergency arose, a sensible precaution to be sure.

What she didn't know because no-one told her, and to be fair she'd never asked, was that it was an automated test, and occurred every Tuesday morning at one am.

There was some residual power in the capacitors, of course, so disaster waited a few moments, but at one oh-two am, that red light had blinked and everything changed.

Kim reached for one of the many stacks of papers piled around a nearby workbench, feeling some tension under her arm, and then unexpected freedom as the seam in her precious top gave way.

Thinking back to a strategy taught by her school behavioural therapist, she counted to ten in her head, but just as it had at age seven, all it did was delay the inevitable screaming rage by around ten seconds.

"Well, that's just some flaming bull-poop right there!"

She shouted at no one before pulling at the torn fabric and ripping a hole big enough to fit an overweight Dalmatian through.

The clock clicked over to nine thirty am. In the before times, others would now filter through security doors carrying coffee and packed lunches, and there was that one guy with his flask of one twenty proof 'tea'. That didn't happen anymore, but there could still be a visit and she didn't like the colour of the bra she was wearing today, so felt it best to cover it back up.

The complex was enormous, taking up the entire third and fourth basement levels and built around an atrium that funnelled outside light into sun pipes that provided free light during the day. The store was on the far side, past the lab and just outside the secondary test chambers, which meant quite a hike. She headed out, but as Kim rounded the first corridor and turned toward her destination proper, an orange-purple tint in the natural light caught her eye.

The damned clock was wrong again. It wasn't nine thirty at all, but much later. She made a mental note and continued.

Since arriving, the key panel had developed an exotic fungal growth covering the three and six, so she grabbed a repurposed screwdriver and chiselled off the fruiting bodies. They scuttled away after bouncing with a low squeak, leaving her to enter the access code. Inside, she chose a navy-blue coverall, considered her ensemble, and removed the ruined top along with her skirt, before climbing into the scratchy cotton romper.

The zipper stuck halfway. Second attempt it wedged solid three-quarters up, better, so she shrugged and left. The morning hue was a colour that defied explanation but resembled green if you squinted. Purple meant it was late after-noon. Kim liked the purple, so detoured via the atrium to soak in the light from the second, smaller sun. The observation room view didn't disappoint. A crystalline cloud passed over, refracted the light and painted the walls with a beautiful shimmer that was over far too soon.

The return trip took Kim past the lavatories, a modern marvel of self contained plumbing that defied reality enough to still function. With no one to care, she used the gents. They were cleaner, nearer, and the graffiti was informative. Adorned with varying levels of depravity, she chose by mood, and today was a 'Creepy Kim likes it in the butt' day, stall two. The lettering slanted a little to the left, and the i's topped with an upright line that would have taken longer, and wasn't any clearer than the usual dot. Paul. She'd seen plenty of his handwriting on inter-department memos, but since H.R. was long gone, she didn't dwell.

Now her zipper wouldn't budge a millimetre, so after a minute of awkward contortions, she decided not to go after all and headed for the lab.

Some more fungal outcroppings had appeared since she left, so getting back in required more screwdriver action and a deft hop to prevent the small balls of weird running up her leg. They weren't bites; it was more that they settled and became sentient skin lesions. Once part of her, Kim could feel everything they did, and they didn't like soap at all. Lesson learned, Kim kept the outside air from entering the lab without detouring through many filters, but the spores already inside provided a sometimes welcome distraction.

Once she returned to the central laboratory, she made for her desk and organised the papers back into piles. Happy with the order, she moved onto the thousand dollar radio clock that, without the MSF signal from Cumbria, ran fast to the tune of ten minutes a day.

The lab had a bespoke atomic clock, which was accurate to nanoseconds over millennia, only it wasn't connected to the network, or other clocks, so Kim got an accurate reading, climbed a stepladder, and moved the arms by hand. Nearly seven o'clock in the evening. No wonder she was tired.

There were still two lines on the monitor, but it was too late to care today. She shut everything down and stared at the red light for a while. Solid now, un-flickering, reliable.

"Damn straight. Too late for a meeting now, bedtime?"

Words spoken aloud as if to someone else in the room, but not. She'd always talked to herself, but there were other things that marked her out. She fumbled with her shoes, unable to tie them long after others could, and she wet her bed into adolescence. Her parents and teachers had furrowed their brows and talked in concerned whispers, at first anyway, when they thought she could change. But as time moved on and she went from cute and quirky to just quirky all the way through to weird and shunned, only her therapist kept caring, and he was being paid to see her, at least until he ruled out any publishable mental health issues and ended the relationship. She needed to hear the words in her head out loud to process their meaning. Also, being fair, she hadn't heard another human voice since that day, which was now six months ago.

"Anyway, I'm not weird. I bet loads of people talk to themselves all the time." She looked down at the stuck zipper on her coveralls and felt her breath catch and her chest tighten a little. "I really liked that top."

The living space was a floor above the lab, and the elevators didn't work, so sleep was a five-minute walk away up a flight of stairs and through a scary corridor.

It wasn't always like that, but the wormhole wasn't stable, so when the lab bubble warped, things melded with some of the surrounding flora and fauna. Now there was a glowing tree thing right in the middle that liked to ogle her as she walked past. It was worth it though, as her room was quite agreeable, with high ceilings and a polymer screen-paper on the walls that projected the outside environment, and more than that, it was quiet, and it felt safe. Once inside, she used the scissors from the bedside table to cut through her zipper, inadvertently cutting through the front of her bra, before giving up on the day and throwing herself on the bed, still clothed. The outside world filled her vision, three suns in the tangerine sky, the largest always visible.

"Computer, dim display by.. Crap."

The A.I. was in the main building, which was presumably still on Earth. She knew that, but four years of conditioning had her still asking it to do everything. Kim rolled over and poked a jury-rigged control panel until the walls dimmed enough for sleep, closed her eyes and tried not to think about the future.

* * *

They came five minutes later. The favoured plan of attack meant full on assault, aimed at the obvious entrance on top, the central stairwell. The planners specified state-of-the-art security throughout the building during construction, including that stairwell, so this always ended the same way.

After failing to enter from the top, the raiding party changed tack and tried the emergency access tunnel on sub-floor three. More security, this time aggressively fatal, to humans at least. Kim watched from her bedroom wallpaper-screen as a highly decorated general in their army absorbed thousands of electrical volts mixed with dozens of amps. The air ionised around him, or possibly her, but provided only a minor deterrent. They waved what Kim presumed was an arm and directed the bulk of the force into a flanking manoeuvre directed at the only other visible entryway, an outflow pipe for the mains sewerage system.

Same result.

The first time they'd come, Kim had been terrified and wet herself, huddled in a corner with head in hands. It was something she hadn't done since college, over twenty years before, when she'd got engrossed in a juicy maths problem and then forgot to eat, drink, or go to the toilet for nearly twenty hours. She was calmer about it now, but much as they hadn't yet affected entry, the assaults were noisy. Kim wasn't fond of noise, especially when it was unpredictable, and this army was that in spades.

As the weeks progressed, however, and the attacks became less frequent, Kim almost missed the contact with other living creatures if they didn't show.

Not tonight, though. Her eyelids were fighting a losing battle with gravity, and the yawns were getting more frequent.

"Sod off!.. Oh, wait."

The panel she used instead of the missing A.I. was coming apart. Only ever a temporary measure, and mostly held together by faith and electrical tape, it buzzed with an angry tone when she activated the external P.A. system, and then filled her nostrils with an acrid odour that was becoming more and more prevalent.

"Yeah, look, I'm trying to sleep. Any chance you guys could piss off and try again in the morning?"

Kim looked up at the ever present middle sun and wondered how people in Scandinavian countries with endless days stayed sane and then rephrased.

"Ah, a few hours? You guys have hours, right? Come back when the little sun, the, uh, green one? When it comes back around. I'll make some cake!"

Their leader, a tall leathery cylinder adorned with a cape that seemed to be part of his or her physical being and festooned with colourful disks that might be medals, stopped moving. It had taken Kim some time to get the hang of hearing the creatures. They didn't vocalise by disturbing the air and creating sound waves. Instead, they projected a fluctuating sense of meaning mixed with applicable grammar straight into the subconscious mind.

The first time they addressed Kim, she thought she was having a stroke. After a few days she could approximate English, now she was pretty adept.

"You offer surrender? This 'cake' signifies understanding of your unworthiness?"

"Oh, hey, Joseph! You haven't been here in ages."

She couldn't tell them apart on sight. Being honest, she had the same trouble with humans, where identity could boil down to a combination of odour and hair colour. It was fortunate that although the creatures didn't have hair in the same way humans did, their 'voices' were all individual and distinct. Along with the vocabulary, they projected some of themselves into her cerebral cortex.

"That cape new?" She continued. "Oooh, and medals? Those are definitely new."

"Surrender?" Was that disappointment?

"Yeah, I will not be doing that. Look, I'm sure you're sweet and all, but I enjoy being alive and, you know, in here where you're not. I'll be going home soon. Could you just leave me alone until then?"

Rehearsed words, a repurposed script taken from a daydream. Thousands of scenarios played out millions of times, just in case she needed to sound normal and spontaneous.

Joseph signified his response by ordering a volley of weapons fire.

Kim still got nervous when they started shooting. She was in an uprooted basement dropped onto the surface of an alien planet that wasn't supposed to survive as a fortress. The projectiles pounded the walls, disturbing the video feed into Kim's room, blinding her momentarily. Although she couldn't see, their words still filled her mind, and what she felt was anger. More missile explosions thundered through the subframe, moving the bed a solid inch to the left. That was new.

Kim scrabbled up and out of the room, ran past the ogletree, did her best to avoid physical contact and jump-sprinted down the stairs toward the laboratory area. Getting to the lab took her a few minutes, enough time for another terrifying barrage of projectiles and thunder. Once in the complex, she bee lined for the control desk where the red light was still on, not blinking.

Not a disaster just yet.

Some button pushes switched audio visual to the terminal screens. Joseph's team had a new and gnarly looking weapon floating above and pointed down the atrium. The electromagnetic fields preventing entry were top quality, the best available in fact, but they were there to stop human sabotage, not alien death guns.

"What in the flipping flip, Joe? I thought we were friends."

They responded with a single 'word', no longer a question.

"Surrender."

"Not an option, Joe. Don't do this, please?"

She was close.

Despite the interruptions, her progress during the last few weeks was solid. With the calibration fixed, Kim could go home. Life on Earth was a party-sub full of crap from dawn till dusk, all comfort-eating despair cycles and workplace antagonism. But she wanted it back. Oh God, how she wanted to sit in a room full of people that hated her again and experience the disappointment. She needed the awful television and junk mail, the cat turds in her slippers, and the dreadful smells from her food bin. Was anyone feeding her cat? Christ, he hadn't been out in months. If he was still alive, she would need to prioritise buying new furniture.

"Surrender."

Loud enough to hurt like a migraine, including the aura. The vision to Kim's left ended, replaced with bright dots of light that danced and made concentration difficult. She blinked away the associated nausea that had lurched into the pit of her stomach and squinted the lights down into a narrow slit of sight. One more button press diverted power to the lockdown protocol, sealing the lower part of the atrium just in case.

Kim watched as Joseph ordered the weapon fired with a gesture, a flick of the cape. Radiation flooded the space, followed momentarily by a concussive force beyond anything Kim had experienced. The red light kept steady, but the rest of the room didn't. Weeks of work scrawled onto reams and reams of paper in handwriting only Kim could read scattered. More concerning was the precision equipment keeping a tab on the planet Earth, signified by one of the two lines on her monitor. Kim climbed back into her chair and powered up instrumentation, being careful not to divert from the security measures.

Three lines.

She couldn't risk another impact like that. Maybe she didn't have to. The chatter outside was full of disappointment and discouragement. Joseph had apparently believed this would work, and he couldn't understand why it hadn't. While they recharged the battering ram, Kim reviewed data through the lifting fog in her vision and saw an opening. The impact was from high-density shock waves and not a projectile. If she was quick, she had an all-in-one solution to both party crashers and weapon but it would only work if they targeted the same area again. If she was wrong, it was over.

"Joe, please, stop." Did she sound sufficiently scared? "Oh God, no, please stop!"

They fired again before Kim was ready. Fifteen seconds later and the lab would have been unprotected. As it was, the field held, but just barely. Another check of her monitor showed additional lines, but they seemed to converge and that was a sign, right?

"Surrender."

"Not cool, Joseph. Do that again and I'll retaliate. Do you hear me? All of you, jog on."

This time, she would be ready. It took around half a minute to charge, which left her twenty seconds.

On screen, the creatures convened in one spot near an

exterior waste vent. Convenient, right in front of a camera. Hundreds of them milled about like sentient eldritch clutch bags carrying guns. Around eight feet tall and with no discernible limbs, they seemed to float unless you looked past them. Peripheral vision could see something off-putting and indescribable that was definitely not tentacles, but also kind of was. Besides some occasional adornments, they were identical in all but voice.

Ten seconds, give or take.

Kim redirected all the power she could spare to the electrical countermeasures protecting the atrium. All at once, the power would create a thin layer of super-heated plasma, which should absorb the shockwave while dispersing it all over her unwanted guests. Well, that was the plan anyway. It was time to check her theory in the real world. Kim fired everything into the grid and held her breath.

Joseph fired.

The burning smell was permeating the lab by this point, not just the bedroom, but at least there was a lab, and a red light that was still steady. As the monitors came back online, Kim saw the fruits of her labour floating around outside on fire and sounding quite annoyed. She couldn't resist and flipped the P.A. back on.

"So, do you fancy surrendering dipshit?"

The beings dispersed in a matter of seconds. Alone again, Kim looked at the unholy mess now covering the floor, and then at the clock. Nine-thirty, bed-time part two, and this time she definitely needed to use the toilet first. A nearby scalpel made shreds of the remaining zipper, after which Kim climbed out of the coveralls, leaving them in a heap on the floor with the remains of her bra and all her paperwork.

When Kim regained consciousness, she couldn't feel her legs any other way than with her hands. Still not awake in any genuine sense, the surroundings confused for a few moments. Then the smell hit, clogging her nostrils, reaching down into her lungs and robbing them of clean air.

"Shit!"

Figurative and literal. After the evening's trauma, she'd passed out on the toilet wearing nothing more than a pair of green socks.

After a failed attempt to stand, she reached round to flush and knocked the toilet paper onto the floor, where it bounced with energy that defied physics, rolling under the partition into the next stall. She glanced to the left, more in hope than expectation, finding nothing to replace it, so she dragged herself upright and waited for the pins and needles, then waited for them to bugger off before hobbling round to retrieve the errant two-ply wadding.

As she walked, alone, back to the stores, a thin sheen of sweat accumulated on her bare skin before evaporating almost as quickly, like a gentle mist, cool where it met the air but heavy in her socks, and leaving damp footprints on the tiling. It didn't help with her mood, which was whipping up a dull ache behind her left eye that ran down and into her teeth where she was clenching her jaw tight. Opening the door didn't help either. Shelves once loaded with stationary and sundries of all kinds had deplcted after six months of all take with no give. Palettes of bathroom supplies had dwindled to a handful of toilet paper rolls and a single refill for the deodoriser. Food choice, which wasn't great to begin with, had reduced to packets of freeze-dried protein and long-life powdered milk. She'd eaten all the pen lids, and missed the instant noodles even if they'd tasted how cheap cat food smelled. She had access to endless blue coveralls, but no underwear, so today would be a commando day.

It didn't matter. As long as the power held out, she could get home.

While adjusting yet another uncomfortable onesie until just about bearable, Kim daydreamed about long hot baths and fish-finger sandwiches, before giving way to intrusive thoughts about her cat. She chased those away with a delicious pot of chocolate memory-mousse before sealing the room and making her way back to the laboratory.

Eleven-thirty AM, probably. Things were better than she remembered, although not outstanding. Back to two lines was fantastic, and they really were getting closer together, which meant no damage to the antenna arrays. If she couldn't reconcile them, she might have to roll some quantum dice, but it would be worth it. Thinking back to the toilet situation, right now, a straight choice between death and home looked tempting. Kim sighed and got down onto the floor, dragsliding herself through an inspection hatch under the main desk. Although the bulk of the beacon lived in the concrete walls, a single computer system ran all its functions. Kim knew it better than anyone, a given since she built nearly all of it.

The inside was like its creator's mind, a cramped and disorganised affair, which was in contrast to the lab outside. Dozens of cable miles filled the colour-coded conduits criss-crossing the space. Kim hauled herself further in, helped by a low wheeled trolly. Past the redundant power stacks and under a load-bearing gantry, separating tonnes of steel and plastic from Kim's soft torso. Further even than that, lived six feet of lead shielding behind which a highly reactive gamma source was providing endless ionising radiation through a microscopic aperture. Just beyond the aperture, but still within the safety of the lead bubble, was the magic. A huge superconducting core. One of a kind. Kim wasn't interested in the core right now, having more pressing concerns about the linkage between the sensors and the microprocessor that adjusted the core alignment millions of times a second.

It had been making mistakes, and those mistakes made calibrating the beacon impossible.

She stared at the panel for nearly two minutes. Removing it was a prerequisite to fixing the bloody thing, but once off, she wouldn't be able to stop working until it was done.

Another two minutes passed with no interruptions.

She couldn't put it off anymore and reached for the toolkit that lived in a purpose made niche by her knees, getting the tip of the screwdriver into a screw-head before she heard him.

"Surrender."

Not Joseph this time. Whoever spoke felt much more

important, speaking with inherent authority. Whoever it was, this wasn't a good time.

"Mother.. God damn it!"

Kim balled her hands and hit the ground as hard as she could, which wasn't wise, sending most of the toolkit flying and embedding a scalpel blade deeply into her skin just above her wrist.

"Son of a BITCH!"

The journey out took half the time, and she trailed blood the whole way. When she stood, a few tools dislodged from her coveralls and joined the growing pool of blood at her feet. She pulled the blade out and, when satisfied the damage wasn't too great, pulled her hand into her sleeve and tightened the material enough that she could feel the seam bite and her hand warm up like a kettle element before becoming cold and eventually numb. On-screen stood a new creature. Resplendent in a glittering toga-style fabric covering, she hadn't seen this one. To his left, Joseph floated with what Kim sensed was abject humiliation. He certainly had fewer shiny disks decorating his torso.

She flipped the P.A. on and cleared her throat before considering her words with care and then speaking.

"WHAT?"

"Ah."

Was this new creature a leader? His words felt commanding but also comforting. That single syllable slowed Kim's heartbeat and smothered the worry in her mind. More followed.

"You burned my army."

"I.."

Kim felt like a scolded five-year-old, filled with pent up

energy looking for an angry outlet, but also empty and needing reassurance. The contrition only lasted a moment.

"They tried to kill me. I'm bleeding!"

It didn't feel like enough, so she embellished.

"And you ruined my favourite top."

"I don't understand all your words. This 'top' was important to you?"

She looked down at her current garb and felt salt tears welling up.

"Um, yes."

"Then you have my apologies. I will do what I can to replace what you have lost."

"You can't replace what I've.. Wait, what's happening here?"

Kim's mind fogged. She could feel a second presence driving her subconscious toward a fleeting memory from school. History class with Mrs Benson. When her classmates weren't abusing Kim's short fuse for entertainment, they liked to give teachers nicknames, and Benson earned hers.

"Your designation is Kim? Mine is.. Oh, Benito."

Kim chased the memory back out of her mind. The after-image alone ran icy fingers down her spine.

"You pulled that out of my head?"

"We have no need of designations. You do, so we'll use yours."

"The hell, dude! Stay out of my mind!"

"Be not afraid, Kim. We cannot steal any thoughts you hide."

"I hid that one!"

"No, you dwell on it, savour it."

Kim couldn't help but relive some more of that afternoon. Benson was called away. Once safely gone, Kate Waterhouse had asked Kim what her favourite position was loud enough for the entire room to hear. Still being a sheltered twelve-year-old, she hadn't understood the question, which, of course, was the whole point.

Kim felt the blood rushing to her face as she spoke.

"No, I flipping don't!"

But maybe she did. Secretly, at least. The warmth in her face travelled downward, leaving goosebumps in its wake, before fading suddenly a few seconds later. The sound of her heart beating loud in her ears, the coolness of the draught through her coverall, already stained with blood, reminding Kim just how fragile she was, and driving any remaining school memories back into the crevices of her subconscious.

"Why are you here?"

She couldn't see an army on any of the screens and there were no weapons trained in her direction, but when Ben spoke again, she felt disinclined to believe him.

"I'm here in peace, Kimberley. Your fortress withstood the machine. Your technology is beyond ours, in its magnificence and durability. You built this place?"

His words came into her head as a question, but his delivery felt more like a statement of fact. Kim glanced around the room at the equipment and gadgetry assembled around concepts that were hers, even if never acknowledged audibly.

Well, until now, at least.

The goosebumps returned, and her chest swelled, an unfamiliar sensation, so Kim took a moment to be sure it wasn't acid reflux from the spoonful of powdered milk she snuck into her mouth before leaving the stores earlier. Time that allowed realisation Ben hadn't answered her question. She tried again.

"Right, but why are you here? I mean now, why are you here now?"

The red light was still solid, but there were limits to her remaining source of power and she probably needed most of it to get home. Another assault could maroon her.

"I rule this place, Kimberley. I am here offering partnership that is a benefit to all of us."

His toga was very shiny, like a shimmering plane of stars woven into a shifting pattern that formed and reformed endless geographic structures, beautiful, practical, and it looked like it had good breathability. Kim was suddenly conscious of her lack of underwear. Maybe she could play this to her advantage if she stayed cool.

"How, I mean, ah, what are you suggesting?"

Smooth.

"An exchange. I provide an ambassador from our ranks to teach you of our ways and provide for your needs while you teach us how your technology works."

"Yeah, I'm kinda hoping to not be here in a day or two."

"It would be a shame to waste this opportunity to learn from an intellect such as yours. I promise not to interfere with your leaving if you wish, but surely you are, ah, curious about us?"

She was. She was also hungry and tired and sick of worrying every day.

"You'll kill me as soon as I let you in."

"Not me. Unless you request it, of course. I recommend you allow entry to another, more qualified to foster amicable relations between us."

The pod was small, but well proportioned. Green light emanated from the icy walls that, though tacky to the touch, were unencumbered with dust or debris. Precipitation was a memory so distant that reportage was now myth, so the flat and solid sheet of black overhead was there to absorb energy from the fiery suns for later use while also preventing a scalding life-end. Visions hovered mid-air throughout, projections of thought distilled from revered philosophers across their region of the globe, and then beamed from mind to mind across vast distances to termini in every abode. Endless, unedited streams of consciousness covering any conceivable topic rendered visible by concealed emitters buried in the obsidian floor. To the left, a representation of the primary tactician, Hanibal, was discussing the benefits of purity in the species. To the right, à propos of nothing, an artistic concept of the alien, built from the latest deep scans, was cavorting while thinkers dissected its physiology and considered the threat it posed. Someone speculated that it existed in just one reality, that its coming signified an impending singularity. Another theorised about its many orifices.

"Filth!"

All around, the floor was spotless, and the ceiling was unblemished. Outside, the fungal spores settled and colonised every surface with aggressive sentient moss. Inside, not a spec.

The reason for the lack of dirt, Caruthers, busied himself with what the alien would probably call a book case but more civilised entities referred to as an info-nook. He'd spent so many solar cycles polishing the shelving that a patina was developing, which was not agreeable.

Everything looked clean but felt dirty. Everything.

Since the appearance, which was long enough ago now to have quelled the immediate panic, all anyone had done was hypothesise. Much to his chagrin, the initial belief that this thing heralded an invasion waned. Now the consensus was that the creature stranded itself with an unwise attempt to harness the outer dimensions. All he knew was that it was ugly and unclean. That it was a lesser form of life was clear as the towers of Pride on a bright light-cycle. It should be in a capture-pod, he thought to himself. That thought quietened all the view-streams except Hanibal's, which grew in size to fill all the space. It was his favourite, so he put down the clean-tools and communicated his thoughts aloud.

"Yes, get in! What wisdom do you bring today?"

Below, and just slightly to the left of the vision, was a caption showing the answer to his question.

'My soul-bond mated and brought forth Quiana, the destroyer of worlds. Now they are demanding life-cycle payments. I wish to compare flesh and prove they cheated with my pod-brother! Later in this stream, should we make those of low-means toil in the crystal mines until sterile?'

The topics pleased him. Flesh-tests could be quite entertaining and the impure should be sterile, although in these liberal times that was not the most popular concept.

'It is good you think these things, Hanibal. You have the courage of ten!' Caruthers thought to himself.

Quiana's life-giver appeared to raucous braying from an invisible crowd of peers. They bore the destroyer before them. As with all younglings, this one was gormless and plain. If the tests showed it was from an impure flesh-line, he would happily see it sent to the mines.

"I did nothing wrong and this product of seed and ova is pure. Also, nutrients are expensive and we desire occasional toil-rest and it's only fair that the seed-bearer accepts some of this cost."

"Hah! But I am not the seed-bearer. My cousin tells true of your dalliance with my brother!"

"Nuh-uh. I have bonded only with you and one other, and I came clean about him immediately!"

Another being entered the vision from the right. The brother, it went to the destroyer, which was wailing and expectorating in that unpleasant way younglings have. The audience vocalised their displeasure with a round of boos. One among them lobbed a projectile at the newcomer, narrowly missing their left view-orb.

"Son-of-a-goober! You want a piece, huh? I'll be intercepting you outside."

The vortex of endless, spinning thoughts in Caruthers' mind eased as he watched an inevitable fight break out.

He had been at odds with the day since the moment Benito appeared before him earlier, swaddled in the garb of state he insisted on wearing. He was a pompous and insufferable ass, full of words but lacking in action. Alas, he ruled the realm, and had Joe with him, so Caruthers had no choice but to grant him an audience. The last time they'd communicated was in the palace many cycles past, and it didn't end well. An exploration of views and opinions that ended with Caruthers discovering the current administration and he had grown incompatible, and that he was now unemployed. They had offered him the chance to compromise, but Ben wanted to appoint a lower form to government and Caruthers would not stand for it. It was bad enough they moved around freely, without restraint, but he would not share an office with a sub-species that until the recent epoch had eked an existence in far away forbidden zones. And they talked funny, also they smelled a bit.

The holographic fight concluded with Hannibal's sizeable security detail separating the warring family. Quiana's life-giver muttered something distasteful about her former soul-mates forbearers. It riled the brother enough for one more momentary burst of action that ended with him writhing on the floor in apparent agony.

His conversation with Ben had followed a similar route. It opened with a job offer which was nice but that offer turned out to be an obvious insult, and Caruthers' attempt to decline with a thrown nutrient-receptacle had ended with Joe forcing said receptacle into his flesh with enough force to corporealise a scuff-mark. Ben's second offer of employment was a lot more order-y. He knew his place, and it was right at the bottom, beneath even the filth that fell from the sky.

Caruthers returned to his cleaning. He wanted all traces of the impure that had no-doubt tracked in on Ben and Joe out of his abode. Everywhere he looked was grimy.

"Curse you, Benito. May you suffer the death of ever-present itching."

It hadn't always been like this. Once, Ben and Caruthers had been congenial compatriots. Equals even. Things had soured long before the alien appeared in the palace court-yard, right on top of the wisdom-tree, with a thoroughly disconcerting popping sound. Their friendship ended with the treaties. Untold eons of dominance and purity discarded for a peace that only lasted a few orbits. These times, it was no longer even correct to pain-shame the lowers for taking nutrients from the wrong side of the dispenser. Worse, now there actually wasn't a wrong side.

"Show me the thing from the fortress."

He said the words out loud, even though it was unnecessary as the visions were largely mind controlled, but too much time without conversant company had taken its toll. Caruthers' fall from grace initially saw him prostitute himself in many demeaning ways to cover the pay-orders. First, his skill with data-streams earned employment with a paymaster, but that only lasted a short period. A misunderstanding over status demanded an honour-duel, and the resulting death of a fellow employee wasn't conducive to continued workplace harmony. Later, he translated ancient texts for a learn-hub. Until a disagreement over the significance and length of nutrient breaks, at least. Finally, he served rapid-food from a booth to passing compadres, occasionally vulgar compadres. Another honour-duel and another death left Caruthers again without a pay-stream, no matter that the deceased wasn't an employee this time.

He'd barely used his voice in dozens of cycles, so now he spoke to the machines.

Hanibal's feed faded to the background. A re-run of the

earlier discussion of the alien grew to replace it, replete with the artist's impression. A spindly collection of sinew and calcification, wrapped in a thin flesh-tube and punctured at both ends with a multitude of openings. They'd built the model using the latest readings, so accuracy was high. Did this monster truly only exist on one plane? Why did it need so many holes? The mind contained within could hear them, which set it apart from some of the other beings he'd encountered, but did it have intelligence? True intellect was a rare thing, and he'd yet to see evidence beyond the structure it inhabited. Caruthers watched as the vision changed, demonstrating some of the garb that had wrapped it when observed. He phased just a little, unable to contain his disgust.

He downed the tools again, then gave an unnecessary and theatrical sigh before kicking the info-nook and spraying its contents onto the floor, where they formed an untidy but geometric pattern.

"Connect me with the palace."

It took just long enough to cause concern. Caruthers considered for the first time just how low he had sunk. When he appeared, Ben looked smug.

"There is nothing more to discuss.."

"Stop! That is not why I have called. I.." Caruthers looked at the messy pile of once prized knowledge strewn on his otherwise spotless floor. Then he considered how long it had been since he last consumed a full meal. "Will there be compensatory funding?"

"You always came right to the point. I should remind you of your words when we parted at the palace. Hurtful words. You didn't need financing back then. Honour and purity were more important, as I recall?"

"AS THEY SHOULD.." He stopped himself mid-sentence. This would be an honour-duel too far and he really needed to eat. "Apologies, my liege. I.." The last few words stuck fast, needing to be forced out into the world. "I need nutrition. You've seen my existence. Are you going to make me beg?"

"No need. You'll feast as long as you perform your task, and be of good cheer, as when this is over, you are going to have everything you ever wanted."

* * *

"So, how come you're called Caruthers? I mean, like, you guys don't need any names, right?"

He looked at her with what he felt was his most imposing and imperious glare, certain that his superior heritage was on full display before answering the question. Again.

"These designations exist only in your mind. Our identities are part of us, immutable, pure, and they don't need vocalising."

"But Ben called you Caruthers. If you don't need.."

"Enough!"

"I'm just saying, so when you're born, you don't get a name? How do your parents tell you guys apart?"

"Once more, we are not 'born', at least not in the way you describe." Her words were still vivid in his memory, eliciting a shudder. "We came to be and have always been."

"Oh yeah, you said. It's just, I'm trying to get it straight in my head."

He'd learned much in his time inside the fortress. That the creatures had differing genders amongst themselves was taking time to process. Since his kind had no requirements for such differentiation, being all of one flesh, the idea of these things all being individual was confusing. That, for them, coming into existence involved gestating inside each other before being pulled, partially formed, from an orifice was horrific. He observed she was still loitering in his presence with mouth ajar. He really wanted to get back to cleaning the sty that was the fortress interior, so distracted her rather than answer more questions.

"Is this not a nourishment period?"

She gawped open mouthed for the briefest moment before looking down at her hands. One of them held an unnamed fruit that their scientists had determined was compatible with her physiology. It was part eaten, then somehow forgotten.

"Oh. Yeah."

Caruthers was now thinking these creatures weren't the threat he'd once imagined.

He'd been there for twenty-seven cycles now and still did not know why Benito hadn't used the opportunity to storm the place and destroy this curious infestation, as she was ripe for the taking. Instead, he'd been making visitations upon her, showering her with his attention and protection. She was not to be touched by any of their kind, much less harmed. Caruthers had wondered if this was a unique punishment created just to make his existence even less bearable. As the cycles wore on, though, it became apparent this wasn't the case. Ben valued this clumsy, bumbling thing and his time spent with it.

Could it be the technology she possessed?

Caruthers had attempted to strip the knowledge directly from her in the way they could with others of their kind, but her mind was impervious. No doubt a consequence of her base and un-developed nature. The tech itself didn't seem to be anything beyond a collection of minerals and power, poorly contained in hollowed out rock. She had somehow harnessed the outer dimensions and travelled among them, though, something that was admittedly beyond Caruthers, Ben and their kind. All these cycles he'd spent inside the fortress, and he still couldn't see how it worked. There was energy here, though, and the source seemed as boundless as the suns above. Some sort of fusion, no doubt, and certainly dangerous in the wrong hands. Yet even after he'd briefed Ben, he still played games while she wielded this power unchecked. Worse still, Ben and she seemed to build a relationship. How could he stoop so low as to consort with this alien? He must see that it is not higher in status than a disease ridden bug.

"Uh, C. Any chance you could get one of those, ah, tube things? You know, with the electricity inside?"

The alien had broken another vision-plug. The interconnection was fragile, that was a given, but after seven cycles and now twenty-five tubes, even a bug should have understood and figured that out for herself. Watching her stumble around this place with so little focus while in command of such exceptional power was just one more concern.

"How are you still breaking these?"

"I mean, have you guys considered not making them out of glass? I.."

She turned away as her voice dwindled. Inside her flesh-shell, the bones of her upper limb supports sagged to suggest upset. Caruthers thought back to the last of Ben's words of caution after agreeing to this assignment. He then imagined the inside of a capture-pod, which was where he would end his existence if he didn't help the creature in every way she asked.

They did not design them with comfort in mind.

"Wait, Kimberley." Another shudder. "I shall have more tubes delivered to you."

She turned back, but with her view-orbs directed downward. Then paused before opening her maw. She paused again before speaking.

"Actually, I was thinking about the glass. I don't know, these things provide so little attenuation given their volume. I have an idea for improving.."

Not the first interesting words she'd uttered. She'd voiced several fascinating concepts in his presence and Caruthers had considered the tubes design less than ideal himself but could not conceive a better way. Alas, Ben chose that moment to appear with his guard. He ignored Caruthers and moved to the thing. He placed himself between them as just another insult.

"Kimberley! I see you making use of our supplies. Are they to your liking?"

Caruthers couldn't see her reaction, but detected a change in her vocalisation.

"I. Yes, but I was just saying to Caruthers that these tubes.."

"The plugs? Yes, your idea of using their inherent properties to, well, you know better than me. Your mind is a marvel."

What was he up to? She seemed as confused as he when she replied, after an almost imperceptible pause. Almost.

"I. But, I was.. Caruthers and I.."

"You should pay him no heed. He lacks the imagination needed to fully appreciate your brilliance."

Ben's meaningless compliments affected the creature, whose upper flesh took on a ruddy hue. She raised her view-orbs just for a moment, looking past Ben and directly at Caruthers before continuing. He wondered if her next words were for him personally.

"Yes.. Yes! It's a problem I have experience with."

Ben turned to Caruthers with a thoroughly unneeded theatrical flair, causing a corner of his state-garb to whip into Caruthers' side with a crack. An action that in a previous lifetime would have implied significant dishonour and insult, but now just meant there was a sun burning in the sky. He waited to hear the fresh insults of his leader.

"Old fool. You.. You just don't see, do you?"

Disappointing and confusing, but Caruthers had heard worse. In fact, he'd heard worse that morning on a daytime vision-stream that was meant for younglings. He turned the words over in his cranial hollow and felt them for barbs, finding none. He'd meant what he said, and that hurt more than anything Ben had ever done to him before.

Benito turned away without further communication and ushered the creature along with him. He thought back to the time when he was as close to Ben as this creature now seemed to be and all the discussions they'd had. Heat pooled inside his mind, narrowing his thoughts to short bursts of explicit hatred. This behaviour made no sense. Once out of sight, Joseph made an abrupt appearance. He moved close to Caruthers' side before talking in a low and personal voice.

"I think you might be nearly out of chances, old one."

"What's happening here? Seriously, what in the name of.."

"You had a job to do, one job. Provide Kimberley with knowledge and supplies while keeping her happy."

"And I have.."

"You're interfering with her work. You should have let

her do things as she wanted to, any damn way she wanted to."

"I have!" Joe made to speak, but didn't. Instead, he produced a small un-maker and jammed it tight against Caruthers' body. His discomfort was plain. "What aren't you telling me, Joseph?"

"I liked you Caruthers. You alone had the conviction to stand by your beliefs when others were weak."

"Liked? Hey, look, take it easy, Joe. You're going to need to back up a bit here."

The weapon was cold against his side. He'd seen what it could do to a being from thirty lengths. Point blank there would be no surviving. He probed Joe's mind for intent, finding nothing and wondering if this was how he ended, after all?

Benito reentered the room with Kimberley close behind. Caruthers looked directly into his orbs, seeing a dark scowl that lifted quickly as those eyes widened. A shake of the face. Joe saw it too and just like that, the un-maker was gone. Joe moved away, leaving Caruthers alone as Ben approached with the thing. It was rocking gently, back and forth on its perambulatory limbs and smiling.

"It seems I was being hasty. Kimberley has really taken to you. Keep up the apparently excellent work."

Caruthers moved to keep Ben in view as he left the fortress with his retinue, once again leaving him alone with Kim, who was now flapping her arm-extremities. It was something she'd only begun doing after he'd been there a while, and he still wasn't sure if it meant anxiety or happiness. Her orbs remained downwardly directed.

"So, I'm going to be needing more tube.. Sorry, vision-plugs."

She was so small and fragile. Her frame was just a collection of meaty sacs and tubing hung on calcium deposits. Her intellect was just as tiny, that of an insect. She was, in every way, his inferior, a creature to be ridiculed and subjugated. Somehow, this thing had taken what had been his rightful place at Ben's side. That was almost as painful as the unmaking would have been, but what really hurt was that this insignificant parasite had just saved his life. He wanted to crush her right here and bathe in her freed hydraulic fluids, but a growing part of him had developed an iota of respect.

"As you wish."

4 / WORKING HARD, OR HARDLY WORKING?

Kim's eyes opened just a crack. Only enough to be certain she was alone in the bedroom before she kicked the covers off. She was sleeping in the nude and the envoy Ben sent her had been a little, well, clingy since his visit the previous day. That's not to say she hadn't appreciated his help with the ogle-tree thing in the hallway. It had been a gift from a far away ruler who wielded substantial power and influence. Apparently, it didn't leer. What it was actually doing was peering into the soul and identifying her worthiness in battle.

She was relieved to find that everyone thought it weird. That was why it was outside.

Caruthers had it moved into a better position by the atrium sun-room where it got better light. He'd also been a wonder with the cleaning and tidying. It was something she'd never been efficient at, organising her thoughts into a coherent plan of attack when faced with piles of tasks with no obvious starting point was something other people could do. Her skill lay in occasionally making ridiculous lateral connections between scientific concepts and wrangling the resulting theory into practical, life altering solutions. That was all fine and dandy at work, but constantly forgetting to shower, brush her teeth or wash her clothes made her home life frustrating and limited her circle of friends to a disappointing none.

Progress had been slow for those endless first weeks. She just hadn't been able to ease her fears, what with the constant concern about impending death at the hands of the creatures. They seemed as good as their word, though, which was nice, as she now had toilet paper again, and food. And after she finally relaxed, things started happening.

The targeting subsystem had eaten itself during the warping. She hadn't seen it because it still looked as it always had, externally anyway. The components had all swapped internals, which made for some exciting times, like when she realised that a previously inert boxed coil she was holding had become a capacitor with enough current to stop her heart while popping her eyeballs. At first, this meant doom and gloom. She didn't have the parts, and obviously the aliens' technology would not fit.

Then, overnight, it was all sunshine and lollypops.

Caruthers had been doing his job with the broom thingy while evading her questions, like every day up to that point, when she realised it was just a question of perspective. It wasn't perfect, of course. They made everything out of a paper-thin glass material that broke if you so much as thought heavy thoughts. She had an epiphany about that, in fact, a couple of mornings ago.

"You have awakened."

He was in the corner, blending nicely into a coat stand she'd been using as a wardrobe.

"Jesus Christ! What the hell, C!" She pulled the covers back up and waited for her heart rate to slow. "What have I told you about coming in here while I'm asleep?"

He drifted over in silence looking sheepish, propelled by the not-tentacles she could and couldn't see that were, according to Caruthers, in a different plane of existence. She remembered being unhappy with his explanation and made a mental note to ask about it again later. At that moment, she had more pressing things to consider, like the fact that the duvet had turned while she was asleep and didn't cover her feet anymore.

"I'm not wearing anything. Seriously dude, it's not cool to walk in on a lady when she's, you know."

"I'm also not wearing any garb, Kimberley. Is your discomfort because of the saggy tumours protruding from your torso? Our heal-teams are capable of remove.."

"NO! No, they're supposed to be there. I told you. Also, screw you, they're not saggy, just relaxed, okay?"

"Your early-cycle nutrition is ready for consumption, Kimberley."

"I.. Thanks. It's Kim, okay? No one ever calls me Kimberley."

"Kim."

He made the single syllable long and low, like a parent trying to scare their child at Halloween, but she was hungry, and so ushered him away before sliding out of the bed and into the less crumpled of the two coveralls on the floor. She took a moment to swap to the other after sniffing her armpits and deciding that the creases had added character, and then tightly balled the first before throwing it into the pile of retired clothes in a far corner.

You couldn't make out the floor there anymore

Once dressed, she enabled the view-paper and introduced the lab camera feed. Caruthers was already down there with the promised breakfast repast, which comprised a weird fruit thing that looked like a spherical banana but tasted like cornflakes mixed with tuna-mayonnaise. Drink was the purple juice of a large blue furry cube that screamed when being crushed. He insisted it wasn't sentient, but she wasn't all that convinced. It also tasted like cornflakes, this time mixed with barbecue sauce and, unquantifiably, sadness.

Kimberley couldn't explain why, but it worked.

With the tree gone, the walk to the lab was pleasant. When there, breakfast was delicious. Her ever-present envoy was his usual cordial self, ignoring her questions and doing a fantastic job with the crud that had been building up on the tiled floor. She got on with her work, realigning another emitter, with a bounce in her step that took her by surprise. Something was different, so after a few hours lost in quantum adjustments, she stopped and put the tools down. She ran a self-diagnostic, something she hadn't done since university, in which she listed all of her bodily functions and states of mind as imaginary lights in her head, red and green. One-by-one, she honestly appraised the state of play and assigned green for good, red for bad. The probable yeast infection aside, all the lights were green. That wasn't even the case in her teens. Most confusing was the last indicator.

Was she happy? Her first thoughts upon waking up were now of the future, not the past, and she hadn't spontaneously burst into tears in over a month.

The fiery suns of this alien world had burned away decades of misery, and she felt more at home than she ever had on her own planet. The creatures didn't demand eye-contact or belittle her awkward manner, at least not since they'd stopped trying to kill her. They accepted her like she'd never been by other humans. Maybe she'd just been with the wrong people, but here and now it felt more like she'd been on the wrong planet.

Kim chewed on that thought and wondered. Did she still want to go home?

Kim had no time to answer that hypothetical before a disturbance in her vision told her Benito was back. He was already in the lab by the time she extracted herself from the guts of her machine and, this time, he was alone.

So was she, as Caruthers was nowhere to be seen.

"Kimberley."

Ben floated in front of the primary display directly under the lab clock. Six feet above the ground and without the aid of the ladder, which stood just behind. He said nothing more after that one word.

"Huh, didn't know you guys could do that."

He stayed silent just long enough to make her nervous again. Then, in the space of half a second, he covered the ten-ish feet between them and stopped just a few millimetres from her face. Kim felt both the displaced air and her own defensive reflexes pushing her back, but stood firm, which was an instinct she'd learned from years of being bullied. At close range, Ben's skin resembled a deep leathery mahogany that was criss-crossed with silver pulsating capillaries that blended in completely from more than a few inches away. It was beautiful.

"Do.. You guys moisturise?"

Even though she couldn't see the tentacles wrapped around her, she felt the force around her chest and shoulders, and it wasn't pleasant. There was heat and compression, which was to be expected, but the sickening vibration conducting a symphony through her bones? It felt like electricity and death, like her heart had stopped, but her blood was still flowing. She had to force air into her lungs to speak.

"We.. Had a deal? Don't.. Kill.."

Ben lifted her and propelled them both into a side room. It happened so quickly she almost blacked out on the way. The pressure wave that followed slammed the door loudly. As it shut, Ben dropped her onto the floor.

"I would never harm you, Kimberley. We must speak privately on a matter of some urgency."

"You won't kill me?"

"Nothing dies, Kim, not really. But, no, and I apologise if that was what you believed. This is a joyous occasion!"

It didn't feel joyous. Her left shoulder was grinding audibly and felt dislocated, and there was pee running down the inside of her leg.

"I.. What?"

"In honour of our great collaborations here, I plan on giving you our greatest honour. I have prepared to receive you in the great hall at the palace."

Kimberley had been the butt end of a lot of pranks in her life, but she felt like she belonged here. She liked this world, and she was starting to really like Benito.

"Oh. Wow. I mean, that's a lot. Thank you!"

"Tell no other until the announcement."

Ben backed away, and as he did, the door opened to reveal Joseph and Caruthers. The latter rushed in and placed himself in front of Kim.

"What's going on here?"

"Relax old one. I was just giving Kim here some good

news." And then directly to Kim. "I'll be in contact shortly. Remember what I said."

Then they left Kim alone in the room with Caruthers.

"What did he say?"

"I can't.."

Now she felt Caruthers tentacles around her, just as strong but much hotter, vibrating like disturbed hornets and just as much of a threat.

"Listen to ME. I stand between you and Ben. He's my kind, not yours. You would do well to remember the distrust you harboured not so long ago." He squeezed a little harder. White spots floated into Kim's vision. "You need to remember who you really are. You're nothing to him. Never speak with him outside my presence again."

5 / MUTUALLY ASSURED DESTRUCTION

Caruthers stopped to focus himself back into one reality. Everything was happening too quickly, or at least seemed to be. Focus. Another violent movement in the complex's fabric threw the room to the right by several sublengths. A large container of alien clothing dislodged from the racking above and dropped, pointed-corner first, onto the top of his being, before disgorging its contents onto the floor. His immediate concern, that he'd only just finished organising this space, dispersed. More pressing matters reared along with the ground, as yet another shift caused a cascade of failures in the rack supports, blocking the exit.

"Jesus!"

He'd been spending too much time with the alien, Kimberley. Her ways and language stained his being like so much lubricating fluid. He made a mental note to work on it after he got out.

He phased a limb and took hold of the cold metal barring his way. By using a good portion of his strength, he got it to move, albeit only scant micro lengths. Not enough to transfer himself. This impromptu cage had him trapped.

As this new reality sank in, the lights failed.

Their world was tide-locked to the largest of the three stars that illuminated their planetary system. It was always present in the sky above, pouring photons on to every surface that then cascaded off other surfaces like warm liquid. There was only one place it didn't reach and Caruthers had been fortunate enough to have never seen the crystal mines. He'd existed a long time without experiencing total darkness.

He didn't like it.

"Bitch!"

Whatever was happening had to be her fault. Something she'd cooked up with Ben, perhaps? Or maybe now she had his trust she'd signalled an invasion of her kind? He didn't care. When he found her, he was going to squeeze until she popped like a juice-cube and then drink what came out. First thing first, though, he had to get out. He pulled a few more limbs into existence and felt around until he found a bare wall, then rose to find the ceiling. It was a false partition, being a single suspended layer of crumbling tiles that separated the space below from wiring and ducting that lead into neighbouring rooms. The largest of the passageways, the one Kim had called 'air-conditioning', was easy to find, even with no vision. He wouldn't fit inside, but he didn't need to. He just needed to follow it until it met with another wall. Pulling the ducting from its mounts and then forcing the twisted metal back through the opening with enough force to create a hole big enough took a large amount of effort, leaving Caruthers unable to maintain his limbs for a micro-period, and dropping him back to the floor. After a rapid filtering of the atmosphere through his diaphanous membranes, he found he could control the pace of his inhalations and finish the job by climbing out.

Welcome sunlight from the atrium at the far end of the corridor reflected warm onto his skin, lifting the heavy weight pressing down on his spirit, but not enough to prevent another collapse as his limbs deserted him again and he sank back down to the floor. The air moved more easily through his being now he was out, but he couldn't stay. Kimberley was up to something and he had to know what it was, maybe stop her before it was too late.

It took more inhalations and effort than he liked to get moving again, and he felt every cycle of his age pulling him down and draining his resolve. Then the ground moved again, this time downwards and violent enough to leave him airborne before landing hard. Suspended ceiling tiles rained crumbled beige in messy clumps all over his neat-swept floor.

"Agh!"

Paralysis took hold as his orbs darted back and forth across the debris-field, in the end fixing on one small area that was unmarred, shielded from the mess by the rolling cart he used to carry his cleaning tools. One thought took hold, burning hot in his mind, causing him to lash out, smashing the cart into an array of pieces that scattered out and away from the wall. He had achieved nothing, but at least he was mobile again, so he picked his way through growing piles of detritus to the atrium, which was holding up well. The wisdom tree gave him a once-over as he passed and leered, no doubt seeing something disappointing. Since he didn't have time to ask, he moved on.

An alert was blaring over the internal speaker system that he couldn't understand since he needed a consciousness to read for the words to make sense, but it was loud and annoying. On top of this emergency, lighting had replaced the usual tired orange glow with an urgent red that flashed. The sensory assault combined to leave Caruthers disorientated, causing him to make a wrong turn off the main corridor into a side room full of discarded undergarments Kim had been hiding since he arrived.

He tripped over a small hillock of socks into a moist scattering of other assorted bits and bobs. When he righted himself, something was stuck to his back. He materialised a limb and threw it at the wall, where it adhered for a moment before rejoining its friends on the floor.

Only then did he see the fungal spores, which were everywhere.

He reentered the corridor and shuddered before taking a moment to be sure that this time he was going the right way. The announcement looped and restarted just as another event rocked the building. Straight on and round the corner, to the right. When he got there, the door was gone, replaced by a wall of metal, a security partition he hadn't been aware of. Caruthers took the keypad and forced the buttons until they popped off one-by-one and fell to the ground with hollow plastic clacks. He then crushed the remains into a ball of sparks before hurling it at the wall.

None of it helped with the fluttering in his digestion chamber, or the painful lightness in his upper torso.

"I know you're in there, harlot. This cage won't protect you for long."

That didn't help either. He tried the air-conditioning trick again but found nothing that led inside, even after tearing the entire ceiling down and throwing himself at the cold metal. After that, he threw a tantrum worthy of a first cycle youngster, screaming and flailing until all the energy and irrational thought had left his body, which took a good number of micro-cycles.

To his surprise, that helped.

With a slower mind, his thoughts were more cohesive, and he remembered the button panel in the aliens' sleeping chamber, which controlled almost everything in the building. With a sigh, he turned back for the corridor and made for the stairwell, a journey that was much quicker this time. The tree judged him again as he passed, and a deep-set frown formed on its taciturn features.

"Yeah, well, screw you."

The stairs looked dangerous but were the only way up. Once at the top, after a sizeable time spent lugging his heavy and spent frame, he regained composure. The ground-shakes were lessening in both intensity and frequency and they, along with Kim's poor housekeeping, had broken most of the bulbs on this floor, so fewer red flashing lights. Logic infused his thoughts with a more even-brained view of what was happening. Whatever it was, Benito's thought-processes were all over it. It had to be him. What'd he and the creature talked about? Maybe they'd been developing some new weapon to be turned against those that opposed him, and now they were using it to get rid of Caruthers? He was still going to kill the alien when he found her, if he survived.

He was just calmer about it.

She'd been taking her rest-cycles in what had been a security station. A large room that was connected to all the base security systems, enabling the creation of her makeshift control panels. Once he had dominion over them, he would lift the lockdown. Preparing for the worst as he inched along yet another rubbish strewn corridor, Caruthers moved back through his memories and felt the texture of the door and walls surrounding it, pushing, willing a weakness that he could exploit. The fluttering was back, filling his mind with doubt like a first cycle rookie, something he never experienced. He had never seen the door locked, but he'd seen how thick and solid it was being a former security booth.

He needn't have bothered worrying. The door was open wide.

Inside, on the bed, Kimberley had balled herself up with arm-extremities covering her hear-holes. She was naked, and she was screaming something guttural that hurt. Caruthers swept in and directed his attention to the controls, which were just to her right. The sticky-tape, stretched and re-stuck many times, had new singe-marks. Dark smoke was escaping from a hole in the top, filling the room with the pungent odour of dying electrons. Kim's shrieking had become irritating, filling his head with unpleasant images, so he took her form in his limbs, even producing several new ones to prevent any chance of escape, and lifted her off the bed.

That was when he felt it. A catastrophic loss of agency that drained the heat from his body and froze his thoughts into shards of pain. This wasn't something he was used to. He'd been unsure of himself, sure, unable to rationalise an outcome ahead of time, but never to where the worst outcome became an all-consuming reality.

And, he realised, he'd been feeling it this entire time.

Right now, though, with Kimberley in his limbs, it was clear he was experiencing this feeling second hand, absorbing the outpourings of her unmarshalled, rapid-fire, unfocussed thoughts. She was emitting her terror like a soft pink sun that fused nightmares instead of hydrogen, and he'd been tanning himself in it.

Caruthers prepared to crush the life out of her, squeezing

Kimberley hard enough to elicit a pop from an upper limb socket. He looked into her eyes, wanting the satisfaction of feeling her death, but she didn't even register he was there.

"Look at me. LOOK AT ME!"

He threw her back onto the mattress, where she dropped her arms and lessened her screeching. She stared at him for a few eternity-spanning moments before speaking.

"What the hell have you done?"

"What have I done? This is your doing, wench. I.. Isn't it?"

He wasn't as certain as he had been. Kim appeared to have emptied her bladder-chamber onto the bed before he'd arrived. The resulting odour, along with her screaming and general nudity, wasn't projecting the air of control a master-mind would muster. The building sub-structure groaned as reinforcing metal stretched and compressed way beyond the design specs. Kim gawped but said nothing more, so Caruthers took charge.

"We have to get out of here. Now. Kim, NOW!"

* * *

She wasn't moving, and it was making him reconsider, but he still attempted to encourage her with a few prods from a timepiece that was near to a limb extremity. She repaid his help by grabbing the alarm-clock and throwing it with all her strength at his face-area.

"Kimberley, we have to get out of this death-trap before it collapses on top of us."

"NO! We have to cancel the alert."

"So do it, then we leave."

He followed her gaze as she turned to the control panel.

The smoke was still there, but now it had a friend, some fire. He looked back at her face, where he found an expression that combined a frown with a snarl that exposed her upper masticators.

"I'm guessing you can't do it from here, huh?"

"No shit, Sherlock."

She was still in the grip of a dread that would paralyse most. Caruthers could feel it oozing from her dermis even as her countenance betrayed nothing and portrayed calm. The speed at which she donned this practised facade took him by surprise and earned respect. The smell of urine only lessened the effect slightly.

"Why is this so important?"

Another tremor punctuated his words with a convenient rumble which shook Kim's remaining knick-knacks off the makeshift bedside table.

"If we don't, the reactor.. It'll destroy.. I won't, mm. Mmm!"

"Yeah, I mean, that is really more of a you problem. Good luck with that."

Caruthers turned to the door, mentally noting that he had to stop talking like that, getting around half way there before a drink-receptacle flew past and smashed into the adjacent wall. Several pieces of glass ricocheted into his being, but did no damage.

"Seriously? I could break every organ in that fleshy sack you.."

As he spoke, voice low and gravelly, he spun as slowly as he could. She was rocking back and forth on her heels with her arm extremities dancing. Fighting the icy death filling her mind, but still frowning, and now deep red in the face. A low hum was the only sound she made, and he could feel words backing up in her head like traffic jammed into a pinch-point, unable to move either way. The intent in her thoughts was clear, though, and he didn't like what he saw.

"What in the actual hell, Kim!"

"Mmm!"

"Stop! I don't need the words. Just concentrate on the details and I'll feel them. How big? How much power are we dealing with?"

"It's, mmm!"

Enough to destroy everything within several mega-lengths.

"This whole place is a giant bomb?"

Kimberley nodded, still mute.

"How do we stop it? Don't speak, instead imagine the solution with as much detail as possible. Make it into pictures."

The override was in the main lab area. An insignificant toggle switch under a protective flip-cover on a panel right next to the central console, but weirdly not on it. Lift the cover, flip the switch and then disconnect the anti-espionage protocol with a pair of wire-clippers.

"Oh. That could be a problem."

"Why?"

Kim was regaining her composure, which made her less petrified and more pragmatic. This was a good thing, as he needed her calm before explaining their predicament.

"Well, there's an impenetrable wall blocking access to the laboratory."

"Yeah, it's a blast shield. It's easy enough to open with the code."

Caruthers knew where this was going.

"Does this 'code' get entered via a small buttony box?"

"You mean the keypad? Yes. I set the code to.."

"It doesn't matter what the code is."

"What did you do?"

"The important thing here is that it's broken. Is there another way in? I couldn't find an air-conditioner conduit when I.. Why are you observing me in that manner?"

Kimberley had collected one of her customary jumpsuits from a pile on the ground and was climbing in as she stared at him. She had the same expression as the wisdom-tree did earlier.

"I found it broken when I got there all right. You need to move on. How do we get in?"

"I can open it from the other security room."

He felt the relief wash down from his upper regions. Simultaneously cool and exhilarating, with a tangy metallic aftertaste. Kim's next sentence soured things a little.

"You can fly, right?"

Caruthers didn't understand the question.

"I don't understand the question."

"It's in an inaccessible area." She sighed in a manner he didn't like before continuing. "About twenty feet above where the stairwell ends. You can get there from the atrium, but not without climbing a sheer wall of steel-reinforced concrete all the way to the sodding top."

"The.. Top?"

"Yeah, past the security grid."

"Security grid?"

"Yeah, high-powered anti-personnel countermeasures. Relax, I'm pretty sure they're off by now."

"Pretty sure?"

"Stop repeating everything I say and answer the question. Can you fly?"

He wasn't sure he liked this new, slightly more confident Kimberley. He definitely didn't like the idea of elevating himself to the atriums' apex just to experience deadly force and a long drop back to the bottom.

"No."

Now Kimberley's frown was gone, replaced by a single raised eyebrow. He didn't need to feel her thoughts to know why, but he didn't want to go into further detail, so he flanked her incoming question with one of his own.

"Are you sure there's no other way in? These air-conditioning.."

"I've seen you guys flying."

He could tell she wouldn't let it go, which meant there wasn't another way.

"No, you haven't." She opened her mouth to counter, but he got there first. "It's not technically flying, as much as it's standing tall. Like you would stand on the extremities of your bottom limb-nodes."

"You mean Tippy-toes?"

"I don't know what that is, but let us say yes. We can grow our 'tippy-toes' as required for height, but not without risk."

"What's the worst that can happen?"

"The strength required.."

"Is it worse than this entire region being vaporised in a nuclear explosion?"

He didn't want to, but he saw her point.

"Fine."

Neither said anything else before reaching the bottom of the atrium. The wisdom tree was on its side, having tipped over during the last quake. It still pursed its lips and rolled its eyes as Caruthers moved past. When Looking up, everything seemed much further than he'd remembered, but he wasted no time in reaching for the top. He was halfway there before Kim stopped him.

"Stop!"

She said more, but that one word was all he felt and it felt urgent, so he returned to the ground.

"Aren't you forgetting something?"

Elevate to the top, enter the security booth, and disable the blast shield. He ran through the short list a couple more times in his mind to be sure before answering.

"No."

"There's no way you're fitting through the access panel. I need you to head back and disable the protocol from the lab."

"I.. Wait, I'm not sure.."

"Carry me up there. Once I'm in, head to the lab and wait for the doors to open."

He observed her frame more closely. Talkative meaty victuals hung inefficiently inside a sack of fluids and then propped up on a calcium scaffold. She looked more weighty than he remembered.

"Don't you look at me like that? You picked me up fine just a few minutes ago. Where did all the 'I will crush you like a paper cup' shit go, huh?"

She seemed resolute. Caruthers explored her memories of the panel and found she wasn't jesting, so he forewent any further verbal jousting and just picked her up and made for the top. The journey was short and silent, which was mostly because he could feel his limbs failing again and needed all his focus, but didn't want to show it. Kim flinched in his limbs as they approached an emitter and then audibly breathed out once past it, but otherwise it was uneventful until they reached the hatch which was smaller in reality than Caruthers had seen it in Kim's head. A grating, which he was unaware of, blocked it too.

"Bollocks!"

He wasn't ready for Kim's sudden outburst and reflexively phased some limbs supporting her. Catching the alien used most of his depleted energy reserves.

"What's 'Bollocks'? Is this not supposed to be here? Are you not prepared?"

"Well, yes. I was just hoping, you know? Hold me steady so I can unscrew it."

He figured honesty was the best policy at this point.

"I don't know if I.."

The speed with which she lashed out left Caruthers scrambling and confused for a micro-period, but he realised what had happened just before hitting the ground. From his prone position, he watched the distant blob that was Kim slip before re-finding her footing and scrambling into the access way above. The grate, which she'd punched out before jumping, caught an updraft and described a graceful downward spiral before hitting Caruthers midsection just before she got in.

"Go! Get to the lab."

Was he to take orders from this filthy thing? He righted himself and considered shouting back, but reconsidered and charted an unsteady path to the control room where the barrier was already gone. He disabled the alert and then reached in to disconnect the wiring, at which point the alarm started back up. Caruthers considered his options and reached back in, finessing his limbs along the conduits and cables as he searched for power signals. Then he got antsy and seized every conduit he could sense before tearing the entire mechanism out, along with the attached panel, and tossing it into a corner where it caught fire.

Silence. No alarm.

A sudden violent movement brought him back to full consciousness. The immediate threat of a nuclear powered ending gone, Caruthers ignored the growing ache in his body and righted himself once again. A sense of joy filled his form before being extinguished by another tremor, although this was the smallest yet, barely shaking any still-upright equipment.

"Help!"

Kimberley. He couldn't hear her from the lab, but he could almost see the wide-eyed and sweaty expression on her countenance. Thinking about capture-pods, Caruthers hauled himself back toward the atrium and the alien trapped there.

Progress was slow. Retrieving Kim from the high passageway in the atrium took longer than he imagined it would since she refused to jump, and he lacked the strength to rise far enough to grab her. An aftershock focused negotiations, but not before a stand-off that lasted several time periods and almost ended with him leaving the squishy sack where she was. The solution reached involved several lengths of cable, a lot of screaming and some pain as she dropped the final distance into a web of limbs he brought forth just in time. Once on the ground, she delayed and procrastinated, throwing excuses like projectiles as if she hoped to deflect his attention from the precarious state of the complex. But he could see the thoughts behind her words, which were little more than a play-book. A script of utterances such as the view-minstrels would recite as their own. Behind those fake rationales, she was uncertain, spiralling like the grate she'd punched out earlier. There wasn't far to fall and he could sense her thoughts converging on the inevitable. She had no agency, and she knew it. Waiting for her to get there was interminable.

"H. Jesus Christ! Open the portal!"

"I.. Look, the situation isn't that serious. If we shore up the.. Wait, did you say H. Jesus?"

"You're focussing on the wrong thing, Kimberley."

Serendipity provided Caruthers with some help, dressed as a gantry which chose that moment to detach itself from the bolts connecting it to one wall and swing into another. It cut through as a warmed blade would bisect a youngling, but with less life-juice and more sparky explosive partitioning.

"See!"

"But, I need.."

Her voice faded, but the thoughts didn't. Inside her head, Caruthers could see something, but it was just a glimmer. Benito was there. Before he could understand what he was seeing, it was gone, leaving Kimberley standing with her arm-ends balled as tightly as her cranial expression.

"You need to open the portal so we can leave. Or just me. I do not care any further Kimberley. If you wish to end your existence here under a pile of rubble, that is your.. Oh."

It was open. Kim's fingers lifted from the panel as her face fell, with no readable expression. She was swaying again, back and forth. Caruthers probed deeper and felt a loss which was understandable, but not just for her work. She was mourning for her identity.

"Where will I go?"

He knew what he wanted to say. He didn't care. The thought of abandoning her reared like a friendly pet, slobbering for attention. There was nothing left here, and he needed to get somewhere safe, but finding Ben in her thoughts had him intrigued and she had a point. All her cycles in this world spent sealed away inside the complex. All of this required a slight reformulation of his reply.

"I am going to my home."

A crease crossed her brow, then a flicker in her eyes, but nothing else. Maybe she hadn't heard him through the chaos all around.

"I am going to my home. It is near and should be safe."

Another clench of her fists and then movement in her mouth, but no sound. He felt uncertainty build in her again, and it was irksome. Where was she going to get a better offer?

"Are you coming or not?"

"Are.. You being.. Do you mean it?"

At last. He made for the exit with haste as more of the supporting structures were choosing this time to exercise their newfound rights to freedom of movement. He got as far as a sealed outer decontamination chamber, which she'd forbidden him from ever entering, before realising Kim hadn't followed. She was still standing where she had been, but now perfectly still. Her uncertainty was now overwhelming. He could feel it cover her like a heavy blanket, obscuring the truth of his words.

"Yes! I do not say things unless I mean them Kimberley."

Now she moved.

In the time it took Kim to catch up with him, the doorway he was hoping to escape through collapsed. As he tried to lift the debris, more fell, and a large crack in the wall announced itself before reaching for the ceiling via a brief detour through another support lintel. Caruthers felt a hand on his body, pushing him away from the danger and toward the sealed chamber, which Kim opened with a practised dance over the keypad. Once inside, the corners of her mouth opening curled upwards into a smile, creasing the flesh around her eyes and betraying her exhaustion.

"You're going to need to fly one more time."

A series of red lights illuminated the small room before yet another disagreeable alarm filled the space with noise. Kimberley was holding onto his torso tight enough for him to feel some discomfort.

"I.. What?"

Then they were airborne. Not immediately, since the matter evacuation system ran for several lengths, but Caruthers spent most of that period trying to figure out what was going on. The building finished evacuating the two of them just as he got it, and there they were in the sky.

The view was spectacular. Distant fuel fires streaked the sky with a dark smoke that fully obscured the smaller sun while illuminating the devastation on the ground. The vast clean lines defining the palace courtyard blurred and elongated with shifting shadows from the furious red and orange flames. Out on the horizon, the bright green structural force-field that surrounded all municipal buildings in case of attack outlined and supported the palace. He didn't have long to enjoy the spectacle once the horizon began rushing up to meet them. The landing was going to hurt and there was little he could do to mitigate with the strength he had left, and with a sweaty meat-limpet throwing his balance, so he called on all that remained of his reserves and threw out limbs in every direction. One found the ground but slipped on the dusty surface. The sudden jarring overextension felt like blades through his flesh, temporarily disconnecting Caruthers from the realm of forces and dissolving his remaining tentacular protrusions. The momentary contact he'd made had the effect of bouncing the pair away from the structure, imparting downward and lateral forces that slowed their descent enough for a second try, so try he did. This time he could see downward and aimed his limbs with more confidence. The only problem was that none came. Caruthers had faced down many enemies during his life-tenure. He'd won countless honour-duels and bested armies of filthy lesser beings with his superior intellect and breeding, and he'd done so with decorum. Now here he was moments from exploding, such as a nutrient-ova would if dropped from a height onto a searing-plate, and he was struggling to overcome the frosty fingers spiking into his confidence. Not so much that he couldn't shift his weight and position the bringer of his downfall to take the initial impact, though.

"Now would be a good time to do some of that levitation shit, Caruthers!"

He had a retort lined up and wrapped a tendril around her throat to be sure she was paying attention, but realised that the force of impact was going to hurt her far worse. He also realised that he had limbs again, so threw all of them down. The sudden deceleration shook the monster loose, and she tumbled hard. Hitting the unforgiving surface cut her mid-air scream short with a satisfying slap. He followed a Milli-period later, producing a heavier thump and rolling away. He was in pain and had several serious abrasions, but he was alive.

"Jesus! You.. You dropped me! Ah.. Uh.. Shit, I think it's broken."

The creature had deceptive durability and was also still alive. It was also moaning in a high-pitch that he barely registered as it was and was getting higher. Caruthers directed his attention toward the noise and found Kimberley laying prone and breathing in a ragged, irregular manner. One of her upper limbs was bent at an acute angle he hadn't seen before, and her life fluids were draining from a ragged tear in her dermis beyond where the now shredded material of her clothing had failed to protect her. It looked raw, like uncooked eating-flesh. He imagined the pain she was suffering and considered that, whilst impure and lesser; she had undoubtedly saved his life.

Once upright and sure he wasn't seriously injured, he closed the distance between them, increasing his pace as a massive explosion tore through the structure of the lab complex. Large pieces of the outer walls flew outward, defying gravity for a time and then falling toward Kim's position. He raced through, grabbing the alien with little regard for her disjointed limb, which dragged under her body and snapped with a wet cracking and a piercing scream. The vast piece of structure hit the ground some ten lengths from where they'd been, shaking the ground, and then tumbled outward. The inner surface was still ablaze and pushed more smoke into the already darkened sky.

They had to get away to the relative safety of his home and its protective force-fields.

"Can you perambulate independently?"

He could feel Kim's breathing and the warmth in her body, but she didn't reply, so he gave her a gentle shake.

"Uh? What?"

"We must go, now. I cannot carry you."

Caruthers placed her back on the ground and executed a brief outer examination. Life-fluids were no longer seeping from her meat and, in a surprising development, her broken limb was no longer angled unnaturally and was moving as it always had. The grimace twisting her mouth and wrinkling the dermis around her odour inlets betrayed the agony she was experiencing.

"It's all gone."

Now he could feel her pain. Those three words, innocuous in many other situations, floated on a wave of emotion strong enough to stagger his own thoughts. Fluids ran free from her orbs and down her face, cutting tracks in the grime already there. He looked deeper to find some hope he could use to leverage compliance, but found nothing. No thoughts at all. It was as if she was the embodiment of her work, and all that remained without it was a chasm that was slowly filling with hatred.

For the second time in this period, Caruthers felt an icy tremor flow through his frame.

* * *

THE REMAINING JOURNEY TO CARUTHERS' HOME WAS long but uneventful, at least compared with what had gone before. They saw no one and experienced only a handful of diminishing aftershocks. The Kim-creature could walk unaided, and once the conflagration that consumed the lab was no longer in view, more positive ideations returned to her mind, much to his relief. It took time enough, though, for him to consider the events of the day. The hate he'd experienced in Kim's thoughts was consuming her. He'd never seen it before because she kept it a secret. A mask of practised platitudes and learned behaviour hid her true self, but it was always there.

And he was about to bring her into his personal sanctuary.

"How much further?"

He couldn't believe she'd scared him only moments ago. The edge in her voice had left, replaced with petulant whining. He was thankful that, unlike the last time she asked, they were close.

"Near."

"God! You said that ages ago. I'm getting tired, my feet hurt.."

"You can always stay here and perish, if you prefer?"

"I.. No, I'm good. Lead on."

And then they were there. The structure had withstood the quakes with no visible damage. The outer areas were strewn with debris from unprotected buildings nearby, but his sanctuary stood intact on its foundations, wearing its shimmering green force coat. He reached in to open the entrance-portal and ushered Kim through. He followed, sealing the portal behind them.

"Wow. I mean, I didn't know what to expect but.. Wow."

"Move through to the next space. The centre of the building will be safest."

Once he was sure she couldn't see him, Caruthers moved to the hidden locker by the garment support-post before forgetting the security code and failing to open it.

"Shit!"

More of her colourful language. He was spending too much time with the creature.

He gave up on the locker and joined Kim in the central space where he found her refilling his info-nook with scattered tomes from the floor. She wasn't doing an outstanding job.

"Leave them. There is a particular order.. No, I'm serious, leave them."

He enabled the view-streams and tuned the widest range

he could manage. He hoped for something positive but found only horror. The quakes had taken everyone by surprise, leaving countless souls unprotected and unprepared. All but the protected municipal structures had failed, and nearest to the epicentre, even the protected structures had taken damage. Several of the usual streams were unavailable, but those remaining painted the vast loss of sentience in bleak lines and hard screams. Beings he'd known, some of whom he'd even been friendly with, pressed into the next realm like juice-cubes.

Kim was still staring at the projected hell-scape with an expression Caruthers had not witnessed before. The muscles in her face were slack, leaving her stretchy food-hole rims parted just a little. Her upper-limbs raised such that as the extremities waved back and forth, they drummed a rhythm on her torso. There was no emotion he could read, no anger or fear. It was as if she was calculating how best to react.

Cold, like a machine.

Then she laughed. It was almost imperceptible, breath passing by chords in the fragile tube of flesh connecting her thinking centre to the rest of her body. He couldn't be sure at first. Then she did it again, only louder.

Caruthers left the room and opened the locker. The period inside helped calm the torrent carving through his mind and gave him the code, a combination he'd picked based on the past but prescient right now. The plush inside contained several items, things he wasn't supposed to have.

He re-sealed the locker and carried one back into the living space before pointing it at Kim.

A furrow formed in the space between her orbs. He felt the question as it danced across her synapses before she asked.

"What the hell, C?"

He was hoping for more from her last words, but it tracked with her usual retorts so it would have to do. Aiming for her lower limbs, which would prolong the agony, he pulled the trigger and waited to see what the un-maker would do with such a base life-form. Only as she dived behind his furniture did he remember the safety catch.

"You did this! You brought this upon us."

"I don't know what you're talking about! Listen to.."

The blast disintegrated the lounge-stool that it was hiding behind, splinters of light engulfing the smooth bouncy surface before exploding outwards into a kaleidoscope of smoke and colourful sound. The alien was unharmed and showed as much by diving behind his info-nook. She then started throwing tomes with accuracy that could only be luck, catching the un-maker and swatting it out of his grasp. It hit the ground via a convoluted route that introduced the trigger with some floor-junk, causing a bolt of disintegration to remove his favourite rest-nook from reality.

He grabbed the weapon and pointed it where Kim had been, but she wasn't any more.

"I will end you Kimberley. There is no leaving this place for you."

The taunt elicited no response, leaving Caruthers unsure of her exact whereabouts. There were few places she could be, though. He tried the eating-preparation space first, bursting the portal open with a flurry of limbs.

She wasn't there.

As he turned, the portal swung shut, blocking his way.

"I didn't do this. I can't believe you'd even think I could."

There was a higher register to her voice, part way between a shout and a scream, and a new vibrato. The blast caused the portal barrier to expand in its tight-fitting frame before turning to smoke and fire, cracking the load-bearing support structure above, but not enough to cause a collapse. Once the haze cleared, he crept through, avoiding contact with the portal-surround, before heading to the slumber-pod.

"You murdered my kind. I will see you end in agony, filth."

"You're whacked! We're friends. I saved your damn life earlier today."

She was back in the main living-space. He diverted toward her now wavering and panic-flecked voice.

"I could never be friends with your kind. You're fit only for the mines."

"Think about this, please. Just stop for a moment and think!"

He did. For a brief time, the cognitive dissonance that allowed Kim to be both a lower being, devoid of the wit and intelligence needed to clean his waste receptacle, and a genius tactician that had ended many of his comrades unwound. Then he remembered the laugh and complete lack of perceivable emotion. More news in his peripheral vision steeled his resolve.

"They're gone, just.. Gone."

Younglings in a learn-centre, elders in ever-living spaces. A clearer view showed the destruction centred around a crystal-processing facility and had only spread to the bordering regions. Panic was spreading, though, bringing a fresh wave of despair.

"I didn't think you could die."

There was a new cracking in her voice, which broke into a horse whisper at higher registers. Caruthers could feel confusion. Did she do this to test that hypothesis? He didn't care to find out. Her voice placed her on an upper level, the unused observation decking. He fired upwards through the ceiling, being careful to avoid any more of the load-bearing sub-structure. The resulting hole allowed for fast access to his prey.

He rose to find her scrambling for access back downwards. She tripped in her haste, her torso stretching forward as her perambulators stopped fast. The fall tore open the earlier wound in her side, liberating a generous portion of her life-fluids which dripped onto the coated surface of his view-floor.

It looked like it might stain.

"Take it. It's all yours. I'll give you the codes, the notes, everything. Just.. Please?"

Was she begging?

"I want nothing from you but to see you end."

"Then why are you doing this? You can have it. You don't need to kill me."

"Revenge for the fallen!"

"Stop! I'm out now. You don't need to keep up this bull-shit pretence."

It was Caruthers turn to lose the thread. He ran back through the spoken words of the last few periods and probed for missed meaning, finding none. He raised the un-maker and levelled the sights with care, this time aiming for her thought-centre.

Then an unexpected internal conflict, fed by his curiosity, stayed his limbs.

On the ground at his lower limbs, Kimberley was moving with care to conserve her body-liquids. Now sitting upright, she was mute, but he could feel the chaos in her cranium. A stray thought rose above the noise and caught his attention.

"You think this is a trick?"

All she could manage in response was a murmur, maybe an attempt to communicate, but just as likely the result of the pain she was no doubt experiencing. Caruthers no longer cared. He adjusted his aim upwards a little to compensate for the weight of the weapon and to ensure a clean kill, pulling the trigger and once again experiencing disappointment. A squeaky-beep announced that the charge had spent and would need a few more micro-periods to rebuild.

Caruthers expressed his frustration with a roar. Kim used the reprieve to throw herself from the building.

"Just die already!"

A second squeak showed that killing was back on the menu. By that time, he was at the edge, looking down at Kim's broken form. She was moving, trying to crawl away from his wrath, but not effectively. The wound had grown in size, revealing internal tissues that greater minds would dissect and pore over later.

"Screw you, C. Screw you and this entire planet."

"No, Kimberley, screw you."

She just couldn't believe what was happening. Bits and pieces fitted like a cheap jigsaw if you hammered them down and pushed hard, but not everything.

Pain momentarily wrenched her attention from the death-barrel aiming square at her head, narrowing her peripheral vision and leaching colour from what remained. Waves of nausea rolled in from nowhere in a relentless flanking manoeuvre, which, combined with her lack of mobility, produced a lap full of purplish bile. More pain followed, meaning less vision and more nausea, until all she could see and feel was black.

"Ben said you were a good.."

It was her voice, but quiet and distorted, like she was a million miles away and watching through a narrow telescope, hearing the words second hand. Then he had a tendril around her throat, hot like before but numbed by the overwhelming sensations the hole in her sternum was providing. Kim felt herself being lifted, the weight of her body on her neck. The pain in her body ebbed a little as the weight shifted, returning her clarity. Then Caruthers 'spoke', splitting her skull.

"Ben isn't who you think he is. And he can't save you.. Ah, damn!"

Kim threw up a second time, projecting stomach acid into Caruthers' eye-holes. It was an accident, but she didn't have the strength to tell him, deciding to use what remained to avoid soiling herself. She could at least die with her dignity somewhat intact.

Then she didn't.

She expected the heat and the noise. It was as she'd experienced earlier when the sofa exploded right in front of her. What she wasn't expecting was to still be alive to experience it. Kim looked up, seeing that Caruthers had dropped his gun and was retreating toward the building while staring at something behind where Kim slouched.

"Move no further."

A powerful voice, authoritative. It continued.

"I don't need you alive, Caruthers. Give me a reason and I'll gladly add your name to today's fallen."

Then there was a gap. Kim wasn't sure how long. It was like being asleep apart from being partly aware of what was happening, albeit in an abstract and incomprehensible way. A dream where unseen shapes made plans and discussed the future while she lay motionless on the floor. No, while she became the floor. Hundreds of shoes filled with sweaty feet trampling on her dirt encrusted surface. Then movement, starting with a jolt and stopping with a gradual deceleration that came with an indistinct ache she couldn't place. Over and over, hours moving through darkness while people climbed on and off. It was a metaphor for something, but just as Kim was grasping enough thought to work it out, reality intervened.

"You don't get to die just yet, Kimberley."

The last vestiges of her fever-dream faded, leaving her propped up in something that passed for a chair. Her wound was no longer bleeding and the smell of cooked meat permeated. Kim hoped that whatever they used to cauterise the opening was clean.

She tried to speak, but a crushing force limited the intake of breath. Was she having a heart attack? Sweat overwhelmed her left eyebrow and invaded the eye beneath. Her breathing, already fast and shallow, got faster, but not fast enough, and her air-starved brain shut down once more.

When she woke again, Kim found herself naked on what could have been a bed. It was smooth and supportive in all the right places, but had an aroma that was difficult to place, both pleasant and something you would try to wipe off a shoe. Creatures surrounded her, she could see Joseph and several of his team. She could also see the contents of her chest cavity floating about eighteen inches above her body, which was quite disconcerting.

"I believe we have them in the correct order this time."

Offal. That was what she could smell.

"I.. Think.. Those are mine."

Kim could see her lungs inflating and deflating as she spoke, her heart beating a little too fast and the fatty deposits on her liver. Blood pumped into her arteries, and she could see the vessels twitch with each beat. Then, once more, she was unconscious.

She dreamed about her cat. He was playing with a ball of red wool, batting it around as it unravelled around him, leaving red yarn laying in an increasingly untidy pile that just grew and grew until she leaned forward to pet his furry tummy and saw what all the wool represented.

This time she woke with a start, fully alert in a moment. She was back in the chair, although still naked, but now she was bound with her hands tightly confined behind her back. Kim glanced downwards and found everything where it should be, barring a slight bulge under her left breast that she didn't remember seeing there before, and a few bloodstains. Joseph stood in front with Caruthers' gun. He wasn't aiming it at her, so she followed his line of sight the best she could, given the constraints.

Caruthers.

He was bound just like her, but wasn't being as calm about it.

"I'll have you erased. You have no authority to.."

"Silence, old one. You dare to question my authority? I know what you did, what the two of you did."

Kim watched as Caruthers' restraints tightened, cutting into his torso.

"I.. Don't know what you.. mean! Release me now.. And you.."

"What? What can you grant me from your current position?"

"Ben.. Ito. He'd never allow you to.."

Joseph fired the weapon, producing a much smaller ball of light than the ones Kim remembered heading her way. A portion of Caruthers' front glowed an angry orange before flashing a blinding white and lifting outward with a glittery haze that was quite beautiful. His scream was less aesthetically pleasing, blinding Kim for a few seconds. When the vision returned, she realised some of the noise was coming from her.

"You have something to add, bug?"

It was Joseph, and he was talking to her. Kim composed herself the best she could, but her mind was racing, just like it always did when she stressed or found herself unprepared, which was often. Words filled her head but proved illusive when she reached out. Sentences wouldn't form no matter how hard she tried, so after what felt like an eternity, she gave up and shook her head.

"Are you sure? Which ever of you confesses first will live."

Still no words. Caruthers wasn't having the same difficulties though, and made this plain by projecting what looked like a cup at Joseph's head before speaking.

"What the hell is your meaning? Tell me so that I can give you what you want."

"That you two conspired to steal from the mines? That your clumsy attempt to transpose the crystals brought about this destruction, this.."

Joseph's voice broke as he tailed off.

"What are you saying? I could never.. Ask Benito.."

"Don't speak that name, traitor. We know he was involved, which brings us to.."

He moved back over to Kim. She didn't like where this was going.

"What were the two of you discussing at the fortress that day? What secrets do you hold in that fragile little egg?"

Joe poked Kim with enough force to bounce her head off the back of the chair, but said nothing further. The seconds combined into a minute or more. Enough time for Kim to gather herself and start assembling some sense from her brain-maelstrom.

"We didn't."

"You are going to need to do better than that."

"Are you saying this is real? I.. Thought this was a trick, to get me away from.. I don't even know what 'crystals' are for. What the hell would I do with them?"

Her peripheral vision showed Caruthers pulled against his bindings. Joe turned his back on Kim and mused at the wall.

"Maybe I have this wrong? Could it be that the only two not affected by this disaster, found fighting to the death not more than a few periods after the fact are, in fact, innocent?"

Caruthers answered for the wall.

"Yes! I.."

"That was rhetorical. Unless you have a confession to give, your demise will be quicker if you keep quiet from this point onwards."

More bindings wrapped themselves around the being. Kim could see marks appearing all over his torso where perhaps circulation had stopped.

"Kimberley. May I call you that?"

"It's.. I mean, I prefer.."

"What did you plot in that room? What treason did Benito concoct with you?"

"Nothing!"

"WHAT DID HE SAY TO YOU?"

Now Kim had a problem. She could remember every word. The elation she'd felt still gave her a happy-jolt of serotonin when she thought about how accepted she'd felt in that moment, but it was double edged. In the past, with very few exceptions, letting her guard down had been a one-way trip to humiliation city, population one. Had she missed something? Was it a set-up?

She could never tell, not for certain.

If she told Joe the truth, would it turn out that, however unlikely, this was still a ploy to separate her from the beacon and her way home? Benito's insistence on silence buttressed Kim's reluctance to test this hypothesis. She was obsessive about following instructions, and this didn't seem like the time to challenge that personality trait.

"Nothing."

She was staring at her knees. They were both scuffed, and a bruise was forming on the left one so she couldn't see Caruthers, but she could still hear him and he sounded surprised.

"What is this? What are you doing here?"

"All right, I've seen and heard enough."

Kim wasn't ever going to forget that voice and the sense of certainty it carried into her head.

* * *

KIM PULLED ON THE NEW COVERALLS. THEY WERE A reasonable facsimile of the clothes found in the lab-stores, being ugly, scratchy and a bit too tight, but they were a nicer shade of blue, though, and the material was lighter and stretchier, which helped with the lack of underwear. On the far side of the room, Caruthers was engaged in an argument with Joe that mostly involved threats and poking each other so hard that Kim could see their tendrils even in the daylight. From what she could make out, Joe was holding back, and they proved her theory a few moments later when Caruthers flew across the room into the one bookshelf that was still upright. Its contents joined him on the floor, along with a suicidal shelf. As he rose, hurling said shelf at Joe with ballistic force, Benito moved between the pair.

"Enough!"

Kim flexed her back, stretching her arms and feeling for injury. There was a dull ache in her belly that she didn't want to contemplate too much, but other than that, and the bruising, there appeared to be no lasting harm. Thinking about it, the ache could mean she needed the toilet.

Yes, that was it.

"Guys, I need to 'go'."

"You won't be safe without our protection. You should stay until we've finished talking.."

"No, I mean I need to 'go', you know, the little girl's room?"

Nothing, Caruthers usually understood her, but even he was silent.

"I need to empty the waste from my body."

Joe was his usual understanding self.

"Absorb it. We have no time for your disgusting rituals."

"It doesn't work that way."

Benito joined the discussion between his warring peers.

"You saw her internals. She is truthful about this."

"Jesus, I wasn't dreaming that?"

"Go to the rest-space adjacent. You may void your waste on Caruthers' slumber-bay."

"No, she may n.. AH!"

After doing her best to avoid making too much mess, Kim returned to find Caruthers squatting in a far corner, doing his best to appear nonchalant while Joe hovered nearby. Benito was in the centre of the room, amongst Caruthers' scattered possessions. He was immobile even as he spoke. His explanation seemed simple and hit enough verifiable pointers to put Kim simultaneously at ease and on edge.

The planet was dying. Over-mining had exposed the

core, and the resulting expansion of molten rock and gas had overwhelmed a central power-generating station. The explosion, which they'd felt as the first quake, then split the mantle on which the ground stood and caused several seismic events. The death toll was huge, running into thousands.

It wasn't a pretty picture, but it all made sense, given her experiences on the ground. There were a few pieces missing though, and she still wasn't sure where she fitted in to the puzzle.

"So, this was a test?"

"We had hoped to have more time with you, Kimberley.."

"Just Kim."

"Ah, yes, Kim. More time. This event has taken it all away. I had to know that you were trustworthy, that Caruthers would hold his nerve."

"And you couldn't think of another way? I nearly died."

Joe piped in from across the space. There was an annoying smugness to his voice.

"More nearly than you think. Your physiology is fragile, just Kim."

"Yeah, that's hilarious. Seriously though, Caruthers could have killed.."

"Oh, he wasn't a part of the plan."

Benito, and there was a sharp edge to the words as he spat them out.

"This fool nearly ruined everything."

"Perhaps if you included me in your scheming, I could be of more use?"

Joe threw a book at Caruthers, who parried it with a deft flip of some tendrils before swinging it back. Joe drew his weapon and disintegrated the tome mid-air before it was half-way back. Kim watched as the gun remained out of its holster and pointed at the older creature just long enough to imply a threat. Caruthers saw it too, slumping back to the ground with a submissive sigh.

Benito continued.

"This disaster has been a long time coming, Kim. Our scientists have been observing anomalous behaviour in the crust for a significant number of cycles. Alas, our greed for energy wrought a dependance on the mined crystals that leaves our planet on the verge of destruction."

"Yeah, I get that. We have that problem back home too, just without the imminent exposure of the planet's core. I'm, I.. Yeah, I still don't quite get why you need me?"

"Your technology."

Kim took a moment to think before replying. The silence stretched out long and thin while Kim worked through the scenarios in her head. The relative safety of the current situation allowing reality to permeate the bubble of hope she'd been hiding in since leaving the lab. It seeped in slowly, smothering her enthusiasm like an ice-cold blanket steeped in treacle.

"But it doesn't work. You know that."

Benito emitted a moment's doubt, carried without words on a wave of thought, and then it was gone, but there was still some sharpness, and inside it Kim felt she could see something secret. He was searching inside her head, giving her a connection to his thoughts she hadn't noticed before, and it was there, hiding in the back. She couldn't quite grasp it before he severed the link, happy with whatever he'd found inside her.

"You can make it work, Kimberley. You have potential, but you cannot see it through all the self-doubt."

"I.. But the lab is.."

"That is not something to worry about right now, Kim. Preparations are being made, and all you need to do is trust yourself."

"Hah!"

Caruthers didn't sound impressed. Kim watched as he rose back to his usual height and squared up to Joe, who didn't move. He then turned to Benito before speaking with words drenched in ire. Kim could feel the fire burning in her head like it was her own.

"Trust? You've known about this impending disaster for how long? How many lives would still be here if you had told of your suspicions rather than waiting for it to happen?"

Joseph turned to his leader. Kim thought she could feel a question in his mind, but it went unasked. Instead, he moved aside, allowing Caruthers an obvious line to Ben's position. Caruthers spoke again, but didn't move.

"Well? I have lost friends. I've known Joseph's family since he was a youngling. They would have been in the region most devastated. Tell him why you allowed them to be extinguished."

Ben sank just a little, almost imperceptible but Kim noticed. She always noticed.

"There was nothing that could have been done. The damage was already too great when the notification came. We had hoped that things would hold long enough to evacuate in an orderly manner. Then you appeared, Kim. At first they thought you might be the vanguard of an invading fleet.."

Caruthers thought-grunted in agreement. Everyone ignored him while Benito regained his train of thought.

"Where was I? Oh yes, invading fleet. Anyway, once we figured out you were simply a lost traveller, we thought instead of using your machine and its limitless power to re-seal the rift that is tearing our world apart."

He paused. Kim wondered if she was supposed to applaud, but waited for the rest.

"And that is why I provided you with help, Kim. I hoped to get you home while learning enough to use your technology to build a clean source of power for my world and heal the harm already done."

The speech felt rehearsed, pauses included. Kim thought about the micro-fusion reactor that powered the complex and all the waste it produced, finding herself feeling queasy, and Benito saw it in her face.

"I would never have stolen it from you. I always hoped you would become an ally of our cause."

"That isn't the problem. The power I use it isn't clean. Not even close."

Caruthers interrupted, his words slow and deliberate, ensuring everyone present understood what he was saying.

"An understatement. This creature brought a bomb into our midst, one capable of destroying everything in this.."

Ben stopped him with a glare while rising another five feet into the air. Kim could feel electricity fill the space, ionising around her and rendering his limbs more visible, like red lightning. Caruthers drooped back to the ground and pouted.

"We need your help, Kim. I can't put it any more plainly than that."

"I.. I mean, of course I'll help if I can."

Another thought-grunt, this time from Joe, and it felt much more cynical.

Benito's ire abated enough to clear the static in the air, too late for Kim's hair, which was standing on end by this time. Across the room, Caruthers had no fight left in him, so Joe stood down, returning to Ben's side. Kim detected a slight curtness in his words as he addressed his leader, deliberately loud enough for all assembled to hear.

"What of my family? Is there any word?"

"I promise you I will pass any word I receive in an instant, my friend. Right now, we must focus on the things we can control. I hope you can understand."

A momentary pause. Just a beat, not long enough for anyone without Kim's familiarity with awkward silences to detect.

"Of course I understand. I am sorry to have mentioned.."

Another beat.

"The preparations are almost complete, my liege. I will prepare just Kim for the journey ahead while you attend to this. Are you certain you won't be needing my help here?"

"Go, Kimberley will have many questions, and I need you with her to ensure safety. I'll be with you in just a few micro-cycles."

Joe was at Kim's side before she'd fully registered Ben's words and up close, she could feel the tension orbiting his torso like an electric overcoat, wrapping him in danger. He gestured toward the exit. She needed no further encouragement to lead them out.

As she left, her peripheral vision picked out Benito moving toward Caruthers.

Once Joe was gone, taking the creature with him, Caruthers pulled himself upright and squared himself off against the advancing Benito. He hadn't much liked the way Joseph had spoken. In fact, he hadn't much liked anything that had happened since awaking to find his entire world was wrong-side-out. He glanced at the devastation filling his home, a prescient analogy for the destruction outside and seeing, on the floor, just a few lengths from where he stood, was a holo-image taken in better circumstances. In it, Caruthers was resplendent in military garb with gaudy citations, medals dripping import and announcing his place at the top table.

Happier times.

It had been his prized possession, the only reminder of where he came from but a double-edged sword, in that it was also a reminder of how far he'd fallen. Now it lay amongst broken nourish-pots and preparation vials, a visible crack marring the once pristine finish of the view-window. The world had changed beneath him and who you were was no longer mattered.

Caruthers reached out and picked the image out from the other jagged pieces of his former life, swept rubble from a nook-shelf, and placed it alone in the centre. The crack ran its entire length, bisecting his avatar with a heavy forked line that glowed with the energy of escaping photons. Already visibly dimmer, it probably wouldn't last through to the next cycle. Frozen in time, captured with older technology that was barely understood now, let alone used. Irreplaceable and irreparable, just like the moment itself, and just as lost.

"Seriously, you still have that?"

Benito's voice had a sombre key, low and quiet, not what Caruthers had expected. The leader touched the image with a new limb, buzzing with power and imparting sufficient energy to bring it back to life for a brief period. It shone bright and clear, looking just as real as the shelf it stood on before disappearing altogether with a large splintering. The now empty frame exploded outward, showering both of them with pieces of grained plant-flesh and crystallised stone fragments. Caruthers brushed it from his body before talking, using that time to compose himself and at least partially camouflage the slight quaver in his voice.

"Get to the point. What do you want?"

"We don't have to be enemies. We really are working toward the same goal."

"I doubt your honesty. In fact, I doubt you have any relationship with the truth at this point."

"There was a time I would have ended you for less than that insult."

"You would have tried."

Caruthers readied himself for the inevitable fight, a dull

aching in his fluid-pump sapping his will and raising the pitch of his voice. His earlier exertions left him low on energy, but if he was going to meet his end, he was going to do it on his own terms. He brought forth some more limbs and pushed all his attention into them, just like he always did when cornered.

"Easy, old one. I keep telling you we're on the same side. Just stop opposing me for one cycle, listen to what I'm saying."

Benito dropped to the ground before him.

At the last moment Caruthers realised he wasn't making any attempt to defend himself and pulled all his strikes. The wasted effort was exhausting, quenching what remained of the fire in his belly, leaving just the aches and a need to understand.

"Old? We're the same age."

"I'm younger by nearly half a cycle, but maybe it's time to stop counting."

He moved over to Ben and dropped next to him. This could be an opportunity.

"She's evil, you must see it. Even if she didn't bring this disaster upon us, she's still taking an advantage."

Ben didn't respond right away, instead issuing an opaque sigh. Caruthers felt the weight in his words when they came.

"You are thinking too short term."

"I don't understand?"

"No. That was always your problem, and it has only got worse as you aged."

He observed as Benito fully relaxed, a rare moment of vulnerability that only he would ever see. There was always a plan, a scheme that benefitted Ben, often at the expense of others. If he could figure out what it was, there might be some advantage for him to take. After a momentary pause, and before he could muster enough words to articulate an idea, Benito beat him to it.

"You've worked together. What do you think of her?"

It was a strange question.

"The creature? I.. I don't know what you mean?"

"Intelligence? Abilities?"

"She's a lower being. I have spent no time considering her anything more. The thought that.."

Benito turned a stony gaze toward Caruthers, orbs narrowed to tightly focussed slits, withering any further words on the vine before they could ripen.

"It is not true though, is it? Don't forget, you could never deceive me. I know what you think before you do."

He was right. It wasn't true, even if he didn't want to admit it publicly, and he didn't. But Benito waited with surprising patience, leaving him no choice.

"She has.. Moments."

The gaze remained.

"I will admit to being surprised by the creature's resourcefulness.."

"Her."

Ben's interruption derailed his thoughts. Did he detect feelings for the alien?

"Your obsession with this thing will be your undoing, maybe for all of us."

"She can save us. Until she arrived, my vision was small. I wasn't sure I could.. I didn't believe. Now I can see the entire universe all at once.."

Caruthers made to argue, but Ben kept going, ignoring the distraction and drowning him out.

"Her world must be full of wonders. Now tell me, and be

honest this time, and respectful, is she as brilliant as I think she is?"

He considered his words.

"Her mind is a contradiction. She has doubts. I'm sure you can feel it in her, but there is something there underneath the neuroses."

"Go on."

"When she is alone, or thinks she is, her mind is capable of lateral movement worthy of even some of our most influential thinkers. When she is with others, a facade of bravado and strength hides that skill from even her. It is as if she tries to become her companions, absorbing their mannerisms."

"Yes. I've experienced this firsthand. My presence affects her performance, but not yours?"

"I.."

This was hard to say, almost shameful, but the look in Benito's orbs wasn't providing him any latitude to escape from it, so he took the pain.

"She considers me a friend."

He felt dirty, as if the camaraderie, even unrequited, sullied him. Benito's laughter in response didn't help. Caruthers tensed, creating enough limbs to rise and move away, but Ben stopped him.

"Don't misunderstand me, please, you know I meant no insult. Stay and continue with your assessment."

"She is comfortable with me and does not hide her inner being. It can be exhausting. Her ways are so disorganised, so messy."

He looked around his once pristine floor, catching glimpses of his world as-was, now reduced to rubble. The detritus was everywhere.

"I suppose that is an observation that applies to me in equal measure."

"Don't start feeling sorry for yourself now, Caruthers. Not after so many cycles of dignified rebellion."

"Why did you send me? There were many more qualified to work with the thin.. Ah, the.. Kimberley."

"I trust you. I knew you wouldn't let me down."

"It was a humiliation. I may as well have been her servant, fetching and cleaning up after her and indulging the easily distracted whirlwind in her cranium. Me. I once led.."

"That is exactly why I picked you."

An idea began forming around the nucleus at the heart of Caruthers' pain. Ben had just handed him the advantage he was looking for and all he had to do was grasp it and maybe he could get what he wanted at the beginning.

"I could still be of use. My rapport with Kim, if your belief in her is genuine."

"It is. What do you propose?"

It was so clear. Even if the creature's guile had blinded everyone to it. She was a lower being, a thing to be worked to death in the mines along with all the others they had subjugated. She may not have wrought the surrounding destruction, but she would certainly not be the one to resolve it. He could follow her work, waiting for her to screw up and then be the one to crush her spirit, and then her body. Maybe he could even be the one to provide a solution. As saviour, his path back to the upper echelons was certain. No one, not even the head-of-state could prevent it. Then he would make everyone see just how right he had been, and just how wrong they all were. Once he was back where he belonged, he would see Joseph flayed, sliced, and fed to the slaves in rotting pieces.

A road opened up in his mind, clear and level and lined on either side with wisdom-trees, every one of which exalted him as he made his way toward the synchronised sunrise on the horizon.

"Hello? Caruthers?"

Daydreaming wasn't something he did often, preferring to face reality with weary pragmatism, so it surprised him when he clung to the fading vision.

"I.. Uh? Yes?"

"You said you could be of use?"

"Yes! Of course. I have her trust. If you will allow it, I could assist her as I have been doing. I'm sure I can spur her on to be her very best."

"You remember you tried to end her lifespan only a few cycles ago, right? I am not so sure you're the best choice. To be frank, I am not so sure I can trust you either.."

"This situation is bigger than us, than me. If she is the one who can save us, I only want to help. Please?"

Feeling safe to do so, Kim surveyed the landscape outside Caruthers' home. It was beautiful, or it had been. The foliage in what she supposed were trees shimmered with a light that moved between hues as the breeze took it. Climbing vines accented trunks that were so black they erased the wood behind, and they dripped with berries, also black, that were lighter than the surrounding air lifting their stems. Every once in a while, a fruit broke free and shot upwards toward the ever present central sun. Where they collided with a branch, they exploded into a fine confetto that caught the light like a cloud of sequins, emitting a popping sound that she could hear even from thirty feet. On the ground, there were pavements inlaid with what looked like solid gold trim. Where the ground broke open and rucked from the aftershocks, she could see the malleable metal was an inch wide and a foot deep, an ostentatious outline that glistened like it was wet even though it wasn't. The slabs making up the pedestrian thoroughfare were a stone she couldn't explain, solid and reassuring, but also a little translucent. Light passed through, or maybe trapped itself and then released from within. Where they cracked, the breaks were indistinct and blurred. All around flora filled the space with textures and colour that demanded attention, leaving Kim struggling to focus on any one thing. The squeaking fungus from the lab was present in several low columns, demarcating the turns in the road. Fruiting bodies, that were far more mature than any she'd seen, protruded like fur covered melons. A small creature scuttled into view from the left. At first it looked like a rabbit, then, after pausing underneath one of the squeaky balls, it turned towards her and all she could see were teeth. The furry fungus dropped on the creature's head just before it could hop Kim's way, absorbing it into a new hybrid being that rolled away after Joseph shot at it with his weapon.

"You'll want to stay away from those, just Kim."

"That's wearing thin now."

Kim realised she sounded churlish but was beyond caring. They'd been stood outside for at least half an hour by this time and beyond being introduced to yet more of their kind, whose names she'd already forgotten, nothing seemed to happen. Still, Joe had tried, which was more than she could say for herself. She wiped the slate clean and started again.

"Sorry. What are those things? They started growing in the lab."

Joseph spoke without words, filling her head with the sense of something she couldn't quite name. Familiar but indescribable. It left her itchy and feeling a little like she needed a scalding hot bath.

"Wow. I.. I think I'll just call them fur-melons."

"Have you had physical contact with the fruits?"

Kim thought back to the one that bounced into her leg. It seemed like a lifetime ago, but it was probably only a month.

"Um.. No? Why?"

Joseph laughed, forcing Kim to take a step back. It wasn't too unpleasant an experience, but she didn't want to be that close if he did it again.

"Fear not, Kim. The effects are only temporary if the fruits are not yet ripe."

"What happens if?"

"It is for the best that you do not dwell on that thought."

Kim thought about the toothy bunny Joe had scared away moments earlier. It didn't seem all that happy after being absorbed.

Behind her, the door opened with a loud reverberating crash. Kim flinched as her hands shot over her ears, another reflex from early childhood. In front of her, Joseph drew his gun so quick she missed it, by the time she realised he was already re-holstering.

"Are we ready to move?"

Ben's voice. Kim stood and smoothed the material of her coveralls before turning. He stood in the doorway with Caruthers behind, still in the gloom. For a second she thought she saw something malevolent in the way his eyes darted, but it was gone before she could be sure. Joseph pushed past her, causing Kim to fall sideways into one of the fungus-adorned columns.

She only avoided contact with the fruit by a thin margin.

"Jesus! It could've absorbed me. Come on.. What's so funny?"

Caruthers reached a tendril past her and picked the fruit before levitating it back to where he stood and taking a large bite. After eating another chunk, he threw the remains at Joe.

"He told you that these are dangerous? You should not believe everything you are told, Kimberley."

"But I.. Saw.."

Ben moved over to Kim with a smooth glide and ushered her away from the building with a gentle bump.

"They have appraised you of the preparations, Kimberley?"

"Um, no?"

At first, Ben said nothing in response. He shot a fast glance Joseph's way, looking back before the soldier even noticed and then continued to pressure her away from the group with gentle nudges that burned slightly where they touched bare skin.

"What will you need to continue your work?"

Kim thought about the structure of the lab, how they built it with a singular purpose, integrating the antenna and dishes to generate and then focus sub-atomic particles with enough energy to pierce time itself. She considered the decades of theory that had gone into every fixture and fitting, informing everything down to the colour of the coffee table in the lounge. Then she thought about the years of experience that the place had given her, and how she would do it if tasked with rebuilding from scratch.

"There's a really nice screwdriver. It's in the hall by the storeroom."

"I will send a scout to retrieve it."

He paused a beat. Kim could feel a question forming in the foggy atmosphere surrounding his thoughts.

"It's a long pointy thing about so big, with a shiny handle that has 'Kim. class 4a' scratched into the side."

No response.

"I'll write it on a piece of paper so you can compare."

"Excellent. Do it now and I shall despatch the scout right away. There isn't much time to waste. We must get to our destination before the end of this cycle, the next one at the very latest."

With the sample writing scratched onto a piece of surrogate paper, a flimsy sheet of metallic gauze that pouted telepathically into her mind when touched, everyone but the scout regrouped by Caruthers' door.

They were twenty strong. Most of those assembled appeared to be younger beings. Their thoughts were less organised than their leaders and betrayed a large amount of distrust for the alien in their midst.

She also saw a lot of furtive glances and fidgeting.

"What do you propose?"

Kim assumed the question was for someone else until she realised everyone was looking at her.

"What?"

Benito put her out of her misery straight away.

"Forgive me Kimberley. If this expedition is to succeed, it must have one leader, and the technology is yours."

She couldn't speak. In the pit of her stomach, a small furious ball of trepidation birthed some gas that she first tried to hold, before then attempting a quiet evacuation.

"I.. Don't know where we're going."

"Of course, Joseph!"

The soldier's thoughts invaded hers without warning, pushing against her ego, but this time not unpleasantly. A map formed in her head, showing their position. A mark showed the destination, about 2 kilometres to the north if she was seeing it right.

"Well, we'd better get going?"

"At your command, Kim."

Caruthers snorted loudly enough to frighten a nearby tree. It felt like there might be a retort desert, but another of Ben's iron glares kept it from the daylight.

"North.. Uh, that way, right? We can get there in a few hours if we double-time it."

No one moved. A few of the younger team-members looked to Ben, who gestured to Kim. After what Kim guessed was a mental game of rock-paper-scissors between them, the shortest turned and cleared his throat with a blast of mind-static before speaking. The way he spoke left Kim wondering if this was his first time.

"My.. Queen?"

"It's just.. Ah, Kim, okay."

"Kim. Destruction blocks the roadways in that direction. The rapture has wrought wrinkles into the moving surfaces, leaving them hazardous to one as fragile as you."

"I'm sorry.. It's.. Perhaps you?"

Kim looked at Ben, who shook a metaphorical no. Joseph followed suit. Caruthers ignored her altogether.

"Do you have any.. Suggestions?"

She mumbled the last word such that even she couldn't hear it. Ben chose that moment to interject, once again pulling her away from the group with a stinging limb. When he spoke, it was with purpose.

"Lead this team, Kimberley. I have faith in you. I know what you can achieve and I know that this is something you've always wanted."

It was. But she knew that her best work came when someone else was calling the big shots, or was she just afraid of the responsibility? In the theatre of her mind, memories of being passed over, ignored and belittled, fought for attention.

"Yes, I feel that anger with you, Kim. Use it, believe your instincts. Take charge."

Ben was in her head again, muddling her thoughts, making it hard to be sure which were hers and which were his. She pushed him back with a childhood memory from her ninth birthday, alone in the kitchen with tears running down her face. It was enough to evict him and he moved out and away with a smile, leaving her with a red flush that extended well below her face. She strode back to the group, right up to the spokes-thing.

"Blocked right? I mean, that information would have been useful before you asked me for an opinion. Is there anything else you want to add?"

The creature moved back with a deliberate crawl, eyes down.

"That's what I thought."

* * *

"So we're agreed then?"

Joseph's mind nodded, and he took a small group from the assembled beings. Kim assumed they were probably all soldiers, but in reality, she didn't care. They were to scout ahead and report back if any part of the route proved too difficult to pass.

It was a good plan. Ben told her so, although she became less sure a few minutes later when confronted by a sheer wall of native rock twenty feet high and smooth as glass.

Caruthers, who had visible wrinkles in his once high sheen leather exterior, looked Kim in the eye, then Benito, then back to Kim before opening his thoughts to speak.

Benito shot him down before whatever it was he had to say could take flight.

"We take our lead from Kimberley. Quiet yourself and wait for her instructions."

And then to Kim.

"What do you suggest?"

Her first thought was, 'why didn't Joe and his team warn me about this blockage.'

A few of the scientists elevated themselves above the wall and climbed over. They could fly. No, Caruthers said it was something else.

They could 'stand tall'.

Twenty feet was nothing to these creatures, so it just wasn't a problem.

She waited. No one spoke. Over Ben's shoulder, Kim watched as Caruthers began his ascent, only to be stopped again by a slew of tentacles. Back on the ground, he leered at the remaining group, making sure Kim could see that his ire was manifesting as a gentle vibration in his left orb.

Kim waited a little more. Still, no one spoke, so she broke the deadlock with what seemed to be the obvious answer.

"Could one of you maybe lift me over?"

"YES!"

Benito almost shouted. Kim's vision defocused just a little before settling. He carried on, though the rest came in a gentler tone.

"This is the sort of thinking we need. You."

He pointed out Caruthers with a tentacle.

"Why didn't you think of that?"

Both his orbs were dancing now, Kim wasn't sure what was keeping them in his cranium but felt now wasn't the time to ask and since Benito's question was rhetorical, she looked away before he got angry enough to think violence might be acceptable.

"Take a firm hold of her and let us go, there isn't much.."

And Benito was gone, leaving the sentence unfinished. Caruthers grabbed Kim from behind, tightly enough to hurt but not do any permanent damage. Well, not straight away. As she left the ground, she could feel the same vibration in his arm-things as they restricted the movement in her chest. By the time they were at the top, the restriction was preventing Kim from filling her lungs, eliciting a burning in her chest that tapered into lightheadedness and tunnel-vision in her head. Unable to breathe, she lashed out, striking Caruthers in one of his eyes with a sticky slap that was both funny and horrific. His response was to tighten his grip and force more air out of her body, then release her altogether. As Kim fell, she screamed, but not for long since there was only four or five feet between her and the ground when he let go.

The rest of the team were milling about nearby, where she'd sprawled. At least two of them were laughing, but she couldn't tell who.

"Not.. Cool! Not flipping cool."

Caruthers joined her with a much more graceful descent, slowly blinking away the violation of his eye, but much more jovial in his manner.

"My apologies, Kimberley. I forget just how squashy you are. I trust no harm has come to you?"

"Screw you. Let's.."

That was the moment she saw just how difficult the journey was going to be. Fierce fires burned across the landscape where residential buildings had reduced to their parts, and then some of those parts reduced yet further. Immense tree like plants had fallen across access ways, blocking passage to everyone. The routes left to them were only slightly less hazardous, the acrid smell of ozone betraying the vast currents of power waiting to trap the unwary with a sudden blue bolt of forked death. The hairs on Kim's arm stood on end, and where they met the air, singed a little in the unnatural heat. Here and there scattered furnishings and household equipment interspersed with what looked to be bolster cushions of all sizes. Even as Kim realised what they were, her mind still filled with mundane images of people placing soft furnishings on chairs and sofas while fretting about the colour, and whether it accented the blue fleck in the curtains. Except these beings didn't use curtains, and those weren't cushions.

They were dead. All around, everyone. Scorch marks to the flesh showed how some met their end, some simply couldn't get out of their dwellings before being crushed and then ejected by an aftershock. Some were much smaller than those Kim knew, being only a few feet long, some even shorter.

Children.

"Shit."

It wasn't much, a single word, to represent the turmoil in her head as waves of ice cold flowed through her body before ebbing away to leave first numbness, and then a flush of heat that tore her stomach into pieces. She wanted to say more, be more, but it was all she had. That and tears, which welled and then freed themselves as a stinging curtain that dried instantly to a salt crust on the skin of her cheeks.

Joseph emerged from inside a structure that had once maybe served as a shop. The large gash on his left side told a story, the punchline being that he was now alone. He said nothing as he approached, leaving a trail of fluids in his wake.

He didn't need to. Kim watched as Benito met him half way before embracing the soldier. She could feel all the pain, physical and metaphorical, in his head and body even from ten feet away.

"So, what's your glorious plan now?"

Caruthers barged past, leaving only those words and a hit to the back that again knocked the wind out of her. She didn't respond. He was right. What could she possibly say to make any of this right? Benito, though, had more faith.

"Joseph has informed me that the quickest way is not passable. He instead offers the option of retracing our route back to the palace courtyard and attempting to move across the decorative plains, which have their own problems. The decision is, of course, yours, Kimberley."

They'd wasted most of the day getting as far as they had, and she could still feel the bruising in her ribs from the helping hand Caruthers had provided at the last impasse. Joseph's injuries looked significant.

The full force of the lab security measures hadn't put a scratch on him, yet here he was, bleeding out.

Kim pressed at the ache in her side, feeling movement where there shouldn't be. It still wasn't a hard choice.

"Back we go."

The atmosphere among the group, which hadn't been jovial to begin with, soured further as they returned. Caruthers held back, making Kim nervous every time Benito moved far enough ahead to be out of view, but he never came within six feet of her, moving back outside this self imposed exclusion zone if she stopped too quickly for him to react. She tried to read his thoughts but found nothing, not even the contempt that she'd felt building again since rejoining the advance scouting party. Once they were no longer moving away from their goal, turning onto what had been a beautiful, wide, tree-lined avenue leading away from the palace but was now an intricate obstacle course full of shining hazards and acidic smoke, Kim decided enough was enough.

"What?"

Caruthers ignored her, so she moved to block his path when he tried to circumnavigate and join the group ahead. He didn't speak, so she did it for him.

"You don't like me, do you?"

It felt like that might be an understatement, since he'd come close to killing her several times already. She was used to people not liking her and could count the number of actual friends she'd had on one hand, but hating her enough to want her dead was new. Kim didn't like it.

Caruthers didn't speak, didn't move, didn't even look at her. She tried again.

"Come on, this isn't my fault.."

"Nothing is ever your fault, is it, Kimberley?"

Now she felt him, and the barbed wire tying his insides into bitter knots, but there was something else. Before she could pin whatever it was down, he barged past her again, only this time he took care not to hurt her as he did.

"I'm sorry. About everything, I'm just trying to do my best. I don't want to be here any more than you want.."

"This is my home! I live here! Lived, anyway."

He paused before changing tack.

"I am also sorry, Kim. I find myself unsure of why Benito is placing so much of his faith in your terrible, terrible decision making."

This was progress, and in all honesty, she wasn't sure either. It was still hurtful to hear it put into words, though.

"Hey! I've got two degrees.. Ah.. No. You're absolutely right."

"Indeed, your ability to strategise is appalling. Is that the right word? Beyond stupid?"

"Thanks for that. I think we'd better catch up to the others."

Kim followed Caruthers into a clearing just off of the ruined road where everyone else was waiting, allowing Kim to see the problems Benito had mentioned for herself. The decorative plains were less flat open space and more gigantic, endless forest of hundred foot high hedge thickets. The foliage was dense enough to block the light. Caruthers turned to Kim and gave a metaphorical shrug, as if to punctuate his earlier assessment of her decision-making prowess. Benito, however, saw only solutions.

"This was a wonderful suggestion, Kimberley. We will make our way through the light planting here and into the inner geometric designs where we can make our way with more speed."

Kim stared at the wall of purple leaves which, on closer inspection, weren't leaves at all but small flat metallic disks with scalped edges. She brushed a finger along a nearby disk, which sliced through her skin with no resistance. The slice was so clean that for a moment Kim wasn't even sure it was there. Then she flexed the digit and watched it bleed.

* * *

EIGHT HOURS LATER, KIM HELD UP A HAND AND clenched her fist. The universal sign of 'halt!' The group ignored her and moved past. She sighed as loud as her burning lungs allowed, which wasn't very, but it did the trick, stopping the party in their tracks. Joseph slow-rotated to face her. He was, as ever, expressionless, but Kim could detect some scorn in his mind.

To be fair, this was the eighteenth time she'd stopped, but the pace was relentless. After convincing Caruthers she couldn't just walk through the razor bushes like they could, he gave her a lift. He was much more gentle this time, enough that she was concerned he would drop her into a pile of death-leaves, and while she was grateful that he hadn't, he instead dropped her onto what looked like an enormous granite boulder, that turned out to have the consistency of set yoghurt, breaking her fall with comical farting noises that did nothing to mask her high-pitched yells. It would have been funny, but she tensed up so much on the way down that she rolled her ankle, extricating herself from the unexpected gloop.

She was struggling to keep her thoughts jovial while fighting a losing battle with sleep, and both of her damn feet hurt, like, a lot.

"What is it now, Kimberley?"

On top of everything else, the heat and humidity in the air combined with her metabolism to soak everything she was wearing in sweat, which dried enough to become sticky before mixing with more sweat, but that wasn't even the worst part. They'd made her new jumpsuit from a miracle fabric which became almost translucent when wet. She hadn't realised until one of the science team began asking her about her navel and the strange split in her rear end. Even that would have been bearable if Joe and Caruthers hadn't chimed in with a detailed explanation of her physiology based on the vivisection they'd performed earlier in the day. They'd made several wrong guesses, and she didn't feel comfortable correcting them, so now the group all believed that the purpose of her genitalia was marking her territory with scent. That lead to inevitable discussions surrounding the odour that she was producing.

Ben, who'd kept quiet the entire journey so far, was now also staring at her.

"I'm tired! I can't keep going like this."

"You require sustenance?"

Kim fought to block thoughts of food from invading her mind. It was only a partial victory.

"Chicken pot-pie.."

Her voice was so quiet even she wasn't sure she'd spoken. Since no one responded, she changed tack and started again.

"Yes, and you know it. I've been telling you for ages that I'm hungry."

"There will be nourishments at our destination.."

"Where is that, exactly? We've been walking for hours in what feels like circles."

Some others grumbled a combined agreement. Their support, however ethereal, fed Kim's confidence. She continued.

"Well? And another thing.."

A loud, deep blast prevented her from finishing the sentence. It sounded close, and it felt big. Bass frequencies vibrated their way through her skeleton, filling her senses with electricity and pounding her head with a white noise that scrambled her thoughts for a moment. Everything slowed and then stopped, like someone had popped a flash bulb for a photograph, painting the world in frozen light and pinning it in place. Then it all exploded into chaos as the resulting shockwave tore through the surrounding foliage.

Kim fell backwards, sheltered from the full punch by a

tall shrub that splintered into thousands of pieces ten feet in front of her, hurling the sharp fragments like shrapnel instead of liquifying her major organs. Most of the debris missed, striking Caruthers, who was standing behind her, and ricocheting off harmlessly. The chunks that hit her felt like she imagined bullets would, tearing through her clothes and drawing blood. She laid on the ground with her eyes closed and waited for the tinnitus to ease, and in that time, the others regrouped around her. She opened her eyes to find everyone accounted for and staring down. No one was talking with their mouths, but all at once, and unrestricted by decorum, their thoughts were deafening. She blocked the loudest of the intrusive imagery filling her head, looking into Ben's eye-sockets and using them as a key to focus on his voice alone. What she found was unbridled chaos, with untargeted synapses derailing his train of thought before it even left the station.

She pulled herself upright, leaning on Caruthers for support. He did not stop her.

"Jesus! What the hell was that?"

The noise dropped, but no one answered.

"How far? To wherever we're going? Seriously, this time."

The size of the blast was like nothing Kim had ever imagined. She didn't want to be outside if it had friends, so she slapped Ben across where his face should be as hard as her aching arms could manage. A foreign body now lodged in her shoulder meant it wasn't as hard as she'd expected, hurting her more than it would him, but it was enough to get his attention.

"Not.. Not far."

That was all he said before whirling away in a tangential direction to the one they'd been following to that point. Joe followed along with all the others bar Caruthers, who raised a quizzical eyebrow-mound. It only lasted a few seconds, then he too was gone, leaving Kim to run after them as best she could, given her new array of injuries and her already exhausted state.

Ben hadn't been kidding. It wasn't far. They left the gardens two-hundred meters from where they were.

What Kim saw in the distance was breathtaking. A vast open space walled on three sides by a sheer seamless material that reflected, like day-glow orange vinyl and stretched thousands of feet into the air. Inside was a city, just as a child would draw one, at least two miles across. Dozens of skyscrapers reached upwards past orbiting roadways and lower buildings with flat roofs. The whole thing was sitting on a gold-coloured disk only a meter thick, that was floating twenty meters above the vast, level ground beneath. Kim bent down to be sure it wasn't an optical illusion, finding no supports, visible or otherwise. It would have been perfect other than the thick plumes of smoke billowing from a built up area in what she decided was downtown.

Joseph was moving toward the smoke at a terrifying pace, leaving the rest of the group in his wake, but all still with a solid head start on Kim. She started towards them and stumbled, feeling tentacles wrap themselves around her body before she hit the ground. Ben, and after he made sure his grip was sure, the two of them flew toward the flying miracle ahead. This close, and with physical contact, she had a clearer view of his thoughts and he while some of the mania had lessened, his head was still racing in tight protective circles, like a child telling themselves 'it'll be okay' over and over. He hadn't been this scared the entire time she'd known him, and it was contagious.

Something was wrong, more wrong than it had been.

Even with enough speed to blur the surroundings into colourful streaks of light, it took a few minutes to arrive. Close up, the city was even more impressive, reaching outwards and upward away from Kim's view. They slipped underneath, stopping below a glowing panel that hovered independent of the primary structure. The remaining contingent of nerd-aliens were flipping feverish tentacles at a holographic control panel a few meters away. The increasing pace and pressure used wasn't inspiring confidence. Joe approached, his thoughts guarded, his limbs clenched and humming with furious energy.

"I warned you this could happen.."

"This is not the time! Can we board?"

Ben's words were urgent, and his head matched. Kim reached in further, but Ben must have felt her probe as he dropped her, severing the link, and then pinned her head to the cold ground with an unpleasant amount of force. For a moment, she thought he was going to crush her skull into the unforgiving surface, long enough for her to wonder at how calm she was becoming in the face of death, but then he released her.

"Stay out of my mind."

Ice cold, and then with much more warmth.

"I am sorry, Kimberley. This situation is unexpected and is causing me considerable stress right now."

The glowing panel above lowered, slow at first but gathering speed. It hit the ground in complete silence, bouncing a few feet like a vast, flat rubber ball and then settling an inch or two above the ground. The nerds issued a collective cheer and hustled onto the platform, followed by Caruthers. Joseph threw out a loud sigh and joined them. Benito picked Kim up with reverent care and then moved with speed to the platform's edge.

"This is going to feel a little strange. You need to relax your musculature as much as possible."

There wasn't much she could say in reply, so Kim arched what she hoped was a sarcastic eyebrow and smirked instead, a facial expression that proved ill advised when the matter translator they were standing on projected the group into the loading bay above. Her skeleton went first, leaving organs supported in space by phantom bones. Then her organs moved up to join her calcium supports, leaving her a hollow skin balloon that contracted slightly in the face where muscles clenched. It didn't become a problem until it appeared in place to complete her translocation. Her left eyebrow didn't quite match up, causing some slippage and a lot of pain.

"Mother.. Agh!"

"What did I say? Look, it will be fine, just stay still! Do not move, not at all!"

Then her skin was gone again. It didn't hurt. Regardless, she wasn't enjoying the sensation, and it was about fifteen seconds before she was whole, albeit once again naked.

"Jesus H. Christ! What was that?"

She could see furtive glances. It was Caruthers that replied.

"This is old technology, Kimberley, such that hasn't seen use in what you would call millennia."

And then to Ben.

"I know this vessel. We mothballed it in the dark times. Does it even function?"

Another explosion answered before Ben could express any words in response.

The chamber they stood in was cavernous, at least a hundred meters square and stacked floor to high ceiling with crates, a huge proportion of which looked old, but a smattering appeared to be recent additions. The explosion knocked a wall of them over like a house of cards. Ben ignored the clattering and turned to the scientists, who did their best to avoid his gaze. In the end, the one who identified with a name that Kim couldn't pronounce, full of sounds that couldn't exist, cleared his metaphorical throat and pointed at the holographic control panel that had followed them up from outside. It looked incomprehensible at first glance, but Kim was quick to see discernable patterns in the hovering lights.

It was a three-dimensional representation of their surroundings. She could see power circulating through systems buried deeply in the structure, beginning and ending in a complex at the centre of the city. Like blood flowing around her body, and just like her, it had injuries.

"Your highness, there is an issue.."

"I know there's an issue! Can we do anything about it? We have to get away from here, now, this instant!"

The scientists didn't offer a positive reply, instead slinking back into the group as if the others would shield him from Ben. Kim could feel the sharp wire tightening in his head area, and she could see the subtle shift in hue of the limbs supporting his body, green-ish to a magenta that suggested his self control was waning. Worse, she could still feel the self-reinforcing hamster-wheel of doubt polluting what thoughts broke free with blind terror.

"Bypass.."

Still reeling from having no skin, it was the only word she could get out before her stomach vented its displeasure onto the ground. She hadn't eaten a full meal for hours so most of it was bile, acidic, leaving an aftertaste that transported her back into childhood memories of afternoons spent on the sofa under a duvet while her mother felt her forehead and decided if she was going to school the next day. Then more recent experiences involving copious quantities of beer and kebabs that were both more and less pleasant.

"Ugh.."

It was the best she could manage as a follow up. Everyone was staring, so she tried again.

"Can.. You.."

No good. The group went back to ignoring her, so she used the opportunity to empty the remains of her stomach lining onto the ground and blow the acid out of her nasal cavities. Once she was breathing clearly again, she marched up to the control panel, ignoring the assembled creatures, and scrutinized it. It was significantly more complicated when you could make out the detail, but it still appeared to resemble a blocked coronary artery.

"The power needs to be here, right?"

Kim reached out a hand to point to the glowing blue-ish shape that resembled a cube. The leader of the nerds lashed out a wiry tentacle before her hand could reach the panel, grabbing her by the wrist while shrieking, which caused a whole body shudder in both of them. In the uncomfortable silence that followed, he let go and apologised, explaining that if she'd touched the cube, they would all be dead. He also acknowledged that, as she'd guessed, the power needed to be there.

"Right. So why can't you just feed it through this entire section here?"

She gestured toward a vast network of conduits, over half of which were not glowing, which she figured meant they were unused. It transpired that she was wrong, but not so badly wrong that the suggestion wasn't helpful. Ben placed a fatherly limb on her shoulder and leaned in.

"The workings of this vessel are ancient and complicated, Kimberley. It is something even our deepest minds have struggled to comprehend."

Only she comprehended. Maybe not how it was flying, or why it even existed, but she'd had a keen interest in both medicine and mechanics as a youngster that bordered on obsession. More important, she'd also spent a lot of time playing logic based puzzle games on the computer her parents bought her because they couldn't buy her any friends, and the man in the shop had said it was the next best thing.

"So, what does this do?"

"That is where the problem is."

She wasn't absolutely certain what the shape was. It had a lot of sides, some of which had unnatural intersections, but it was bright red-purple and was pulsing in an unnerving manner. She waited for more explanation, receiving none until she performed a theatrical shrug and shook her head.

"Sorry, the, what's the wording? Anti-matter converters? In order that we don't flood the citadel with radioactive death, all the exhaust filters through this contraption.."

"You're making this up as you go along, aren't you?"

She only half meant it as a joke. There wasn't a lot of confidence in the scientists' words, or tone, and the looking at the ground while his eyes did a furtive dance wasn't helping either.

"I.. No. It's.."

"Don't tell me it's complicated. What you're saying is that you can't turn anything on without killing us, right?"

"Right."

"And there isn't a spare? Jesus, who built this thing?"

"This vessel is a marvel that your species could only dream.. I mean, yes, okay, in hindsight, the design isn't perfect."

Ben was pacing. He wasn't even trying to hide his panic now. It was justified by a low rumbling sound from beneath them, followed by a sudden lurch-tilt to the left that threw Kim back to the ground.

Another quake. Kim figured someone had to take charge, and since no-one else was volunteering, she might as well do it herself.

"How does it work?"

"It absorbs the.."

"NO. I know what it does. How does it do it?"

Nerd-creature thought for a moment before giving his reply.

"The lining. The material reacts to produce harmless gasses which are evacuated through.."

"And is that material used anywhere else on the ship? Is anything else made from it?"

She could feel hope building in his mind.

"Almost everything. It is one of the hardest materials we know. We use it in the walls and the conduits.."

"All the conduits?"

"Yes. Are you suggesting that.?"

Kim hauled herself upright and limped over to the panel. One toe on her left foot had taken a knock in the fall and gave an audible click when she put weight on the foot. It was that sound that stopped the scientist mid-sentence.

"All these.. Ow, shit. All.. These pipes and vents and things. No one is in any of these areas, right? Can you just vent everything through all of that? Would that.."

"YES! Oh, but.."

He left it hanging, but Kim guessed what the problem was.

"Can you use this thing to transport me there? Also, you need to teach me how to set it up.. In fact, let's be honest, is there any chance you could come with me?"

Caruthers spoke up from a few feet away while pushing his way into the group, his voice resolute, his stride purposeful.

"I'll go with you."

The familiar, horrifying feeling of having her body dismantled layer by layer and then reassembled somewhere else from the inside out was more bearable this time around. Kim kept everything loose to avoid alignment mishaps, so her eyebrows ended up where they began, which was a bonus. Another plus: there weren't any contents left in her stomach to vomit up. Caruthers was already positioning things on a much larger control panel, arranging the vents and conduits as best as he understood the solution. Kim didn't need to make significant corrections, taking only a few minutes to be positive all the alignments were correct.

Moment of truth.

They could only align the vents from the room they were in, an auxiliary control office next to the failed filter complex. The reason it needed more than one creature to complete the task was the main control panel being in a different location in the room from the manifold release that would flood half the city with deadly gasses. Once opened, the vents would need to be controlled in order to set up the new circulatory system that would, she hoped, remove the danger before harmlessly pushing the gasses out as a warm wind, bypassing the failed systems altogether. If it worked. If it didn't, and to be fair, she'd only eyeballed what she thought were the relevant gauges, the resulting explosion would kill everything on board before they got any further off the ground.

"Are you ready?"

The question was more for herself than for Caruthers. She answered herself with a nod, which he mistook for encouragement, and 'nodded' back. Since he didn't have any bones or joints, much less a neck, it was more of a telepathic suggestion, but it was a gracious gesture.

"On three, okay?"

"Yes. No, what is three?"

"It's after.. You know what, I'll shout 'GO'."

Kim aligned the shapes in a pleasant sequence of hues, ran her hand through each to be sure they linked, and shouted.

It all happened at once. Caruthers could keep up, flipping through pulsing holograms at breakneck speed, using at least twelve tentacles in sequence. In front of Kim, the manifold held, or she hoped that was what the purple peristalsis meant. The noise was deafening. The entire wall screamed under the additional stress it experienced, bulging a little where it had thinned with age and fatigue, but it held. Near Caruthers she could see conduits aligning and the irregular heartbeat in the filter slow and then die away. Then she noticed the whole panel glow red-blue and sparkle like a cheap cartoon. She had little time to enjoy it before Caruthers' yelling overpowered the exterior noise and splintered her vision down the middle. He was already disintegrating, giving her a view of his internal organs as he'd seen hers. Her brain struggled to reconcile what she saw. It was full of beauty and horror, like an infinite nest of spiders with long, thick legs and translucent bodies that writhed in unison around a core that defied rational explanation.

As she passed out, her mind wandered to a childhood memory of waking with a scream after a dark nightmare, and being unable to explain the eldritch terrors that plagued her mind to her parents.

This, this was what she'd seen.

* * *

KIM AWOKE ALONE, STILL NAKED BUT NOT COLD, IN A small quiet space and on a comfortable mattress-like structure that felt a little like a waterbed but also like a pile of straw. She rolled off and stood, finding that her ankle no longer hurt and that the gnawing in her stomach was gone. There was a pile of furry food-things emptied and messily discarded next to the bed with drained drink-cubes piled on top. Hanging from a superfluous looking pipe that entered the room over a door before snaking its way across the ceiling and exiting down through the floor in a dark corner was a jumpsuit. It had a shiny disc hanging from a flap of material over the right side chest area. She put it on and had a closer look. It was just like the medals Joseph wore occasionally, glinting in the subdued lighting, suggesting luminescence.

Once dressed, she opened the door to an empty corridor that funnelled the busy sounds of earnest discussion from a nearby room. She was there a few minutes later, finding another massive room that would house a jumbo jet, full of glowing holographic controls and industrious creatures pointing and shouting. One entire wall, forty feet high and three times that across, projected an image of the outside so immaculate that Kim wouldn't have believed that it wasn't a screen at all but for the lack of noise accompanying the visuals.

She was on the bridge, in the citadel's heart, all still in one piece and now in low orbit. Her plan had worked.

"Kimberley! You have awoken. Come, join us."

She could hear Ben but couldn't see him at first, then she spotted tendrils waving from the middle of a scrum next to a large, throne-like seating arrangement. As Kim made her way over, several creatures turned away and began 'whispering' amongst themselves. They weren't good at it, or they wanted her to hear, either was possible since their words weren't kind. One voice was louder than the rest.

"Filthy thing. How could he?"

There was a mark on his torso which combined with a feeling to identify him as the scientist she'd spoken with before transporting over to the filtration complex, and he had a deep frown rucked into the leather above his eyeballs. A few others stared as she passed, but said nothing, making the walk uncomfortable. When she got there, the scrum parted and Ben flew over to greet Kim with a buzzing-burning hug that knocked the wind out of her.

"The hero of the hour!"

"Ugh."

It was the best she could do until he released his grip, which he showed no signs of doing.

"Kimberley saved us all. You would all do well to pay attention to her schemes in the future. If our mission is to have any chance of success, she will be at its heart."

Kim felt dissent washing over her in waves coming from all directions, again and again. Ben must have felt it too, as he chose that moment to release his grip and rise above the assembled throng. He didn't vocalise, but his intent shone brightly and the hushed voices fell silent. He waited until they directed all orbs his way before using words.

"Do any of you question my decisions?"

No one answered. A toddler would have seen the question was a rhetorical trap.

"Do any of you question Kimberley's decisions?"

A few dozen feet away, the marked scientist nudged a subordinate forward with enough encouragement to send him flying into the clearing that had opened up around where Ben was pronouncing. He didn't look happy and when he spoke; it was with a small voice that struggled to carry his words.

"Your highness, it is, um, just that, well."

Benito stared him down, absorbing the rest of his resolve with a steel-sponge glare that pushed him back into the safety of the crowd.

"While the best of you wailed and surrendered yourselves to doom, she planned our salvation. You all should feel shame!"

Kim could sense what they were feeling, and it wasn't any shame. She worried that if he kept this up, one of them might lynch her, so she put her hands up and gave the best self-deprecating smile she could. As she did, the medal on her chest glowed. It was the first time some of the assembled crowd had noticed it.

Their mood dipped even lower.

"The order! How is she worthy?"

It wasn't one being that spoke, but an amalgamate of several. She felt a sudden pang of self-consciousness, lowered her arms and slipped behind Caruthers, who forced her back out and glowered.

Ben spoke over the again rising chatter.

"Briefings, you are all to make your findings known to me and Kimberley. Convene in the captain's ready-room in two micro-periods from now, do not be late."

Thirty seconds later the entire room was empty bar Kim, Caruthers, Ben and Joe. The latter only remained long enough to see that there were no threats to his leader before backing away and out, staring at Kim the entire time.

She had nothing to say, so followed Caruthers as he made his way to a seating arrangement at the farthest point from the main view-screen. There followed an awkward silence while Kim waited to find out how long two Milli-periods were in actual time.

It was long enough for things to get socially uncomfortable, and leave her needing the lavatory, around fifteen minutes.

Just as she was about to ask whether anyone had considered her need to void waste, Caruthers stood, and without saying a thing marched an abrupt pace to a portal that Kim was sure hadn't been there moments earlier. Kim did her best to keep up, slipping inside just as the door closed.

Inside, the room was much smaller than the bridge but still boasted a whole-wall view-screen that was displaying images of the terrain below them. Most of the space housed a slab of the translucent rock Kim had seen during their earlier trek. Four feet high and twenty feet long, it had niches cut into the sides that allowed the creatures to stand close and manipulate the holo-controls floating over the glass-smooth top surface. Beings occupied all the spaces but one until Caruthers picked Kim off the ground and deposited her there. Everyone but Ben stared as if he'd just thrown a warm steaming pile of offal onto the table. Ben took no notice, bringing the meeting to order.

"Reports, you?"

He gestured toward a being whose wrinkles had wrinkles, Kim wondered if he'd slept at all in the last few days.

"Sire, esteemed colleagues, other assembled, ah, things."

He glanced at Kim, then continued.

"The situation is dire. The explosions have exposed the planet's core, leeching energy and causing a gradual solidification of the molten materials there. If this were to happen, the protection afforded us by the magnetic fields surrounding our world would dissipate. Solar winds would blast all life from the surface, leaving only barren rock."

Kim could feel Caruthers from across the room. The same spiral was inside his head that Ben had earlier, along with a new twitchy mannerism, only Ben didn't have any of that anymore. She reached around the table. No one else did. On the big screen, an info-graphic appeared which detailed the planet's composition, from core to surface. A cone of light-red showed where most of the damage had occurred, with tectonic plates shifting to fill the new void, explaining the earthquakes. Everyone watched in silence until the worst-case scenario had played out in charming pastel shades. Ben pointed to another seated being, but didn't speak.

"I, uh, Sire, my news is no less dramatic, I fear!"

He waited for a reaction. None was forthcoming, so he carried on with fewer theatrics, no doubt feeling the shine wear away from his big moment.

"The quakes have released a significant amount of radioactive vapour into the atmosphere. There is a cloud billowing outward from here.."

He pointed to the screen, which blinked some static images of mundane home-life, a child and life-partner posed around some expensive-looking furniture, before settling on an animation that showed an expanding circle of blue covering more and more of the underlying green-painted land masses until they were all gone. A long silence followed, punctuated in the end, when the screen image changed to a solo shot of the scientist posing above a bright-coloured sheet of what appeared to be linen. There were some gasps around the table, and a hasty grab for the controller by the pictured subject, who apologised profusely and swiped the image away. Kim wasn't sure what she'd just seen, but given what she could feel from the others, she decided it wasn't something she wanted to dwell on. Ben rolled his eyes, gave a polite cough, and pointed toward Kim with the flick of a tentacle.

She stared back, unable to think of anything to say, the medal on her chest weighing heavy.

She didn't know why she was there.

There was nothing she could add to the briefing, but more panic, so she lowered her eyes away from Ben's gaze and said nothing.

No one did.

More than that, though, no one felt anything, either. All the beings assembled had seen the end of their world spelled out in ugly infographics and not one of them felt anything, not even Ben, and he'd been terrified only hours before. Kim kept quiet, feeling the familiar frost cooling her veins and tightening her sphincter, then she realised that there was one other just as unnerved as she was, and just one, sitting just behind her just as quiet. Caruthers.

11 / THE GROWN UPS ARE
   TALKING

Kim followed Caruthers into an ante-chamber away from the main control-space.

There was an endless supply of these rooms branching outwards from the bridge, like a maze that kept growing organically. Every one of them connected in some manner with another, often at a jaunty angle, small, big, all different shapes. There were multiple routes through that led to the exit and loading areas, with transfer-pads that could beam them anywhere else in the citadel. Kim spent a bit of time bugging her new best-friend to teach her how to manipulate the panels and select destinations, but he'd been a less than ecstatic in his delivery so she'd learned little. The room they were in now was well lit by a complicated series of floating coloured cubes that hovered around four inches below the high ceiling. They could sense mood, turning bright turquoise when feeling anger and off-white when happy. There was a detectable blue-tint to the illuminations when Caruthers pivoted and blocked Kim's route further into the room.

"What?"

He answered her with a sigh, which didn't tell her much, so she shrugged and raised an eyebrow. The prompting proved fruitful.

"Why are you following me?"

"So I.."

"NO! No, do not answer that. You have done nothing but follow me around with constant questioning since the meeting last cycle. You are exhausting me. I just need some space to be alone. Do you understand?"

A familiar sensation flushed through her body, like a tingle that made her whole body sensitive to light and turned her face beetroot-red.

Thinking back, she hadn't left his side since the disaster several days back. When she got nervous or anxious, she needed to vent and sometimes doing it alone in her personal quarters just didn't do it, so she would find a friend to share her thoughts with, all of her thoughts, no matter how personal. The biggest problem was that sometimes she didn't realise she was over sharing, or that she hadn't stopped talking for hours, or that the people she was talking to weren't her friends at all and were sharing everything online. Sometimes, often in fact, she just didn't figure any of these things out until it was too late and the rumours were spreading like a wildfire that scorched anything positive, leaving her social world in its ashen wake, sucking the oxygen out of her as it burned.

"I'm sorry. I didn't mean.."

The blue tint changed to a muddy brown that reminded her of old nineteen-seventies decor, flammable velour wallpaper and dirty-looking shag-pile carpets. It was the colour of pity, and she didn't want any right then, so she stopped before finishing her sentence and traipsed out a sullen exit through a nearby door, but not the one via which they'd entered, her feet punching the ground.

She found herself in a circular nook boasting a dark, unsettling dome and sunken seating, all apt for her self-esteem, so she sank into a settee that was way less comfortable than it had looked and thought about what was happening.

The briefing ended with a consensus that both major problems needed to be dealt with separately but simultaneously, so Ben had split everyone into two teams. Each team reported to an overall division head that reported back to an overall project supervisor. That supervisor then reported directly to Ben. It all made sense right until the moment Ben announced Kim was the supervisor, which dropped like a vast bucket of sticky, fresh-laid diarrhoea, smothering everything in shit while pissing everyone off. Ben then made everyone swear allegiance to her while explaining what they planned to do.

If she'd had any chance of making friends in that group, it was gone for good now. All except Caruthers, who'd stayed out of the line of fire and said nothing while each of the team-leaders took turns grabbing Kim's wrist and keeping their desire to rip her to pieces at bay long enough to say the words Ben had prepared. When it was over, He'd come up to her without prompting and warned her to heed any advice, listen to any ideas and not just bulldoze her plans through. It was the only nice thing anyone had said to her in days, and she could feel he'd meant it, even though he finished up by comparing her intellect to that of a reticulated crystal-spore. She didn't even know what that was. Did that make him a friend?

With all sensation on the left side of her body diminishing to a numb ache, Kim pulled herself upright and clambered out of the sunken nerve-trap masquerading as furniture. After a short internal debate, her hurt feelings won out, and she exited through a new door that she knew would take her back to the bridge, albeit after a circuitous tour of the outer suburbs surrounding the control centre.

It took an eternal fifteen minutes, but when she arrived, there was a new dense atmosphere smothering the room, and quieting the usual chatter. The main view-screen split into quadrants, each displaying a different facet of the problems at hand. Top-left was a massive chasm in the ground that was at least four miles long, half a mile wide and with no visible bottom, just an ominous red-orange glow. Underneath a data-readout showed the relative strengths of magnetic fields surrounding the planet along with deltas showing fluctuations and their direction. They were all down, a long way down. Top-right showed an image of the surface, maybe taken by satellite, showing the area to the immediate north of the new hell-trench. Overlaid were bright holographic lines that marked settlements and other structures that were otherwise invisible because of the thick grey-white cloud, flecked with black and the occasional eruption of flame, that covered everything. Underneath that cheery image was a collection of glyphs that flickered on and off, sometimes in different places. It looked like a countdown and it was descending fast.

The citadel captain, who had thus far evaded naming, and who had taken being passed over for her as a personal slight, was on the central throne barking telepathic orders at underlings. They milled around trying to look busy, but even Kim could see how listless they were, shooting furtive glances at the screen, muttering and drifting like flotsam caught in the Captain's wake. Benito was nowhere to be seen. He'd been running a personal project with a small cabal of the most trusted scientists. It would be big, he assured Kim, but it wasn't something for her to worry about right now. It meant she had had no meaningful contact with him in over a week and in his absence, the chain of command had wrapped itself around her neck and hung her out to dry like jerky, until all her authority was gone.

Still, she had to keep things on track.

She walked up to the captain with a swagger she hoped showed purpose and confidence, ignoring the whispering behind her back, which wasn't easy since every unpleasant word was being beamed direct to her subconscious. Once in front of him, she waited for him to acknowledge her, which he didn't, so she kicked the chair, causing a dull clang that suggested it was hollow. The creature looked down with a gaze that punched a hole through her resolve well below the waterline.

"You are blocking my way here, flesh-sack. Entertain yourself elsewhere. Maybe there are some youngling play-things nearby that you can use to tax your intellect?"

This new normal had endured for a considerable period and was getting irritating.

He had inserted himself as project-leader, ignoring every-thing Kim had suggested while throwing belittling barbs at every opportunity and it was wearing thin.

"Listen to me, ah, whatever-your-bloody-name-is, however much you don't like it, Ben put me in charge.."

He jumped down with ferocious speed, landing only a few inches from Kim, causing her to take a small step back-wards to maintain stability. He then filled that space, almost touching her. She could feel the warmth of his body, smell the other-world in his skin, which was a lighter colour than Caruthers', and writhed in just perceptible ripples.

"I lead this vessel, ME! I will never answer to a lower being such as you."

Kim felt a growing sense of déjà vu. She'd already had this conversation too many times to count, with this guy, with Caruthers, with teachers and bosses back home on Earth. Experience told her to concede and let him get on with it, but she was tired and desperately needed to return home.

Kim was over being treated like an inconvenient child.

"Yes, you will. They put me in charge.."

"He only indulges this charade to push me, but I have stepped up now. What? Did you think we would take orders from you? Listen with care, if you do not remove yourself from my bridge I will have the dermis stripped from your meat strip by.."

Kim didn't want to hear what else he planned to do with her meat, so she slapped him in the area that was as close to his cheeks that she could reach, with all the force she could muster. It mottled his skin with dark spots as he issued a mind-scream that came close to emptying Kim's bowels. Everyone else in the room stopped what they were doing and turned their way.

Kim looked around for support, some sort of handhold among the throng she could grasp to stop her confidence from floundering, but found nothing friendly. Suddenly, she wasn't so sure she'd employed the best tactics, given the captain's volatile temper and lack of oversight.

Still shrieking, He grabbed her by the throat, lifting her clear off the ground by a few inches and cutting off the supply of oxygen to her brain. With all her weight pulling downward, no hand or footholds, and no air supply to her brain, Kim couldn't find any leverage to break his grip. Time slowed as her hearing took on a hollow timbre. Then, just as she was blacking out, he dropped her and flew backwards into the control-throne. He bounced off to the left and slumping to the ground where Kim made silent eye contact while choking oxygen back into her lungs. As the roaring in her ears cleared, she heard one voice in the otherwise silent room.

"If you harm this being, Benito will have you unmade. Do you wish to be returned to your kin in an urn, Captain?"

Caruthers, and his voice was hard and loud, with a low, thunderous tone. Kim looked up at him. He stared directly back.

"And you. What was your plan here? Get up, go to your quarters, and clean up. We will revisit this conversation in the next cycle."

K im stared up at the ceiling, just like the sinking feeling in her stomach. It was still there and unchanged since yesterday. She coaxed an uncooperative arm into shielding her from reality, swinging it a little too hard and low, contacting the bridge of her nose and filling her vision with sparks of light before settling into its rightful place over her eyes. Then, just as the pain dulled to a manageable ache, a copper taste infused her already laboured breathing.

"Shit."

She rolled onto her side, cupping her nose with one hand while throwing the duvet-substitute off with the other in a smooth, practised movement. Fast, but not fast enough. Spots of blood found their way onto the material, where they bloomed like ink in water, dying the entire covering red in a matter of seconds. The duvet then issued a gentle purr before scrunching itself up into a ball, taking Kim a little by surprise.

"Jesus!"

Her former bed-clothes reacted to the exclamation by

growling at her, so she kicked out, sending them onto the floor where they scuttled off into a corner, passing a stationary Caruthers on the way.

"Aaaah! Seriously, come on, dude. How many times? I'm naked in here."

"As am I, I do not see where this causes.."

"Fine! Whatever. If you're here to gloat, I'm a little busy right now, okay?"

The elder being said nothing at first, keeping his eyes at a respectful floor level and shuffling with embarrassment. Then, after a pause long enough for the bleeding to have stopped, he looked up, catching Kim's eyes.

"There may be a way."

Kim waited for context, getting none.

"A.. Way?"

"You must be ready in.. Ah, you would say fifteen minutes?"

She looked down at the pool of coagulating blood in her left hand, then the spots of crimson drying on her chest and legs before sniffing to test the clot now damming further flow. It was solid. She got dressed and was ready less than twelve minutes later.

Three minutes after that, she was standing in an ante-room she hadn't seen before. The lighting was dim and followed you around like a personal eclipse, and they'd adorned the periphery with refreshments and beings doing their best to avoid getting swept into the dance-maelstrom throbbing at its centre. After following Caruthers to a small group of nerd-things guarding a diminishing stack of juice-cubes, Kim fished a handkerchief out of her coveralls pouch and wiped, but didn't blow her nose. Instinct required some-thing to hold, a comfort blanket of sorts, and the square of fabric would have to do. One of the science-beings giggled and asked the floor a question.

"Is.. Is it true you have to excrete your waste?"

Caruthers sighed and moved away, taking and emptying a cube as he went, leaving Kim leant against the wall and wondering if they were talking to her. They were. A tentative tendril reached out and nudged her right breast.

"Ooooh! It's warm, and like, squashy!"

"Hey!"

The tentacle disappeared as the group and their chatter shrank back. With Caruthers nowhere to be seen, Kim found herself stranded, which she now realised was the idea, so she pushed her burgeoning disgust back into the pit of her stomach and offered an olive branch.

"I'm Kim. What's your name?"

It included sounds that would require a second larynx, so she simplified it to Kevin. Over the next half an hour she learned he was a senior adviser on the poisonous cloud project, that the project had no proper direction or leadership, that his group linked like a hive-mind and that they found the idea of breasts hilarious. He learned Kim had no conversational skills and wasn't fond of lasagne, but only restaurant lasagne. The microwave-packet stuff was fine. When they finished talking, Kim felt better than she had done in months.

"You guys are alright."

"And you are not as we expected. Your grasp of our language is exceptional."

"Heh, yeah. Look, I've had a few thoughts about the cloud, and I am sort of in charge.."

"Oh! We adore this sequence of chords! You must join us in a rhythmic series of motions."

Kevin grabbed both of her hands and tried to lead them into the dancing crowd, but Kim resisted enough that he stopped, returning to his group with the look of a scolded puppy. Some in the crowd laughed, some mocked, most ignored him altogether, but Kim could tell it hurt Kevin enough for an explanation.

"It's not you. I'm serious. It's just that I can't dance."

"Understandable. I, too, struggle with disfigurement and shame."

He turned to highlight a darker patch of skin on his left flank that stretched from the ground to where Kim imagined shoulders should be, shaped like a hockey stick. Muted moans of agreement came from the rest of the group. One made a wrenching sound that could only have been for Kim's benefit.

"It's not that.. Hey! What's wrong with how I look?"

"It's the bulges."

Then, out of nowhere, she laughed. A chuckle at first, building to a belly laugh that drew enough attention to first embarrass her new pals, then draw them in.

They were having fun. She'd missed having fun. Kevin then added a respect filled cherry on top.

"I have observed your work, Kim. I believe your idea to neutralise the cloud can work."

A blush warmed her face. Although not fully looped in, Kim's nominal leadership allowed for access to the data. There were anomalies to be sure, but thinking back to her bachelor's degree, and a misunderstood project experiment that nearly closed down the university, she knew that there was a way to neutralise the cloud remotely. With a good aim, they might even do it while killing no one else. It was nice that someone agreed, although maybe not enough to steal the idea for himself. Kim reached over and touched Kevin on the shoulder-region. He and his collective reached back and prodded her protuberances.

"NO! Come on, we're having a moment here."

The tentacles moved to more acceptable regions. Just enough time passed for Kim to wonder if the beings ever kissed before Caruthers reappeared and swatted Kevin away, sending him back through his hive and into the wall.

"You are not to harm.."

"Stop! It's fine. We're getting on fine."

She had her hands on Caruthers torso. He looked down at her without moving, making eye contact and then moving his gaze, and a tentacle, to her hands in a slow, deliberate motion. Kevin raised a tendril and gave an attention seeking cough.

"Ahem. I was just discussing work-related matters with Kim, your high.. Um, what is your rank here?"

With a snap, Caruthers switched his attention, and his tentacles, to Kevin.

"To you, I am a god."

Kim felt the need for an interjection before things got too serious.

"Why are you here? We're all getting on just fine?"

"What?"

There was an upward lilt to his voice, like a question, but a chuckling rhythm that made it an expression of incredulity.

"Yes. We were, you know, just about to dance."

If Kevin could have blushed, he would have. She could feel his embarrassment explode like an airbag, then deflate just as quick.

Caruthers had other ideas.

"There is no time for rhythmic nonsense. Benito requests your immediate presence."

"Oh, okay. Um, we'll speak later, okay, Kevin?"

Caruthers led her through the crowd at breakneck speed, leaving her just able to keep up and taking them out of a side door that was, on any other day, locked. On the other side, she found a long narrow corridor, Benito, Joseph and four guards, all armed, anxious and aiming at her. Ben waved them down.

"I apologise for interrupting your nuptials with our gas expert.."

"Eh?"

"Please, let me finish. You know that I have been involved with a side-project? I did not wish to tell you of it until fruition for fear of raising your hopes, only to dash them once again. However, my plan was a success. Follow me."

The corridor ended in a large sliding door that filled an entire wall and when it moved; the ground vibrated. Once open, Kim could see why. It was at least six feet thick and sold rock. Beyond was a lab-space that felt familiar, full of desks and chairs and a view-screen that, while not as impressive as the citadels, served its purpose with distinction. Undulating piles of paper adorned every surface like disappointing mountain ranges punctuated by coffee-cup volcanoes filled with pens. In the middle, underneath the single monitor on the lead desk, a single red light held steady. Above, on the screen, a single line traced its way from left to right.

"What the actual hell?"

The illusion broke when she stepped in. The papers were all blank, and the pens, although colourful, were solid pieces of glass with sharp, dangerous points.

"We built it as close as we could. We could not transport the complete structure, unfortunately, as an energy field still prevents us from gaining access. But the mechanisms work as Caruthers described them, and your technology functions as it should."

"Why?"

"You transported here through dimensions we cannot access. Our greatest minds cannot fathom the methods by which this device functions.."

"Yes, but why?"

"Originally, I had sought a method for us to leave this world for somewhere safer, but the power required would be too great. Instead, we could use this to pull matter into our realm and enclose the rift, exposing our core. This machine could save our world."

He fell silent, casting his eyes around the replica lab and then looking back at Kimberley.

She could only think of one thing to say.

"You can't make it work, can you?"

* * *

IT ACTUALLY COULD WORK, IT ALL STACKED UP. THEY could easily source the matter needed from a nearby asteroid belt which, although much less dense in reality than science-fiction films would have you believe, still held trillions of tonnes of rock, ready to be picked. The replica beacon technology was sound, too. Kim spent an entire day poring over the schematics and probing access points, to be sure. There were issues, since they built it from data purloined by Caruthers, who'd never been into any of the tunnels connecting her core material with the antennae arrays. This meant no sliding trays to ease mobility, causing a lot of uncomfortable crawling. It also meant that a lot of the space was better optimised to her particular physiology, since they'd had to guess about the ceiling heights and light levels. Of interest was the core itself. Since they did not know what it was, the science team had simply replicated the readings Caruthers had surreptitiously taken with matter sourced locally within their ecosystem. Their sample had significant benefits, being much purer and producing no stray emissions. This meant it didn't need shielding in the same way, making the whole assembly much lighter, like, carry around in a briefcase light. It was an excellent compromise, and she felt hopeful that they could absolutely get it working with a bit of luck and a lot of hard graft. Another benefit was that once they were done, she could use this novel sample core to augment her original beacon and, perhaps, get back to her own planet.

Kim would have been all aboard the fix-the-beacon and save the core train, ticket stamped and ready to leave for exit-the-hell-off-this-planet city, but for one minor issue. She felt that dealing with the poisonous gas cloud should take priority, and she had a plan, which didn't take ages to explain since it was uncomplicated.

"Right?"

She looked into his facial area for some signs of understanding, maybe a question that showed he was listening.

"Indeed. But I am sure you can see we need to fix the core before more of our comrades expire?"

"I mean, yes, of course. But if there isn't an atmosphere left when we're done, it won't matter."

And so on, for ten minutes at least, round in circles. He was insistent that she didn't need to oversee the gas cloud project, as Kevin was more than capable of getting it over the line, but Kim really wanted to be there to be sure it ran smoothly. He'd assured her they would switch back to the cloud as soon as the surface was safe. Several times, in fact. If there was going to be a compromise, it was going to be on her side.

"Look, I'm supposed to be supervising both projects, anyway. I can do that."

Ben looked down and gave his best impression of a shrug. It wasn't much to look at, even if you knew how to see his arms.

"My team has tried to understand the workings of this machine, and all have failed. Your presence would be of much greater use here in this space, helping us get the equipment working."

He stopped. Kim felt something akin to anticipation, but it passed a beat later when an alarm that wasn't in her original lab started flickering a purple-red and blaring a siren-like noise that was not natural. A few switches flicked later, and the screen showed that the condition of the crust was worsening at a faster rate than first thought. Just as she turned to acknowledge the incoming 'I-told-you-so', Kevin entered the lab with a floating tesseract that Kim had learned was a data-device. He inserted it into a toner cartridge that they'd replicated as a knowledge-orifice. Additional information showed that the radioactive fallout was covering a narrower area than the original estimates had showed.

"So, how long do we have?"

Kim asked, but it was in Benito's head when she did.

"You would say.."

"You don't have to say that every time! Just tell me in earth-units and leave it at that."

She felt bad about losing her cool, but not for long. Other things took precedence.

"Maybe a month."

"Until?"

"Until our planet destabilises enough to implode. But it won't matter since everything on it will be dead a few days before that."

Was that enough time? They'd wasted so much already with the stupid games.

"Okay, you win. What do you need me to do?"

"No one has won here today."

Ben let that sit for a brief period before continuing.

"Can you teach us how this machine works during that time? Leave me to get the core stable while you neutralise the cloud?"

She could. Bringing up the schematics on-screen she spent the next eight hours talking him and the occasional science-bod through the methods by which the emitted radiation focussed before being fired at a curtain of high-energy atoms, scattering sub-atomic particles at faster-than-light speeds over incomprehensible distances while tracking their movement. The eventual object was to locate 'spaces' in the travel that could be combined, creating an entire wormhole. Kim made sure they knew it had only ever worked once, by accident, without containment, resulting in her current predicament. Ben didn't seem to care, instead pointing out a few obvious tweaks that would allow them to bring the matter back rather than projecting it out.

It had been a strange day, even judged against current standards.

"Yeah, so that's it."

Even Kevin and his collective appeared bored by the

time she finished explaining, and once she was, he ushered her away and retraced their route through the party, which had wound down and evaporated by then. Furry food-things and juice-cubes littered that space along with a few inebriated creatures, one of whom was wearing some of Kim's newly made underwear over its head. She let it pass.

Once on the bridge, Kim felt herself being pushed to the command chair. The captain was standing there, alongside Joseph and another unnamed soldier, who was holding a de-maker to the captain's temple.

"You will have no more difficulties with this one. He has agreed to 'volunteer' his services to you, whatever you may need."

"Thank you, Joe. Is that necessary?"

Kim nodded toward the weapon.

"It was. I am sure it won't be though, moving forwards. Isn't that right?"

The Captain couldn't nod, so he projected his assent with a quick telepathic yes. Then the soldiers were gone, leaving Kim alone with the remaining creatures, one of whom lifted her onto the throne without asking. From her new perch, she could see the entire room with no obstacles, and it was impressive. At her feet, minions milled around, awaiting orders, so she wasted no more time in giving them.

"I need a sample of the gas cloud."

"It shall be done."

It seemed a tad odd that no one had thought to gather a sample without prompting, but Kim didn't want to dwell on anyone's failings, an ingrained character flaw that had derailed so many of her past personal projects. On the throne, on a screen inset into an ornate cross bar that didn't really work if you were human-shaped with protruding limbs, a vision blinked into existence and projected a holo-gram of Benito so real that she could feel emotions from the light. He was speaking, but she couldn't hear him. She shouted back, eliciting concerned glances from those around her but nothing from holo-Ben, so she thought about telepathy as hard as she could and hoped he got the hint. When he didn't, and she could sense him getting angry, she jumped off the chair and told one of Kevin's collective where she would be.

The new-lab was further away than Kim remembered, or she walked a different route. For whatever reason, it took nearly fifteen minutes before she arrived to find Ben circling the control console at a frantic pace.

"Why did you not speak over the communication viewer?"

"It doesn't transmit sound."

"Oh."

That was all she got. Ben continued pacing while she stood by and watched. In the end, she took a chance and blocked his path.

"What is the meaning of this?"

"You called me, remember?"

"I may have been a little rash."

Kim blinked, but said nothing.

"I have followed your instructions and used the controller thing over there to target some mass out in the void above. It gained a good lock, with only one line on-screen, see?"

She saw, she also saw, that the red-light was steady, and that the second-stage firing indicator was off, which was a positive, since they hadn't talked about containment yet. Ben seemed much too jittery for this to be the entire story, and the tense energy contained a contagious quality that asked questions.

"What else did you do?"

His answer was to throw up several fizzing tentacles and gesticulate wildly around the room. Kim followed his lead, looking at everything he pointed to, a deep stabbing pain behind her left eye building as she did. Joe entered through a side door that should have led to a broom-cupboard but now appeared to link with the central ship-maze. Ben stared at him until he was stationary, then shook his head, causing the soldier to leave just as quickly and without saying a word. In the room, Kim noticed the increasing static energy. She ran over to the console and brought up the patched in status display, which was a confusing mix of hers and their technology.

"You started the sequence?"

The words came out as a rapid squeak and were more of a factual statement than a question. She could see what he'd done.

"There isn't anything to stabilise the field. You could pull in a whole fucking moon, right into this space!"

Caruthers was having a good period. He was back. Around him, lower beings tended to their work while granting him the reverence he'd been born to wield. In front of him was a surface full of fine eating-things and drink-cubes piled neatly, and above him, the fates were finally returning what they owed. It was unfortunate that this miracle had been achieved via the near destruction of his species, but he felt certain that henceforth, events would play just right and everything would be well. The alien was proving to be useful, which hadn't come as a tremendous surprise since he'd seen her work, but she'd integrated with the science-cluster she now called Kevin. That was huge. No one got on with Kevin.

He'd half expected her to be eaten by them.

There was definitely something unusual occurring between them, and he would work hard to understand what. Until then, while she still proved useful, he would keep a close eye on her activities and put a stop to any sabotage he may spot. It would make no difference if she attempted betrayal, since they would find solutions to both problems, of that he was certain.

A lackey moved forwards, taking care to avoid eye-contact, before standing motionless before him.

"What?"

"Car.. Um, your highness? You asked to be notified if the alien creature made further contact with our leader."

Nothing more.

"And?"

"Oh, yeah, and she has re-entered the new-lab room. They are alone in there together."

What was she up to now? Her briefing had been thorough, and she had no business being there. The lackey was still stood before him so he threw a partially drunk juice-cube at him as thanks for the news and stood in as theatrical a manner as he could before striding forth for the command deck. He'd picked his quarters with care, being as close as possible to equidistant from both the new-lab and the bridge. It was also the closest thing to quiet that he could find, and it had heated rest-pads and a nice view-screen.

He had covered about half the distance to the lab when the deep boom of an explosion halted his progress. At first he considered it could be a trick of his thoughts, a waking night-mare echoing his experiences of the deadly quakes below, but then he felt the vibrations in the airframe and stepped up his pace, flying as fast as he could to see what had happened. There were guards at the entrance, but not sufficient to prevent his entry. Inside, Benito was crouched against a far wall, with several marks showing he'd endured a significant impact of some kind. On the central console, Kim-alien was tending to the controls while cowering behind a large plate of metal. She had a familiar expression on her face, wide eyed and agape.

The creature was also white in the face and visibly vibrating.

What had he discovered here? Had she made a move to seize power? Caruthers moved over to protect his leader but stopped half-way there after being paralysed by a Kim-scream. It wasn't the sound so much as the unfathomable whirlwind inside her brain, in which he could read danger, so he backed away from Ben and made for Kim instead. Just a few paces later, and around where he had been when she yelled, an eruption of photonic energy burst from venting he'd never paid attention to before, or noticed, if truly honest. A burst of heat that he bore the full brunt of followed, only lasting a few Milli-periods, but warming his outer dermis such as when hit with an energy projectile, only covered his entire physical form at once. Once the heat faded, it was Kim that reacted first, running in her ungainly way to Benito's prone form. He watched her as if in held in a trance, reeling from the blast and unable to make himself move. When he coaxed himself upright, there was a worrying crackling and resistance from his rear-side.

He reached Ben just after the alien, finding him awake and lucid enough to stop Caruthers from grabbing Kim and throwing her across the room. With a single intense thought, he conveyed what had transpired. It was enough to warrant another attempt to render Kim-thing to pieces. This time Ben spoke with words.

"Stop!"

"But it sabotaged your experiment and set us back, maybe for whole periods. It has to pay a price for this treachery."

"You will leave her unharmed! This was my mistake. I was foolish enough to believe I understood when I did not. Kimberley saved us all."

He read her mind to a greater depth, finding, in amongst the chaos, truth in what Ben had said. He also found something else.

"It is un-repairable?"

He stared at Kim, waiting for a response. When she shook her head, she was just confirming what he already knew. It was Ben that spoke next.

"But surely you can rebuild. We can provide you with the materials.."

"I don't know how!"

Then there was silence. Inside her head, Caruthers could hear her thoughts screaming, each one fighting for her attention, but they were slippery, like eels, and she could not hold on to any of them.

"Kim, KIM!"

She didn't react until he touched her shoulder, at which point she flinched so hard she fell backwards, before curling herself up into a body-fist. She was of no practical use, so he turned to Ben.

"Why did she destroy the contraption?"

"I was testing the machine's capabilities, only intended to bring down a sample of matter from above. The regulators and containment systems were not engaged when I did so. I tagged an asteroid big enough to end all life."

"Could you not just disengage?"

"It became apparent that we could not. We did not replicate the systems that allow for it."

He wrapped his last sentence with razor sharp barbs and then aimed it directly at Caruthers. Had he missed something when cataloguing the lab-complex on the ground?

Everything looked as it should.

"Imagine our surprise when Kim went to activate the fail-safe and found instead a dispenser of soiled nether-clothing."

Caruthers looked to the floor where he observed a small pile of the creatures stained, dainty garments, and above was a low unit permanently strewn with such items back in the real lab.

"Are you saying that is not where these fabric-coverings originate? There are always so many.."

"No. It transpires that under the clothing is a direct vent that allows the harmless ejection of the radiation while disengaging the matter transport sequence."

He was seeing how someone might interpret this as his fault. Ben continued, getting louder and deeper as he did, humming tentacles whipping against his side with a rhythmic cracking that was getting faster.

"In the absence of any safe options to stop the sequence, Kim had no choice but to employ more drastic methods."

Caruthers didn't like where this was heading.

"She destroyed the core. Brilliant, really, you should have seen the speed with which she manipulated the systems governing power supply and thermal extraction. She was a marvel."

At that exact moment, the marvel was a trembling, tightly wound ball on the floor. Her head was clearing, though, and he could feel it.

"Right, so we can re-make the core and re-align the power and energy systems? This should be elementary work for our skilled technicians."

"This is what I believed. Kimberley disagrees, though."

An increasing amount of anger was heading the alien's way, and Caruthers could feel Ben's trust in her worth melting just a little, just not quite enough to get what he desired, but that eventuality was drawing near. Right now, his planet needed her machine, and if there was any way to repair the apparently substantial damage, only she would know.

"Kim?"

He placed a limb on her back with care to avoid causing her alarm. She responded by unfurling and sitting against the wall. Her head was almost clear of hindrance, and her thought ordered once again.

"I didn't design the interface. Sodding Paul cobbled it together, and he never felt the need to tell me how it worked exactly and I didn't need to know, so I just let it go and did my own things."

Caruthers tried to ignore the free-fall in his digestive-re circulatory system and pushed a little just to be sure he had things straight.

"So you don't know how this core functioned?"

"I didn't say I didn't know how it worked. Most of the theory was mine, at least in the end. It's just a few bits and bobs here and there that I, you know, didn't work on directly."

"Now I am confused."

He was.

"It's just.. Look.. I didn't need to know everything because it was all documented. I could just look up the fine detail if I needed to know how to wire something up. The stuff they all did was pretty trivial, and I didn't need that in my head."

His confusion was growing. He could feel that everything she said was the truth, no matter how boastful her words were.

"So why not consult with this documentation?"

"It's.. I.. I don't know, why don't I? You can re-make this core stuff right?"

Benito projected an emphatic yes he could feel vibrate through Kim's mind, and ricochet off new found pain. When she spoke, it was through a grimace and gritted teeth.

"Jesus! Could you not do that when we're so close together? How long?"

This time, Ben used words.

"There is a supply. I have access to it now."

"Great, let's go get the files. I can get this thing running in a few hours. The damage is.."

"Get?"

Caruthers elation soured only a little. With access to the citadel's transport system, even compromised and power limited as they were, everything within the current hemisphere was within range.

"Yeah. They're in storage at the lab."

"Let us waste no further.."

Benito pulled himself fully upright and threw out a cautionary limb that caught Caruthers midsection like a hook, halting him on the spot.

"Is there a problem?"

* * *

ONCE SAFELY ON THE BRIDGE, CARUTHERS BROKE THE awkward silence that had lain over them like a thick spore-mist the whole way. He did it partly to dispel the hold it had over them, but also to verbalise the problem, make it tangible.

"And you are certain?"

"The reports are clear on this. I am afraid that it will be quite impossible."

Benito ordered a quadrant of the main view-screen re-tasked to display the courtyard area around the creature's displaced lab-complex. A hatched area overlaid, showing that fatal levels of radiation had indeed infused the building and all its surroundings.

There was no way to return.

Even if he could withstand the onslaught of ionising particles and somehow reach the files, he wouldn't know which was pertinent, and would therefore require the guidance of Kim, and her distended lumpen form would disintegrate within very little time. Much as he wished to see it, his own lifespan was simply too high a price to pay. On top of that, the transportation beaming equipment on the citadel, which was only ever experimental to begin with, struggled to maintain focus around too much atmospheric charge, and Caruthers was certain he did not want to experience the displaced horrors Kim had done during her forays into local matter transfer. He preferred that his internal form remained as such, so he would not risk it. This news brought a pout and some moisture to the Kim-creature's face.

"But I need those files! Without them we're sunk."

Caruthers was also struggling to maintain a positive outlook while the gigantic countdown still overlaying most of the view-screen kept diminishing. Something needed to be done, and no one else appeared to be doing it, whatever 'it' was.

"We must continue with the other project, dispel this destructive layer of fatality. You.."

Caruthers pointed an angry tentacle at Kim-thing, then drove it into the squashiest part of her torso with enough force to elicit a backwards stumble and a deep-set frown that wrinkled her olfactory intake nub.

"You have a plan for dealing with the gaseous issue?"

"First, asshole, that was rude! Second, yes I do. I've been trying to.."

"Excellent. I will assume leadership. I wish you to enact your scheme right now.."

"No."

He needed a beat to realise that the refusal had come from Benito. Ben then moved himself between Caruthers and the creature, but near enough to Caruthers for him to have to move backwards. He tried to read his ruler's thoughts but found himself excluded, so he asked.

"What would you have me do? We cannot sit still and watch our planet die."

"The beacon technology takes precedent. We must get it ready. Kim, prepare.."

"But there is no 'beacon' without the files. We know this, and must do what can be done, not dwell on what cannot."

Kimberley sidled out from behind Benito, sly thoughts papering her face with smirks and other unsightly twitches. He was being excluded from events.

A situation that was unacceptable.

"Tell me exactly what is happening here, this instant."

He still could not access Benito's thought, but Kimberley was an open tome, projecting her mind like an errant holo-screen for all to see, and she agreed at least partly with Caruthers. But there was hesitation, and he could see why.

Her plan involved a focussed high-energy beam, as most of her plans did, but one that would fuse sub-atomic particles together, transmogrifying one isotope into another and reducing the half-life to negligible amounts.

There were a lot of unfamiliar words and ideas floating around there.

"What is sub-atomic?"

In reality, he didn't care to know; it was enough that she knew and understood. Still, hesitation clouded the back of her mind, obscuring it from his gaze and preventing him from seeing the complete picture. He pushed a little harder, feeling her defences rise as a transparent wall in her head, failing to cover what he already knew but preventing further progress. As he was making headway, Ben cut him off again with a blow to the cranial region.

"Kimberley remains in charge. She must complete the beacon tech as soon as is possible."

"I don't understand your insistence on.."

"She understands the technology better than you."

"No, I get she is more familiar. What I don't understand is why we must adopt this order of priorities."

Caruthers watched as Ben sighed, ushered over a science-bod, and gave a hushed order even he couldn't hear. On-screen, the entire view changed to that of a rotating planet-wide graphic that showed fissures appearing and then lurching across the continental surfaces like clear-rock shattering in slow-motion. It was beautiful or would have been, if it wasn't real. Everyone else stopped what they were doing and watched in silence as the lines crossed and merged, each crack growing until there was no realm left untouched, then exploding outwards with a bright flash that dulled away, leaving nothing.

A simulation. The screen returned to its previous configuration, and Caruthers took the breath he'd been holding during the show without even realising.

"I don't understand?"

"Our projections may not be as accurate as I was letting on. The lifespan of our world could be lesser by several periods. We must stabilise the surface, then save any lives that remain."

Kim-thing, who had watched with her food-hole ajar the entire time, turned and stared, first at Benito, then at Caruthers. He looked back into her and observed deep conflict, as if both halves of her consciousness had fought to a stalemate over the best course of action before moving forwards.

It was Ben that broke the deadlock.

"I will return to the surface myself and return with the needed papers. I alone will take this risk. There is, I believe, a way to achieve this safely, but I must leave immediately. In the interim, Joseph will represent me aboard this vessel. You will all report to Kimberley, then she will report to Joseph and he, then, to me."

"This is preposterous! I have seniority!"

Caruthers turned to Kim-thing and articulated his fury the best he could without lips or eyebrows, which, judging from her subsequent grimace, was not a pleasant sight. That lifted his spirits for a moment while he took stock of the situation.

"I think Caruthers is right. We should do what we can with the cloud, and my theory should be sound.."

"You will do what I ask!"

And that was it. Benito turned sharply away, his perambulatory limbs giving an audible snap as he hustled toward the doorway, alone. Joseph remained with the group, and his demeanour, which was twitchy and erratic, betrayed the same bewilderment felt by all creatures present. In the time it took Ben to leave the room, Caruthers could already feel the doubts rebuilding inside Kim. She rolled her eyes up, then squinted, then moved over to the command throne and sat on the floor next to it. Joseph watched, then 'shrugged' and exited the bridge, using the same door as Benito. That left Caruthers, and he wasn't certain what to do next, choosing to storm over to Kim's location and play on her insecurities.

"You are not qualified to lead this mission. I can see your thoughts, even you do not believe you are capable. You will hand control over to me this instant, and I will put you to work repairing the damage you did to our great hope."

"I never believe."

She was telling the truth, and he could sense it. A kaleidoscope of memories tumbled through her mind, colliding, combining, and coalescing to form a picture of her life that betrayed her constant and worrying lack of self-confidence. Knowledge Caruthers was sure would prove handy later, or now.

"Yes. I am assuming command. Report to the laboratory immediately. You need to prepare the room for new material and ensure that everything is ready for when Benito returns with the papers."

She remained seated, so he tried again, this time with a little more force.

"Go, now!"

"You don't know how to prepare a proton beam, so I'm needed here to make the radiation safe."

"I will.."

"NO!"

He didn't need to feel her mind, he could see her confidence crumble all over her body as limbs clenched and then not, and a sheen on her face that stressed the pale complexion splashed with blotches of red, but somehow it wasn't lessening her resolve. Suddenly he felt Benito's influence on everything, clear as the mid-sun that baked his land. The two of them were plotting something. It explained why this being would not follow his orders. She had a plan, and Ben was in on it somehow. All around, science-nerds wittered and rustled as they did their best to look busy. No doubt they were also aware of what was happening. Was he the only being not privy to the master-plan? No matter, for now the danger was real, and there seemed to be a way forwards. He didn't like it, not at all, but for now he would play the game, just a little more, until she slipped up and he could swoop in.

"As you wish. What would you have me do, highness?"

"You can knock that shit off right now. We're friends, Caruthers, and I'm scared and I need you. I could really use some advice. Do you think we should listen to Ben? I'm really not sure, and the beacon is in pretty awful shape. It'll take ages to fix, even with the schematics. We could have a prototype beam tuned and ready in a day."

It was a test. She was testing him to see if he would remain loyal to Benito in his absence. If it really was that simple, then perhaps the situation was salvageable. After all, he had played this game many times before and won.

"I believe we should do as instructed. Our glorious leader sees, and I trust it will prove to be the best way forward."

The hairs on Kim's neck stood to attention as static energy infused the air around the magnetic field. Thankfully, it was holding, keeping the highly charged contents inside. The whole experiment sat inside a seamless box of transparent rock. That was a contingency in case an emergency arose and Kim wasn't quick enough to contain it.

She stared at the readings, uncertain what to make of them. No, that wasn't true. She understood what to make of them, but she wasn't clear why they were telling her what they were. The makeshift instrumentation was sound. It was something she'd tested when setting up this little broom-closet test-bed and her calculations were meticulous, checked and rechecked.

Kim spent hours calibrating, when she was supposed to be asleep, to the extent that it was interfering with her day-job, where she was supposed to be awake.

Only yesterday, there'd been a hairy moment on the inner gantry. A vivid daydream about seven foot tall raspberries which gained enough momentum to bulldoze its way through her subconscious mind into her conscious.

It transformed a blink into a ten-foot fall off of the walk-way, and into the tendrils of one of Kevin's collective who, conveniently, was replacing shielding tiles that had broken when she dropped a spanner from that exact spot a day or so earlier. Or it could have been the same day. She really didn't know anymore. Without demarcation, and lacking even the crappy, inaccurate lab-clock, which they hadn't replicated, she did not know how quickly time was passing. The count-down on the bridge wasn't helpful, since it didn't measure passing time in any direct way, but the thought-cycles of a network of 'great-thinkers' that dotted their globe. A beep announced a fifth round of analysis was complete. New read-ings replaced the previous, but the same result prevailed.

It wasn't working.

In fact, it was making things much worse. The gas became deadlier no matter how she calibrated the beam. Kim reached out to Kevin with her mind since one of him was often hanging around the off-limits room, and he didn't disap-point. She asked him to retrieve another sample, to which he reiterated that someone was going to notice at some point, so she pointed out that it would probably be a member of his collective, in other words, him, at which point he agreed and then sent another body to get her sample. She had it in her hands around ten minutes later. However, as she was about to inject the gas into the magnetic flask, she remembered that the definition of madness was repeating the same actions while expecting different results, or something sounding similar.

She stopped everything and stared at her fingers for a while instead. Kim wasn't certain about anything anymore, not even her sanity, and she thought that she'd lost even the basic grasp of chemistry that got her through high school and into university.

She needed to do something different. There was an alternative method, something that had worked historically on Earth. But for it to happen, she needed a more accurate idea of the exact composition of the cloud.

A few button presses later and she had the console reconfigured, the sensors redeployed and the flask full of poison. At first, the machinery was reluctant to report any useful results, pointing to a faulty sensor. She felt elated that her earlier failures could have such a succinct explanation, so she reached out to Kevin again, asking for more equipment. He duly complied within minutes while reminding her she would need to be on the bridge in less than an hour.

An hour. Would it be enough time?

Kim unscrewed the panel that housed the sensor array, unplugging the modules with care since they were breakable and difficult to calibrate. Once removed, she picked up the box containing the replacement components, once again taking her time to avoid any chance of damage, which would set her back another day. The box felt secure in her grip, and the top was tight. Inside, metal and glass jostled to a comforting tinkly sound, as if they were excited to be splitting the gaseous atmosphere into its component atoms and then identifying them all one-by-one. Maybe a little too excited.

The lid popped up at one corner, something Kim compensated for by gripping what she had even tighter and then watching as the container deformed, throwing the array into the air where it hung for a second, fighting for its existence, before falling to the floor with a tinkling of shattered glass that reminded Kim of Christmas.

"Bollocks!"

It was a major setback, that was for certain. Then she had a brilliant idea. There were alternative sensors in the main lab that, although not designed to interconnect with her more primitive set-up, she could coerce with some duct-tape and prayer. Without saying why, she got Kevin to provide her with the pieces and then ejected him from her space. It took most of her remaining forty-five minutes, but with just enough time to run her analysis, she fired everything up and waited for the numbers to settle while sweeping up her earlier mistake.

Kim did not like what came back.

"Bollocks!"

Now understanding why her earlier attempts to nullify the danger weren't working, she changed tack altogether, putting all her eggs into basket number two. There was a way to transmute the material into harmless matter, relatively speaking. She just needed to come up with the correct formula, and it would bind with the death-particles that could penetrate your skeleton and eat you from the inside, turning them into death-particles that were stoppable with modest clothing and a better attitude toward hand-washing.

Kevin knocked gently in her mind, her ever faithful alarm.

Only she didn't want to go. This was important and there was finally a pathway forward, so instead of leaving, Kim begged Kevin to stall for additional time. She would be there eventually, Kim assured them, but it would be a short while later. He muttered something about petunias before leaving, which seemed odd, but his internal monologue often brimmed with words that didn't properly translate, so Kim was used to it by now.

Alone again, she pulled knowledge from every corner of her mind and wadded it up into a sticky ball of hope, making sure that her creepy fifth-grade science teacher was stuck in the middle. Formulae came forth, but only part-formed at first, then whole. The result of months of cramming for her A-levels, in which she memorised an entire textbook word-for-word. She could still remember the page numbers that dealt with explosive reactions.

The matter transporter could synthesise nearly any element by pulling molecules from the air and combining them before materialising them on a pad, so raw materials weren't an issue. It still took far longer than she wanted to complete the compound.

When it was done, it was a solid at room temperature. A jar of nondescript blue-green dust that was simultaneously both greasy and powdery. In order to work, it needed to be gaseous, so Kim tried to heat it, gently at first, then more aggressively since nothing seemed to happen. All at once, the entire jar exploded. Kim ducked just in time to avoid the razor-shards that radiated out, pinning themselves to the surrounding surfaces like tiny daggers.

"Bollocks!"

Another hour, another jar of powder that was stubbornly inert in its current form.

This time, Kim had a prototype atomiser ready and waiting. A much more robust take on the use of heat to convert things into gas, it was highly effective. The powder fizzled into a light fog that filled the atomiser with twinkles, before settling into a dull greyish smog that didn't look like it would smell very nice. When injecting it into the sample, it had no effect at first, just mingling and increasing the density inside the flask, and then it did. All at once, the material contained within the flask cleared. It took less than a second for the entire space to be crystal clear apart from a layer of dust that coated the lower surfaces.

Kim measured the radiation present inside. The original equipment was still registering residual emissions, no doubt the result of an explosion driving matter into the sensors at some point. The newer equipment, however, registered almost nothing. Nada. Needing to be sure, Kim reached out to Kevin one more time, requesting a final sample. At first, when they didn't respond, Kim thought nothing of it since he would be busy stalling for time. After a few minutes, when he still hadn't responded, and when she could no longer sense his presence anywhere, she worried.

Kim synthesised another batch of the formula and loaded it into her mark-one atomiser, making sure that there was enough charge to fire it before leaving her hidden space and making for the bridge. It was a short walk, a direct route through two empty rooms and something that felt like a sauna but smelled like an ice-cream shop. She stopped, just for a beat, to enjoy the butterscotch, although not long enough to get sweaty since that sometimes made the alien fabric of her jumpsuit completely transparent, before striding with confidence into the command centre.

There was almost no one there.

Over by the throne, Caruthers stood with a Kevin, across whose torso, a mesh of welts stood proud and red. They split his skin, making it look like someone had hit him with a huge spatula. Two feet from the door Kim had just entered through, Joe stood motionless. Kim made her way to

Caruthers, shooting an apologetic glance at Kevin as she did so. Joe followed, but Caruthers spoke first.

"What is the reason for this treason?"

* * *

To say he was angry would be to understate the obvious, like saying burning-hot coals would sting just a little if you ate one. On the main screen, the countdown was still flipping through random shapes with no discernable meaning while charted data spelled out the death-by-a-thousand-cuts being experienced by their world. Joe, still silent but no longer motionless, had moved up close enough to Kim that she felt uncomfortable. He had a weapon, but he wasn't pointing it at anything, something she took as a positive, unlike the brooding darkness filling his eyes. The raised marks on Kevin's body had receded a little, giving the impression that he was wearing a single giant fishnet stocking that he'd pulled to his chin area. It would have been hilarious, only Kevin wasn't laughing. In fact, he wasn't doing anything. His mind was blank. Nothing came out, and, as far as Kim could tell, nothing was going on in there.

Joe nudged Kim closer to Caruthers. She resisted at first, but he was strong and she was tired. Now sandwiched between the two beings, she felt that maybe now could be a good time for an explanation.

"Look, I'm just trying to help."

"By dooming our world to a fiery death?"

She wasn't sure which of the two had spoken, so she picked one, addressing Caruthers.

"For the thousandth time, if the air poisons everyone, it won't matter if there's still a planet."

He stood silently. Joe prodded her in the side with a pointed tentacle. Kim figured she had to add more, so she unveiled her trump card a little earlier than hoped, and with much less fanfare.

"It works! I can neutralise the danger. Well, we can. Obviously, I need some help to get this stuff made to scale."

More silence. This time, however, she could feel some doubts in Caruthers mind and see the brief glances up and to the right. Joe was still vibrating with a heat that was both menacing and quite pleasant, given the lack of heating in her hidden lab had leeched a lot of her body-heat. Kevin had now rejoined the world but was keeping pointedly quiet, wrapping his thoughts in happy memories and fighting the urge to grimace, a heroic effort given the state of his body.

It was Caruthers that spoke next.

"You can show this miracle?"

Kim pulled the atomiser from her pocket, holding it like a gun. In hindsight, not a wise decision. Joe threw limbs at her with a speed that whip-cracked in the air, sending her flying across the room and into a low console. The impact, which caught her left side just above the hip, knocked the wind out of her lungs and triggered a nerve-ganglion into first paralysing, and then spasming her lower torso and legs, which shot out from under her in comic fashion. Her coccyx took most of the brunt, hitting the ground unprotected. Still, she clung onto the atomiser with a sure grip that she found as amazing as it was unexpected. Less helpful was the fact that the combination of angles she'd pool-balled off things left her facing Joe full on with the gas-container pointing at his head area. An accident, of course.

He had his un-maker out, and his aim was deliberate.

Kim lowered her arm as fast as her mind could put the

pieces together, which was just quick enough to prevent the soldier removing her head. She then dropped her implement and raised her hands as far as the ache in her side would allow, which was an unimpressive thirty degrees, way below her shoulder. Joe eyeballed, and she stared back while Kevin thought uncertain thoughts loud enough that everyone in the room could read them, and this time, it was Kevin that spoke.

"I've never seen that thing before in my entire existence, Joseph. Believe me. I don't know where the hell she got it."

"I made it! Look.."

Kim reached out, but Joe raised his gun, so she sat back.

"It's not a weapon! Unless you're fighting radioactive isotopes, in which case I suppose it is."

Caruthers reached out and picked it up, turning it in the air before his eyes. There was a small crack that had appeared in the incineration chamber. He ran a tendril along it before withdrawing the limb and handing the tool to Joseph, who handed it straight to Kevin. Kim continued her explanation.

"The compound binds with the isotopes in the cloud and forms other isotopes that have massively reduced half-lives. They then fall harmlessly to the ground and, you know, abracadabra!"

"You will show us."

So she did. The return walk to the hidden lab was slow, but there was no opportunity to savour the ice-cream odour, which was a sort of dark, comforting chocolate-chip concoction when passing this time. Once inside, Joe closed the door and took in the surroundings. He felt much calmer than Kim thought he should be given the deception, so she pressed a little and tried to read his emotions. Not only was he not filled with any expected, there wasn't even any surprise. She looked to Kevin, who avoided her gaze by apparently counting rivets in the bulkhead, and understood why.

"You told him about this, didn't you?"

He waited for unspoken permission from Joe before speaking.

"I didn't need to tell him. It was his idea."

She was sure he wasn't lying. Kim took a moment to consider this new information before formulating a response with care.

"What?"

It was a disappointing culmination of thoughts, but it did the job, and Joe joined the conversation.

"I knew we could not dissuade you from this course of action. Benito, also, felt this was your most likely course, so we facilitated, provided you with tools and time, kept you docile and compliant."

Joe moved around, laying smug limbs on the equipment.

"I monitored your progress, authorised your.."

"Docile? Screw you."

Kimberley clenched her fists while Joseph picked up one of Kim's redesigned sensor parts and observed it for a moment, turning it carefully in his limbs, savouring each curve and facet before turning to Kevin, who looked at the floor like a five-year-old in trouble. He shrugged a telepathic apology as Kim continued.

"Careful with that."

Joe looked up, still holding the piece. Kim could feel something akin to concern in his head, but he didn't betray any when he spoke again.

"This is an interesting toy. Explain its purpose to me."

He was probing her mind. She could feel him there, but not deep, like he was waiting for her to make a mistake.

There was something wrong here, but she couldn't quite put her finger on what it was.

"It's a sensor."

"It doesn't look like anything that we provided. Kevin."

He drew out the last word, sounding a lot like Kim herself did when calling out for her cat after discovering he'd decided that her new kitchen basin made an ideal litter box. This time Kevin answered with words.

"I.. I don't know whee she got that."

"You didn't provide it from the surplus?"

"I.. Yes.. Um, no."

Now what Kim felt from Joe was icy fear, thick and juicy enough that Caruthers picked up on it too. The sensor flew across the small room and dismantled itself, with a grinding, tinkly sound, when it hit the far wall. Joe went back to examining the lab equipment, but this time he was frantic, searching for something. When he got to Kim's new testing chamber, he all but screamed, the telepathic echoes rattling in Kim's head, nauseating and loud.

"What? What did you find?"

Kim didn't understand what was happening. She had done nothing wrong, and this was a triumph, not a disaster.

"I found a solution?"

Kevin moved over to examine the chamber, holding up a tentacle, then two when one wasn't enough. Everyone fell silent on the outside, but Kim could still hear some of their thoughts, the ones on the surface that always escaped no matter how disciplined you thought you were. Kevin radiated intrigue and wanted to know what she'd found. Joseph was angry that his little ruse to keep her working on the beacon had failed, but also amazed that she had succeeded somehow.

She wasn't worried about them. Everything she felt there was to be expected.

No, it was Caruthers she was worried about.

He was incandescent, as hot and irrational as he'd been back on the planet when he tried to end her, but try as she might, she couldn't figure out why.

Joe turned back to Kim.

"There is no solution. We designed this equipment to provide only the readings we want them to. There should be no change whatever magic you bring to bear. This is.."

"You son-of-a-bitch. Days of wasted time with faulty readings, and it was on shitting purpose? I could have solved this issue last week. I probably did!"

At this, Caruthers snapped, shouting something loud and untranslatable with sounds that fell outside of anything Kim had heard before and made her teeth feel like small marshmallows dipped in cheese. After the brief outburst, he pushed past Joseph and toppled the test-rig to the floor, showering everything in glass and the residual inert powder that remained. Then, while Joe and Kevin watched, he grabbed Kim and threw her against the same wall that had destroyed her sensor a few minutes before, this time dismantling her shoulder but with more of a splintery thud than a tinkle.

"You see!"

He sounded triumphant. Joe moved in front of Kim, blocking further access but doing nothing more. Caruthers continued.

"You see! All along, I have said she is playing games with us. I have gone along with your schemes, allowed you to indulge this creature, hoping something in her primitive thoughts might be of use. Time and time again she has showed how useless she is, how unpredictable. I said she needed closer supervision. I have told you I should lead this programme."

He jabbed Joe in the chest area. The soldier didn't move, so Caruthers kept talking. Kim was getting worried about the direction his ramblings were taking.

"I am taking charge. You do not have the authority to prevent this, so stand aside. I will put the creature to work in shackles so that she may remain focussed on her tasks."

Kim watched as Joe pushed Caruthers back, mind-shaking his head. Then, just as she thought things were calming down, Caruthers lunged past Joe, getting at least eight tendrils around Kim's body, and a few around her neck.

"I am finished with you!"

Everything happened in slow motion, like watching a sports replay, only much more personally painful. Caruthers limbs burned and twisted, wrenching disparate parts of Kim's body in unnatural directions, like wringing a dishcloth with a chainsaw. She felt a disc pop in her spine and the feeling leave her torso below, then her already broken shoulder grind in the ruined socket splintering the nerve endings. Then, all at once, his grip was gone, and she tumbled to the ground. Unable to move, her view of the subsequent altercation was limited, but she could hear the bass zip of Joe's weapon firing and the dull, heavy thud of Caruthers hitting the floor behind her. She could also hear his threats, all directed at her. He was blaming her for everything that had happened, just like on the planet.

And just as then, he wanted her dead.

Tears formed and then fell from Kim's eyes, not because of the pain, which was ebbing from her upper body, and non-existent below the break in her spine. It was because she'd missed something that was probably obvious to everyone else, and because of her blindness, she'd lost another friend. It had happened so often she couldn't understand why it still hurt, but it always did.

The room filled with additional soldiers, all under Joe's command. Some lifted Caruthers from the ground behind where she lay. Kim could hear his ragged panting rise to a grunted scream as he moved. The rest tended to her, gently lifting her with a mesh of tentacles before throwing her onto a gurney that one wheeled in when they arrived. Kim still felt nothing below her waist, which was a concern, so she brought it up.

"I think he broke my back."

Her words came out shapeless and undisciplined, and when Joe's face appeared above her, leering down, he had no expression that she could read. To her left, a being she hadn't seen in quite a while threw an exotic appliance over her that fitted with a comforting click into grooves on either side, before powering it up and projecting all of Kim's internal organs into the space above. Now numb and dissociated from events unfolding around her, Kim watched through a fog that defocused and over-saturated, seeing the dislodged disc in her spine, but also some discolouration on a lung and some fatty deposits on her liver, so she made a mental note to cut back on the food-cubes.

They tasted nice, and universal law said nothing that tasted nice could be positive for your health.

Above, the med-tech prodded her herniated disc with a device that looked like a miniature cattle-prod that hummed on contact. After it was back where it should be, in her spine, he injected something from a gun-shaped syringe and re-inserted the bits-and-pieces into her skin-sack. The pain hit her all at once, pushing the air out of her lungs in a protracted, hoarse rattle. The shoulder and spine had a quick fight for dominance, and after a few seconds, the shoulder won, relegating her back-spasms to a dull ache.

Kim stood, unsteady at first, then strode with confidence to where Caruthers was standing, barely conscious and flanked by four guards. She wasn't sure what to say, so said the first thing that came into her head.

"Screw you."

His answer felt more rehearsed.

"This equipment told lies. Your 'solution' is a sham, designed to poison our world so that you can invade with the rest of your vermin breed. Mark me, I will end you before you have the chance to enact your plan."

"There is no plan other than helping you. I know you can read my thoughts, so you know I'm telling the truth."

"You lie, even to yourself. You are always hiding behind a mask, pretending to be something you are not, someone you are not. How can I trust your thoughts if you yourself do not?"

Kim felt the words like a punch, hard and fast to her gut, and again bringing tears to her eyes.

"I'm just trying to help. The compound works. You'll see when it's deployed."

Guards hauled Caruthers away before he could reply further, leaving Kim alone with Joe, Kevin and a few soldiers and medical-nerds. Kim picked up her atomiser and checked it for damage, then handed it to Joe.

"Test it."

Joe waved a tentacle at Kevin, who already had a sample container to hand. Kim watched as he inserted the nozzle end into her workbench and injected the atmospheric gasses into the containing flask, noting that the emission indicators showed a pattern that matched with the previous samples.

Then they went haywire..

It was only a split second, enough to worry her, but not quite long enough for anyone else to register.

"I think you broke it."

Kevin moved round and tapped the dials before unplugging and re-connecting the data-cables. The readings spiked a second time and then settled. As he moved away, Kim spotted a crack in the outer rock-glass, slowly etching a spider web across the tank. Just before Kim could react, Joe spotted it, too.

"Kim is correct. We must vacate this room now!"

He was already pushing Kim out of the door before the sentence was done. Kevin followed, then the others. Once everyone was out, Joe sealed the door. Inside, a muffled explosion preceded a large quantity of glass hitting the floor.

"No one is to re-enter this space. We will test your compound on the bridge."

No one moved at first, then Kim walked over to the door-way, only to be intercepted by a flustered Kevin, who blocked her using his torso.

"That room is no longer safe. I will bring a new test-chamber to the bridge where we will try your compound."

And that was just what they did. This time around, everything went much more smoothly, with the atmosphere and compound reacting just as Kim had calculated. Once the sensors showed that the reaction was a success, she threw the now empty atomiser over her shoulder in a gesture she was certain looked like triumph. All she got in return was stunned silence. Behind her, the implement bounced off a desk with a clatter and then skidded across the floor. Ahead, at the readings panel, Kevin pored over the readings a third time and then laughed.

"She has done just what she said. This compound will solve the second problem. It will make the atmosphere safe for our people once.."

Then he was quiet, staring wide-eyed over Kim's shoulder, along with the others. Joe moved past Kim to whatever it was, which, when Kim turned to find out, wasn't a what, but a who.

"Kimberley, I have returned with your documents."

Ben didn't look well. The colour was all but gone from his skin, which was now marked with a series of weeping sunken lesions and angry raised welts. He stumbled, revealing the container behind. It was the filing cabinet Kim had requested, the whole thing, including the concrete floor it had stood on.

It looked heavy.

"I.. Ah, hello?"

Benito was scanning the area, noting things that shouldn't have been there, missing things that should. Kim felt his confusion through the mist clouding his mind. After Joe checked him over, Ben moved over to the throne area and sat himself down, flicking the right combination of controls to update the main viewscreen and list the goals achieved while he had been gone.

"I do not understand. The tech should have been ready by this time."

Kim shuffled her feet the best she could, which wasn't well as pins and needles in both legs had replaced the dull ache in her spine. It was Kevin that interjected, saving her from a drawn out silence that would otherwise have ended with an embarrassing climb-down.

"Very little work has finished on the beacon, but she has neutralised the cloud, sire. This is wonderful.. Ah."

Ben looked over at Kim, his face neutral and his eyes cold. She felt much needed blood abandoning more important tasks to light up her face the second he made eye contact, but kept quiet and looked down, waited for the fireworks. When he spoke, she could hear the effort needed to push his words out, feel the lead slowing his thoughts, heavy enough that she nearly missed the words.

"This is wonderful. I knew you could.."

"Look, I know you didn't want me to do this, but I still think.. Wait.. Ah, what did you say?"

"If you will let me finish. I knew you could do this. Your motivation and desire to help were never in any doubt Kimberley. Can you show me?"

Kim looked over to the test-bed, then to Kevin, who nodded and waited for another of him to bring a sample. Meanwhile, she moved over to an unused console and entered the formula for her compound before double checking and then sending it to a replication station. The prototype atomiser was still good for a few more shots, she figured, so once the compound was ready, she loaded it up.

"So, this works by.."

"The details are of little use to me. I trust that you, in your brilliance, understand it."

"Oh.. Kay. So, anyway, this is the gas cloud."

Kim watched as Kevin injected the sample and fired up the sensors, going over the formula in her head as the data appeared on the main screen. Everything was exactly as it had been in the lab, so she atomised the compound and introduced it to the tank.

Once again, the results were immediate and spectacular.

"So there it is. I guess.."

"You understate your achievement here. This will save many lives. We must begin the manufacture of this compound straight away."

"Don't you want to run more tests? Check.."

"Do you believe these results are sound?"

Just for a moment, Kim wasn't sure. Ben continued.

"Your genius is singular, Kimberley. I can feel you have been unsure of yourself for most of your lifespan, but now you can trust in me. You are as good as you think you are. Do you believe in these results?"

She hesitated again.

"DO YOU BELIEVE?"

"YES!"

* * *

AFTER A GOOD FEW HOURS SLEEP IMMERSED IN A DREAM where she was a giant starfish with fifty-foot arms and a craving for gummy-bears, which were always just out of reach no matter how she stretched and climbed, and then suddenly a new dream where she was extremely naked back in elementary school gym-class, hanging off the climbing bars while the entire school laughed, she awoke in a puddle of sweat. The sheets she'd replicated weren't porous although there were large holes between the threads, something she fixed in the past by perforating with a needle, but not last night.

She was so tired that she'd forgotten.

Climbing off the bed and then using her pyjamas to towel herself dry, she considered the crazy events of the last few days. It had been a wild ride. Caruthers was god knows where. Her formula to fix the death-cloud hanging over the planet worked and Ben had all the notes she needed to fix the beacon. She sniffed under her armpits to gauge cleanliness. Today's bouquet dictated a shower day, so she balled her PJs up tight and threw them into the corner of the room, where they joined at least a week's worth of laundry that she would incinerate later. The shower was a Jury-rigged device that replicated something approximating water in real time before dropping it through a repurposed conduit into which she'd poked a few holes. The 'water' was cold, and the drainage wasn't fantastic, making the experience unpleasant, which was the main reason Kim kept the showering to a minimum, but after sleeping in a bowl of her own bodily secretions, a clean set of coveralls just would not cut it.

Once dry and dressed, she returned to her work.

The beacon lab had seen extensive remodelling since the previous attempt to power the device had destroyed a good part of the equipment and supporting tech. There was a new central console that now included an integral ejection system, allowing any overheating core material to be fired out toward one of the nearby suns. It was an innovation that could have saved a huge amount of time and effort if it had been installed previously. There had also been a complete redesign of the user interface that allowed for dual language controls and remote access from an auxiliary panel in one of the adjacent rooms. All-in-all, it was a massive improvement, capped off with a lovely new colour-scheme that Kim had supervised herself, with lots of pastel blues and greens. On a functional note, they were nearly back where they had been before the unfortunate explosion. New core material had integrated easily with the other systems and was stable. The antennae array had to be reconfigured to work with the differing levels of shielding that surrounded the room in order to promote a less nervous disposition in those working nearby. It hadn't proven excessively difficult though, and this newly improvised configuration was, if anything, more accurate than it had been previously. The targeting calibration screen, one of the few pieces kept from the old user interface, showed a steadfast single red line, which was an excellent sign that things were progressing in the right direction.

Benito had recovered well. It took a few days. Kim couldn't be sure exactly how many since there weren't any clocks, but not over three. At first, she thought the lesions would kill him. They boiled up like a carpet of angry bubbles that covered most of his torso, before popping down to the texture, and colour, of overcooked lasagne. Once they cleared up though, and he dulled back to his usual dark-brown leathery consistency, there was no stopping him. Like a clingy toddler desperate for approval, he rocked up every few hours to garner a progress report, and to give Kim a rundown on how the compound manufacture was proceeding. Ben thought there would be enough to neutralise the entire cloud within a week. News that brought a smile to her face.

At her end, even with his interruptions, the work was almost complete.

Kim arrived at her workstation to find, just like every other day, Ben was already waiting for her. He was, as always nowadays, alone.

"Ah, Kimberley. I trust you have enough rest and are ready for today's tests? I must say, you are looking most fetching on this fine and potentially momentous morning."

She had made it clear several times the previous night that she would not sign off on live testing again until all the simulations had returned good data. Ben argued for hours, but she'd held firm, no matter how many platitudes he threw in her direction.

"Feeling fine. It'll take a while to recheck the settings in the central computer before we can run the simulation. You might as well get some more rest."

Ben's words were still a beat slow, and without his distinctive power, so she didn't think it was an unreasonable request. He disagreed.

"We do not require such measures. Your work here has been exemplary and we are ready to once again use your marvellous machine."

He'd been like this from the moment he'd returned, brushing off her concerns like cheap confetti at a wedding he hadn't even wanted to attend. Just as she had before, Kim squashed any thoughts of actual test-firing as quick as she could.

"It'll be ready when I say that it's ready. Come on, we don't want to screw this up again. I'm not sure I could face putting this back together a second time."

Ben channelled his inner teenager and threw a virtual pout, saying nothing.

"Not long, I promise. Just bear with me."

And then, pivoting the subject onto something more positive.

"How's the compound coming? We must be pretty close to using it by now, right?"

While Ben explained the latest hold-up, Kim picked up her favourite screwdriver. It wasn't because she needed it, as the newer design was all hidden push-clips that she didn't understand the design of, but because she'd always used it and it made her feel confident. With tool in hand, and Ben's excuses following her around the room like a noxious fart, she began testing the settings. If she was being truthful, they didn't even need checking. She'd set everything up the previous evening before turning in, and this exercise was more about building her own confidence than anything else, but she didn't want to tell Ben that, so kept him busy discussing other topics.

"Great! So, a few days then? Anyway, how's the skin? Those lesions look much better."

The simulator itself was just an AI module that attached to the main targeting system and interpreted inputs as if real, returning the results as output that was charted on the central screen. It wasn't really an AI, though. Since it channelled the data through the same network of interconnected hive-minds that provided the countdown on the bridge, it was more accurately an actual intelligence that spread like a messy spider's web over the inhabited part of the planet's surface. It had weakened a little in the last week, as more members perished, but it was still strong for now.

Convinced at last that the beacon wouldn't explode when fired up, she nodded to Ben, who was explaining his morning skincare regimen in excruciating detail, including the various grades of sandpaper that he was using to remove the necrotic outer flesh. He was at the controls before his sentence finished, leaving an unpleasant image hanging in Kim's mind, and the smell of burnt haddock in the air as he flew past. Ben had the targeting system up and running before Kim had time to join him, and when she arrived, he'd targeted a rock with the mass of a large saloon car, which was a manageable test.

"Remember, this time I'll count us in. Tune the array carefully as I bring up the charge in the core."

In his exuberance, the last time they'd tested, Ben had

fired without fully tuning the system and the resulting scattered beam had tried to combine the mass of every object behind the meteor into one lump and then pull it down into the virtual target area. Even at sub light-speed, the beam spread had accounted for about a tenth of all the matter in the universe before she'd realised what was happening and shut it down. She suspected that the resulting data-surge caused the death of at least one of the collective in Ben's AI group.

He seemed unconcerned.

"Fear not. I have a controlled view of the screen and will take care to focus in one place this time. You have my word."

He didn't speak the last part aloud, and for a moment, Kim wondered if his words were worth anything if he hadn't vocalised them. It was a fleeting thought, interrupted by the bright flashing alarm system that she'd insisted on so she'd know if the machine was being used when she wasn't present. The noise was overwhelming and made it impossible for her to hear her thoughts, though, so she disabled it from her console and then fired up the beam. As the charge built in the core, she watched the screen to be sure Ben was targeting the right piece of rock, which he did well all the way through the sequence.

One red line, solid and unwavering.

"Okay, I think we're ready to go. Are you ready?"

Ben didn't speak, instead projecting the impression of a nod into her brain from his station. Unsure how much longer he could maintain his aim, she decided it was enough and fired.

The alarm restarted as soon as she pressed the button.

It worked. All of it. After the initial results rolled in, the remaining tests whizzed past in the blink of an eye.

One by one, they targeted larger and larger objects with increasing accuracy, and helped by the AI collective, Kim could devise a method of automatically stabilising the targeting lock once they calculated an object's mass. Better than that, once she'd figured out the logistics and built the system, all with Kevin's help, of course, she did it. Her one goal since landing on this rock.

She'd targeted the Earth. She'd really done it. It was there, and it was stable.

Benito hadn't believed her straight away, saying it was impossible that she could have managed such a feat in such a brief space of time. Then, after he'd reviewed the data himself, he was almost as ecstatic as she'd been.

After that, there was the usual double and triple checking of data preceding re-runs of every single test. Following that, they installed a newer guidance system that

Ben himself worked on, with Kevin, that improved the efficiency of the targeting by over 60 per cent.

All of that took a week, maybe.

Kim could only see one issue, although it was a big one.

Where were they going to get sufficient energy to actually transfer the material from space to where they needed it? There was heaps of power at the lab, a unique reactor. It was the smallest ever devised on Earth. It consumed hydrogen from the atmosphere, an element so abundant that there would be an endless supply of it in perpetuity, combining it into larger, unstable molecules that then decayed, releasing huge amounts of energy. As long as air or water flowed freely, she had more power than a moderate-sized town could use.

The citadel didn't have that. Instead, it had the creaking and already compromised conversion chambers that Kim had bypassed when they boarded in order to keep everyone alive.

The power generated was still quite impressive, but nearly all of it was being consumed by keeping them in the sky. She'd run the calculations herself, and there wasn't any spare. They simply couldn't power up the beacon.

While Kim panicked, Benito was more circumspect. She did not know how he was keeping so calm while soothing her with an endless supply of platitudes, as if trying to smother her with cotton-wool kindness. Time and time again she ran the numbers and returned a deficit. Time and time again he told her she was worrying unnecessarily, and that her undeniable genius would conceive a solution.

Another week. That's how long it took her to figure out an answer, albeit not one popular with crew members. By this time, the core was solidifying in earnest, playing havoc with the magnetic fields that kept the ever-present suns from washing planetary life away in a sea of scalding solar flares. Scant few flickering shapes remained on the bridge-countdown now because a large proportion of the collective were dead or dying. Those remaining souls kept projecting, anyway. The mood aboard was subdued to the point of melancholy, with wayward beings skulking around unlit consoles, prodding inert buttons in order to feel useful. Kim needed almost all the power siphoned from the bridge, all non-vital systems, in fact, to find the power she needed. Without the replicators, there were no replacements for her filthy clothing, something only affecting Kim, but there was also no nice food since the stores only contained emergency rations. That affected everybody, and by day six, Kim was naked and suffering serious malnutrition, and most of the crew was considering her as a potential foodstuff. They didn't say it, of course, but they were thinking it, and some of them, those who thought visually, possessed some nasty imagery that followed along with their hunger-pangs.

In the end, smelly and almost delirious, an obvious alternative answer burned her retinas when activating a viewport. The planet orbited multiple suns, one of which was always at the same spot high in the perpetual daytime sky, with the planet being tide-locked to it. An enormous ball of fusion. It was just a gigantic version of her own lab power-source, and all they needed to do was harness a fraction of the abundant heat. The inhabitants of the planet's light hemisphere already used solar power for nearly everything, with the citadel being a notable exception since they built it for deep-space use and the scientists of the time weren't sure if there would be enough solar power in other systems. By the time their astronomers had figured out their mistake, those in charge had given the order to mothball the entire project. This left a slight problem, namely how to get the solar converters aboard without dying.

Then Ben had a breakthrough with the compound production. Twenty-four hours after Kim mentioned the need to get back to the ground, they had enough compound to decontaminate the planet's entire surface.

They already had the means of delivery, since Kim had designed a larger and more practical atomiser array to help clear her mind while trying to solve the power problem. Kevin and his ever-larger collective had it built in no time at all. Once loaded, they test-fired at an uninhabited part of the surface to check that it was safe at scale, which it was, so Ben threw everything into the pot. Small regions at first, with warnings to those left there that they needed to stay indoors and avoid eating the resulting grey dust that fell from the sky and covered everything like grainy soot. Later the same day, larger and more populated regions. Once they cleared the palace area and its surrounding city, Ben sent a contingent to requisition the solar converters. They were much smaller than Kim had been expecting, being cubes of porous, glowing rock around half a meter across, and they only brought four of them, which Ben assured Kim would be plenty. Installing them was easier than she'd thought, too, taking a small team around fifteen minutes to get them in place and connected to the main power sub-arrays.

Once powered, they could finally start the main event.

They were cautious at first, selecting small amounts of matter and transferring them from one point in space to another. Kim spent a day tracking asteroids and crunching the numbers they returned on the controller screen. When she got tired, Kevin took over. A diligent stand-in, he and various members of his collective added numbers to the dataset for a few hours, allowing Kim to catch some dream infested sleep in which she was once again naked in school, but this time holding a laser pointer that could call down an endless amount of rock with which to squash her imaginary tormentors. She awoke with a smile, gripping the pen she'd been taking notes with before drifting off. Back at the main desk, she checked over Kevin's figures before okaying a larger test in which they moved the moon from a nearby planet out of its orbit and into the geostationary orbit of another, much larger planet in another system several light years away. This test was also a success. Armed with some soothing numbers, and badgered by Benito and Kevin, Kim aimed the beacon at the asteroid they'd picked to fill the hole in their world. It had the exact amount of mass needed. It was in exactly the right place at the right time, and Ben already had the targeting coordinates cached on the computer. They'd run hundreds of tests by this time and crunched petabytes of data. There was nothing left to go wrong, but Kim had never felt more nervous at that moment than at any time in her life.

She let Ben enter the last command and press the big red mushroom-shaped button she'd insisted on having installed.

There was a new loud whirring noise, then the harsh white glow of strip-illumination switched to the blinking red emergency lights, but only for a few seconds.

On the screen, the countdown was gone, and the visuals were missing, blank squares of purple-tinged black in their place, so Kim read the sensors to confirm the planet was still there, which it was.

And it was whole.

One-by-one the visuals returned, showing a surface that had seen major damage but was still intact. The readings showed stability in both the core and the magnetic fields it produced, with solar emissions back within safe parameters and no deadly radiation to be found. They'd done it. The immediate danger was gone.

That had been a few days ago, and after a few hours of whooping and throwing things in the air, some of which were quite pointy and dangerous, Kim had retired to her bedroom for some well-deserved rest. On the way out, Ben had promised her something special, and had he delivered.

"Are you sure about this?"

"Yes. Your work on this project has saved many lives and allowed us to continue as a race. You have earned this. Accept your greatness."

She did. In fact, if her ego grew any further, it was liable to burst out of her head like a demented gremlin and start screaming in people's faces about just how fantastic she was. Still, the sash was heavy, and she couldn't be sure what the inscription on it meant.

"So, what does this say again?"

"It is the name of one of our greatest thinkers. This award is eponymous."

"Right, I get that part, but what does the rest of it say?"

"It merely states that your brilliance has saved us all."

"Okay. Yeah. So, why do I have to be naked?"

He didn't answer, not that she heard anyway, instead shoving her hard enough in the back to propel her through the curtains with a stumble and out onto the makeshift stage in front of the entire citadel crew, and, Ben had assured her, the entire planet, via holo-feed.

* * *

THE PARTY LASTED FOR THREE DAYS, OR MAYBE MORE, she wasn't certain. In fact, after the first few sticky-sweet drinks, her brain fogged up, and events became a blur of handshakes and inappropriate touching that she was fairly sure had come from the Kevin collective. All throughout, everyone aboard lauded her while pointing at the sash she was still wearing, at Benito's insistence, and then extolling her genius with a reverence that she was finding a little unnerving. In fact, the whole thing was getting to be a bit irritating. After it was done, she retired to her room to catch up on her rest.

Then things unravelled just a little.

Undressed and under the covers, Kim struggled to get to sleep. It wasn't just the scratchy fabric of the sheets and duvet-cover, and it wasn't the sentient duvet, since she got used to that by the end of the first week, and as long as you fed it snacks, it was fine. There was something gnawing gently at the depths of her brain, something tiny but persistent, and it just wouldn't release its grip.

After an hour laying still in the pitch black, hoping that her horizontal nature would combine with the absolute exhaustion to produce snooze, she gave up and turned the lights back on.

Across the room, on a convenient hook that sprouted in the doorframe during the previous twenty-four hours, hung the award sash. She'd pinned her medal to it, just above the embroidery. It was a thing of true beauty, all glittery semitransparent leather. There was also an inner light that, while not bright enough to illuminate anything, gave the sash an important-seeming aura.

She'd earned it, all of it, the medal, the sash and all the plaudits. All her life she'd been different, unable to fit in, an outcast among her own species, but here in this far-flung alien world, someone had seen her full potential at last. All she ever desired was recognition, someone to notice just how brilliant she was and acknowledge it in public. Maybe that was it? Imposter syndrome was a real phenomenon, so perhaps her own brain was rebelling against her now that she had everything that she'd always wanted. Kim got up and redressed, but in a clean set of coveralls that she'd put aside for special occasions. They'd emerged out of the replicator with a different hue than the previous sets and try as she might, the machine just wouldn't replicate another set the same pastel colour.

Out in the corridor, everything was quiet. The power cubes were amazing, providing enough for orbit. In fact, as long as they didn't move, they could power the whole citadel, so Benito shut down the reactor complex. Kim found she missed the constant humming, without which her mind now struggled to focus, but it meant that all the ship's functions restored to full functionality. Food and drink were abundant, clean clothes covered Kim and bedsheets covered her bed. After an entire month, the pervasive sense of panic was gone.

Everyone was asleep, it seemed, except Kim.

For the first time since he'd gone mad, she wondered about Caruthers, and whether he was still even alive. Joe had shot him up seriously, and his mind was lacking strength, enough that Kim couldn't hear his last words as they dragged him away, although that could have been just as much the near fatal injuries she sustained a few moments earlier. Ben said he was still onboard, locked securely in the brig wherever that was located, but this was the first time she'd been still in thought, and confident enough to consider visiting her erstwhile colleague. Kim imagined the conversation, which would turn to her triumph, and allow her to rub in exactly how right she'd been all along, and how wrong he was to have doubted her. The image brought a smile creeping along her lips, so she went back to get the sash. If he saw her wearing that, it would be the icing on the cake.

Doubts began swirling before she'd walked half the way back. What if he still didn't believe in her? What if he still wanted her dead? Why did it even matter what he thought? She was a one person army that fought adversity and saved their world. But she cared very much, in fact.

She'd thought of him as a friend, maybe her only real friend here. He was a tad rough, sure, and there were times she was downright terrified by his actions. But he never lied to her, never tried to hide what he thought. He'd been brutal in his honesty, when she thought about it, never afraid to tell her how ridiculous her ideas were. The others were nice, Ben especially, but he was always telling her what she wanted to hear.

What she wanted.

Kim felt a chill run up her back, then down into her stomach, spreading out like a drop of blood spreading red tentacles in clear water. It wasn't just Ben; it was everyone.

She forgot about the sash, and in the short term at least, about Caruthers, now charting a course for the beacon lab. There was no one posted to stop her from entering. Not even on the bridge. Once there, she pulled up the test data that Kevin signed off on before they fired up the machine that final time, sealing the core with space-rock. The numbers were correct, at least as far as she could discern. The readouts were translated in real-time by the citadel computers via a module that she'd designed, so she was sure that the data was accurately represented. Or was she? Kim disabled the module and waited for the readout to revert to the alien language. After around sixty seconds, she realised they weren't going to.

"What the hell?"

The coupling for the interpreter was under the secondary control console, easy to access, so she unplugged it altogether and watched as the numbers changed in an instant to something that appeared more realistic. There had been several large fluctuations in the power output during the firing sequence. Not unusual, she thought. The machine drew a huge amount of energy. But why had they hidden them from her? She kept mentally running the numbers, coming up against small anomalies that, on their own, weren't anything to worry about, but collectively showed that the systems still needed bedding in and integrating properly. Everything pointed to a successful run. The beacon had created an accurate lock on the mass in space, and it had transferred that mass across the void and onto the planet's surface. The only issue she now had was a vast discrepancy between the mass stated on the original data-stream, and the mass that the raw data showed being transported. If she'd read the numbers correctly, and right at that moment she wasn't overly certain of that, then Benito had targeted a rocky mass approximating the scale of a beach-ball, and not even a big stadium one.

She pulled the automatic recordings that the lab made, something no one else knew about, and watched the entire evening on fast-forward. It was as she remembered, all except the interactions between Kevin and Ben, that she missed at the time because she was so busy. The console they were using was showing different data than hers, so she accessed the screen-recordings and put them up on the central display, overlaid with the now unredacted data that she got from bypassing the translator. They matched. The machine didn't misfire, and they didn't miss or target the wrong rock. They knew what they were doing and deliberately hid it from her.

The ice in her stomach grew, branching out across her limbs, freezing her in place for a minute while she tried to intellectualise what she was seeing. In the end, it took most of her willpower to break that frost and move past a worrying but indistinct idea that had been in her brain since she'd woken, but was just now beginning to focus. Kim shut the system down, re-enabled the alarm and disabled the override, just in case. There was something more important that she needed to check on.

Kim took extra care with the walk back through to her hidden workspace, as she didn't want to encounter anyone part way and have to explain what she was doing, so she took a circuitous route through some empty spaces surrounding the lab, closing and seal each door behind her, which kept her hidden and allowed her to grab an emission counter on the way. Once outside the room, she faced a seal she hadn't seen before. Ben had it placed there when they evacuated before, to keep the area safe from the radiation inside, something she was terrified she wouldn't need to worry about.

Kim turned on the counter, muted the alert and waited for the screen to show the levels. It returned nominal, or at least no higher than the safe background levels found in any supermarket on earth, even pressed up against the door, which was only half an inch thick.

She worked to disable the seal, taking care not to trigger any alarms. It was a simple affair which bypassed the locking mechanism on the door, allowing a fresh set of biometrics to be installed as key, and others excluded. Unwiring it was trivial, and took only thirty seconds. Inside, everything was as she'd remembered. Machinery hummed a quiet tune while glass covered the floor with gleaming danger.

On the workspace in the centre, her notes and equations defining the compound that had saved their world. In her hand, the emission counter continued to show safe.

The brig was much larger than it should have been. In fact, it was bigger inside than his private quarters. It was also better furnished. Caruthers resolved to take this up with Benito once that fool came to his senses and freed him. This would surely be any day now.

Now fully awake, he looked over the scars on his torso where he'd been punctured by Joe's un-maker. The wounds were clean, almost surgical, with the edges cauterised and sterile. Were the weapon set to default levels, it would have obliterated his entire lower half. This meant that he was alive because someone wanted him to be, something that he had tried and failed to reconcile with the events of that period.

The walls were plain, being fashioned from a darker and denser form of the power absorbing rock that made up the conversion complex. It prevented the use of energy weaponry or excavation tools that relied on the same principal. This rock could absorb almost any amount of power with ease, converting it in an instant into heat that would boil alive any creature unfortunate enough to find themselves still trapped within. Illumination cubes furnished light from above. These were lower in power than those used elsewhere, but provided more than enough photons to make reading comfortable. Or they would have if he had anything to read. This was something else, Caruthers mused, that he was going to bring up during the inevitable apology he was bound to receive. Oh yes.

He lifted himself with care, using the fewest limbs needed to complete the task. Once upright, he scanned the far wall and found the reason for his rude awakening. It was a holo-viewer, embedded deep enough to be unbreakable, which was showing a closed feed from the debriefing suite. There was some sort of party, an award ceremony of sorts, with the alien usurper in its midst. He settled himself down again, oriented to watch the unfolding events.

The view fixated on Kimberley as she loped onto the stage in that way she had, all gangly flesh-spindles and flappy extremities. A rictus split her face into two and exposed those hard, off-white glistening pegs she insisted were vital to her ability to masticate foodstuffs. Surrounding her, menial bods and science-nerds milled in expectation. At the bottom of the view port, a message scrolled showing that she was about to be awarded a great honour.

Caruthers felt his life-fluids boil and a darkness cross his mind, gentle at first and then, as the message scroll continued, with significant vigour. After a few micro-periods, he lashed out a tendril, hooking the utensil they provided for maintaining his sustenance, and throwing it with all his diminished might at the image cavorting in front of him. It passed harmlessly through the photon curtain, of course, bouncing an acute path off of the wall behind and tracing an arc back across the room toward the doorway where it skittered along the floor, leaving a trail of partially eaten flesh-cube in its wake.

With that out of his system, he refocussed.

This shouldn't be happening. He was, as ever, right about this. There was no way that it'd solved the problems it was facing with the poison-gasses down below. He'd seen her workings and knew for a fact that she'd calculated her quantities based on a faulty assumption. He thought back, doubtful for a moment, then happy that his perfect memory still served him. She'd used figures that were mistranslated from the raw data, something Kevin didn't spot. Caruthers observed this in his memories, clearly as if he were standing before the panel right this instant. To compound her basic errors, she had applied the compound to a sample from too high in the atmosphere. The emission readings showed it contained scant dangerous material. These issues should have combined to create a disastrous miscalculation that would cause a compound that would, at best, be so inert that it would prove useless. At worst, it would be a toxic vapour, more dangerous than the cloud itself.

He'd told her all these things himself. She'd chosen, like she always did, to listen only to those who praised her every move.

On the screen, Benito had appeared behind the alien, his fawning limbs draped all over her plain form. He was a little surprised to see that she hadn't donned her usual shapeless blue garb, and had chosen this evening to embrace nudity. Caruthers imagined pinning a medal to her chest. He imagined pushing the pin through that thin fatty layer, preventing her internals from spilling out onto the floor; the puncture tearing open as a slow rip before disgorging her essence in a messy pile. Caruthers hoped it was going to hurt. He hoped it would hurt a lot, like being shot through the chest with an un-maker.

The scrolling message spelled out more of her achievements, including the now stable core down below. This was news to Caruthers, and it was more of a surprise than the compound. He'd worked with her on that damnable beacon technology for entire periods. Endless time poured down the waste-receptacle of existence as she searched in vain for a way to maintain focus and stabilise the matter beams. That she could get it to work was not the news that he found hard to believe. In all the time he'd spent with her, he'd seen beneath the outer layers. Under it all, there was a twinkling of intelligence, something brilliant that might polish up if she could stop concerning herself with what others believed, and focussed only on what she knew. She could make the technology work. He knew that, no matter how much it pained him to acknowledge it. And he'd done just that, in words, to her face. No, what he doubted was that she'd transferred enough rock to stabilise the planet's surface. And even if she'd managed to, the core was cooling too quickly. This rendered the exercise almost moot since there was no way to harness enough energy to restore the temperature and liquidity, and with it, the magnetic fields that kept the surface inhabitable.

The figures on-screen on the bridge were conclusive. Although everyone still worked like there was purpose, the last set of numbers he'd seen showed they would be too late by over 2 periods.

Yet here they were, announcing that the surface was once

again safe and ready for return. Now there were images from below showing friends and family, other loved ones, going about their lives with little care for the air and no worry about errant land movement. Making good on the devastation that was still obvious, but with a good cheer that showed hope, not fear.

The view returned to the party. Kim was still cavorting, only now with a dead juice-cube in her hand and the remnants of its lifeblood running down her hideous chin before dripping below. Caruthers wondered for a moment if anyone had stopped to tell her yet where these succulent creatures originated. How they bred them from beings that had once been a proud warrior species that lived and thrived on a nearby world, before being conquered and reduced to a foodstuff. Traits selected, then encouraged in evolution accelerators over the mega-periods to produce a small fur bound vessel that went well with light-meals and good holo-programmes.

He judged from the look on her face the answer was no.

Caruthers slumped back against the wall, sliding down to the floor in an uncomfortable slouch. It allowed him to continue viewing the projections while punishing himself for his stupidity by bending his torso in a way that stressed the pain from his still healing wounds.

Then something interesting happened.

He had to unfold himself in order to get a better view of the holo-projection, to be sure he was reading the scrollery correctly.

"Son-of-a-bitch!"

The words had left his mind, via a vocalisation, before he mitigated the speech patterns he'd absorbed during his time with the alien. The sound echoed around the dense walls before dying on the plush flooring that provided insulation from the heat of the exchangers that would in ordinary times be running below this cell-block. He was glad no-one had heard, but a little sad that he could not shout these words into her face while driving a full-length serrated blade through her ribcage and into her chest cavity, piercing as many of those squashy bits inside as he could manage. The image sustained him long enough for the view on-screen to change. Behind Kimberley, one soldier was preparing to drape a sash over her arm-sockets. It was an award Caruthers knew well, being one that he himself had given many an unfortunate who had crossed him in the better times, before his unwarranted exile.

He tried to smile, aping the creature's facial movements as best he could, twisting the flesh around his food-intake into an arch. Alas, given the differing physiology between them, it was too painful to sustain, so he stopped, and reverted to swearing again, which he was finding comforting, even if he hadn't quite got the hang of it.

"Yeah, eat it fool-fool bitch!"

"So I take it you approve of these events?"

Caruthers whirled to observe the speaker, even though he knew who it was from their thoughts. He turned so fast that an errant limb tangled in the rug below, causing him to trip sideways and into the wall with enough force to tear open the scarring in his chest with a sound not unlike a serrated knife passing through flesh.

* * *

IT TOOK A FEW MICRO-PERIODS FOR CARUTHERS TO GET his wits back about him, hauling himself upright with great care to avoid spilling too much of his already depleted life fluids into the stained floor coverings. Over by the exit, Benito was watching him with care, not stepping too far into the cell, but not outside of it either.

He was waiting for something. Caruthers spoke first.

"What do you want? To humiliate me as you have her?"

He gestured as best he could toward the holo-screen, where Kimberley was now resplendent in her sash-of-shame, a mark of degradation reserved for only the lowest and stupidest amongst them, those who could not complete even the most menial tasks without encountering failure of some kind.

"She humiliated herself. All we did was provide her enough leeway and encouragement."

"I.. I don't understand what's happening here?"

It was true, and he didn't like it. Caruthers prided himself on always playing the long game, seeing the bigger picture. It was how he'd forged alliances in the past that had proven so beneficial. It was also the reason his downfall had been so swift and unforgiving. He looked over to Benito, hoping for a clue but finding none in his taciturn features and stony mind. If the plan had been to humiliate the alien all along, then why was he forced to spend such an extended period with her, fostering a working relationship that still tainted his language skills? If they were to seize her technology for themselves, why not just do so once they secured unfettered access to her laboratory complex?

Then, he witnessed a glimpse, just a small corner of the complete picture, largely obscured but enough to deduce a tiny amount of detail.

"You need her? What about the earthquakes? The dead in our world?"

Benito stayed silent, but his thoughts leaked a little and betrayed an inner monologue that willed Caruthers to further explore the circumstances of the current situation, so he did just that.

The disaster was real. He'd seen for himself the devastation that had befallen their planet, and the bodies laying motionless on the streets. Well, he'd seen the devastation in their region, anyway. And the dead? Those bodies had been genuine enough. He'd seen enough war to know the aroma of charred and rotting mortality. But other than on screens various, how many of the dead had he seen with his own observation orbs?

"It was all subterfuge?"

Still, Benito said nothing.

Thinking further back to when he'd first entered the creature's lair and observed her technology for himself, he remembered just how difficult she had been to read and understand, just how alien her works were to them. He'd wondered then just what Ben wanted with her, and why he'd indulged her so much.

"The beacon? What could you possibly want with that? Why would you go to such lengths to get something we could have just ripped from her mind?"

Now he spoke.

"You used to be so much better at this. I must admit to feeling a little disappointed. You yourself tried to take her knowledge, at the beginning, remember? It was the original plan to be sure, but you failed me then, and you are failing me now."

"I.. Don't.."

"What you don't understand would fill the great libraries

at this point. Maybe I was correct about you all those periods ago, right to exile you from court."

Caruthers felt the fire again, starting in his torso, then burning a course up into his cranium where it filled his mind with violent imagery and a desire to throw things.

"How dare you! I was nothing but loyal, subservient to a fault. It was I that saw the future you so quickly assumed once you disposed of me like a used clean-rag. I deserved better. You OWE me better than this ridiculous parlour game? Now tell me what is happening here."

Benito moved further into the cell, leaving the door open and no guard was visible. Caruthers considered his options, those being to wait this charade out and maybe gain some understanding, or to overpower Ben as he knew he could and take command himself. Slouching down into a far corner, he cursed his natural curiosity.

"Well?"

"The beacon technology is the answer."

It was a cryptic answer, even for him, but not wanting to feel any stupider than he already did, Caruthers went along with it.

"Yes, okay, so it's the answer. Why the games?"

"She really is brilliant, you know. I don't think you ever gave her enough credit, but that was why it had to be you. I knew you'd push her, make her feel inadequate, make her want to get it right."

That made sense.

"You ripped it from her mind, didn't you? But you couldn't get it to work. How, though, I could not read her inner thoughts.."

"She cloaks her true self, hiding away inside an act, behind a mask. The Kimberley that the world sees is a curated amalgam of what she sees around her, a mirror to the beings that surround. All that is needed to see beneath that mask is to gain her friendship."

Caruthers thought back to the times Ben had given privilege and affection to Kim and at last made sense of everything he'd seen. Well, nearly everything.

"So, my purpose was.."

Ben was alongside now, leaning against Caruthers with several tendrils draped cordially.

"I needed you to antagonise her, keep her wary when I was not around. She was never to feel altogether safe around you, allowing me to uncork her mind when away from your influence."

"Right, but then you couldn't make it work?"

"Yes, the machine was incomplete. Her appearance here in this world was by complete chance, a failed test she staged to bolster her ego back on her home planet. She has no one there, no support, no family. Unfortunately, this tainted her desire to return."

He thought back to the time it'd spent tinkering with unneeded systems, cursing her inability to focus on the beam while avoiding the actual problem with the containment equipment. Her anger was genuine, but maybe her desire had been illusory.

"You needed to create a new impetus? You gave her an additional reason to complete her work, then waited."

Then, remembering what he'd seen on the surface, the charred dead and destroyed abodes.

"You staged the quakes?"

"Yes, and no."

Ben sighed, but said no more, leaving Caruthers curious and afraid of the answer to his next question.

"What do you mean, no?"

Before answering, Benito stood upright and moved over to the cell door, but he didn't leave, instead closing the door and sealing the two of them inside, alone.

"What I say here is classified, and does not leave this room. Do you understand?"

Caruthers nodded, but didn't speak. Unsure if this was a promise he could keep. It was enough, it seemed, as Ben continued.

"I thought I had it figured out, her machine, so I staged a test in the secret complex I had built near a disused mine. It went.. Bad. But I turned misfortune into an opportunity with a plan that I feel would make even you proud. The intent was to scare her into leaving the complex and boarding the citadel. Once aboard, we would show her footage of a dying world that she yearns to stay on, and convince her to build a working beacon to save it. So I primed her with promises of grandeur and then allowed the meltdown to proceed. It destroyed the mine completely. We calculated a collapse that would cause some minor tremors."

He stopped there. Caruthers could see the 'but' coming, but held back from filling in the blanks, waiting for his leader to admit the mistake he'd made. It didn't take long.

"But it didn't collapse, more an explosion than an implosion. Crystal dust, long forgotten, igniting with a fury the scientists hadn't foreseen. The destruction was real, just more local than I alluded to."

His life-fluids running cold, Caruthers, had one question. He could not vocalise it, but Ben answered just the same.

"Yes, I'm afraid they all died in the resulting explosion."

"How much was real?"

"Everything you saw, we staged none of it. I assure you, I am just as disheartened as you, but this was necessary."

"Necessary? What about the soldiers that died getting us to the citadel?"

"They died a warrior's death, serving with honour and distinction."

"And the emergency when we got here?"

"That was very much real. A chain reaction was tearing the ground from underneath us. There were not supposed to be any aftershocks, and my team assured me that the citadel was sky-worthy, ready to escape. They were wrong. It was fortunate indeed that Kim could find a solution that got us airborne in time."

"The poison gas?"

"A mistake on my part. A small leak of this deadly smog occurred at the mine-site, but I can assure you it was local, and is not an issue. I thought that with two problems to solve, her ability to see through any ruse would diminish, so I exaggerated. I had not foreseen her inability to prioritise. Once I saw she could not let it go, I had her provided with materials and a quiet space to work where she would believe we did not know of her intentions. As long as she thought she was getting away with it, her work on the beacon was unaffected."

Caruthers glanced back at the screen, where Kimberley was still standing in her shame-sash and juice-drippings. There was one question left.

"So, what happens to that?"

Ben moved close.

"That's up to you, chancellor."

He looked at Ben, read his thoughts, tried to find the trick, but saw none.

"Are you serious? I do not wish to end up on a stage like that."

He gestured toward the image of Kim.

"It's yours if you want it. You have served, completed your tasks somewhat without question and to the best of your considerable abilities. I would be remiss not to reinstate you."

"And I can do as I please with the creature?"

"Just try not to stain anything nice."

Caruthers looked over his newly assembled personal protection detail. Ben let him pick any amongst the soldiers aboard, with the sole exception being Joseph, who served only Benito. They were a fine bunch, being able, willing to do what needed to be done. Since she'd left the stage before Ben finished his pep-talk,

He instructed his new captain to track the alien and report its location as soon as possible. He did so without vocalizing, enjoying conversation the way it should be, but finding himself sad names would no longer be necessary.

Kim would have given the team names.

As the battle-scarred warrior left the room, he ordered the rest of the team to escort him to his new quarters. They were just off the command deck, suites reserved for royalty, and just magnificent space, he thought to himself, that he deserved. It was an extensive trek, and with no threat, the escort was completely unnecessary, but he wanted to parade his reclaimed status in front of as many beings as possible. He wanted them to see that not only was he no longer a prisoner, but that his influence and power now usurped all but their sovereign, Benito. With that foremost in his mind, he took his sweet time and detoured via several rooms along the way, picking up some food-objects and juice-cubes on the way.

It was enjoyable, to be sure, but not as much as he'd hoped. Deep inside, a burning sensation boiled his digestive tract, fighting for attention and distracting him from the nervous thoughts and glances of those among the crew who had wronged him.

Kimberley.

She was the sole reason this adventure had been so painful, with her inability to listen to reason. What should he have expected, though? She was a lower life-form, an insect, she would say. Her intellect, while impressive and probably responsible for their continued life-span, could not compare to his, or any of the revered thinkers. It was her doing that saw him shot and imprisoned like a common criminal, and her inflexibility that caused Ben's subterfuge, and the resulting death-toll amongst his friends and colleagues. She'd been a thorn in his side since her inconvenient appearance in the courtyard, and he was going to pluck it out with surgical accuracy. Then, he thought to himself as quietly as he could, so as not to disturb his guards, he was going to remove her calcium supports piece-by-piece, while keeping her alive, until she reduced to a puddle of flesh and juices on the floor. Then he was going to use her as a rag and clean the hull, rubbing away until nothing remained. The thought brought an unexpected feeling to his face, forcing creases where there should be none. It wasn't unpleasant, so he set things in motion.

"You, I need you to fetch medical tools, set them up in a

quiet, out-of-the-way room where I may work without distraction."

It was only after he finished talking that he realised he'd spoken the instructions. It was a bad habit he would quash along with Kim once she was in his custody.

For now, the soldiers stared back at him, unsure of which among them he'd been speaking to. He restated his desire telepathically and then waited for his henchman to get to his task before continuing his tour. They were on the bridge by now, with the citadel's captain perched upon his throne.

Time to flex, he mused.

"Get down here, grovel at my lower extremities and you may live to see another period."

More spoken words, but he liked them, and so let it go for now.

The captain looked down and was half way through his insult before he saw the emblems of power that now adorned Caruthers chest. He back-pedalled with impressive speed, but not quick enough to prevent Caruthers getting the gist of what he was saying.

"No, in fact, I believe it will be you that will fornicate with the food-things later, while adorned in your life-givers under garb."

"Forgive me, my lord. I was unaware of your ascension. Things sure happen fast around here."

He'd said the last part under his breath, or as near to that as possible for a species that didn't need to breathe. Caruthers let that go, too. He then waited for him to clamber down and prostrate himself before leaving the bridge for his suite, that was just around the corner from the captain's ready-room, and mere lengths from the royal suite that Benito occupied. Once inside, he dismissed all but two of his guard to join the search for the alien infestation, leaving the remaining pair outside the door with their weapons drawn and orders to point them at anything that moved within half a length of the room.

It was breathtaking, but no less than he deserved. The suite was vast, twice the size of the conferencing space where the party had been, and lit with the most exquisite of illuminating orbs, that hung in the air just below the vaulted ceiling and projected a warm, diffuse light that smothered everything below in a warm comforting blanket of fluffy photons. Opposite the grand entranceway, along a short hall, was a gilded reception room that dripped with the most metallic of elements, reflecting the aura of the orbs back into the hallway and drawing the visual cortex toward a desk carved from a single piece of energy rock, but not the cheap kind, the rarest translucent variety that was so clear that if not for the reflections you couldn't even be sure it was there. Making a mental note to attach some adhesive decorations to avoid walking into it as the sides were each honed to a razor-like edge, Caruthers shuffled awkwardly around one side and sat on the opulent throne that served as the office chair. It, too, came from an energy rock, but one of a differing hue that went well with the sumptuous scheme. It wasn't the most comfortable piece of furniture he'd ever sat upon, but it said what needed to be said to whomever passed through the main entranceway, so it was staying.

Just as the life was leaving the lower half of his torso, as he was contemplating maybe adding a cushion of some sort, one of his guard entered the hallway and strode on visible tendrils up to the desk.

"It is in the old workspace, my lord. Do you wish us to

dispose of it for you, perhaps bring the upper cranial node for your inspection?"

"NO! It's mine. No one harms it but me. Do you understand?"

The soldier projected the instructions to his colleagues, which was something Caruthers could have done himself, but with his newfound appreciation of decorum, did not. Instead, he waited for the report.

"As you desire, my lord. I have ordered the area sealed off. There shall be no escape."

And then, almost an afterthought.

"Do you wish the medical tools to be delivered to the location, or shall you be bringing the creature to the space we have provided?"

Initiative, that's excellent, Caruthers thought to himself while imagining the look on Kim's face when she realised that there would be no respite this time, that he would take her apart piece-by-piece until nothing remained but a sticky mess. He stood.

"Lead the way."

To avoid embarrassment, Caruthers waited until the soldier had turned for the exit before extracting himself from the desk arrangement. He then followed to the location and then instructed his team to prevent anything from entering or leaving the area. Only once he was sure that there was no way to leave did he enter the laboratory area and begin making his way toward the room where it hid.

Then he hesitated.

Memories of the initial blast filled his cerebellum, firing his nerves with a cold energy that filled him with doubt and stayed his limbs. Responsible or not, the base creature in the next room had saved his life, and not just once. It was enough to give pause, but only until the heat of his ire returned to overwhelm his nostalgia. If she had given her technology, as was always going to happen, none of the games would have been necessary, and many hundreds of lives would still be. He thought back to the smug thoughts that filled her head, and the disgrace she had wrought upon him and just like that, a blaze of laser fast plasma melted the remaining ice from his circulatory conduits, leaving only fury.

It did not deserve to live. Taking that life would be a mercy, even in the manner he intended to do it.

The door stuck a little, so after a micro-period he gave up on any pretence of stealth and forced the portal open with a flurry of limbs, destroying the frame. He was ready to snatch the squashy creature by her joints and throw her at a wall, laughing into her head as things broke inside.

Caruthers was expecting to find her concocting more science, self-centred and full of ego. He was sure he would find her, unaware of the humiliation that had already befallen her, ready to show her believed superiority, something he was going to break.

He wasn't expecting to find her already broken.

Kimberley was still in the sash, pacing back and forth with notes in her hands and familiar salty fluids painting her face. She barely noticed him as he entered, but stopped once he threw some equipment at her, glancing a blow off one shoulder region.

"Car.. Caruthers? I thought you.. It's all wrong, everything is wrong. The compound, it's out, my calculations because of the readings.."

She was ranting, her words unable to keep pace with the maelstrom in her thoughts. He only caught glimpses, but it was enough to experience the ache eating her from the inside.

"It's wrong, it's, look."

She held up some paper, but he couldn't read what it said.

"By a factor of ten, maybe more. It's going to kill everyone! I don't understand why it.."

Caruthers had held back, waiting for his moment to seize her. In that time, he'd been replaying the scenarios in his mind, like a favourite home vid-cast, which was a mistake because she'd seen all of it.

She kicked the wall, and a panel dropped to the ground, revealing a doorway that he hoped, but didn't believe, his team knew was there. He moved as fast as he could, but she was out through it before he covered half the distance, slamming the door behind her.

"Well, shit."

Her knee hurt, it hurt a lot. They didn't design the escape hatch for humans and its shape lent itself to catching stray limbs as you passed through, more so at speed.

As she did, she'd felt the tail end of Caruthers thoughts and didn't like what she saw one bit. Did he really hate her that much? After so long spent together, did he see her as vermin? What she'd seen in the lab was comforting, at least. She didn't just kill everyone with a compound that was an entire order of magnitude stronger than it needed to be.

How could she have been so stupid?

No, that wasn't the right question. She was always that stupid. On a normal day, her lab assistant would catch it and then offer polite correction with an arched eyebrow while explaining the error as tiredness, or excessive tequila the previous evening, or both. If the assistant missed it, then the project oversight would find it, usually because they hated her and went looking for mistakes, often visibly disappointed when none were present. That was how it worked, and that was how it was supposed to work. No one is perfect.

Mistakes happen. The question she should've asked was, what in god's name made her believe it was different now? The answer was simple, as it often was.

They'd played her.

Kim slouched against the wall and pressed her knee into her chest with both hands. She hoped, as she'd done so many times as a child, that the pressure and her sad pouting would stop the pain, or at least catch the eye of a responsible adult, so they could stop it. Instead, the pain intensified as the leg bent, and she sat on something sharp that, without clothing, dug into her left buttock with unnerving ease. She stood upright once more and extracted the sliver of rock from her posterior, stared at it for a few seconds, then threw it down the corridor with all her strength. It covered around four feet, partly because it was light and awkwardly shaped, partly because she just couldn't throw. A quick rub of the sagging skin on her behind was enough to convince Kim that the damage wasn't too bad, so she started thinking about the next steps.

The poison gas wasn't real, so no one needed the compound. It was a mirage, a childish distraction so that she would give them the beacon without a fight. That was a comfort. Without the usual oversight, she'd started believing in her own genius, which was the point, of course. Now, though, she needed to reclaim her technology. If the natural disasters weren't real, then they needed her tech for something else, and whatever it was couldn't be good or they'd have simply asked.

Whatever they wanted it for was bad, and she would not let it happen.

"Illuminate."

The black that filled the corridor lifted and dispersed.

What replaced it was a warm orange glow that Kim had improvised from some discarded party decorations and an energy projector that she'd found under the sentient creature that doubled as her mattress. In fact, when she thought about it, shiny things absolutely stuffed her mattress.

If she ever returned to her bedroom, she needed to discuss its tendency toward hoarding, perhaps find it a different hobby.

The light ran the entire length, nearly half a kilometre, with doorways branching off either side that accessed hundreds of rooms, some occupied, some not.

No one else had direct knowledge of this tunnel system.

Kim found it while moving boxes around to make room for a large piece of equipment she'd designed to focus arrays of sub-atomic particles. At first, she thought she'd broken something, but after some exploration, she realised it was an access tunnel left over from the original citadel designs. It allowed effortless movement between sections, and hidden entry to most of the command deck. a few doors had jammed solid in their frames, but the majority opened with gentle persuasion, so the question now became.

Where was she going?

The beacon lab. She needed to destroy the technology, even though it meant stranding herself here.

Kim mused, waiting for the pain of losing her one way home to kick in. Then she waited for it to pass, which took a little longer. Unfortunately, there wasn't a direct route into the lab, since they built it inside a larger space, blocking the hidden access way and preventing entry. The only way in was via the command deck, past the central console. The secret hatch was about five feet away from the throne. As long as no one was present, she could sneak past if she moved quick. Kim made for the right-hand door. It was nearer than it should be, but she'd long since given up trying to make sense of the citadel topology. Once there, she accessed the mechanism, taking care not to make any noise.

Two things happened as the panel slid open. One, she remembered that she'd told Kevin about the tunnels, although not by choice, as he'd picked up on their existence while reading her mind for instructions on machinery. Two, several energy bolts passed through and dismantled the wall opposite with blinding flashes of light that burned white, then blue, and then sparkled like fireworks. Kim hit the panel with her entire hand, since her fingers were far too scared to work independently, shutting the panel again before Joseph could gain entry. Then she ran. Several meters further down and on the left, one of the older doorways led to an uninhabited area deep in the ship's bowels. It was perilously close to the irradiated area near the energy converters. She reached the portal just as the sound of a gigantic explosion filled the narrow walkway. It reverberated around the low ceiling, pushing some light-orbs forwards past Kim's head. One of them hit her across the temple as she exited.

She found herself in a cramped space with only one exit, so she took it without thinking. She ran out into a vast area that was open to space, taking her breath away. Except that it didn't. After a few seconds of gasping like a beached fish, hands clawing at her throat, Kim discovered she could breathe just as easily as she could inside. She presumed some kind of force-field and looked around. She was standing in the power conversion quarter, as she suspected, but it was quiet. The terror of her first boarding, and the flow of plasma that could power half the citadel, was gone, replaced, she guessed, by the energy cubes that Ben had brought aboard.

That she could have expected, what she didn't, was the new construction that occupied the footprint of several championship football stadia to one side of the ruined conversion towers. It was beautiful, a bright blue-green colour with shimmering purple star decals that floated up the walls before converging at the top of a spire that sprouted from the middle. The entire structure appeared to be a neon-clad cathedral, or maybe less gaudy circus big-top. There wasn't time to fully appreciate it, though. An explosion announced Joe had discovered which doorway she'd used and had followed, along with enough firepower to level most of the surrounding structures, so Kim zigged and ran away from the new building and toward the ruins of the conversion towers.

Kim had an idea. She just hoped that they weren't great with housekeeping.

The run wasted significant energy, more than she expected. But she still outpaced her pursuer, allowing her to disappear into an open vent. Once inside, she watched as the soldiers, now with Caruthers at their vanguard, took a punt and trooped the wrong way in perfect cover formation. They ran toward the shimmering construction rather than where she was hiding. It wouldn't last long, she knew that, so after gulping cool air into her tight lungs, Kim picked herself up again and moved through the building, retracing the route in her head before finding herself, at the fourth attempt, in the control room she'd used to save the ship on her first day. In the corner, as she'd remembered, was the transporter system. With a small amount of trepidation, Kim thumbed the controls, breathing a sigh of relief when the panel lit up, then gasping when the lights died with a disconcerting rattle before coughing and sputtering when they returned and stayed alight.

Then she hit a problem she wasn't expecting.

The coordinates were in her head, somewhere, but she couldn't locate them in there no matter how hard she tried. Instead, remembering what Caruthers had told her about how the system worked, she guessed at how they generated coordinates. Then she punched in, and then rotated, the required glyphs for what she hoped was the loading bay. Once Kim was certain she was correct, she took off the sash that she was inexplicably still wearing and lay it on the dusty floor with more care than it deserved. This thing represented everything wrong with her, and how she experienced her world. It was a mirror to her obsessive need to be right. It reflected all the missed cues and signals that could have prevented any of this from happening, right from when she first discovered she wasn't like other children in school, to her somewhat premature testing of experimental trans-dimensional technology that had brought her here. Once down on the ground, no longer weighing heavy on her shoulders, she turned and rejected that part of her life forever. She embraced her new reality with an awkward flick of the wrist that enabled the transporter and peeled her apart, layer-by-layer, until all that remained was her skin-balloon floating around the room, but not a part of it. Then even that was gone.

* * *

SHE REFORMED IN THE LOADING BAY, AS PLANNED. IT wasn't empty, though, which came as a gigantic surprise to everyone present. An insignificant detail of creatures was stacking mysterious crates of a substance that glowed when bumped, and almost exploded with light when dropped.

This was useful since an entire stack of crates fell when Kim's skin attached itself. It created enough of a distraction to allow an exit through the main doorway while the beings tried in vain to herd the erstwhile contents back into a single pile. Then something else happened that Kim wasn't expecting. She found herself lost.

The configuration of this section of the ship was switched around considerably since her pervious visit, with new corridors sprouting from the old ones, and doorways reconfiguring into sold walls. The corridor Kim now sweated loudly in was large, but not sizeable enough to fill the space she knew surrounded it, so there'd clearly been some building work.

What was behind all these new walls?

Rather than find out now, Kim decided that the prudent thing to do was leave, regroup her thoughts and, just maybe, find clothes to wear, since the temperature had lowered sufficiently to raise goosebumps and condense her breath. Her personal quarters were out of the question. She was sure there would be guards waiting for her there by now, and they were obviously going to patrol the recreated lab heavily, so after a quick internal game of rock-paper-scissors that she somehow lost to herself, Kim made for the farthest point. If she'd guessed correctly, it would lead back into the oldest parts of the citadel, areas that no one entered since they all came aboard.

The walk was lengthy, and most uninteresting, providing Kim an opportunity to consider her situation for the first time since the aliens turned on her. In fact, she realised it was the first time since she'd arrived. If a miracle occurred, and she somehow returned home, she would need to change. That was a nailed-on certainty. She couldn't continue the same as always, with no friends to provide comfort and no support network to repair her shattered pieces after her shifts. She always believed it strengthened her, but it made her weaker in almost every way. As Kim finished that sobering thought, she encountered the exit, which led her back out into the open.

It was a marvel. Above her head, space fell away into infinity. Stars were visible everywhere and the smallest of the three suns arose majestically over a series of high-rise tower blocks a few kilometres to her right. The vast ball of fusing hydrogen felt near enough to touch, almost overwhelming in its size and raw power, but she didn't feel its heat, and the air was breathable. She wondered about the force-field that must be present and even attempted to calculate the power requirements before the situation intruded back into her current reality. Kim shook her head, trying to get the thoughts out, in the end settling for a mild headache. She then strode purposefully for a squat but otherwise uninteresting building complex that appeared deserted and wasn't too far away. She covered the entire distance before realising that not only was it not deserted, but it had power and radiated warmth. The exterior was clear, no one was anywhere near it and there were no visible guards. Kim was feeling chillier by the minute. She lost another internal game, this time tic-tack-toe, and headed for one of the side entrances, which was already open. Nearer to the building, Kim realised how big it actually was. It covered enough square-footage to house an international-sized airfield complete with runways and was high enough to allow for a small plane taking off. Inside the side entrance, however, was a cramped compartment with a low ceiling that a short nine-year-old would find compact and bijou. There was only one piece of furniture present. It was a low desk that floated approximately two feet off the ground with no visible supports, on which were stacked a dainty pile of cylindrical rods. Like almost everything here, they glowed, but not with light exactly. It was like they contained an energy Kim couldn't see, but her senses knew about, anyway. She tried to pick one up, but they repelled her hand like a magnet pointed the wrong way or a force-field, sending it off the desk. After scattering several more across the floor, she gave up and stoop-crawled to the doorway that led further into the complex. Opening it, she found an equally low tunnel. Anti-rods like those from the desk lined each side, driven endwise into the wall until barely an inch protruded and spaced around two feet apart. The tunnel disappeared into an infinite inky black that swallowed everything twenty-feet in. Kim was about to turn around when she heard an electronic latch. Only seconds later, the portal closed behind her, plunging her into total darkness.

Kim sensed a Kevin, his thoughts clear enough for her to read even through the walls and doors. He didn't sense her; he wasn't even looking, so Kim stopped moving and held her breath while she waited for him to move on. When holding her breath became impractical, about ten seconds later, she tried to breathe in as slowly as possible to avoid making any noise. She failed, and ended up first coughing, and then sneezing, loud enough to wake the dead.

He still didn't notice her, something big preoccupied his thoughts that she couldn't make out, but he also wasn't leaving, so Kim had a choice to make. She moved her shoulders into the tunnel, felt the force pushing at her body, but there was something else. It was also pushing at her mind. It wasn't unpleasant at first, so she climbed in further, scraping a knee, then a little further. Then the force took her body and threw it down the corridor.

She flew the entire length, at least five hundred meters, in around thirty seconds, which was impressive, but not as impressive as the space she found at the end. Kim exited the tunnel via an opening approximating the size of a cheap flat-screen television into what looked like a conference room. There was another desk, this one old-fashioned, and sitting on four plain legs. Chairs surrounded it, or what passed as chairs in this world. food things piled high on the otherwise pristine surface, along with drinking cubes, to which Kim helped herself while taking in a projected view. The area comprised a gigantic dome, its inner surface a screen that displayed a projected view from within the palace authentic enough that she could have been standing right there. On the farthest wall, a vast mural depicted scenes of war, or at least a victory in battle. At its centre, Benito floated above vanquished foes. They were all depicted minus their cranial areas. In front of the mural, a plain but functional throne, in front of the throne, another desk exactly like the one in the dome, but piled with inscribed papers and unintelligible diagrams instead of consumables.

Kim took a few steps toward the holo-table, but couldn't quite identify the writing. What she made out was a door-way. Nothing more than a faint outline in the wall ahead. It opened as she approached, revealing a startled looking sentry who pointed several limbs but said nothing, instead screaming internal obscenities as loud as his mind could manage. Frozen to the spot, Kim couldn't move her legs, so pointed back and gave an embarrassed laugh while willing her feet to uproot themselves. In the end, a delivery of food through the dumb server she'd entered from broke the spell and got her moving, at speed, past the sentry, who by this time had levelled a weapon but missed the trigger several times. A blast of energy whipping past her head and destroying a section of wall beside the door she was running toward announced that he'd found it. Kim got through just as a second bolt melted the frame, splintering the surrounding stone material, shooting dozens of red-hot projectiles in all directions that somehow missed anything important on Kim's body, instead choosing to impale her right calf. Even in its distorted state, the exit closed behind her, intercepting a third shot in mid-air that was destined for the back of her head. She had scarcely enough time to plan an escape, so Kim beelined for the first exit she saw, which took her past another sentry. This guy, though, was better prepared and had his weapon trained before she passed him.

"Don't fire!"

She'd thought it, but it wasn't her voice. Behind her, the doorway had reopened and disgorged the first sentry, who was running as fast as his tentacles allowed while shouting at his comrade.

"The supreme commander wants to disembowel the creature himself. If you take that pleasure from him, you will find yourself in its place."

The second guy lowered his weapon, radiating disappointment as he did, then emitting a virtual smirk when his friend whipped a pair of tendrils into the small of Kim's back. She tumbled forwards into a gangly heap at his invisible feet.

She took a while to look around, cornering the panic in her brain like a cartoon lion tamer, complete with imaginary chair and bull-whip, and in that instant at least, succeeding.

"It should not be at this location. How has this occurred?"

While they argued, Kim spotted two escape routes. There was the exit past sentry number two, but it was at least ten feet further on and she didn't think he'd contain his enthusiasm with the death ray a second time, meaning that was out. To her left was another dumb server, which, thanks to the shove, was within perhaps three feet and easily doable. Just as long as they remained distracted.

Maybe?

* * *

With a flourish worthy of any professional athlete, she feinted right before throwing her entire body-weight hard left. Both soldiers fired at once. Thankfully, they fired at the space she would have occupied had she carried on straight. The gunfire destroyed a large section of the floor in spectacular fashion, lighting the first twenty feet of the dumb-server tunnel as she sped along at breakneck speed. Once through, projected hard into a storage crate on the other side, Kim stood, vomited her stomach contents, and a little stomach lining, and then screamed.

All around, gigantic creatures hung from sharp looking hooks in the ceiling. They had no obvious features beyond their enormous eyes that followed Kim as she backed into a corner near the tunnel entrance. Below, someone had sliced their bodies open. Entrails spilled out onto tables set below, then fed into a winding mechanism that pulled the viscera out of the captive beings before cutting a length and squashing it into moulds that seared the outside with a flash of heat and then ejected the result onto a conveyor running alongside. The cubes of flesh then travelled the length of the table before being deposited into chutes that connected to pipework criss-crossing the walls and floors. Kim stood back up, picked up one cube and scrutinised it. Even brand new and scalded, fur was growing on all six surfaces.

She dropped the juice-cube back onto the conveyor. All around, the pain of the captive creatures was seeping into her head, poisoning her thoughts with visions of death and wanton destruction. It took her a moment to understand that this visceral assault hammering nails into her senses was simply a mode of communication and not some unspeakable torture. Forcing them out was hard. She filled her mind with painful memories of her own, displacing their torment enough to think freely, then stumbled forwards onto a grating that allowed their blood to drain, tripping on the wide gauge and falling face first into the warm liquid. In her head, their thoughts were already fighting back. Her vision clouded into daydreams of being hung herself, dissected, watching her intestines portioned into party-food.

She needed to vacate this chamber immediately, if not sooner.

Beneath each of the sagging creatures was a duct, wide enough to slip through if she emptied her lungs and sucked her wayward stomach in, which was the exact course of action she decided upon. At first, it wasn't too bad. The piping expanded to a comfortable, although still tight diameter past the entrance, and the slope was gradual enough that she wasn't falling, rather sliding, and with no great speed. Then she levelled out, still in a narrow pipe but no longer falling. Beneath her hands and knees, the warm blood pooled and coagulated, but in the pitch black, she couldn't see anything. She couldn't hear either, but after the onslaught above, that was a blessing. Kim tried to stand, banged her head, then got back down on all fours.

Nothing.

It was so black that she could see the patterns of blood flowing in her retinas. Also, it was so quiet that she could hear that same blood rushing through the structures in her ears a few moments later, or perhaps before. Anatomy hadn't been one of her strong suits at school. Upon reaching up, Kim found the rounded ceiling to her current prison around four feet above the squelching, clotted ground. Not high enough to stand. It was a duct of some kind, probably a sewer, although it didn't smell, no smell at all. Moving forwards, the pipe continued on and on with no deviations, and after what felt like a hundred feet of crawling on painful, grazed knees, Kim stopped and rolled onto her back.

She was tired enough that she'd started having waking dreams in the darkness. Visions creeping in around the periphery, melding with the lava-lamp splotches of bright that already floated there and showing her things that couldn't possibly be real. A Christmas dinner with friends she didn't recognise, and family that showed affection. A primary school setting that came bundled with a strong sense of belonging, surrounded by cheering peers, holding a gaudy plastic sports trophy in one hand while cradling a can of soda in the other. Except she didn't play any sports on account of her innate inability to catch or throw, or coordinate her hands and feet in any kind of useful way. She was also pretty sure that she was a girl, and the memory came with additional sensations that didn't gibe with her physical body. There was more. As she lay there, an eightieth birthday party flashed through, filled with gin and arthritic knees that wouldn't bend. Then it was gone, replaced by a scolding father pointing and shouting at something that revealed itself to be a soiled bedsheet. That felt more familiar, except her dream-dad was clearly of a different ethnicity. More and more dreams came. They mingled with each other and became harder to separate into individual scenes. A minute later, the icy ball of feelings in her stomach became too difficult to ignore. She snapped back into pitch black reality and realised that these weren't dreams. They were memories, and they weren't hers. Then one vision overwhelmed the rest, a voice, one of her pursuers.

They knew where she was.

That wasn't what caught her attention, though. It was more the discussions involving a cleanse of the drainage system by flushing everything with fire.

Back on all-fours and crawling for all she was worth, at the best speed her aching limbs could muster, Kim searched for an exit. All she found were smooth, featureless walls and no light. Above, a Kevin was already preparing the drain-cleaner, waiting on Caruthers to give the order, so there wasn't much time and she knew it. In front, she finally found something different. The pipe joined with a second, similar tube at right angles, creating one fork to the left, which descended slightly, and a second to the right, which sloped upwards with a significant incline. She chose up. After six feet, though, up became extra, extra down, with a near vertical drop of six feet that Kim took head-first into a section of pipe so narrow that she wedged tight.

She was stuck, facing downwards at a drop she couldn't see, unable to move back up as there was nothing to grip inside the pipe.

Above, they gave the order.

Kim pulled her stomach in as far as she could, helping her slick torso further into the trap. She hoped it would open out below her in a short enough distance that she would survive the fall. While she did so, a rushing sound filled her ears that differed from the blood-flow she was used to. It came with a growing warmth and the smell of ripe bananas. Desperate, Kim pushed all the air out of her lungs and wriggled. She slid a further few inches downward before realising that she would not make it, and that the vice-like constriction made it impossible to re-inflate her lungs.

Kim tried to scream, but there wasn't any breath left. The warmth above became heat and the banana smell morphed into burnt toast, or crumpets.

There was light now, too, as a small bevvy of photons wriggled past to show that, as she'd hoped, the pipe diameter did indeed expand, and significantly. Freedom was just inches from her shoulders, but without breath, Kim's peripheral vision was gone, leaving a closing tunnel-view of sanctuary she'd never reach. Her last vestiges of panic played out with a half-hearted nod of the head, reality slipping away just as the soles of her feet started crisping in the fire.

Then, suddenly, she was free.

The heat from above expanded the air in the pipes, which were sealed at all exit points to prevent escape, leaving it nowhere to go but past Kim. She shot downward like a sagging fleshy bullet, bouncing off her arms and ricocheting forwards into a slumped pile just far enough away from the fiery exhaust to avoid being further singed. Her near unconscious state prevented her clenching too many muscles, so other than bruising, she found herself unharmed by the experience. As the fire died away, she moved her eyes around the section of tunnel she was in, seeing a staircase that wound upwards around the outside walls of the chamber. Above, several openings, neatly arranged in rows, all the same size as the one she'd entered through. From a couple, decaying meat was dangling, or had been until the fire scorched it to carbonised dust. At least, that's what she thought it was, although in the fading orange glow it could have been pairs of socks.

Kim stood, testing the soles of her feet, which, although well done and with a nice crispy skin, didn't hurt too much. She pondered on whether that was a good or bad sign, deciding that good was preferable for her mental health, then aimed for her last sighting of the staircase before the light died into impenetrable gloom. She got there in seven good strides, well six and a half, her right shin not quite making the full distance. Now, taking additional care, she climbed the steps to what she hoped was a door.

It was.

There was a mechanism mounted inside that allowed the stays holding it shut to be retracted, but they didn't budge, not one millimetre, at least not at first. With hands still slick from the viscera coating the sewage pipes, Kim struggled to get a grip on the lever, and without clothing to wipe them clean, things weren't likely to improve, so she improvised. After laying on her back, she kicked from below. Her feet were dry, and she only missed a few times. Then, following several failed attempts and right on the cusp of abandoning the entire idea, the portal opened a crack, then the entire way.

"Oh god, no."

Caruthers wasn't looking forward to giving his first report. Truth be told, he was dreading it, not being used to failure despite having surrounded himself with it most of his latter life. The Kevin cowering before him raised a tendril, lowering it again when Caruthers whipped a fast tentacle across his facial area. The violence helped a bit, but not as much as he'd hoped, so he hit him again, this time hard enough to split the outer dermis and expose internals. He was about to strike again when the captain of his guard intervened.

"Perhaps we should allow this one to live, my lord."

Behind this Kevin, several of his collective lay in varying states of dismemberment.

Looking down, his torso was awash with sticky pieces, probably not an acceptable look in court, or when facing his liege, so Caruthers heeded his guardsman's advice. He lowered his limbs, quieted the loud noises in his mind, and slowed his circulation.

"This is a truly lucky day for you, Kevin."

At his feet, the scientist threw a few furtive glances around the room, picking out the bodies surrounding him, before looking back at Caruthers, but avoiding his gaze. He continued.

"Yes, alright, not for all of you. You, however, shall live. I trust you will not disappoint me further."

Not waiting for an answer, Caruthers left the torture chamber and set a heading for the shower he'd installed for just this eventuality. The guards followed a respectful distance behind, all but Jeffrey, who had misinterpreted an instruction, or taken initiative. Caruthers couldn't quite remember what exactly, but it warranted punishment, so Jeff got to clean the equipment for a few periods. Once in the shower, a series of high pressure outlets jetted the detritus from his body and washed it down into the sewerage system below, where it would ultimately meet with the fiery fate that should have befallen the alien vermin infesting his ship.

Now clean, he donned the robe of office he'd had tailored, at great expense, and then bedecked with military awards, some of which were genuine and celebrated past exploits, some of which were simply invented nonsense, but important, because he needed to have more medals than Joseph. Most days, the mirror in his dressing room gave him confidence. Today, though, he looked furtive, with jittery limbs and a gaze that wouldn't stay still. He felt smaller, somehow, so he grabbed another gaudy badge and added it to the cluster below his gallantry citations.

"That is better."

It wasn't, but it would have to suffice. Ben had requested this audience by official channels, sending a herald, which meant that it wasn't optional and he couldn't just blow it off like the last few. Once outside the dressing room, he rallied his troops.

"If there is any news of the creature's whereabouts, you are to convey them to me immediately. Is that clear?"

"My lord, any audience with Benito is strictly private.."

"Immediately! You are to continue tracking it, but remember, I will be the one to strike the fatal blow."

"Yes, my lord."

"Good. Now go. You accompany me."

He gestured toward Jeffery, who looked like he was expecting a punchline, and then swelled with misplaced pride when none came. Caruthers kept him from picking up on the real reason he was coming, which was in case he needed to make an example of someone in front of Ben, because screw Jeff.

The walk wasn't a long one, seeing that Caruthers quarters were in the same wing as Benito's state rooms, only a few lengths away, but he took his time anyway, subconsciously delaying the inevitable. In the end, though, however slow his pace, those lengths really were few, and his arrival came scant moments after departure. At the entrance hall, a contingent of sentries greeted Caruthers with deference, leaving him to enter the audience chamber while they escorted Jeff away. Caruthers prepared himself for the insults, steeled himself for a beating, prostrated himself at the foot of the throne.

"What are you doing? I'm over here."

Caruthers looked up at the empty seat, then followed Ben's voice around to the banquet table, fully laden with delightful treats, and where he was standing with a mild squint on his face and a juice-cube in one of his tendrils while the others rapped an irritated rhythm.

"Seriously, I don't have time for this ceremonial bullshit right now. Come, have a drink."

"I.. Don't.."

And he genuinely didn't understand, but decided that a drink would be nice, so he trundled over to where Ben was standing, helped himself to a cube, and waited.

And waited.

"You asked me to come, remember? Have I got the right period? Shit, I'm early, aren't I, or am I late?"

Benito held up a limb. Caruthers stopped talking and opened another cube. Only after he'd quaffed his third did Benito say anything more.

"You wanted to know why. You have proven yourself these last few periods, well mostly, anyway, so I'm going to show you, so that you can understand the reasons I acted as I did."

With that, the ruler marched to a short, narrow opening beyond the throne that Caruthers hadn't noticed earlier, just large enough for an oldster to traverse if they inclined themselves a little. Without a formal invite, he was a little unsure if he was supposed to follow, but curiosity won out over the ball of ice in his digestive system, so follow he did, albeit at a respectful distance. Behind him, the sounds of Jeff screaming dragged a smile along his face, or would have, if he could smile. Inside the cramped tunnel, Caruthers discovered Ben aboard a waiting vehicle that, once aboard, allowed Caruthers and his boss to lie horizontal while being whisked at great speed along a series of interconnecting tracks. The journey was extensive and left him disoriented, but in a single, still-living piece as they arrived at their destination, another small room with a single exit, already open.

"Where is this place?"

"Save the questions. You'll have more use for them in a short while."

Caruthers did his best to match the pace as Benito left the vehicle and ran for the exit, which wasn't easy. He was in a hurry. Once outside the arrival room, the opening sealed behind them. In front, Caruthers found himself inside the replica of the alien laboratory. He had intimate knowledge of each grime encrusted surface in this setting, and every facet having cleaned and polished almost every one of them, at least in the original back on the ground. But as he ran his visual cortex over the space, something felt wrong, or at least different. It wasn't the mountains of paperwork that always covered the desks, scribbled full of unintelligible hieroglyphs, they were as he remembered, and it wasn't the..

"H. Jesus Christ!"

"Cool, right?"

Above, where the ceiling normally lived, the open sky stretched out into infinity, but there were no stars. Directly over them, however, a vast circular rift gaped open like a pulsating waste excretion valve in the sky, which contracted on cue to drive home the analogy, but the inside of this rift didn't contain unwanted gore, it contained light, and heat.

"What in the.."

"Yeah, so, anyway, we figured out the aliens tech."

"I.. What?"

"That, my friend, is the molten core of a dying planet on the opposite side of known space. Picked it out myself. Turns out the machine can open wormholes, or at least I think that's what she called them. Anyway, wormholes, connecting any part of space with any other part. I hooked us up to this core. It's powering the citadel!"

Caruthers looked up. A ripple in the outer folds of the orifice revealed the fiery contents beyond.

"And this planet is dying?"

"Ah, well, I mean, it is now! Anyway, this isn't what I brought you here for. I just wanted you to hear this from me first, given your history with the creature."

Ben paused long enough to leave Caruthers, wondering if that had been a question. He started planning his answer, but didn't have time to finish.

"Actually, you know what? It's going to be much easier to just show you."

Whatever Ben wanted to show him was some place else, and a significant hike from where they were, taking almost half a cento-period to cover. During the arduous walk, which Caruthers couldn't help thinking would have been easier and more pleasant riding inside a motorised vehicle, Ben said almost nothing, pausing only once to remark upon how many awards Caruthers seemed to have picked up since their last meeting.

"I earned these!"

"Yeah, sure. We're nearly there, okay, let's just let this one go for now."

The structure they were slowly approaching was new to Caruthers. He'd been in the citadel before. It was a special interest of his, so he'd seen the designs and plans, studied the schematics and watched countless vid-casts of tours. This building shouldn't be there.

It was huge, like everything aboard the floating city, but this dwarfed everything around it, soaring into the black sky and obscuring the sun above. As they got closer, he could feel the energy inside, like it was fighting to escape these confines and destroy everything around.

"You get used to that."

Ben hadn't stopped to wait for a reply, so Caruthers assumed he meant the cranium-crushing sense of pressure that was now building around them. As they approached, several guard units intercepted, all with weapons drawn and no hesitation apparent in their thoughts.

"Identify yourself."

Ben had already passed the cordon. Their weapons were all pointed at Caruthers.

"Stand aside! You know full well who I.."

They probably meant the first shot as a warning, the only reason they could have missed at the non-existent distance between them. Behind him, a large section of the pathway disintegrated into glowing confetti and floated up into the air.

"Um, Ben?"

"He's with me. Let him through."

Caruthers didn't wait, rushing past as they untrained their weapons, meeting Benito at the entrance, which was a grand affair bedecked with a security system he'd never encountered. With the wave of a tendril, the entryway, one entire section of wall, slid noiselessly behind another and revealed the interior.

"Oh god, no."

Kimberley dragged herself upright and looked out, then climbed onto a nearby table to improve her vantage point and help absorb her new surroundings. Ahead was a cage, similar to something you'd employ to transport a reluctant cat for wince-inducing surgery, only large enough to enclose half a city, looming upwards and outwards before vanishing into the oppressive, gloomy distance. It rested down below in a vast, level, open plain, and behind a thick sheet of transparent energy-rock that hummed a little with power, preventing Kim from approaching. She could see all she needed from where she stood, though, and it wasn't a pleasant sight.

Well, that wasn't quite true. Under different circumstances, the view before her was all she wanted. She'd spent a lot of time there, in fact, and grown quite fond of the shops and parks. Location was the crux of the problem. It should nestle amongst rolling countryside back home.

The slice of Hampshire before her looked as though

someone had scooped it whole from its resting place with a giant trowel, lifted with little care for the contents, and then thrown it down onto a concrete paving slab. The buildings were mostly ruins, the few that remained upright, showing significant structural damage. A selection at the periphery appeared to be missing large sections, sliced through with an enormous, red-hot knife, with only half the structure, edges bright red, being transported. The ground was intact, mostly, with roads and paths, street lighting and benches, and in the distance, a park, complete with children's play-area and grassed, hilly banks. Cars littered the parking lot, a few of those chopped apart like the buildings, the exposed edges also glowing slightly with heat, or radiation, or both.

This was an area Kim was intimately familiar with, since it was the town surrounding the laboratory. Her flat would have been situated a mile or so further left, past the edge of the cage, so she figured it was still back home, along with her cat. Half a mile further along the road should sit her regular supermarket where she bought her favourite triple-pack sausage breakfast-sandwiches. She ate them most mornings, since the job started at half-five and the supermarket was the only thing open. Kim scanned the skyline, looking for the town hall and its tower-mounted clock, finding it just where it should be, but also not, and showing ten-forty-five. Was that morning or evening? It wasn't easy to tell. Only a handful of cars parked in spaces out front, and none sat on the road, but quarter to eleven meant the school-run would be long since done and dusted, and employed adults would be clock-watching at their jobs. If it was evening, the right-eous folk of this town would already be at home, sipping wine, or whatever normal people did once they'd eaten and tucked their children into bed for the night.

Kim followed the road to the supermarket with her eyes, peering as the distance grew and the light faded, but finding it where it should be. It looked intact, the benefits of a pre-fabricated steel skeleton skinned with the cheapest panels and toughest glass known to man. Kim moved closer to the barrier, enjoying the warmth it brought to her now frozen body, then stopped, along with her heart. There was movement by the entrance.

There were people down there.

Following the perimeter as close as she could stand, Kim ran around and toward the supermarket as fast as she could manage, which wasn't quick. Her legs buckled under the exertion, giving way after fewer than a hundred meters, leaving her sprawled in an ungainly heap, but still pointing in the right direction, so she hauled herself upright and tried once more. Again, after fewer than fifty meters, she collapsed, only this time she didn't have the strength to get back up on her feet, so she pivoted onto her bottom and sat staring at the commotion occurring by the trolley park. It squatted just past the car-park payment machine and next door to what was once an open air smoking area for the staff, but they'd repurposed in recent years as a toddler play area, albeit one still enclosed on three sides by yellow tinged acrylic sheets and half-eaten junk food, with the occasional used condom. Kim had a clear line-of-sight from her current position, but sound wasn't carrying through the outer shield, so she could only imagine what was being said. On the ground, around thirty people had split into roughly equal groups, mostly older or middle-aged people on one side jabbing fingers and shouting silent orders or insults at the younger group who represented a good porting of the shop's staff. The teenagers, all wearing corporate tabards, were mostly examining their shuffling shoes with a deferential downward gaze, something Kim was familiar with so she sympathised. One person was being forthright, a woman in her late fifties, Kim guessed from the clothes and entitled posture. She had a young lad that Kim recognised from the cheese counter, and, occasionally, the checkouts, cornered along with his shift-manager. She was pointing at the car-park, then the machine, then the barrier, all while screaming in the kid's face. To his credit, he wasn't taking it lying down, at one point grabbing the woman's hand and pushing her backwards with much more restraint than Kim would have mustered.

Of course, it only made things worse.

Kim moved her attention away from the fracas, up the road toward the nearby daycare-cum-nursery that she could now see after moving. The lights were dark, which might be a positive sign, but since everywhere unequipped with a backup generator had no lighting, it meant little. She kept looking for signs of life. Then she saw the mobile kebab-van. It moved around a lot because it didn't have a permit, and the grill looked like no one had cleaned it since being fitted, and there clearly wasn't any running water, so the carving guy would contaminate the food with whatever he'd scratched most recently, which was often his arse. Didn't matter though, the kebabs were the tastiest things she'd ever eaten drunk. Much more important right now, though, since it only catered to the wasted sots drunk enough to stomach the fatty biohazards served there, it only appeared after ten in the evening or sometimes later. The daycare would have been long closed.

That meant no kids.

Kim breathed a sigh of relief tinged with sadness that she would probably never taste one of those grease laden calorie-bombs again. She imagined herself peeling away the protective layer of limp, inedible lettuce, throwing it at a nearby bin, and then sinking her teeth into layers of scalding hot meat byproducts, before closing her eyes and letting the exhaustion take her away from that place and back into the assorted dreams of..

"Woah! Jesus!"

Kim sat bolt upright. Shaking the memory that her brain just force-fed her from her head and double-checking that she was still in one piece. Once she'd satisfied herself, she stood and looked back toward the shop, which was now deserted.

"Excuse me!"

Even muted, years of getting her own way apparently conferred a certain authority to her tone. Kim glanced below into the enclosure and found a crowd of hundreds congregating on the stretch of road ahead. Maybe all the trapped people there. The voice she'd heard was the lady from the supermarket, who stood at the vanguard, hands on hips, hair neatly styled, staring back at Kim with the same expression she'd had when admonishing the teen earlier, only it wasn't anger or entitlement that Kim saw in her face.

She was shaking, her eyes wide and pupils dilated. She was terrified.

And maybe a little embarrassed. It was at this moment Kim remembered she was naked.

"Oh, shit, I.. Ahh.."

With nothing available to cover up, an ineffective flurry of hands and an apologetic expression were all Kim could muster, lasting several protracted seconds, after which she gave up and just addressed the point.

"Look, okay. You guys are in a space-ship right now, and it's probably my fault, but.."

"Your fault? What the hell is going on? I need to get home. I've got to work in the morning and I'm tired. There's dinner in the oven and I only came out to get some.. What's happening?"

"I.. There are aliens here and they used my technology to bring you here. I don't know why. I.. Yes, they're breasts. Could you stop staring at them, please? I got trapped here months ago.."

"The lab accident? That was you? They said you'd died in the explosion. It was all over the news, after it happened, and they dug through the wreckage."

Kim's blood ran cold.

"Was anyone else hurt?"

She had to know.

"No. Just the lab-tech.. Ah, you I guess. The scientist in charge said that you'd done some cleaning and accidentally.."

"Lab-tech? Mother f.. I built that flipping place. Wait, who said he was in charge? I bet it was.."

A sudden increase in the light levels cut Kim off mid-rant. It was everywhere, blinding white and all-pervasive, reflecting off of every surface except the outer transparent rock, which didn't seem to reflect anything at all. A sound followed, deep and insidious, vibrating her bones and filling her head with a migraine-like aura, or maybe just causing a migraine. Below, in the cage, the group of people were no longer ogling Kim's nudity, instead staring at the gigantic ball of glittery-black nothing that had appeared above their heads, filling much of the ceiling area.

They looked confused. They should have been terrified.

"Get back here, now!"

Kim screamed as loudly as she could, but it wasn't enough to carry over the bass frequencies filling their cage, so they heard nothing.

Caruthers watched as Ben nudged a couple of controls on the custom-built panel before him and then moved in for a closer look. The opposite wall was now a view-screen, the clarity of which he'd never seen, being indistinguishable from the reality it portrayed. He could be there. He just didn't want to be.

"What is this abomination?"

Benito ignored him, focussing on some fine adjustments to his new toy. As he shuffled a dial, first to the left, and then back slightly to the right, targeting markers that were present on his small display overlaid the images on the larger screen, edging closer and closer together until they aligned perfectly and changed hue to an angry higher wavelength that the alien would have probably called red. Except she wasn't the alien anymore, she was just one of many.

"I demand you tell me what you are.."

Now Benito swung round, his ocular appendages narrowed and piercing, his voice just as cutting.

"You are in no position to issue demands. If you continue

to distract me, you may find yourself down there in the cage. Is that what you want?"

Unable to plan an answer that he felt certain wouldn't anger Ben further, he kept quiet and lowered his gaze, waiting for a polite period before looking back down on the captives. There were hundreds of them, scattered across the space when they arrived, now concentrated at one end of the enclosure, communicating amongst themselves but distracted by something outside that the vision-panel didn't depict. With the reticules aligned, Ben activated the machinery, filling the entire space with photonic radiation that caught Caruthers unaware, inducing a flinch he was immediately ashamed of, but that Benito didn't seem to notice. In the cage, the alien beings were moving en masse toward the singularity that had formed in front of their eyes, all rapt by the ball of infinity that grew and grew.

"I.. Ah.. Permission to speak?"

"What? Oh, yeah, cool isn't it?"

"It is indeed cool. I just mean to ask, if such enquiry would be acceptable, exactly what is your majesty is attempting to achieve with these unfortunate creatures?"

Benito peeked back at the screen, then at Caruthers, then to the control panel. He didn't seem to have an answer until he did.

"Oh, you mean the humans. So, they were a byproduct of the earlier experiments. They're really not important, there's just a lot of them, and they're everywhere I aim. We'll get to them later. The important bit is the wormhole, observe!"

Caruthers moved in for a closer look as Ben made final adjustments to the settings and nudged a large trigger-orb that had risen silently from the console. On screen, the singularity exploded outwards into a translucent plateau filled with ethereal objects that swam in and out of reality, never settling for more than a micro-period before shifting focus and pulling in more curious objects for Caruthers to behold. After a short while drifting, he realised that the non-corporeal landscape was moving, or rather their window into it was flying across the alien landscape, the ghostly view overlaying the contents already present in the cage. After a short while of this, Benito slowed their movement through this unfamiliar world, settling upon a region that, like everything he'd seen, contained signs of over settlement, but also a structure with no discernible purpose. Inside, the alien creatures cavorted in a state of near undress in a gigantic, decadent trough filled with fluids. Some struggled from end to end, some bobbed up and down while displacing some of the liquid into their compadres faces with their hands. In another, smaller trough to one side, much smaller creatures were splashing in a similar but far less coordinated manner. Caruthers struggled to imagine so much liquid in one place, wondering at the number of creatures they'd massacred so that they could float in that much blood.

"Is.. That?"

"Kimberley's home planet? Yes. It's infested with her kind. They build on everything and fill all their space with machinery and toil. Honestly, I can see why she wanted to leave. Still, if you ever complete your task, her problems will be over."

"It wasn't my fault, Kevin.."

"I'm joking! You'll get your opportunity. My security detail has been following your progress closely. We have her scent, or had it anyway, recently. We'll find her, and when we do, she's all yours. Anyway, check this out."

On screen, the vision became more solid, merging with

the matter already present and becoming real. Then, in a flash that would have been apt in a late period entertainment-cast, the buildings popped into existence, disgorging the fluids where only part of the trough had materialised via the wormhole, and emptying the creatures within onto the ground with scant dignity.

The new material brought forth by the machine consumed the matter that had occupied the space a micro-period before, disintegrating everything it touched.

The newly transported humans were picking themselves off the ground, pointing out wounds and then, almost simultaneously, rushing to access the smaller bowl, in which the mini-humans were now thrashing with even less coordination than beforehand.

"Yeah, they come in a variety of sizes. The small ones seem quite important to the larger ones, offspring maybe? I'll get a crew to dissect a representative selection and find out."

The original inhabitants of the cage were also dusting themselves off, or at least those that weren't absorbed by the new material, or worse, partially absorbed. Even without a mental connection, or the sound these creatures utilised instead, Caruthers understood what they were feeling. They moved at pace around the small region of the enclosure they found themselves in, bumping into each other with comedic consequences, hitting each other with their puny limbs.

"So, what are you showing me? How does this benefit us? We already had one of these things. Wasn't that enough?"

Benito sighed with internal disappointment, then vocalised it with a louder, more theatrical sigh.

"You are witnessing the now, but you should imagine the future. This wormhole works both ways, or at least it will when it's done. Experimentation is a tad behind, if I'm honest, but most of the backup-backup-backup team made it through unscathed!"

Caruthers didn't want to ask, but since Ben wasn't volunteering more information, he felt it was the best way to push the conversation forward.

"By 'most', do you mean?"

"Yeah, so only their top halves survived the journey, still an enormous improvement, and they lived sufficiently long to report that the atmosphere was breathable, or something approaching that. It was difficult to understand through the incessant screaming."

In the cage, the liquid from the trough was already drying on the ground. As he watched, he realised that an earlier question had gone unanswered.

"That liquid? Where are they getting it from?"

Ben draped a tendril around Caruthers and leaned in, joy radiating from his thoughts.

"Oh, you're going to love this. Their planet is absolutely swimming in the stuff, lakes of it, oceans! It's just as the ancient thinkers imagine our world would have been once, before the first cataclysm stripped it all away."

"That's just a theory.."

"Yeah? I'd say this proves it."

Ben moved back to the controls, dialling in a new location with speed that betrayed muscle memory and prior knowledge. As Caruthers wondered just how long these experiments had been going on, the wormhole reappeared, exploded into view and then filled a large amount of the space with a view of something that refracted the light, obscuring and distorting far off objects. The most recent guests began running as fast and as far from this terrifying new vision as their bipedal frames could manage, with those carrying little-ones enjoying less success. It was all for nothing though, as Ben activated before any were clear, bringing forth the most liquid Caruthers had ever seen, drowning the contents in an instant. He watched as it flowed across the floor, covering everything in its path, lifting large objects and washing them away. He looked at Ben, but his shell-shocked mind couldn't find any words.

"You like that, huh? I told you, it's everywhere, and it's safe to drink. I had some a while back. It certainly has a unique taste, bursting with tangy minerals, but it has to be better than juice-cubes, and a hell of a lot cheaper to 'manufacture'."

In the cage, several remaining creatures, still clutching at life, had formed a huddle, waist-high in the liquid, clothing soaked and sagging, clinging to themselves and the others. The littler ones were all gone now, crushed under the weight, or absorbed into matter that materialised alongside the fluids. Near what had been some kind of construction, there was a small, person shaped rock wearing a brightly coloured bathing suit, around which several survivors had slumped, defeated and wailing. Without sound, the scene took on a tone bordering upon comedic.

"They're pretty resilient for such a squashy species."

Caruthers nodded, keeping his orbs trained on the viewscreen.

"They'll make excellent slaves for the mines. They don't seem to possess lengthy lifespans, but if we put a range of them together in a darkened enclosure, 'boom' there will be new ones! Although there are different sub-types, so you need to make sure some possess front appendages."

"You've seen this?"

"Oh, no. Scientists found literature amongst some of the

first material we transported. Not that hard to translate. Our attempts to make it happen have failed so far."

"How long have you had this machine working? Why didn't you tell me any earlier?"

Ben shut the machine down before answering. Caruthers watched the light fade from the view-screen, plunging the cage's inhabitants back into almost total darkness.

"A while. It was important that we kept Kimberley on our side while we translated her books. Then, when it didn't work, we needed her to fix it, which she duly did, even though you nearly ruined everything by trying to usurp her."

"If you had told me.."

"If I had, she would have seen it in your thoughts."

* * *

BACK ON SCREEN, ONE OF THE FEW REMAINING LIVING humans was storming toward the lower edge of their view, upper-limb appendages balled up tight and her cranial features furrowed with many creases. Behind her, another being, one that was attached to the first, followed close behind with a gait that suggested age and insecurity. A few of the smaller ones, having survived the secondary reintegration after all, were congregating around a similar sized group of larger aliens, who were grouping around a metallic object inside the ruins of one building. A source of heat? Caruthers wondered how long they could last in the box without sustenance, without heat. The evidence suggested that it wouldn't be long. The creature displaying the angriest mannerisms had now reached the view-screens lower portion and begun gesticulating with wild abandon to someone, or something just out of sight.

Something that seemed familiar to them, maybe?

She stood for a few short periods before advancing upon the security mesh that laced the inside of the enclosure.

"Oh, cool! Watch this."

Benito was excited about something. Caruthers felt unease and suspicion sprout roots throughout his form. They didn't wait long for confirmation. The creature reached the edge, partially obscuring the view, so Ben nudged a tracking nodule and lowered the view a little so she was clearly visible again. Without further hesitation, the being struck the inside of the cage with both her upper limbs. The effect was spectacular, and surprising in its intensity. The creature first began glowing a little from the points of contact with the outer enclosure, a glow that grew and then tracked through her limbs into her torso, where it grew yet further. Her cranial features contorted into a series of expressions that, at first, showed a lack of understanding, but after a short while, after her body expanded, became unreadable. Then her clothing gave way, stretched far beyond its outer tolerances, ripping and then exploding outward like the skin of an over-ripe juice-cube left in the suns for too long. Her outer dermis went the same way a short period later. With nothing left to hold her form together, the remains dropped to the ground, but kept expanding until, one by one, each of the internal organs popped like party-decorations, disgorging their liquids in all directions.

Behind the spectacle, the nearest human was now on the ground, holding his cranium and screaming. Behind that specimen, the little ones were stunned out of motion, all standing perfectly still while a group of their chaperones, those not also weeping, attempted the futile act of shielding their vision from the horror.

"The elders declared that weapon illegal generations ago."

"I rule this realm. Nothing is illegal to me."

But it was. The constitution made no provision to grant unlimited power to the liege, and they removed this abomination from their arsenal for good reason. The effects were indiscriminate and unpredictable, rendering victims that came into contact with its molecular distortion field into their constituent parts in a variety of different ways, all slowly, all in indescribable pain, but not always in a way that proved fatal.

"Anyway, I thought you'd like it. She's, like, the fifth or sixth that's done that now. I lost count. One of them, a few tries ago, transformed into a sort of ribbon that blew away and upwards until they hit the ceiling and combusted!"

He didn't like it. Caruthers didn't like any of it. Since Kimberley had popped into reality, his world had been a series of catastrophes strung together with pain-wire and then draped around his being, before being pulled tight into his feed pipes and choking all the fun out of his life. But this? This was too much. Benito had opened a portal to their world, dragged innocent beings into this reality, and then delighted in their torment and demise.

"Shit! Is that?"

With the camera lowered, the thing that had drawn their captives' attention now stood visible. Still intact, still breathing and very much incandescent with rage, as evidenced by the visible teeth and tight muscles, she was striding purposely toward one of the inspection panels that fitted the perimeter.

Kimberley.

Ben re-trained the vision to centre her and then

enhanced the view by zooming closer and filtering for low illumination. She was accessing the controls with frantic movements of her digits, enabling fail-safes, disabling couplings. Her commands seemed random, Benito concurred.

"She does not understand this system's functions or format. Her attempts to intervene will be fruitless."

As Caruthers watched further, though, it became clearer and clearer that she knew exactly what she was doing.

"Are you sure? She designed the.."

"Not this one! I built this one, and I made it work, me."

The panel behind Ben activated and immediately disengaged, showing an error where there was once targeting information.

He tried to reconnect, but it was in vain.

"Oh, come on!"

Back inside the cage, the wormhole had reappeared, but it was unstable.

Kim could be seen flipping several controls simultaneously, before engaging and causing the singularity to collapse.

"Shit! No, no no no NO!"

"I thought you said.."

"I KNOW WHAT I SAID! If she doesn't reengage immediately, the regulator assembly will fuse, and if that happens.."

But it was too late. Much to the surprise of Caruthers and, evidently, Kim, the wormhole reappeared, only this time it seethed with angry, unstable power. A series of minor explosions destroyed the panel she was working from, throwing her back and again out of view. In the cage, the wormhole had shifted its hue to a longer wavelength that bathed the entire space in a cold, unnerving light that washed away shadows and didn't look like it would end well. Kimberley had, by this time, run to a second panel further up the view screen and was now engaging the safety override, trying to wrest control of the cosmic phenomena now consuming everything it came into contact with.

"What? If she doesn't reengage the gadget, what will happen?"

"The portal is open to a random point within reality. There's a significant chance it may not even be this reality. It could let something in, something bad or, I don't know.."

Caruthers watched Kim, now an indistinct blob of bright photons in the distance as she wrestled with the controls, a fight which she wasn't winning, as evidenced by her demeanour. She kicked the pedestal supporting the controls and then hopped backwards on her one remaining good foot, yelling silent obscenities at the enclosure as the wormhole grew again. Then her shoulders slumped, or so it seemed. It was hard to tell at this distance, and she returned to the controls. Ben watched the results from what remained of his panel.

"What the hell is she doing?"

On screen, Kim was talking to some of the caged inhabitants. They weren't happy about whatever she was saying, pointing angry limbs back in her direction before walking away. The littler ones were all corralled into a group nearby, and one chaperone slumped to the ground when he heard Kim's words. Back at the panel, she'd activated something and was now waiting.

"NO! You need to stop her, NOW!"

Caruthers hesitated. He wouldn't make it there in time to stop whatever she was doing, and Ben knew that. He was desperate. In all the periods they'd known each other, he'd never known Ben to panic about anything. It was the reason he was in charge.

"There is nothing I can do. You must have a detachment of guards nearby?"

"That area is.. I.. No, there's nobody nearby. This is a secret installation. If guards were milling about everywhere, then that would somewhat defeat the whole secret part."

The wormhole chose that moment to collapse, contracting in the tiniest timeframe into a point of brilliant, ultra-focussed darkness that pulled in all the surrounding light, hovering for a micro-period in a photon aura, before exploding outwards and filling the cage with unimaginable energy. Caruthers could feel the force of the explosion, even from where he was standing. Such was the power in the room.

When it faded, nothing seemed changed. The enclosed contents were as before, partial buildings, vehicles and humans stood where they had, but then, slow at first, then gathering pace, the objects and people disintegrated into a fine powder that floated upwards, hovering like a weightless miasma, mingling with other dust, thickening and combining before falling back to the ground as a muddy precipitation that gathered the remaining dust as it fell. Outside the cage, Kim was still alive, and she was shaking, cranium in hands. Caruthers reached out with his mind, wanting to feel the pain she felt, but couldn't find her. He could, however, feel the fury radiating out from Benito, who was gawping in disbelief at the readings that were now filling his panel.

"I don't.. Mother f.. BITCH! She destroyed it."

"You can rebuild, surely?"

"Of course I can rebuild it. That's not the point. This one

worked. The targeting array was perfect. You don't understand how much effort.. Enough!"

He flipped a communicator, setting it ship wide, and waited for the popping and static to die back before addressing his crew.

"This is Benito. The alien creature is loose on board this vessel. Anyone that encounters her from this point onwards is to consider her a threat to our species and destroy her on.."

"NO, wait. I want her. You promised me vengeance!"

Caruthers could feel Ben consider the request before continuing.

"Anyone encountering her is to contain her, but not kill her. Caruthers will be the one to have that honour. Understand this: I will have anyone who disobeys this order thrown into space without their dermis attached."

Then, to Caruthers, after disengaging the communicator.

"Well, get her."

The faces of the children filled her mind, refusing to leave even with her eyes closed so tight that spots of light filled the black backdrop. The confusion on their faces as the swimming teacher tried to shield them from the explosion, then the panic as their mortality became real. A little boy, maybe six or seven years old, in cartoon print swimming shorts, had refused to duck away from the cosmic events above his head. Instead, he stood pointing directly at the collapsing neutrinos as they formed a perfect black hole, his finger elongating just a little as the gravitational forces grew. Kim refused to look away as she closed the wormhole, wanting to see the suffering she'd caused, needing it to burn away the guilt. With the regulator destroyed, the entire system should have shut down. That was a central fail-safe, born from fear of this exact eventuality and ingrained deep into her original design. But Ben had taken shortcuts, or perhaps not understood that sometimes events don't go as planned? It was over for everyone inside as soon as the wormhole reopened without a regulator to control density and energy flow. There was nothing else she could have done that would have been humane. The alternative was allowing the gravity well to grow uncontrolled, ripping everybody inside to pieces before starting on the citadel itself, and, perhaps, in time, destroying all matter within the star system.

And she'd considered it, just leaving an unmanaged black hole to grow and consume everything.

Except, it wouldn't have been fair, not to those trapped inside the cage, who would have suffered hours of unimaginable pain while being torn atom from atom. It also wouldn't be fair to those innocent souls back down on the surface if they existed. So she'd disrupted the power source before the reaction could become self-sustaining and drained all the life from the enclosure instead, instantly killing every living thing in there.

Now she had work to do. While the original beacon still existed, Benito could rebuild this monstrosity, keep targeting worlds, maybe Earth, maybe others, and she couldn't have that on her conscience. First port of call would be the replica lab onboard, she could sabotage the guidance systems and remove the core-couplings easily enough. Even with her copious notes, Ben would need a sizeable dollop of luck to get it working a second time. Then back to the planet's surface, and the ultimate destruction of the complex she spent years building and months defending. Everything she'd dreamed, she could make it work, get home, but he would follow.

It had to be destroyed.

With resolve in abundance, Kim found the corners of her mouth curling upwards, just a smidge, around the edges. She even covered some ground, several meters toward the exit, her plan at the ready, before all the wheels detached at once.

It started with an innocuous ping from the door activation circuit, a small sound with huge ramifications. The door slid open to reveal four heavily armed soldiers, all radiating a single-minded desire to destroy her, all moving forward with an assurance that told her they knew she was there. Kim ran through her limited options, settling on the only viable thing she could do, turning back into the hangar and running full-pelt down the enclosures' far side, hoping to hide among the many panels that dotted the perimeter. It wasn't a poor plan, apart from the fact that the enclosure was transparent, and that the creatures were telepathic, and, of course, that Kim was several decades and mounds of fatty snacks from her athletic peak, one evening during her high-school years. She'd covered one hundred meters in a little over fourteen seconds while running from a group of bullies that wanted to throw her over the side of a bridge into the muddy ditch bisecting her home village.

Not world record numbers, not even fast for her school. It wouldn't, for example, have qualified her for the track team, but it was the fastest pace her wayward legs would ever manage, and it hadn't even been enough then. She finished that day covered in cold clay, and with no shoes, the river having claimed them as its own.

Now, burdened with years of cheese and movie marathons, she was much slower, and her pursuers were much quicker, and armed, and filled with a rage that permeated the space, making Kim very nervous.

They caught up with her before she got to the third panel along.

"Where do you think you are running, vermin?"

She didn't know the voice. This one must be a recent addition, maybe coming aboard with Ben when he returned from his trip to the surface. He stood a little taller than his comrades, his skin hued a little differently, but everything else was the same, apart from the crystal pinned to his torso slightly below where a human might keep their belly-button. He lashed out an angry tentacle from behind as Kim ran. She heard it fizz through the air, hoping that a little hop to the left might be adequate, but it wasn't and he struck her thigh, throwing her off balance and into the outer, surrounding wall. The contact knocked all the air out of her lungs and brought flickering stars to her peripheral vision, taking her legs out from under her and leaving her, once again, in an untidy heap on the floor.

She didn't reply, instead closing her eyes and waiting for the end. But it didn't come, at least not there and then.

"It thinks it can run from me. It's very mistaken."

She felt something cold press into her side, maybe the muzzle of a weapon. She didn't want to see.

"See how fragile the creature is? And you feared this thing?"

The alien rammed the whatever-it-was hard into her stomach, hard enough to have broken a rib if a few inches higher. Now Kim opened her eyes and rolled away, gasping for breath as the beings watched, their heads filled with curiosity. She could read their thoughts, and they weren't making any attempt to hide what they wanted to do to her, but there was something else holding their enthusiasm.

"You.. Can't.. Kill.."

The words were hard, breathing having become a chore, but she persevered.

"You can't.. Kill me!"

The new soldier levelled his weapon, jabbing her forehead with the muzzle, then running the cold metal down past her face until level with her heart, where it stopped.

"Oh, we very much can."

"No, you can't, not unless you want to end up just like me. Caruthers would tear you to pieces."

She felt heat from the weapon as it powered up, fighting to keep calm as it burned the skin on her chest, wondering if she'd read his thoughts correctly, until.

"You are going to wish I had killed you here. When he has you, your suffering will be unending, you will beg us for an end."

He kept the weapon trained on her as she stood up. Kim flexed her left knee a few times, making sure all the connections were still connected, then squared up the best she could. Considering she was naked and that her adversary towered at least three feet over her head, carried a gun that could vaporise her intestines before she even felt the shot and had all his friends with him, it wasn't too bad. She fought to suppress the smile sitting on her upper lip.

Then they waited.

This was a useful time. She needed a plan and the longer their boss took to arrive, the better that plan would be. At least, that was how it was supposed to work. After about five minutes, Kim had no ideas, and was wondering if Caruthers was ever coming. The others sensed it, too.

"Into the cage."

"I'm sorry. Are you talking to me?"

The soldier struck her across the temple with a whipped tendril.

"For Christ's sake, if you're going to keep being a dick, I'm going to need your name so I can complain to your manager later.. Oooh!"

The second blow hit her in the stomach, doubling her over. One comrade had moved past her and was activating controls with confident prods and swipes. He deactivated the security grill before Kim could take a full breath and get herself upright again.

"You will get into the cage, where you will await whatever punishment our lord decides."

If they got her through there, no plan was going to work. Caruthers could execute her without ever hearing her say a word, or Ben. Ten minutes had passed by now, and she still hadn't come up with anything beyond pointing and shouting 'look behind you!' Kim didn't rate her chances of success. A loud siren filled the entire space with noise that made Kim nauseous, as loud sounds sometimes did, especially if unexpected. It announced that the entryway was opening. At least that was what she read from the guy manning the controls, but there was something else there too, something she hadn't felt in any of them since landing here.

Nausea, of a kind, and a listless weariness in their thoughts. They were sick.

She didn't even realise they could get sick.

Kim felt tentacles wrap around her body and push her toward the now fully open doorway, a hexagonal orifice ringed with more of the security grill material, still glowing and active. More pangs lurched in her stomach, filling her mouth with bile, finally giving her an idea she could use. It had worked once already, a long time ago.

"Ugh, I feel terrible. I don't think I can walk."

She followed with a theatrical pratfall that took her to the ground without hurting or causing further injury and waited. The illness she was feeling wasn't hers, it was all coming from her captors. If they felt anything like as tired as her parents had when she last pulled this stunt, then they should also choose the path of least resistance.

"You pick her up, throw her into.."

The goon made a half-hearted attempt while Kim flopped in his tentacles like a toddler trying to avoid bathtime.

"I am sorry, Colonel, I.. Ah.."

That was all she needed. They all wrapped limbs around her, but the portal was narrow, so some had to go in ahead to avoid disintegrating her on the security mesh, the others having to follow to be sure she made it in one piece. As they lowered her back down to arrange themselves, she pulled the crystal away from the general. Once on the ground, she was up and away, just as quick and naked as that self-same toddler, still avoiding their bath, making sure she kicked the poor guy nearest the door on her way out. His flailing attempts to avoid contact with the death-grid toppled him into the rest of the group. Once out, Kim swiped the panel with her forearm in passing, resealing the cage before anyone managed a coherent response, leaving all of them trapped as the grid powered back up.

She didn't even glance at them as she left the hangar and headed for the bridge.

* * *

THE CORRIDORS WERE CLEAR, MOSTLY ANYWAY, allowing Kim a clear run to one of the transporter stations she'd spied on the way down. The jewel she took from the colonel glowed different colours depending on the doorway you presented it to, and after a brief excursion round a circular route that returned her to the hangar, Kim figured out that those colours corresponded with an eventual destination. That wasn't all, though. It opened doors that were previously sealed. All she needed to do was figure out which colour led her where she needed to be, and that colour appeared to be a bright neon pink that glowed with an intense, ethereal aura and reflected blue from every surface.

There was only one moment of panic. She felt Caruthers' presence, almost overwhelming her senses after connecting the transporter to a destination pad that might be the one in the loading bay. He was close, and his thoughts whirled with unfocussed ire, but he wasn't paying attention to anything outside the sphere of fury burning a metaphorical hole in his mind, and a very real and painful hole in the side of one of his lackeys, after pointing out that Kim had gotten away again. It was consuming his thoughts, but Kim still caught glimpses of his underlying state of mind, and it wasn't good, at least not for her.

Kim teleported before they reached her and then disconnected the system from her end, hoping it would obscure her destination at theirs. Then she had second thoughts and reactivated the system, leaving her location engaged if anyone tried to transport themselves in. Or that was the hope. After that, it was plain sailing. She reached the bridge a little over half an hour after setting off. When she arrived, everything was different. All the emergency displays had gone, and the central view-screen now showed a real-time view of the planet surface that appeared nothing like the one she was used to. There was life everywhere, and the devastation which was still there around where the palace stood only affected the smallest area, in a strangely linear shape that lead to the launch site. She knew it wasn't real, but seeing it with her own eyes still felt like a gut-punch, and it hurt. The entrance to the replica lab was already open when she got there, but it wasn't her first destination so she passed it by, heading instead for her secret lab, where she destroyed everything in as quiet a manner as possible, which given that everything was glass and electricity, wasn't. Kim also took the time to put on the spare set of coveralls she stowed there for emergencies, the slightly ratty set that had rips along the seams, leaving gaps that left nothing to the imagination.

Wearing them, though, felt like donning armour.

That done, Kim aimed for the bridge, a short slog away, where she discovered the Captain had now appeared. He was alone and distracted, entering coordinates into the guidance systems and flipping an extensive set of red controls that made funny squeaking sounds and served no real purpose as far as Kim could see. He was there for a few minutes, with Kim squeezed into the void under a nearby control desk that allowed her to see him clearly, but also allowed her to duck away if needed, shielding her from view behind a seating sphere that, up close, smelled an awful lot like the juice cube creature in the lower decks, and seemed to breathe. Once the Captain left, she moved over to the throne and checked his inputs. They were returning to the landing-site, or would be soon. She was running out of time.

The replica lab was just as she'd remembered it, since it was just as she'd remembered the original. A few things had moved, with the central console now a few feet nearer the main view-screen, obscuring the data output and the console directly underneath it from where she entered. She took a few steps further into the space, running her hand over the replica stainless steel finishes as she went, wondering what they really constructed it from and getting all the way to the core circuits before realising she was being watched.

"The.. Hell?"

He was standing in the blind-spot, tentacles mid-flurry on the controls, no certainty in his thoughts. There wasn't anybody else present, just him and her, and she didn't see a weapon. Kim tried to work out in her head if she was quick enough to activate the self-destruct system before he could override her inputs, or overpower her, or both. She knew he was strong, and he was fast, just like she knew he was remorseless and prepared to do anything. After a stalemate probably lasting a couple of seconds but dragging out to countless eons in her mind, she took a deep breath.

"Hi, Ben."

She activated the panel under her left hand without turning away from him. He continued to flip controls on his panel, deactivating the power supply as she entered the core ejection sequence.

"You are no longer wearing the sash of shame? A pity, it suited you. I had it made specially, you know, to fit your physiology. I tried to have it made just heavy enough that it would become uncomfortable. Was I right? Did your puny frame buckle under the weight of your failure?"

Kim flexed the shoulder that had borne the offending award, wincing involuntarily as the dull ache became acute for a moment.

"N.. No! I'm stronger than you think."

Something was wrong. The sequence she'd entered was right, but nothing was happening. Kim needed to look, but knew that if she turned away, he'd read her panic and overwhelm her in a jiffy. She needed to distract him, just for a second or two.

"I see you still don't know how the power grid works."

It was worth a try, just to see if he would engage, which thankfully he did.

"How dare you! I built this complex. I am the only one here that understands how it functions.."

"Then how come you reconnected the backup supply? You know, I can help if you'd like. I know you struggle to understand.."

"SILENCE! Your input will not be required."

She watched his movements as closely as she could without giving her interest away. In her peripheral vision, which wasn't all that reliable if she was honest, he was wildly striking a button that wasn't in her original design. It took little to realise it was a communicator, meaning he was playing her for time too. Kim used her panel to open a remote access request to the data from his terminal, or she hoped that was what she'd done. It was getting increasingly hard to tell now that crippling cramps were taking control of her hand. A ping from her end indicated some sort of success, so she hoped for the best and disabled his access. The result was immediate, with all the lights going out on his end, including the communicator. He turned to investigate, giving her an opportunity to check her own work, realise that she was half an inch to the left of where she needed to be, and reenter the destruct sequence before returning her attention to Ben. In those two seconds, he had covered half the distance between them, but he stopped when she raised her other hand.

"Don't come any closer! I'll destroy everything, even the citadel. Look into my thoughts and you'll see I'm telling the truth."

Kim felt Ben push at her mind and not be gentle about it.

"Come on! You need the beacon technology to get back to your planet. You're not going to.."

As he pushed a little harder, Kim's vision blurred a little, so she pushed back enough to avoid a migraine but didn't expel him completely. She needed him to see she was serious.

"Seriously? You're being serious? Look, we can make a DEAL!"

As he said the last word, Ben threw a tentacle at Kim's body, looking to knock her away from the platform and disarm the controls. What she knew, but he didn't, was that she was reading his thoughts at the same time he was violating hers. Kim knew what he was going to do before he did, so she sidestepped his move with ease, then parried his limb with a backhand swipe, carrying her hand over to the control panel, where she enabled the self destruct sequence.

"Woah! There's no.. Wait! I made a mistake, I can see that now. We can just talk about this. Just.. Disable the sequence, and let's talk this through like equals."

"Equals?"

Kim protected the sequence with a passcode. It wasn't one she could repeat, being a random jumble of glyphs she entered without looking at the keypad. After locking it down, the full weight of what she'd done pressed into her consciousness. She wasn't going home. This was the blueprint, the original working model. She designed every system in the room, but once it was gone, even she wouldn't be able to rebuild it. There was, however, still the cage, and even though the monstrosity had sustained damage now, she would also need to destroy it to be sure that the Earth was out of immediate danger. She'd kept her telepathic link to Benito open through the exchange, and now she pressed his subconscious for the control-room location and he didn't disappoint.

"Thank's Ben, I have enough now. I think it's time for you.."

It happened so fast Kim barely registered that the dynamic had changed. One second she was in his head reading his thoughts, the next he was in hers laughing while Joseph threw her to the ground, tendrils wrapped tight around her throat, restricting her airway and squeezing the life out of her.

They had her. Benito's message had been short, but its meaning was clear. Caruthers would have his prize to do with as he wished.

They'd caught Kim in the laboratory complex attempting to destroy her machine. He wasn't told whether she'd succeeded, but the anger present in Ben's communication showed that she may have. In either case, she was surplus to requirements and, as promised, was being delivered. By the time the message reached Caruthers, though, she wasn't in the lab anymore, since they'd moved her to the incarceration cubes, where he himself had spent much of the trip. They were on a lower deck, far from the living quarters, and sealed within solid, seamless energy rock. The only entry point was a single heavily fortified transport point in a side chamber just off the command deck. Control was only possible from the bridge, and required top level access crystals that only the Captain, his second and Benito possessed, so while getting in was difficult, getting out was almost impossible without an escort and explicit permission from the Captain or Ben.

Unlike his brief stay, which had been in one of the holding pens, they had her in a torment cell, which was built with only one thing in mind: pain, and inflicting it without causing fatality. The problem, though, was that the jagged, probing implements available followed designs for native physiologies, which were robust, not human forms which were puny and fragile. So unless he hurried, there wouldn't be much left of her to claim.

She had to be breathing when he arrived. He needed her alive. He had a special surprise planned, something from the far recesses of his conscience, a deep splinter that he simply must remove before festering.

He entered the restricted access portal chamber with his retinue, but they were all turned away by the duty guard. Before a conflict ensued, Caruthers dismissed his team, instructing them to await his return in his chambers, where he would rejoin them for a celebratory feast once the creature was paste. They seemed unsure, but a little additional prompting from the guards un-maker convinced them of the wisdom of Caruthers words. As they left, he stepped onto the pad and awaited the order confirmation from the bridge. While they waited, the guard kept his weapon aimed at Caruthers' cranial area, where any wound would be fatal. Far away on the bridge, the Captain, a being that Caruthers had browbeaten and humiliated frequently, and was probably enjoying the power he now had over him, waited long enough to cause concern, but did eventually signal his acquiescence. As he peeled apart, the last thing he saw was the duty guard holstering his weapon and returning to the desk. As he again became corporeal, the first thing he saw was another guard un-holstering his weapon and aiming it for a kill shot. Once whole, there was an additional wait whilst they confirmed the Captain had allowed the transport, and that they were to expect their new guest. That done, they led him back into the series of narrow corridors that ended at the brig. They had changed little in appearance since his incarceration, which wasn't surprising given that it was only a few short periods ago, but there was a new ambience, brought about by the shrieking echoing around the hard walls like game-spheres in a Rico-match. It was, of course, deliberate. Any sound produced in a torment-chamber fed through an amplifier and got played out over noise emitters in a slightly higher key, to foment terror and compliance in any that occupied nearby cells. Judging from the sounds he could hear, Kimberley was nearing her end, with the screams tailing off and lacking the energy she'd had when he first met her. The duty guard at this end intercepted Caruthers as he stepped away from a narrow exit and into an ante-chamber that housed the desk and surveillance panels.

"My lord, you have arrived just in time for.."

"You are to stop her torture this instant."

"But, I.."

"NOW. Or do you wish to test the sharp end of the equipment yourself?"

He didn't answer, instead projecting orders into a communication brooch pinned to his chest. The screams stopped almost straight away, with just a lingering moan left to fill the void.

"The creature is mine. If it is harmed beyond repair, I will see that you and your team will never leave this location again. Am I clear?"

There was uncertainty present in the guard's inner thoughts, like this was new information. It was making Caruthers nervous.

"My lord. I.. That is, we have orders to break the creature."

He didn't need to, but he asked anyway.

"Who gave these orders?"

"Our liege, Benito, the most beneficent."

For there to be any possibility of getting to her whilst she lived, he had to move immediately. Without waiting for an escort, Caruthers swept out of the chamber and towards the cell where she lay dying. He met two more guards half-way there, who apologised while he pushed past them, and then followed a few lengths behind to avoid further ire. It was an excellent decision on their part, Caruthers mused as his fury grew. When he arrived, the room was as he'd expected.

He'd never seen a torment cell for himself, but had heard tales from those that had. The ceiling was low, and only sparsely dotted with illuminating spheres, all a short, cold wavelength, to bring fear and hopelessness to those bathed in their light. In the spaces between, hooks hung from chains fashioned from heat-rock, a type of energy rock that proved too unstable for practical use, but got hot at random, causing annoyance and scalding in equal measure. The walls had on a thick coat of sticky goop that one of the lesser beings ejected as a defence mechanism when squeezed in a clamp; it looked smooth, but cut like razor-disks if touched, bringing agony, but no serious harm, at least, to their kind. Kimberley was on the floor, naked once again, razor-milk running down her back. Where it had pooled, her epidermis was near to being stripped through, with bone and muscle protruding through patches worn thin enough to split. Perforations punctured her sides with a series of wounds that leaked internal fluids into a growing puddle that formed in the dip at the centre of the room, a design that made cleaning easier, but the drain cover remained closed so the gore was coagulating into a sticky pool. Caruthers did his best to avoid contact, moving around the slick lumps and reaching her slumped form, still untouched by the mess. As he approached, the two guards that had inflicted the torment upon the creature took a few steps back, looking down upon their handiwork with what felt like pride.

They certainly possessed an excellent work ethic.

He felt for her thoughts, but found nothing coherent. Lost in a long series of daydreams, her mind was shielding her from reality. Her memories coalescing into a comforting blanket of rationalisation, draped over her as a tent, deflecting the endless rain burning through her nerves and pain receptors. He reached out a limb, nudging her torso, lifting her clear off the ground for a moment before dropping her back down. She was cold, her breathing was shallow. There wasn't much of his prize remaining to claim.

"You. How long has she been in here?"

"Just over a period, my lord. I must admit to being surprised at her resilience."

He was just as surprised. She should be dead already. That kind of pain would break any of the lesser beings remaining on the surface, as it would a significant portion of his own kind, however robust.

"This thing was mine, and you sought to end it before I arrived?"

"I.. No my lord, it's just that, Ben, he ordered us to.."

Caruthers made a quick mental calculation, based on what he'd already seen, what he already knew, picking Kim up from the ground and throwing her across the room toward an extraction module that filled one side. The wall there was all bedecked with sharp, grabby, hooky things that were usable in a variety of ways, all painful, some fatal.

"Good choice, my lord. I'll strap it in right away."

One guard picked her up and placed her on a mobile platform the other brought in, attaching her with clasps that prevented escape but, given her demure size, would allow for her to see everything that happened next.

While the guard distracted himself with Kim, Caruthers slipped a tendril out and relieved him of the weapon hanging from his holster unnoticed, then moved over to Kim.

"Do you have anything left to say?"

He lifted her head with a tendril, dropping it back onto the platform with a dull thud when she didn't respond.

"I don't think it can speak anymore lord, all it does now is moan and drool."

Caruthers wrapped several limbs around her broken form, feeling the life-fluids running through her body, pumped around in ever decreasing bursts by her failing heart. He squeezed tighter, thinking back to all the times he wanted to do this, to the one time he nearly did. He squeezed just a little more, slowing her breathing, then releasing just enough to let her catch her breath. She was fighting, even now.

It wasn't too late.

"You, bring me the grind-blade, the longest one."

"As you wish."

The guard selected a wicked blade from the wall, bifurcated at one end with serrations along all its edges. It hummed just a touch as the guard waved it through the air, then turned the handle toward Caruthers, who took it with care, felt the weight in his limbs, and then used it to decapitate the guard before he had any chance to react. A single swipe, almost no resistance.

"What the.."

The other guard would not miss something that obvious, but Caruthers was ready for him, pulling out the un-maker he'd stolen from his now very dead colleague and firing a single shot that landed between his orbs, removing the nerve-ganglion that lived there while cauterising the wound. His corpse dropped to the ground like a sack of food, but with less life. His compadre had, by this time, also stopped twitching and moved on to the next phase of existence, so he dropped the knife and pocketed the gun before lifting Kim clear of the platform and making for the exit.

Back at the central hub, the full weight of what he'd just done pressed down upon Caruthers' conscience. He propped Kim up beneath the desk, in case anyone else arrived to look for them, but that shouldn't happen for a while. The guards' schedule called for regular contact with the Captain, but there should be no further communication for at least five Milli-periods. That should provide sufficient opportunity to figure out his next steps.

He activated his communicator and formed a message to the head of his personal team, then shut it back off without saying a word. Once his actions became public, no one was going to support him. He'd taken his second chance and turned it into a death sentence, and for what?

Kim mumbled something. She was delirious, running a fever so badly that he could see it in the air around her body.

She was the reason. This puny, annoying creature he'd known for such a miniscule period, and who had been the bane of his existence every period during that time? This creature that had belittled him, ignored his advice, destroyed his home. Since she arrived, his life had been nothing but miserable.

Caruthers took out his weapon and disintegrated a few of the illumination orbs dotting the ceiling, lowering both the levels of light and his mood. He tried something else, ricocheting energy pulses off of parts of the desk, reducing several chunks down to their atoms, something he used to find hilarious.

Nothing.

Kim murmured again. This time her hands jumped and writhed, an excellent sign that any damage inflicted might not prove permanent. She would need the machinations of a trained medical team, along with their knowledge and technological wizardry, though, and promptly if she was to survive into another time-slice, whilst still drawing breath.

Why was he here? He was high-caste, destined for tremendous things, including a place around the table with the ruling elite. All that ended because he dared to consider that lesser beings might not have worth enough to continue existing. He didn't even demand action, merely suggested that they should consider his words. For that, he lost everything. Now here he was, harbouring one such lesser being.

He aimed the weapon at her head, feeling the trigger with his mind. He could go back, return her charred corpse in the torture chambers and blame everything on her, go back to his life. Then what? Ben could fix the infernal machine, conquer planets full of beings who were just trying to get by. From his throne, he could enslave entire systems, drain suns of their power, drink the life out of whole worlds like they were juice cubes.

Would he be okay with that?

Kimberley was a flawed creature, from a weak species,

easy to manipulate. But she was the source of the great power Benito now had at his disposal, and she'd given it to him without hesitation, believing she was saving their world. She hadn't done this for her own benefit; she had sacrificed her one chance to return home in order to protect it, and all life existing there, just as she willingly gave every meagre thing she possessed to protect his planet, not for status, or personal gain, but because she believed it the morally correct course of action

He knew that and he'd felt it in her. Now he'd pinned his entire future, maybe the future of his entire species, on that feeling of blind hope.

A communicator activated on the main desk, patched from the command deck. The Captain was checking in. Unfortunately for Caruthers, the corpse of the guardsman propped up behind the desk wouldn't be able to give a satisfactory answer, so he flipped the control over and answered himself, hoping to buy some time.

"Captain, why are you interrupting my interrogation?"

"Caruthers? Where is the sentry?"

"I won't ask a second time! Why are you distracting me from my work?"

"I'm sending a detachment of troops to your location, Caruthers. You had better pray they find nothing amiss."

With that, the communicator disconnected, leaving only the occasional grunts from Kim to break the silence.

"Shit."

He didn't say it to anyone in particular. He'd only heard the word for the first time when he met Kimberley, and didn't understand its many meanings until she explained, albeit unsatisfactorily. It seemed apt, though, as a measure of his worth right now. He scooped Kim back up, ignoring her delirium induced squeals, and placed her behind the central desk where she would be out of the line of fire when the additional guards arrived. Once she was no longer visible from the transporter pad, he collected all the weapons he could find, stashing two on his person and the rest with Kim, where he could retreat if necessary. Then he waited.

Caruthers had fought wars, several of them, always confident that what he was doing was right, or at least justified. He'd commanded armies that slaughtered entire cities, then razed the buildings into dust with younglings still inside, all in the name of progress and stability. He'd killed thousands to protect millions, and he'd done it without a second thought, maybe even revelled a little. Now, for the first time in his existence, he just didn't know where right was, and the destruction his younger self had wrought weighed heavily upon his thoughts and circulatory system.

He didn't like it, not one bit.

He checked the control desk. Still no one on the transporter. As he looked back, Kim opened her eyes a tad. They had a glazed sheen. Nobody was home.

His certainty, that feeling of divine power and authority, had been his undoing. Not just him, everyone. Benito, after so long without oversight, wouldn't see he was wrong. The deaths that his scheming caused didn't feature anywhere in his thoughts. He didn't see them as real anymore. Everything was a game that he had to win at any cost.

Just as he had until recently.

He turned again to the semi-conscious alien slumped next to the pile of guns he hoped would get him out of this situation.

"Screw you, I was happy. Why did you have to appear here? Why couldn't you have materialised nearer the sun, where the lack of atmosphere would have boiled you like tea? Whatever the hell that is. Why did you have to invade my life, my existence? You've ruined everything."

But she hadn't. Even as the words left his mouth, something stirred deep within his psyche, a feeling he hadn't experienced in so long, a comforting sensation that reminded him of past exploits when he led great armies. He felt purpose. This was the righteous course and one he should have followed, even lacking interference from this infuriating alien creature.

Illumination from the panel announced four troops, all armed, all with orders to assess the situation and report back. He could hear it all in their thoughts. He could also hear uncertainty. They understood who Caruthers was, and the magnitude of these circumstances. Good, that was something he could use.

Materialising on the pad required several moments as each layer wrapped the previous. Caruthers used this time to check their formation and identify the quickest way to get off the four shots needed to remove them from his path. Then, fortunately, he realised as the final layers unpeeled, that he would require their help, willing or otherwise, to leave the brig and return to the outside.

He hid his weapons and strode down the hall to intercept.

"What do you mean by this?"

"We have orders to check the brig, move aside, or we'll shoot."

Behind him, two of the guards had their weapons aimed for fatality. Caruthers moved aside.

"Where are the duty guards?"

"They are both in the torment cell, and both quite dead."

The party stopped, circling Caruthers and preventing him from moving further.

"Explain yourself!"

He hoped his reputation still counted for something, banking his life on it, in fact.

"They damaged the alien before I could extract my prize. Benito gave it to me, to be disposed of at my pleasure.."

This was true.

"They disobeyed a direct order to contain it while I made my way here. I rectified their insubordination with swift rebuke.."

This wasn't true, but they had no reason to suspect that.

"If you continue to impede my work, I'll see that the same fate befalls you too, and not just you, your families. Do you understand?"

It was a bold play. If any of them were paying attention, it would end badly for everyone, but, if they believed him, then he could walk out of here with Kimberley before Benito realised exactly what was happening. After that? He'd give it some thought if this worked.

The lead guard, a newly minted lieutenant, was considering his options. It was an evenly poised choice, so Caruthers gave another little nudge.

"I don't have time for this! Do you doubt my credentials? You know who I am, and you know where I am quartered. Escort me to my chambers with the prisoner so that I can take my time with it. If there are any issues, you can come and get it, but it's life draws thin and I want my satisfaction. What say you, and take care with your words, as I will remember this interaction and your continued liberty may depend on that recollection being favourable."

He laid the words on heavy, perhaps too heavy, even for

him, but the effect was as desired. The lieutenant moved aside, allowing Caruthers to dip behind the desk and collect Kim with no one seeing the weapons.

Of course, someone would check after he'd left, so he was going to move fast.

* * *

CARUTHERS LEFT THE ENTRANCE ROOM CARRYING KIM as nonchalantly as he could while not breaking anything else that might be difficult to fix later. It was, in every way that mattered, a juggling act. His personal guard met him outside, and they stood firm as he passed, preventing any further interference from the troops that were there, in all likelihood, to kill him. That meant one thing. With his immediate activity no longer a part of their itinerary, they would return to the brig and discover the mess. They might quickly determine what transpired there, or they might not figure it out at all. Caruthers had to assume the worst-case scenario that an eagle-eyed sentry would see through his ruse straight-away. He ordered his captain to clear the route to his quarters, mumbling something threatening and creative about what would happen if anyone disturbed him en route, while shaking Kim's limp form. The soldier scuttled off, barking orders to his subordinates, emptying the interceding corridors of anyone that might prevent Caruthers from getting to his destination. He wouldn't have much time, but when he was sure no one was watching, he stopped to probe Kim's mind once again.

He saw nothing. Almost nothing. There was some activity deep inside, where her broken brain had imprisoned her as a protective mechanism, but the surface was little more than a meat shell, disconnected from the human inside.

He upped his pace, confirming by communicator that the medical equipment he needed installed was in his rooms, then ignoring the follow-up questions, cutting his guardsman off mid sentence.

The rest of the journey was unimpeded, with doorways sealed either side and rooms emptied at the barrel of a weapon and he made good time, reaching his quarters before they discovered anything untoward in the brig, maybe. Once inside, he ordered everyone inside to leave, drawing his own weapon when a few dissenters lagged, but thankfully, not having to fire a shot. He sealed the door, a handpicked and reinforced affair he bought from stores after a sleepless rest-period brought on by memories of his own incarceration. It could withstand an augmented crystal drill running at maximum power for four or five periods, which was fantastic, but the surrounding walls would survive half that, and there wasn't another way out of the suite.

He placed Kim on the medical slab with care, avoiding further injury, and then took a tour to make sure there wasn't anyone left inside with him. He only engaged the equipment, performing the scans, when he was certain. Her internals showed significant damage, with life fluids leaking into cavities all over, and internal organs either shutting down or on the verge of doing so. Caruthers activated a stasis protocol, freezing the deterioration while he considered his options.

If she died now, he'd thrown away his entire existence for nothing. Ben would have the dermis flayed from his body and flown like a macabre flag. He would live long enough to see it, too, his life-force slow-dissolving into a vat of pain-gel.

However, if he stuck to his cover story and just told everyone she died at his hand?

It could work, but it probably wouldn't.

"Caruthers? I.. I'm glad.. Agh!"

He wasn't sure it was real at first. Kim was still motionless on the slab, frozen inside a stasis field and with most of her insides outside, only nominally attached by a strong faith in the technology. At first, he ascribed this vision to stress. He'd been under a lot of pressure, most of his own doing if he was honest, but it must be having a detrimental effect on his think-health. Then she broke the silence again, but didn't. Her voice was in his head.

"What happened? Am I dead? It really hurts, I mean, like everywhere."

He moved over to her, checking the observational display where her mind-waves were spiking. He brought her back together with a swish of the controls and activated a recovery subsystem that worked by rebuilding internals at the cellular level from earlier scans. It was hit-and-miss, even for their kind, and had never succeeded when used on a different species.

"Be quiet, Kimberley. This process is delicate."

"I.. Thank you. I hoped you'd come. It'll be alright now, won't it?"

The short wavelength of the illuminations on the panel suggested otherwise, but the pleading in her thoughts suggested she needed a more positive version of reality.

"It will be alright. You need to rest now, though. Be silent and allow the medical machinery to do its work."

"No!"

She was reading him, just like she always had, seeing

through his poor attempt at deception. The resulting single syllable conveying all her pain straight into his mind where it exploded outwards, filling his whole being. Warning symbols pinged across the observation panel, filling the view with negative glyphs that obscured her life-signs.

"Stop talking! I can fix this."

"Why doesn't anyone like me?"

"I like you. Now stop.."

"No, you don't. I thought you did, for a bit, and I tried so hard, I really did. I gave you guys everything I had, but it wasn't enough. It never is."

Caruthers stopped what he was doing, which had quickly become firefighting a series of serious medical emergencies that grew in threat. Alas, with little success, since as one fire extinguished, another arose, often accompanied by friends. There wasn't a lot of time remaining, so he was honest. She would see any lies he told, anyway.

"You were arrogant! To believe you were better than us, a lesser creature!"

"I wasn't.. At least I didn't mean to be. I thought you'd seen that and that was why Benito was so nice to me. Do you really think I'm arrogant?"

She was wide awake but still disconnected from her body, so he strengthened the field that was holding her together and used her emotional pain as a distraction. She could tell when he was lying anyway, so why pretend? Caruthers engaged the pattern matching and began rebuilding her organs from a scan taken when she was in his lodgings only periods ago, but still nearly a lifetime.

This was going to prove excruciating in several ways.

"You come to my world with this technology, a way to

travel vast distances in an instant, and then fight our curiosity with near lethal force. Then, only when you needed something did you invite us in, but not before making it clear you see yourself above our very best thinkers. You! Your species has barely moved beyond cave dwelling, from what I understand."

All he got in return was a scream, loud, but inside her head.

"I saw you with Benito. I saw you change your behaviour, your language, even your clothing to suit. Your attempts to manipulate were as transparent as they were futile. I told.."

"That's not true!"

"Yes. Yes it is. I observed with my ocular facets, heard with my auditory enhancements."

"I just wanted to help."

And she did, even now. He could feel it in her, consuming her like a compulsion, or an itch she couldn't reach with any of her spindly flesh-tube limbs. But that wasn't the only thing.

"I don't have any friends. Caruthers. Not at home, not here. At least, not anymore, I guess. I just wanted to fix the beacon and go home, and if you guys had left me alone, that's just what I would have done. I didn't ask for any of this."

The rebuild was reaching a crucial stage, where the first of her exposed organs would settle neatly back into her system, get plumbed in and then perhaps fend for itself. First up was a sizeable spongy meat-piece from her chest cavity that quivered rhythmically, the purpose of which proved mysterious even to the most learned zoologists. He needed to keep her talking.

"You still performed a lie for our benefit, to twist Benito's perception and sway his opinions. You could have chosen honesty from the start. I would at least have had some respect for that."

"Honest? You're not listening to.. Agh.."

Her breathing organs were next up. The system had removed several masses from the insides that seemed to serve no purpose, which was a safety mechanism designed to prevent poor scans from killing the recipient. The problem was that with no means of assessing the usefulness, or not, of these fibrous nodules, removing them could prove counter-productive or fatal.

"I don't know who you are, Kimberley. None of us do. You conceal everything beneath this mask like an entertain-ment-stream performer playing a part and keeping your intentions hidden from view. How can anyone trust you if they don't know who you are?"

"I don't know.."

The machine was done. Everything had returned to whence it came, and life-fluids were again pumping through vast webs of pipes throughout her gangly form, all without leakage, but she wasn't waking up.

"What do you mean 'you don't know?' You don't have a story to relate? Some justification involving your shitty colleagues back on Earth?"

"I don't understand who I am! I never have. My whole life I've lived in a bubble that kept me from connecting and I have to hide it from everyone.."

Caruthers continued to watch the panel without speak-ing. At that juncture, he had no salient words to give. Nothing changed. He'd made a mistake, he thought, throwing his life away, his legacy.

But he had hoped. He'd believed in something greater

than himself, even if that belief only existed momentarily, and no matter the consequences, it had been justified. It had been beautiful.

"I.. Ugh. Jesus, I feel awful. Are you sure you put everything back in the right order?"

When Kim looked over the wrinkled skin covering her body, there were few scars telling the story it had lived. A small line across her right side, below the belly button, marked the spot her appendix had left, aged twenty, after a night drinking alone at home ended with acute abdominal pains that started out comical but ended a few short hours later in hospital with a concerned-looking consultant probing her with an extended forefinger and muttering serious but indecipherable incantations at a junior doctor who'd earlier left her on a bench seat eating crisps. Later, grateful that she hadn't aspirated partially digested prawn-cocktail flavoured potato snacks into her lungs during the surgery, she asked if she could keep the offending organ, only to be told it had gone to be incinerated with the rest of the bio-waste.

The only remaining souvenir from this experience, one of her most significant and traumatic up to this point, was the insignificant scar, later hidden from view by rolls of sweaty fat, to where nobody but her was aware it existed.

A grumble from her belly told her she was hungry, or that her kidneys hadn't settled yet, or maybe she didn't even have a stomach anymore. The scanner wasn't easy to read.

"Lie still, I still need to finish this scan."

Caruthers had busied himself with ensuring he'd accounted for all the parts, saying very little since she woke, and that was at least an hour ago. She felt his thoughts, though, like balloons filled with emotion pressing against her skin, warm and sticky.

"I'm fine."

She didn't feel fine, but the discomfort she'd felt at first had given way to actual pain in her joints, and a numbness deep inside her buttocks that both didn't hurt and very much did, a lot. Now that pain was making space for a flat-mate, agony.

Above her, the alien creature who'd done so much to cause her current predicament said nothing while pushing some glowing levers that had sprouted from the console near the far edge. The lights had changed colour, from a dark red to a pleasant light green that reminded her of childhood. He flipped both levers and swept a gaggle of limbs across the switches, hitting all of them and disconnecting the medical unit.

"You seem to be, although I am at a loss to explain how. You should have expired, Kimberley."

"That's a cheery thought."

She swung her legs over the edge of the platform and leant forward in one swift movement, practised over the years of sleeping in single beds and on desks. This time, instead of ending upright on her feet, she collapsed into a nauseous and light-headed pile on the floor. Again.

"You must take things at a reduced rate of speed,

certainly until you acclimatise. The life-fluids in your body are mostly synthetic, and they are untested. They may not convey the nutrients your cortex requires as efficiently as the original specifications."

Kim picked herself up with care, leaning on anything she could reach and ending up sitting back on the platform. While she waited for her vision to stop spinning, she counted to ten in her head, over and over.

"What are you doing?"

"Trying not to throw up. I'm not sure how successful I'm going to be. You should probably scoot backwards a bit."

"I am sorry."

Three paltry words that can carry so many meanings. She'd used them herself to avoid trouble, or to smooth over an angry interaction, or to atone for disappointment, wearing them thin like favoured underwear, comfortable but no longer fit for their intended purpose. Not Caruthers, though. He chose his words with care. Maybe she'd misheard? Maybe he had?

"I feel sick, that's all. I don't enjoy the experience of.."

"No. I am sorry, Kimberley. For the situation you find yourself in, and for my part in making it happen."

Caruthers' lower half moved into her view, filling the space on the floor she'd been staring at to focus on something other than projectile vomiting. She could see the tentacles keeping him aloft, hundreds of them moving in chaotic order, achieving their one goal in thousands of different ways. Probably the synthetic blood affecting her brain, but maybe not. She could also feel his thoughts more clearly than she ever had, like someone wired their brains together, and he was being serious. She allowed him to continue, partly out of a need to hear what he had to say for himself, mostly because she was struggling to summon coherent words of her own.

"This world has stagnated. We were once an outgoing species, looking to the skies for advancement and enlightenment. For generations, we explored, seeking life and adventure, finding nothing and exhausting our resources. In the end, we turned inward, fighting amongst ourselves for the scraps that remained, congratulating ourselves when we bent everything to our will, believing we were gods, that the very rock we stood upon was our divine right. We have done terrible things, I have done terrible things.."

He petered out, leaving a silence that Kim felt powerless to avoid filling with her own wisdom.

"Yeah, me too."

It was the best she could manage. Caruthers radiated a small amount of confusion but offered no more exposition, verbal or otherwise, instead returning to the control panel which he had repurposed in order to monitor security alerts.

She couldn't possibly know that, yet she did.

"That doesn't look good, right?"

The amber orb that was flashing a direct route along the diorama representing the citadel appeared angrier than it had any right to, being a ball of photons with no anthropomorphic features.

"They have discovered the slain guards' corpses and will come here in order to locate and end us."

He used the matter-of-fact manner a toddler might employ to point out faeces filling their underpants, or the mother might use to explain, later, that the washing-machine was faulty and in desperate need of repair, or that the father might then have used to point out that their marriage was dead and had been for months before quaffing several alcoholic beverages and passing out on a pile of filthy laundry. There was minimal emotion, such that Kim almost missed the meaning. Almost.

"Corpses? Wait, what the hell happened?"

"The guards did not want me to take you, so I improvised a solution."

"You.. Did that for me? Why?"

"The world needs saving, and I believe that you.."

"It was fake, all of it. Benito did it to steal my technology. I thought.. Were you not in on it?"

A ripple of light pulsed upwards from the lowest tendrils, through the torso, outwards from his centre body mass and then up and out of the top of Caruthers' leathery form. Kim felt the static electricity build around him, and the hair on her head lift and stand on end. She pulled her hands away from the glinting metallic-looking platform edges, but not quick enough.

"Ow!"

"Indeed, he planned it that way, although he did not make me privy to all the detail until much later.."

"So.."

"Stop talking, please. The explosion was accidental, and orders of magnitude bigger than expected, but Benito repurposed the disaster to lure you out of the laboratory. He demolished a crystal mine, once decommissioned, but it didn't fully contain the energy and fissures opened that have been seeping deadly radiation since."

She waited to be sure he'd finished, which seemed to be the case.

"And?"

"You have plans where we do not. We can make this right, with your great ideas and my authority."

"I.."

The orange ball turned red and started tracking back toward their location with a great deal of speed.

"We have to go, now."

The main entranceway opened, revealing some of Caruthers' personal guard, who seemed surprised to see Kim breathing and mobile, enough so that Caruthers could get his shots out before they drew their weapons. He didn't aim to kill, or if he had, he missed, by a lot. Kim watched from behind a chair as they lifted themselves and squared off against their boss.

She could not hear, or feel, what was being discussed, but it ended with a positive tone.

"Kimberley, we must go now. This pair will escort us as far as the engineering deck and then prevent our capture as long as their life-force allows, but we must depart immediately."

Kim remained light-headed from the whole nearly dying drama, and running wasn't a strength, so the journey was a more lethargic affair than planned. Along the way, they ducked through several detours designed to disorient their trackers, and also allowing for collecting provisions. Kim wanted to ask about the food-cubes, but given a lack of vegetarian option, and a desperate need for nutrients, she held onto the question for a less manic time and enjoyed the meat, which in that instant tasted yummier than anything she'd ever eaten. Up ahead, Caruthers was emitting confident thoughts while forging ahead, well, mostly ahead. Behind, the escorts were thinking less polite things, bordering on insurrection, but never quite getting there. She wondered if they would survive being caught since they were just following orders, but wasn't confident.

"We have arrived."

The space felt familiar, bearing a striking resemblance to all the others. It was dark, with what appeared to be brown velour covering the walls, and it was big enough to fit at least three tennis courts with enough height to engage in exuberant lobbing. At its centre were a couple of contraptions she hadn't seen before, large and mechanical, and unlike anything else aboard. Their outer skin was metal, or maybe rock that looked like metal, with pipework protruding from every surface. A panel with actual mechanical switches stood to one side of the nearest machine, each of which occupied less than a couple of square meters of floor space. Caruthers forged ahead to the first, dragging Kim along with him, dark thoughts clouding his mind from the bottom up, becoming thicker and angrier the closer they got until a spark fired across his synapses.

"Bollocks!"

Kim checked the straps around her shoulders one more time, hoping to find them loose and unsuitable, instead finding that she couldn't move her arms and that the circulation to her feet was becoming suspect. Outside the pod, Caruthers was making final preparations to send her to the surface. He was fussing around the controls while one of his guards pointed to lights that blinked on and then off while he tried to wrangle the locator dots into a pattern that approximated a safe landing. It needed to be somewhere she could survive that wasn't too far from her final destination, but if they didn't hurry, would instead be a hypoxic death inside this tin can.

"And you'll follow behind, right?"

She'd asked a few times, never quite receiving an answer, or at least not one she liked. Caruthers looked up from the panel and fixed his eyes on hers, something she found uncomfortable, but he'd earned it so she endured. He said nothing. From the far side of the room, where they'd entered a few minutes before, the second guard projected a loud telepathic warning that they'd discovered their location. The silent screaming preceded some audible banging from the other side of the portal, showing weapon fire.

"The doorway is extremely sturdy. It will secure me enough time to complete this task, so do not worry unduly, Kimberley."

An extra loud bang suggested that his assessment might be optimistic, a feeling reinforced by his immediate sealing of the pod, almost mid-sentence. Even though the interior was soundproof, she could still hear his thoughts racing, and she finally understood why she had to leave first.

"You're not coming, are you?"

"There is damage to the second pod, and it is beyond repair. I cannot follow.."

"What the shit, C. I'm screwed! What precisely am I going to achieve without your help? I need.."

"No, you don't need me. You don't need anyone. That's why you are the only one capable."

A change in his attitude suggested a breach. She couldn't see anything since there were no view screens inside the pod, but she could feel Caruthers and his team arguing between themselves. Then a loud click brought all the outside noise in, filling her tiny space with angry shouting and explosions.

"I.. Don't know how.. Long we can.. Hold this room. I will.."

A series of thuds followed by a comical scream that was pure B-Movie, then a lull.

"I will attempt to maintain open channels of communication for as long a period as possible, but our enemy draws close. Reinforcements will arrive in short order, and they will have made better preparations, carry superior weaponry."

On a panel in front of Kim, five lights appeared, each a

different but equally pleasant shade of lilac, dark to light. After a short period, the leftmost changed hue to a deep red, then popped and fell dark.

"I'm scared. What do I do?"

"I shall be with you in a short while, Kimberley. Bear with me for a moment or two while I.."

A sudden cacophony that filled her space drowned him out like a sudden flood, knocking the air out of her lungs and immersing her so completely she couldn't breathe. Spots floated in her vision that expanded into pools of light as the explosions rang a bass sequence. High-pitches accompanied them, ricocheting off mid-tone screams and projectile percussion that knocked the pod just off straight and vibrated through the subframe into her body. The jolt broke the spell that had kept her from breathing, instinct taking over at that instant and filling her lungs with air, which she then expelled with a scream of her own, no doubt just as comical but impossible to hear over everything else.

Then there was silence, or a few seconds of it, broken by a thump-squeal that she felt in Caruthers' psyche, practically seeing through his eyes as he pumped an energy round into the cortex of the one remaining attacker. His thoughts then returned to her destination, which she could now see was the courtyard where the lab complex still stood stranded. Hopefully. In his mind, she could see the route from the landing spot toward the palace, and then inside, where she would meet a troop of comically large caricatures representing some sort of security. They were two-dimensional and not very intelligent, and the daydream version of her defeated them with ease, but it wasn't the reality either of them was inhabiting.

"I can't do that! I can't use your weapons, and even if I could, I don't have access to any. They're.."

"Be quiet. Get out of my mind and listen carefully to my words. You can do this. With focus and belief, you can over-come anything. That is the reason I enclosed you within the pod, and not me. You have vision, something we haven't had for many, many periods. You just have to believe in.."

"I'm sorry, but that's just bullshit. You get that from my head? Because I've heard that crap so many times that it sometimes pops up without me even realising it's there! I believed in myself, and all it got me was bullying and loneli-ness. Then I thought, maybe? So I tried it again, and this time it's got me nearly killed half a dozen times, by you at least twice, and then stuck in a tube aimed at a fucking army that wants to pull out my organs and turn them into food, or something, I don't know, I wasn't really paying attention. Worse, I nearly gave you guys the means to take over my fucking planet. I'm guessing here, but I don't think that would have helped with my popularity back home."

She ran out of things to say, receiving nothing back but silence. For a moment, she couldn't even feel Caruthers outside the pod, which had taken to vibrating with a frequency that was proving problematic for her overfull blad-der. The number of lights on her panel had reduced to two by this point, not helping with her overall vibe.

"Are you finished?"

There he was, as indignant as ever. She let him continue, not wanting to risk making him any angrier while he was in charge of the trajectory she would trace through the atmosphere.

"You are correct. Wishing for positive outcomes will not make them so, but not believing in the possibility of success guarantees your failure. Also, I did actually wish to end your existence. So, case in point, I guess. I.. What was I saying?"

"I think you were trying to convince me not to give up."

"Yes. I didn't like you. In fact, I despised your very being to the core. Still do, to some extent.."

"Gee, great talk, coach. I feel so much.."

"Shut up! For too long, I was comfortable with the way things were. I grew so accustomed that I feared change, which is what you brought, what you represented. I didn't want to believe it was necessary, and I certainly didn't want to believe that a lower life-form would be the catalyst that wrought it upon us. No. Sorry, I'm doing it again. You are not a lower life-form, just different."

"I.. Um, thanks."

A single light remained by this time, a beautiful puce colour, and the vibrations were now making their way into her bone marrow, which couldn't be healthy. Then they stopped. For just an instant, there was perfect stillness, silence. Then her entire world took a violent lurch downwards, nearly evacuating her bowels into the seat. The movement compressed her spine from the neck, which was why Caruthers had strapped her so tightly into the seat, but the limited mobility left to her made swallowing difficult, so she nearly choked on the bile that rose into her throat in sympathy with her stomach. On the panel, all five lights had relit, albeit in a different colour. Then, just as rapidly as it had started, the acceleration abated, and she found herself weightless in the small space. That lasted long enough for Kim to realise she didn't enjoy being weightless, before a gentle sagging in her protuberances combined with a series of aches in all of her limbs to remind her that having weight wasn't that great either. She heard a click from the intercom, followed by Caruthers voice. It felt odd hearing the words without being able to feel the meaning behind them, this being the first time it had happened.

"You will set down a short distance from my abode. Inside, you will use the following code to access the weapons vault that.."

"No way. I'm just going to wait until you arrive, and then.."

"I won't be arriving. The barricade erected here will not survive further incursions, and once it has failed, I will perish alongside my men inside this chamber."

"No. That.. Can't be right."

"I have sustained a fatal wound. A guardsman punctured a ganglion connecting several of my internal functions to my cortex, and most of my internal fluids are leaving this plane for another. I can only barely hold this conversation. My remaining strength certainly does not allow for wielding a weapon."

"I.."

That was it.

She had nothing else to add, so she ended with that fragment and listened as he explained how to access the cache under his home, describing the symbols with care since two of them were similar and a mistake in the sequence would trigger a self-defence mechanism that would probably make the situation untenable, being an explosive that would incinerate anything within two lengths, which Kim worked out to be around five miles.

"Be yourself, Kimberley. Don't change who you are for others and don't let Benito.."

The last few words stretched out, syllables drawing to breaking point, like an unfamiliar language coerced into a parody of meaning. The 'to' of Benito's name followed a pause that almost made it a unique word of its own, with a downward lilt suggesting nothing further would be forthcoming. A loud electric thump, punctuated by a terminal click that shut the communication channel, guaranteeing that would be the case.

* * *

THE POD LANDED IN AN ISOLATED PATCH OF VEGETATION. It was just outside the walls that protected the palace court-yard from prying eyes, or insurrection. Kim would need bucket-loads of each to breech that sanctuary and succeed in her mission.

Taking her bearings from the ever present larger sun triangulated with the relative positions of the other two, or one, since one of them was below the horizon, she made for what she hoped would be the pathway that lead to Caruthers' home. In the clear, minus the distracting explosions and land movement, she could clear her thoughts and consider the route. This was handy, since there were several additional obstacles on the ground since she'd last traversed the area.

It took half an hour to find the path and assume the correct orientation. Behind her, the palace walls were standing repaired. In front, now that she was back in what passed for civilisation, the decorative planting was clear, and the buildings were all fully rebuilt or torn out of existence altogether, depending on the level of damage they'd sustained. Kim knew her destination lay at least a further hour's travel away, if it still existed. The efficiency with which they'd affected repairs was almost unreal. There was always a chance that someone would demolish Caruthers' home. It'd sustained severe damaged after all?

She pushed the negativity out of her head and concentrated on the noises filling the surrounding air. Kim was listening intently for other life, knowing that avoiding it would give her the best chance of living to see sanctuary. What she found was disconcerting.

Nothing. It was as if they'd had a complete evacuation of the area, with even the sentient moss gone from its usual perches. like they had started the rebuild and then just disappeared into thin air.

Kim kept to the verges, affording her cover and safety if a group of armed soldiers were to turn up and start firing. Even inside the margins, though, she sensed that something was wrong. The tall shrubbery, once so imposing and dangerous, now seemed sparse and substantially less sharp than earlier. She'd brushed against it a few times now with no blood loss whatsoever. At a corner where cover grew scarce, and she needed to break into a run and cross sides, Kim inspected the vegetation, which was indeed thinner and less full of danger than before. The razor blade leaves had taken on a dull lustre, with the edges barely sharper than children's scissors, the plastic ones that can't cut butter. As she moved her hand through the thicket, those leaves fell to the ground and joined a pile of their friends already there and rotting. She moved onto the path, a sense of dread building inside that was comforting, in that if she was right she wouldn't meet anyone today, but also terrifying in that if they abandoned the area, and everything was dying, that couldn't possibly be a good sign.

It was getting late when she arrived. The house was still standing as before, with large sections collapsed and several hanging on by sheer luck, or bloody-mindedness. The entrance was open, so she wouldn't need to remember the entry code here, which was helpful since she couldn't. Inside, a thick layer of dust was settling on what was once clean, blanketing the floor, furniture and extensive collection of nick-knacks rendered to debris by the quakes, and the fire-fight, and, well, her. She picked up a tome, resurrected the living room bookshelf, and placed the book carefully on a middle shelf. Kim then watched as the structure listed to the left and fell forwards, narrowly missing her toes, which she withdrew at the last second, willing the shelving to stay upright as a sign, a good omen.

"Christ on a flipping bike!"

The vault lived in Caruthers' bedroom, which she now understood wasn't actually a bedroom but a rest-space in which he communed with the part of themselves that extended into the outer dimension. While laying down upon a comfortable padded mat that most definitely, according to Caruthers, was not a bed. It didn't move, not one inch, no matter how hard she pushed, so Kim laid herself down and tried not to cry. Caruthers had given his life for her, sent her back to his home, believed in her ability to put things right, and she couldn't even move the bed to get to his stash.

For a second she wondered if he'd hidden anything else under there, imagining alien pornography, magazines full of well written 'articles' alongside double-page spreads showing. Well, she wasn't sure. The creatures didn't wear clothes most of the time, and she was pretty sure they reproduced using technology, or some-such, and they most certainly didn't..

"Huh?"

They didn't sleep, and this wasn't a bed, it was a yoga mat, a glorified floor covering. The opening wasn't under it; it was inside it. Kim rolled onto her elbows and pushed herself up onto all fours before crawling up to where the wall met the mat, rummaged along the seam, and then pushed the sticky lump that she hoped was a button. The floor fell downwards like a trapdoor, dropping her into the opening, which was deep enough to be scary, but shallow enough that no permanent damage occurred when she hit the floor and spilled backwards into the hidden stairway. Once at the bottom, a cursory check of various joints was enough to calm the nerves before pressing her hand into the glowing gelatinous rectangle recessed into the anonymous wall. It felt cold, then warm, then hot, then cold again. Then Kim remembered she was only supposed to use a couple of fingers and withdrew her fist just in time to avoid being scalded.

Warm, then hot, cold, hot, and hot again.

The rectangle changed colour, from blue to green, meaning there were only a few seconds to remember how to build the unlock code sequence. She thought back to what Caruthers had taught her.

'Lesser being.'

That didn't help.

"Come on! Think."

'If it is a higher temperature, then the code begins with a warmer hue, the higher..'

"Got it!"

Kim dragged her hand through the gluey rectangle, right to left, watching the colour change until it hit a pleasant cherry red, then, after a pause, moved further right until the lights went out. A loud click showed success, or impending death, with Kim's continued existence a few seconds later favouring the former.

A short while later, after an eternity of internal panic, the door opened to reveal the inner space, the size of a medium walk-in wardrobe, every surface decked out with weapon shaped technology that almost screamed.

Some had lights that blinked a repeating pattern and Kim decided that they probably needed some kind of specialist knowledge to operate, so she stuck to lightweight guns she could hold without cramping, and either had no lights, or in a pinch, lights that stayed off, or on.

This limited her to four weapons. One of them was the size of a matchbox, but weighed as much as a car, or at least something she couldn't carry, so maybe only as much as a small pony, but still too much.

Of the remaining three, one was a comical orange and green colour. It made a muted farting noise when she picked it up, so she put it right back down. On the rack, it emitted an unpleasant retching noise that could have been a sample of her own voice, and on closer inspection, Kim discovered an unflattering portrait of her with comical buttocks and stink-lines.

With the remaining two items, a pistol sized, pistol shaped thing Kim was hoping was a pistol, and a rifle shaped like a rocket launcher, neatly draped around a shoulder, or tucked into a belt loop, she thought about her next move.

It wasn't a pleasant thought.

She'd been wrong about the radiation, back up in the citadel, isolated in her laboratory, but only because they misled her. The samples were all prepared to trick her into thinking she was making progress. Even then, though, she'd made a series of mistakes, perhaps overestimated the required amount of reagent by a factor of ten, at least. Any apparent success was probably because of a lack of accuracy in the measuring and testing equipment. She could see that. In fact, tainted samples explained any effects. That all made perfect sense, too. What made little sense, now that she considered it, was that the sample she smuggled on board without supervision also reacted to her formula, and positively. There was only one straightforward explanation. There were a bunch of convoluted, complex concepts she could wrangle into a plausible set of ideas, but sometimes simple is best, and this time she was going to trust her instincts. That, and the fact everything was dead or dying all around her.

The radiation was real.

Maybe Ben didn't realise. Someone did, otherwise they wouldn't have abandoned the area, but it wasn't common knowledge, at least back up in the citadel. She had a clean read on the creatures' thoughts now, probably because of the synthetic blood running through her body, but she'd had a lot of practise too, and all she could feel when nearby was triumph.

This meant she had two problems to deal with. One, destroy all the remaining beacon technology at the lab, including the remaining notes. And then two, neutralise the radiation before it rendered everything uninhabitable.

Now back upstairs, Kim collapsed into a chair and stared up at the ceiling. There was a scorch mark, from an unmaker, where it had reflected, or ricocheted, whatever energy weapons did. Caruthers had meant that shot for her, a kill shot. He'd missed her, but she had a deep-seated feeling that it had killed her just the same.

Kim threw her right arm out at an unseen assailant, rocking backwards and over the edge of her perch, falling with a thump off of the chair and into her usual unco-ordinated pile of limbs on the floor. Now fully awake, she unfolded herself and tried to stand up, finding her legs still very much asleep and, therefore, failing. There wasn't an easy way to gauge how long she'd been unconscious. Even if she could read the patterns that formed on what she imagined were probably clocks, she hadn't made a note before she passed out. It had the hallmarks of a lengthy sleep, aching limbs and creases cut deep into her cheeks, but in reality, she'd only been out for a couple of minutes. Long enough to sink into REM and dream about whatever woke her.

Then she felt it. All around. An ionising energy that permeated the air and made her hair stand on end, that buzzed through her synapses and added weight to the lead already in her stomach. It was something she'd only felt a few times before, and it meant that somewhere, probably nearby, a vast amount of energy was being wrangled into one place in order to coax a reluctant wormhole into existence.

Benito was firing up his beacon.

Out of the door a few seconds later, weapons draped uncomfortably around her form and lacking the fitness to get anywhere with any speed, Kim lumbered back along the road that lead to the courtyard and her laboratory complex. She knew Ben had been there. He 'rescued' her notes when she needed them in the citadel. She'd also taught him how everything worked, but there was no way he could have got the original equipment to fire up. The power was there. The reactor they installed would last another thousand years. Of course, it would then turn into a tiny black hole and compress the building into a sphere the size of a mid-range sedan, but the targeting equipment was still a previous generation. She hadn't been able to return and retrofit any of the discoveries and improvements concocted aboard the citadel. Either he'd figured it out himself, or one of the Kevins had, or maybe he was just stupid enough to try it anyway after she destroyed his new toy.

The road was shorter than she remembered. After half an hour of puffing along, taking little care to avoid any patrols since there still didn't seem to be anyone around, she made it to the courtyard. Once there, she could see her lab standing isolated in several hundred feet of clearing in every direction. After catching her breath, she took a few steps toward the structure, hearing the chatter before covering more than a few feet, and still hidden by a large ornamental tree-like statue, or bush, or whatever it was. There was a patrol heading her way.

"..am not feeling so well this period. I have been experiencing several symptoms of ailment. How about yourself?"

"I informed you of your folly! Consuming such a weight of celebration-foods was always going to result in the loosening of your recycling-sphincter. Pay it no heed, instead focus on our task."

"But why us? When they issued the recall, everyone else returned to the palace.."

"Because we are the strongest, the vanguard that will pierce our enemy and leave her empty dermis drying under the sun."

"And you are certain it has nothing to do you with spilling clotted slop all over.."

"Enough! The creature could be nearby."

The voices sounded clear and loud, enough that Kim couldn't believe they weren't within a couple of feet, when, in fact, the guardsmen stood clear across the opposite side of the courtyard. Their ceremonial medals reflected as pinpoints of intense light set against the matte leather of their remaining, unadorned skin. The voices weren't voices at all. They were telepathic projections, which Kim was receiving much more strongly than she had previously. Alongside the clearer connection, there was a burning in her arms and legs, or more precisely, a pulling in her blood vessels that, where exposed to the suns, drew heat into her skin. A familiar pounding announced a headache would arrive soon.

"Just great."

"What did you say?"

Only she hadn't. It was just an idea, which meant that they could read her just as clearly as she could read them.

"I think I can feel the alien presence. Over there!"

They ran in the wrong direction, but it wouldn't take long for them to figure that out, so Kim took off as fast as she could for the building, trying her best to keep the towering structure between her and their ocular sensors, while forcing a simultaneous effort to keep her mind as blank as possible. It worked, to some extent.

"I feel a growing sensation of fatigue, as if I could not lift my legs, and pain in my fleshy extensions where they flap free. I.. I don't have legs or any extensions."

"Quiet, idiot!"

Kim covered half the distance before the guards turned, but all they glimpsed was the building.

They kept moving in the wrong direction for another sixty seconds, enough time for Kim to reach the entrance. It was already open, which she'd expected, and sentient moss infested every surface, which was typical of the day she'd been having. Kim wrapped her arms the best she could in the short sleeves of her suit, then tiptoed inside and hit the lock-down panel, which made a pitiful squeaking noise, lit up amber for a second and then died.

She couldn't help herself.

"Shit!"

"The alien craft! It is there, hurry!"

Ominous dread, rooted in the lack of power at the entrance hatch, overcame Kim. It grew outwards into an enormous tree of amiss. Cutting across the dusty floor was a track deep enough to mar the metal grating, and a crisp energy permeated the atmosphere, assaulting her tastebuds with a tingly metallic sensation akin to licking the terminals on a battery. Unable to seal off the entryway, Kim sprinted for the stairwell that would carry her first to the atrium and then onwards to her personal quarters, where losing her pursuers was possible, being the only portal in the entire building fitted with a mechanical lock. She'd only covered the first corridor when their presence filled her brain. Near the entrance but staying put, unwilling to follow deeper into the structure. Now that their proximity had shrunk, untangling their emotions from hers proved more difficult, taking seconds she didn't have. That everybody was simultaneously experiencing the same emotion made that task even trickier.

Fear.

Their nervous systems heightened to ultra-vigilance, tendrils tensed, intrusive thoughts begging them not to enter. This gave Kim enough time to clear the stairs and cover the distance to the atrium, where high suns were reflecting a beautiful pattern on the walls as they had twice every twenty-four hours since she arrived, but even here, something was wrong. There were cracks in the concrete spider-webbing their way up from a cavernous dent at the base near where one of the ballistic-glass walls had towered up toward the sky. Along with the dent, the glass was gone. Well, not gone, rendered into a gigantic transparent jigsaw puzzle and then scattered across every surface. In fact, there was ample glass to account for the dome itself, which, now that she checked properly, was also gone.

Outside, the two cowards were calling in her position, and while they might be reluctant to enter, Kim felt certain that Joseph and his elite crew probably wouldn't be, so she pivoted, mentally, to Plan B and physically, on one leg, heading back for the command floor.

The wave of nostalgia lasted a few seconds, overwhelming her with familiarity like a giant hug from a favourite relative. A deep-seated tightness set into her chest as she set to work, destroying everything she could find that related to operating her machine, shortening her breath. The smaller weapon made light work of document management, disintegrating everything she pointed it at, apart from the metals in the desks and chairs. Once she'd reduced the notes to black confetti, she turned her attention to the equipment itself, only then realising that it was missing. All of it, the entire central console, along with the core and all the connecting cables, were just not present anymore. Kim climbed into the space it had once occupied, finding her tools left behind at the bottom of a deep trench dug into the floor so deeply that it exposed the reinforcing metal bars. There was a secondary trench furrowing a deep route off the floor via the exit, heading for higher ground up the stairwell and then outwards, which explained the missing dome. The beacon wasn't here anymore, but she could still feel it powering up, which meant it was nearby.

"She is inside, sir. We have prevented her escape by covering.."

"Be silent, or I will silence you."

Not Joseph, but someone equally confident, someone she hadn't met. There wasn't much time if she stood any realistic chance of preventing the machine powering fully.

She had to leave.

But not through the main exit, since that would draw their attention, and probably significant gunfire, which would reduce her chances of reaching the palace to around zero. Kim stowed her weapons again and doubled back, heading once again for her quarters. The new guy was inside before she reached the sanctuary, but it wasn't important now. He wouldn't find her soon enough, so she got redressed in the one remaining set of clean coveralls. They were the ones she'd been saving for the trip home. Kim then added the guns and then climbed into the waste chute outside the room, as quietly as possible, slid into the narrow channel before plummeting the twenty feet down into the pile of desiccated and decaying matter that sat in the trash compactors below.

* * *

THE LANDING WAS HARD. IT WAS ONTO A PILE OF DRIED mould-enriched food waste wrapped in old underwear atop a heap of rotting something that was still moist and hot even after months alone in the dark. It helped a little, but not sufficiently to prevent the impact hurting quite a lot. Getting upright was just as hard. Not because it hurt, although it did. Kim banged both shins hard into projecting pipework as she fell, drawing blood with a gloomy thud that refused to echo, and then while standing she found it a second time, hurting worse. The oppressive darkness was deep enough that she wasn't certain where upright was, or what sticky horrors her hands were encountering. She brushed off what she could and hoped in silence that no one heard or sensed her plan. One foot eased out of the quagmire whilst the other stuck fast, so after a clammy stagger that tasted of vomit, Kim fought herself free and headed for a wall, any wall. Once there, she felt along and around, clockwise, for the emergency alert panel. It wouldn't work, of course. Even with full power, which wasn't an option, the compactor backed up several months ago, jamming fast in a manner she wasn't able, or willing, to repair. No, the panel wasn't her final destination, but it did mark where the inspection hatch sat. Probably. She hadn't been paying a lot of attention during the safety briefings since it was Carl's job to keep this stuff moving. When she located it, a large flat panel with written instructions she couldn't read because of the dark, and braille she couldn't read because she never learned, she reached up and grabbed the highest rung she could reach on the ladder, with both hands, hauling herself up far enough to get her feet on, before climbing the ten feet to the door. After banging her fist, then her head, and then one already bruised shin on the frame, she made it out and into the space beyond that was supposed to be bathed in emergency lighting that had its own power source. It wasn't, but she was certain this passageway was clear of obstacles, and of where it led. Once through, another hatch swung open outwards into a central walkway. Kim took her time. The walkway provided a link between the lower level and the central stairway, taking her past the atrium. Any noise would draw attention from anyone inside, so she felt for any minds that might be nearby, finding nothing. She pushed outward with more vigour, eliciting a thunderclap-headache that eased as fast as it appeared. Still nothing, then just as she grasped the lever to unseal the portal.

"Are you certain it hasn't perished? I haven't felt a presence in several periods now."

"No! We will find it. We must. Go on, inside the great hall where it nested."

Only two, the pair she encountered previously in the courtyard. There was no sign of the others, and given that these guys were idiots, Kim felt safe leaving, so she unlocked the heavy hatch and pushed. She allowed just a crack of light to enter her hiding spot, giving her eyes time to adjust and her thoughts time to settle down to a moderate panic.

Kim got as far as the entrance without being seen by anybody other than the creepy wisdom tree, which offered her nothing but scorn but didn't expose her position. Then, after picking her way between the fear-fungi and out into the courtyard, she tried one more brief scan of the thought-waves to be sure she was alone prior to heading toward the palace. It was a beautiful clear morning, or evening, with no wind and a pleasant warmth in the air. The bushes were humming; the fungi screaming in harmony and the way gentle underfoot.

She managed around ten feet.

"You will halt! Now!"

It came from behind. The structure hid the creature from sight, who was waiting quietly in the shadows for her to leave. Stupid. How hadn't she read them? Kim ran. There was a lot of ground to cover, and she wasn't quick, and she was lugging heavy equipment that banged annoyingly into her sides with every stride, but.

But nothing. It was a doomed attempt, and she knew it. A pair of alien creatures sped past her to one side, then another, both converging ahead and cutting off her route to safety. She tried to dart to one side, a zig where she hoped they were expecting a zag, but only tripped on her own feet and sprawling out onto the ground, which, close up, wasn't as clean as it had appeared. A long shadow eclipsed hers, looming from behind as another creature moved in front, tendrils sweeping the dirt away as he hovered up to her.

Kim gave up. She rolled onto her back and looked up at the sun as silhouettes gathered into a dark halo around her vision. She could feel their anger and triumph, but there was something else there, too.

"We have it! Now we can take it to Benito, and he will reward us with.."

"No!"

The voice was scratchy, broken but still confident, reasoned. It continued.

"This is a chance. We may not have another."

The statement was confusing to everybody, not just Kim. She could feel anger building into fury, eclipsing everything else. Something cold and hard pressed into her shoulder, easily piercing the fabric and several outer layers of skin. It was a fight to stay still and face her end with some dignity. Kim clenched everything and waited, feeling blood run into sweat and soak her skin. The lance pushed a little further but stopped short of serious wounding.

"We have our prize! Flay it where it lies and take the hide. We can fly it as our standard as we approach."

The blade end nudged downward, slicing a neat incision and letting more blood. Free-flowing adrenaline numbed the pain at that moment. Kim started wondering whether that would still be the case if they skinned her alive.

"Enough!"

The older voice returned, croaky and unsure, lacking some of its previous reason, a measure of nervous tension filling that gap.

"Harm this creature and I will end you where you stand."

There was a momentary silence that stretched out over five seconds, or maybe thirty-five, before the spear withdrew from her shoulder. As she watched, the weapon swept upwards in a short arc before lunging forwards over Kim, as if thrown, but clasped in semi-visible tentacles that grew with distance travelled. It reached as far as the creature standing at her feet, where a tree-limb parried it hard left and then continued round, carried by momentum, before being hurled back at the attacker. He wasn't as quick, taking the full force of the throw into his torso and falling backwards. The tree limb, in actuality more like an entire tree, roots included, then dropped to the ground mere inches from Kim, who had rolled hard-left out of the direct path of descent. The spear jerked backwards, still attached to its erstwhile wielder, before he dropped it onto Kim's back, where it stayed for a moment before rolling to the right and falling to her hand. Overtaken by sudden bravery, she grabbed the weapon and jumped dramatically to her feet.

Or tried to.

It was much heavier than it looked, and although she could get her fingers around the shaft, it wouldn't leave the ground with her, so what should have been a dramatic fighting pose followed by a heroic lunge, then escape, wound up being a comical stumble backwards into one creature, who reacted by jumping backwards while throwing her forwards, where she tripped over the spear and onto her hands and knees, grazing everything. While Kim stumbled, the first attacker regained his footing and produced a second, shorter, angrier blade full of topographically impossible edges, which he thrust forwards with lethal intent, but not, as she was expecting, at her. It sailed over before cutting an arc toward the tree-thrower, humming as it split the air, then flew into the distance as he ducked under it and sliced through the attached tendrils with his own.

By now, the bystanders were getting restless, and minor squabbles began breaking out at the fringes. Kim took a chance and rolled out underneath one pair that was engaged in the slap-wrestling you'd expect from toddlers, all holding and shoving but no genuine risk of harm. She got a good number of feet back toward the lab before the tree from earlier flew over her head and landed just past her feet. Kim was too close to stop so she ran straight into it, taking a branch to the solar-plexus and knocking all the remaining bravery out of her system.

The spear followed, burying itself pointy-bit first into the tree limb, splitting it into two pieces that fell away, one of which rolled into Kim, pinning her to the ground. As she lay trapped under the weight of the whatever-it-was that the tree comprised, and it definitely wasn't wood, she could once again see the creatures surround her, blocking the light from her peripheral vision and focussing her eyes up toward the sun. A kick to her flank emptied the remaining air from her lungs and sent stars swirling through her peripheral vision, but she didn't react, hoping that playing dead would be an acceptable substitution for the genuine article.

"It is still alive. You nearly ended it with that throw."

Kim looked to her left, where the kick had originated, straight into the tall leathery form of Joseph. She followed his torso upwards, meeting his eyes for an uncomfortable moment before looking away. There was anger there.

But not directed at her.

"We need your help, Kimberley."

She'd figured most of it out before Joe started speaking, but if the last few months had taught her anything, it was to stop making assumptions and take more advice, or perhaps less advice, Kim wasn't completely certain about that second part yet, but it couldn't hurt to hear everyone out once in a while.

The original plan had been Joe's, and it was a doozy. Since she wouldn't leave the beacon lab, and since they needed her to tell them how it worked, and so couldn't just kill her, they needed to give her a reason, and saving the world seemed like just enough stakes to get the job done. Benito, however, wasn't sure that they would convince her so easily, so, unbeknownst to Joe, he doubled the explosives, and the resulting explosion was much larger than originally planned, blowing a hole in the disused crystal mine and damaging a nearby reactor.

Of course, nobody realised that until later, no.

It wasn't until they started clearing up and rebuilding that things had gone wrong and a new and unexplained sickness swept through the crews working in the immediate vicinity, killing a few weaker souls, incapacitating the rest.

"Go on."

"This radiation idea of yours. I had Kevin look into it, observe the readings as they came in and there is a stubborn cloud of matter that refuses to disperse.."

"Because of the mountains, and.."

She was doing it again. Kim stopped herself mid-sentence and adjusted her back to a more comfortable position. They'd camped out in Caruthers' living room and it was tight, but there were snacks.

"I'm sorry, please go on."

"Yes. It won't disperse because, well, yes, mountains and the atmosphere is poisoning anyone that comes into contact. It would be fine if the terrain contained it, but it seeps and expands as more gas escapes the mines and reactor."

She put up her hand like a schoolgirl, hoping the gesture would translate.

"I.. Do you wish to void your internal waste receptacles again?"

Close enough.

"Ah, no. It's just.. Has anyone shut the reactor down?"

"We have, but the gas cloud escaped the mine complex, vast amounts of it, that are now unconstrained and adding to the increasing deadly.. What now?"

"I'm so sorry. How are you still alive? Is it getting less deadly?"

Joe pulled himself upright and pressed into the skin of his upper body with a few tentacles where Kim saw a dull, red glow, and beneath that, she could see the creature he really was spreading across the dimension most of his impossible form occupied. The skin was so thin that she could see his soul.

"Oh. I guess not. How am I not affected?"

A familiar voice answered the query from within the ambient hubbub, albeit in a lower register and containing a new and uncomfortable sounding rasp.

"Your form exists in one plane, one dimension and this radiation is harmless to matter here, penetrating only a few nano-lengths into solid matter, but it permeates our sister-dimension, and the damage it does there is enormous."

"Kevin? I thought you were.. Look, I guess.. Hang on. Caruthers used a synthetic blood to save my life. Would that be affected?"

Kevin projected a telepathic laugh that wasn't entirely full of good humour.

"The fluids in your body provide combustible elements to our machinery. It is entirely your good fortune that they approximate your biological life-liquids, and frankly, I am astounded that your body didn't reject them."

Kim suddenly felt quite itchy, all over her body, but also inside. She rubbed her torso, then pinched the skin on her arm and inspected a vein near the surface, which, now that she really checked, wasn't the right colour at all.

"So, am I going to die?"

"Of course, all things perish."

"No. I mean, today, or this week, will this stuff kill me?"

Joe coughed a full stop to the conversational detour, an abrupt sound pushed through a clenched mouth. Or maybe he just needed to cough. She'd never heard him do it before, and it sounded rough, like a chain-smoker with emphysema rough. Everyone stopped talking or thinking about talking and waited for him to continue.

"We watched you work up on the citadel and you said you had found the solution, so we manufactured it once everyone abandoned the facilities. I have many cubic units at my disposal. I just need your help.."

Kim felt a sudden chill.

"Destroy it, all of it. Don't let anyone anywhere near it, do you understand?"

The sudden outburst brought all eyes onto her. Kevin broke the silence.

"I.. Don't. Why? Your solution worked on the sample. You were certain of that."

"I screwed up. When I checked later, I was an order of magnitude out. If you use any of it, you'll kill everything in the region."

Murmurs of discontent rumbled into the room, enough that Joe banged the base of the weapon he'd taken from Kim earlier onto the floor hard enough to splinter the tiling. He didn't speak though, Kevin did.

"Then all is hopeless. I had believed that you could save us, that you.."

"Woah. I didn't say we couldn't contain the damage. I just said don't use the even more poisonous gas. My initial plan was the better choice, but I need someone to help me get my notes from the citadel. They're in my room. I worked out a way to, you know what, the details don't matter. Just collect everything with the words proton or pump printed somewhere."

An uncomfortable silence smothered the room, this time tinged with hot emotion that warmed Kim's neck and face with an involuntary blush while she clenched her fists and pounded a thigh.

"Well?"

"We have no access to the citadel. Benito has it secured, and everyone of us here is a declared traitor."

Kim wasn't sure she'd heard Joe correctly.

"I.. Wait, what? Does he? He doesn't know about any of this?"

"Oh, he knows. The monster watched as several of his inner circle, those he'd sent to this region, perish slowly over periods and he had me banish any who spoke of this illness, making me complicit in these endings. When I tried to reason with him, he banished me as well."

"So what the fuck is he doing?"

More of the embarrassed silence, now with added furtive glances. It was Kevin that spoke first.

"He is preparing to enslave your people and take your world as his own. A new utopia free of.."

"Stop! What? How is he planning? I destroyed all the tech. He has no means.."

"The machine you destroyed was a mere prototype. He had a much more powerful system constructed here at the palace, once he integrates the power source from your laboratory, well."

Just like that, icicles clogged Kim's heart and froze inside her veins. When Joe picked up the proverbial ball from where Kevin fumbled, his voice carried a heavy weight and a reluctant vibrato.

"I will understand if saving us is a second priority. We will assist you in the curtailing of Benito's plan.."

Kim raised her hand, but didn't wait for anybody to acknowledge her.

"How long until he can make it work?"

"I.. Kevin?"

"The last I saw, he was still having difficulties with the

couplings. Without my help, it will take him into the next cycle at least to.."

"Perfect. That's like, what, a week? Whatever. We need the notes from the ship. I already did the calculations and we don't have the time for me to redo them. Can anybody figure out a plan to get aboard without getting caught? What range does the transporter have?"

Kevin cut her off.

"This isn't science-fiction, the transporters can only cover.. Oh."

"What's 'oh'? Can we use them or not?"

"We can, but you will not like it."

* * *

He was right. She didn't like it. It wasn't her problem, though, and she had more pressing matters to attend to right now. While the largest contingent of their team had been gone for hours now, bringing their plan to get back aboard the citadel to fruition, Kim and Joseph had left for the palace on what she hoped wouldn't prove a suicide mission. It sounded good when they were discussing it in the study, with a bunch of friendly creatures covering every doorway, and a ready supply of something that looked, smelled and tasted exactly like smokey bacon flavoured potato crisps, but were, apparently, not something she wanted to ask questions about. Now she was out and exposed, in the field, with a Joseph who was just not the super soldier he'd once been, the tight knot balled up inside her stomach combined with a flop-sweat she couldn't shake to tell her she should have gone with the others.

"How far is this entrance?"

Kim had asked already, several times, and just as before, Joe refused to answer. His skin was now so thin that patches had worn away completely, revealing a writhing mass of other worldly inexplicability that itself was not in the best health. She tried not to stare, in part because she understood it was unacceptable, but also because she was going to be having nightmares about this if she survived, and didn't want to feed her brain too many gruesome details.

They had been following the outer wall of the palace, which was seamless rock as far as she could see, an unbroken straight line running for miles and stretching upwards into the wispy clouds dotting the tangerine sky. It was of a colour that blended with the sky, making it almost invisible unless close up, a deliberate choice that protected the structure from aerial attack during the many wars that had erupted there, but it also gave a nice unbroken view across the courtyard from pretty much any angle, so that was nice. The only problem was that it made finding the entrance difficult. Not the main entrance, a grand steel hued arch that was more than a kilometre tall and guarded on the outside by auto-killers, a type of self-targeting machine gun that fired balls of un-matter, a material that was technically illegal, but, you know, Benito being the king and all made that a moot point. No, the entrance they sought was the significantly less cere-monious side portal once frequented by trades-creatures plying their wares and services, but had lain disused for a lengthy period that Joe didn't explain well, but was probably over a millennium. They'd sealed it from inside and covered it over on the outside, but only enough to be aesthetically pleasing. Joseph, until recently the head of security, had inti-mate knowledge of all potential points of ingress, and he hoped he was the only one.

"Here."

He stopped dead in a manner that left Kim unable to avoid colliding head on. Joe was warm, and a lot more supple than the last time she'd made physical contact. He still possessed the old anger, though, and didn't hide it.

"Must you be so clumsy?"

This section of wall looked like all the others, at least until Joseph struck it with a barrage of tentacled fury, at which point a panel the size of a small filing cabinet fell away, revealing a recessed portal blocked by stone. Joe fired a single shot from the rifle Kim had purloined, disintegrating the blockage and clearing their way inside. He then handed her the weapon.

"Fire upon any who obstruct our way, and I mean anybody. Do you understand?"

"I.."

"Without hesitation! Our passage inside will be fraught. They may not be expecting us to gain entry from here, but they will expect us, and they will not hesitate."

He waited for a response. Kim didn't like the idea, but it was clear he wasn't moving unless she was all in.

"Yes sir. Without hesitation."

That was the full extent of her pep-talk. They slipped inside without saying another word, finding themselves in an old ante-chamber that had once welcomed traders and locals looking for employment, but no-one had used it since before human life existed on the earth. There was a blanket of dust thick enough that the bottom layers had fossilised.

"I don't think.."

A barely audible creaking that grew into a loud crack deep inside the shadows engulfing the farthest side of the chamber halted Kim in her tracks, creating a hyper-aware-ness that allowed her to spot the glint and lurch hard right away from the imminent danger. That threat turned out to be an ageing overhead sign, which fell from corroded hooks set in the ceiling, clattering to the ground around fifteen feet from where Kim stood.

"I believe you may be a little tense. You must relax or your focus.."

"Yeah, yeah."

Trying to style out the unnecessary move, Kim had rolled into a desk, causing a mini-avalanche of particulates that almost buried her, but also uncovered a picture frame that showed the king in full regalia, a king that wasn't Benito.

"Caruthers wasn't lying, was he?"

Not waiting for an answer, Kim headed for the exit into the palace, which wasn't sealed in any meaningful way, and swung open into an empty, spacious, and brightly lit corridor. Joseph clarified they weren't to speak past this point, something he now reinforced by squeezing at her brain a little, numbing her left side. They covered twenty feet, as far as a large hallway, before being discovered.

It wasn't much of a fight. There were two on the patrol, and they seemed very surprised to see them, enough that Kim fired twice before either raised their weapons. She missed with both shots, but Joseph had a truer aim, and took care of it.

"I am proud of you, Kimberley. You shot without hesitation."

It felt like a participation trophy. A pat on the head, such as a patient father, might give his wayward progeny after their first dry night. Kim didn't care. It was the nicest thing she'd heard in days. That lasted until the subsequent wave appeared, or around fifteen seconds, not quite enough to reach the next chamber.

The new guys had superior training and came fully loaded. Three concussive blasts passed over Kim's head as she ducked behind an ornamental pedestal. A fourth shot disintegrated her cover into glowing embers and the resulting shockwave pushed her over onto her back. Kim instinctively squeezed the trigger mount on her weapon, sending another shot wide and high into the decorative ceiling, dropping a large section of it onto the attackers. To her left, Joseph picked off a straggler with a precision shot that vacated his cranium, leaving the remaining meat to fall to the ground and empty unholy contents over his now deceased comrades.

"They are aware of our presence."

"No shit.."

"The sanctum lay in this direction, but there is significant ground to cover. I will rush ahead and draw their fire. You must follow behind. Use me as a shield, I will.."

"Woah! Stop right there. I need you to.."

"You need to stop Benito! I cannot reconfigure the machine. That is your task. I am merely here to get you the chance to perform it."

Kim could see beneath most of his skin covering now. Joe would not survive past the sun fall and they both knew it, but it still hurt. Kim felt tears welling in her eyes.

"Your body is leaking again. Have you sustained injury?"

"No, I.."

"Then we must go. Now."

He turned and rushed out through the chamber, via the enormous doorway set deep in the far wall, and into another corridor. Kim did her best to keep up, catching glimpses ahead when she could, feeling her chest burn as her lungs fought to keep up with the sudden demand for air, but what she saw of Joe was glorious. He established hundreds of tentacles, all an angry buzzing red, that swatted ahead, disarming enemies and absorbing projectiles. The effort needed just to stay with him left no capacity to help, so she took him at his word, keeping his body between her and the deadly fire raining down upon them. This got them into the chamber before the throne room, where Kim could finally do something useful, shooting dead the single remaining fighter left behind before he could adjust his aim sufficiently to hit them. In front, a blast door guarded by a contingent of elite guards wearing medals, Kim recognised them.

"Joseph, why are you doing this? Why have you turned your back on our leader?"

Joe raised himself up, ten feet into the air, allowing light from the crystal skylights that peppered the vaulted stone above to shine through his almost non-existent skin. He was disintegrating in front of them.

"You know why."

J oseph's breathing, if he'd ever breathed at all, laboured in short bursts. He sucked in air through porous membranes concealed within the leathery skin of his torso, then pushed out waste gas from a pouch, once just as invisible, now a proud mottled cherry coloured bulge to the right of where his chin would be if he was a squid.

A small but not insignificant vibration punctuated each breath. The elite guard had backed away, taking positions that prevented any further advance, but held off attacking for now. Each soldier maintained a vice-like grip on their weapons, and haunted eyes darted about with little under-standing and an unhealthy energy that permeated the atmosphere with a sense of approaching calamity. It was something that Kim was all too familiar with from successive failed attempts to understand human interaction. Now back on the ground, with no limbs visible to keep him upright, Joe watched his former friends with cold, hard eyes rapidly sinking into his disintegrating body.

"Are you telling me they don't know?"

Someone had to ask. It might as well be Kim. A twitch from the nearest flanking group drew her attention, but didn't develop into an answer. After a short stand-off, Joe pushed the point home.

"Well? Do you still not believe? Answer her truthfully."

Ahead, covering the portal that lead to the audience chamber, a sentry lowered his weapon and moved forward into a sunbeam. A small patch of discolouration, no bigger than a grapefruit, shaped like a melted candle, marred the otherwise perfect chestnut hue of his left side. He pirouetted slowly to ensure maximum visibility, then, once everybody got a clear look, then abandoned his post, leaving unimpeded and without speaking again. Two more followed suit, with another moving to Joseph and laying a reverent tendril across his shoulder region. The leader of the guard, however, was unmoved.

"This is a trick. Benito would not lie to us. We are on the verge of conquering worlds and these traitors and their ilk are all that remain to derail our greatest triumph."

The mood from his team didn't show a unanimous agreement. Kim could feel a lot of uncertainty growing. It fed her soul, slowing her heart and steeling her for what needed to be done. They just needed a gentle nudge, and she could get inside without further death, something Joe picked up on too, as he picked himself back up to speak again, this time with help from his former colleague who lent a series of tentacles for spiritual, and physical support.

"Just like you, I believed. I have served Benito faithfully for mega-periods, longer than some of you have existed in this dimension, many times a lot longer. I have never had cause to doubt his word. He gave no cause. So when he assured me that my family was safe in the blast zones, I trusted his word.

When I hadn't heard from them since the rebuilding, I believed his reasoning that they were simply too busy helping our glorious cause. When they remained unreachable only a few periods ago, I continued to have trust, just like you. I also equated the tales of unexplainable demise growing from the region to the discontent that always springs forth during periods of change. What reason did I have to doubt? Why would anybody? That is why I had no fear when I requested leave to visit my home region. I knew I would find my kin and their younglings, one of whom was close to an anniversary. I would celebrate this with them. When he denied my request on spurious grounds, I still believed.."

A crack broke his monologue off there, like the rotten limb of a tree grown too heavy. There was a sag in his chest cavity that Kim only noticed an hour ago, and it was now deep, and weeping a fluid that was burning tracks into his skin. A hissing sound, long and wet, like hot air leaving a bleeding radiator, showed he was gearing up to continue.

"I left anyway. What had I to fear? The danger wasn't real and our leader is secure here in these walls. I was of more use on the ground, identifying the roots of the building insurgency and pulling them out, casting them into righteous fire."

He chuckled, or at least that's what Kim hoped it was.

"When I reached the region.."

He paused again. Kim felt for his thoughts, finding nothing but pain.

"When I.. When I arrived, I found my kin huddled around a view-screen. A recording was still playing, in it our dear king.."

The last two words left his mouth-organ like gunshots, hard, flat and monotone, one syllable following the other. He waited for them to hit something, but the shots flew wild, high and wide, so he continued.

"They were deceased. My family crumbled to dust, their life force draining through cracks in their form as they watched a recording of Benito assuring them that their sacrifices would be worth it. I found their younglings in a lower storeroom blanketed in survival sheeting, with a note asking me to take care of them, but the radiation permeated their hiding space as it did everywhere, and their coverings only prolonged the exposure, trapping it with them. They perished in agony and fear, with a portrait of Benito overlooking them from the door that trapped them there. They died not understanding how he betrayed them, how he betrayed me. And now, the exposure I endured burying their remaining forms according to custom is eating me just the same. This isn't something any among you can deny.."

"Enough!"

The corporal slammed the butt of his weapon into the ornate railings protecting his flank, producing a long hollow noise that reverberated throughout, and a deep dent that would require substantial remedial work to repair. Once he had everyone's attention, he made a show of aiming the gun at Joseph, who did his best to draw himself upright with the help of his comrade, who stood firmly with his friend. Then another joined them, positioning himself between the gun barrel and its intended target.

"Move! This is treason. I will have you eviscerated in a pain room unless you stand aside this instant. Ah!"

A single shot ionised the air, passing at near light speed across the divide with a bright cerulean flash, leaving the smell of burned toast in its wake. The corporal lowered his gun, watching closely as Joseph fell prone, bouncing a little and then rolling to his left, the weapon he'd been holding skittering across the floor before coming to rest at the foot of a decorative column.

"I.. Don't.."

Now it was the corporals turn to fall. First his weapon, which bounced off a step, chipping the stone, and then stood upright for a few seconds on the tip of its barrel before succumbing once again to gravity and tottering forwards like a well tossed caber. His lower half followed, separated from the top by the blast so cleanly and suddenly that his mind hadn't reacted, although by the time his upper half had dropped, he knew exactly what had happened. The two pieces reconnected briefly on the ground, the upper landing almost perfectly on the lower with a sound like two coconut halves imitating a horse, then after sitting upright for a second or two, he toppled forwards like his weapon and spilled out onto the floor.

Kim sat still, gripping her gun tight, not sure how those present would receive this turn of events. All around, everybody's attention flitted between her, the now dead corporal, and Joseph, who was picking himself up with the help of four guardsmen who surrounded him with a web of tendrils. More joined, and then more. It quickly became an exodus. They moved aside as Kim approached, allowing her to hear Joe as he spoke.

"It is up to you now. I have done my part, do yours."

Then nothing. No more words, no more thoughts.

He was with his family.

The portal opened like the aperture of a film-camera, but with a glacial pace, each individual section folding into the outer frame with the urgency of a relaxed sloth on holiday. Beyond, in the throne room, she watched helplessly as Benito fled into a panic room behind the glimmering golden throne, sealing the space behind him and activating a security system that lit up like homicidal Christmas lights draped around a series of aesthetically placed chainsaws. They looked angry. In the time the doorway needed to open wide enough to pass an adult human through, Kim's newest companions had explained why doing so would be a terrible idea. As she waited for inspiration to provide an alternative course of action, a series of gigantic view-screens rose from the throne-room floor, each taller than a bus and just as wide.

Benito appeared on all of them.

"Kimberley, how pleasant it is to see you again."

She could feel him since he was only a couple of rooms away, and the sentiment wasn't genuine. Still, he waited for a response that she didn't have, like a comedian waiting for applause after telling a poor joke. His gaze dropped slightly, then darted to the left, where he gesticulated at an unseen individual who was presumably operating the camera. This gave Kim an opportunity to look past the liege at the space behind. It wasn't a safe room; it was a laboratory filled to the gunnels with familiar technology.

"I.. Is this thing on? I'll have you eviscerated if I find out.. Wait, hang on. There we go! Ah, Kimberley. Nothing to say?"

She didn't.

"You're not usually so quiet. In fact, I normally can't get you to stop yammering. You'll tell me anything if I pretend to be in any way interested in your inane and worthless existence."

Another pause, still no applause. Behind her, the remaining soldiers had arranged themselves such that they wouldn't be visible from whatever camera he was using to look into their room.

"You were so easy to manipulate, with your insecurities and desperation to fit in. You were so needy that you gave me everything I wanted without even needing to take it from you. Please, regale me once more with tales about how you never had friends. I want to hear all about your youngling period. Perhaps I can be the father figure you never had! Seriously, are you not going to say anything?"

Kim didn't need to feel his emotions to see the twitch fluttering in the corner of his right eye and hear the subtle increase in the volume of his speech. He threw another glance off the camera at the hapless minion.

"Are you sure she can hear me?"

It was all true. She'd told him in confidence, but it mattered no more, not now. Kim had lived a whole lifetime, maybe literally, since leaving the palace alive was unlikely, without ever connecting with anyone or anything other than her cat. There was always something between her and the world everyone else lived in, an impenetrable, invisible force-field that kept her feelings from escaping and left her unable to reciprocate others. She thought she hated everyone, that she just hadn't met the right people, but it wasn't them. That was the reason she could allow nobody in. She didn't want everyone to see how different she was, didn't want them to hate her as much as she hated herself. Here, though, without judgement and alone on an alien planet, she allowed everybody in, did everything she'd been taught not to. She over shared, flapped her hands, avoided eye-contact, and she focussed on her obsessions.

She was herself.

And it worked. Okay, perhaps not as well as it could, but Caruthers realized eventually.

"Okay, I am assured by my technician here, Kevin, that you can hear every word I am saying.."

Unable to resist, Kim cupped her hands to her ears and squinted, mustering the best confused expression she could manage at short notice, then shook her head. A single loud blast announced that Kevin was no longer employed, or in any way alive.

"Woah! Shit. Jesus. I was joking. You need to calm down a bit, Ben."

"You listen here, you little shit. I've won, you've lost. At any moment, a contingent of my most elite guard will converge on your position and eliminate you from reality.

Your lifespan has reduced to nothing, but know this. I have perfected your beacon. Behold it's might.."

The view panned back and up, showing an aircraft hangar sized room occupied by a transporter pad that was surrounded by security screens.

It resembled the prototype aboard the citadel, but this version was bigger, much bigger.

"In moments, it will achieve enough power to transplant half the population of your world into slavery in my mines. In exchange, my troops will enslave all who remain on the Earth, stripping your resources to feed this planet."

The twitch in his eye was still there, tapping morse code gibberish through his eyelids. The view panned back further to show Kim's nuclear reactor plumbed into the grid array that powered the machine. It appeared intact, which was really positive. She would need that power pretty soon. Ben flipped a control on an offscreen panel which lit up, bathing his upper torso in an unflattering light that stressed the creases. His gaze dropped while the corners of his mouth lifted just a smidge, baring what should have been teeth. As this happened, Kim heard a commotion behind her, but she fought the urge to glance back, needing to know what Ben's next move was.

"There! It is done. It will achieve critical mass in micro periods, and there is nothing you can do but watch as my guard tear you to pieces for my amusement. In fact, here they are. Take her."

The noise had died back, partly because there was less happening, but mostly because a gigantic creature was standing close behind her. She saw tentacles move around her at waist height, then a few more close to her neck, which wrapped around her, pulling her back and into the soldier.

Once he had her gripped tightly, the lower tentacles whipped forwards into the throne room, veering hard left and down, striking a series of coloured tiles on the ground just inside the door. At the fifth strike, the security system disengaged with a dimming of lights and a disappointed whine. Once it was inert, the tentacles released their grip and nudged her into the chamber, following close behind. After him, everybody else filed in, making an orderly line in front of the throne, and the screens before it.

Kim said nothing, keeping her gaze fixed on the screen-Benito, who was throwing things at the camera.

"Well, shit! I guess you guys have figured it out, huh? So, yeah, I lied to you. Everybody in the region is probably going to die, but it's worth it. Look, see, we're going to conquer a whole new world. We will speak of their sacrifices for generations. Seriously, just kill her. I'll give a promotion to whoever twists her head off."

No one moved.

"Fine. Look, Kim, I'll make you a deal. I'll send you back to your Earth. You can rule over a section, the north bit. Just do nothing rash, okay?"

"We have done what you asked."

The team had returned from the citadel.

* * *

BACK IN THE AUDIENCE CHAMBER, KEVIN HAD PATCHED in a series of terminals to the central intelligence grid with makeshift cabling and willpower. It wasn't perfect, but it allowed enough information for them to observe the radiation levels in the most severely affected region. With him was the citadel captain, who said nothing initially, eyeing Kim with a squint that suggested constipation, but thoughts that suggested regret tinged with a tiny amount of distrust that clung on like a child with separation anxiety being dropped off at the nursery.

"Our time is growing short."

It came from the throne room, where a small contingent of creatures were monitoring their erstwhile leader as he brought the beacon fully online. It was a lengthy procedure, requiring patience and precision even at the smaller scale Kim was used to. Planet-moving sizes would require a couple more minutes. She could still tear success from the jaws of failure.

On their significantly smaller screens, the incoming data was trending in the correct direction, which was downwards. The proton beam from the citadel had all but neutralised the larger population centres, so they were now concentrating on more remote regions where it was slightly less effective due to increased arboreal cover. Still, it was working, and that was all she could ask for.

"Thank you. I don't know why you have done this for us. We have done nothing to deserve it.."

The captain had loosened up on his distrust, although the squint still marred his face. Maybe he actually had constipation. Kim stopped him there. They all had greater concerns than exchanging meaningless platitudes.

"Don't sweat it. It was nothing, really. I'm just glad I could be of use. On that note, how's the whole breeching the doorway thing progressing?

What remained of the Kevin team was doing its best to open the blast door that stood between them and Benito, but it was proving more difficult than she'd imagined. She hadn't considered this tiny hiccup would derail her plans, since with everybody on her side, surely they would just open the portal for her. However, this entrance was brand spanking new and coded to the royal line, making it all but impossible to bypass.

"The locking mechanism is proving most troublesome, Kimber.. Er, Kim. I may need you to distract Benito in order to allow more time."

"I don't think that's going to work. Anybody else got a plan?"

At that, the citadel captain pushed into the throne room, moving up to the nearest and largest view screen, squaring his whatever he had instead of shoulders and, as Kim watched, addressed his ruler.

"This has gone on for too long, Ben.."

"That's Benito, or my fucking liege to you, Adolf. What do you want? I'm kind of busy in here, you know, bringing purpose to our peoples and uniting the planet while providing a much needed injection of freshness to our food supply."

It didn't surprise Kim that his name was Adolf, since all the names came from her subconscious and it was cribbing from a textbook on dictatorships she'd read in primary school. She was a little surprised he'd never told her, and that he'd grown a spine in the last ten minutes. She couldn't take her eyes off him.

"This is wrong! You have murdered innocent beings to follow a dream that has transformed into a nightmare."

"You've been talking to Joseph, huh? How is the old dog?"

"He's dead. He passed some short periods ago, defending the honour of his people and this world. Something you know little about."

Ben paused. The twitch was gone. When he spoke again,

it was slow and deliberate; the words forcing themselves out of his psyche despite his disdain.

"He was a good soldier, served me well, served his people well. We will remember him well."

Then, with more anger, as if spitting an unpleasant taste from his mouth.

"He turned on me and got exactly what he deserved, what you all deserve, and mark my words, you will all receive at the end of an un-maker."

With that, he whirled away from the console screen and started calibrating the targeting system. Kim could clearly see the colour of the single line tracing its way across the replica screen, red, the wavelength of Earth, probably. She needed a way in, and soon. Surely Kevin had something by now?

"Kevin, dude, I really need you to magic up some of that fine tech-shit and get me inside, like this second. How we doing?"

"This is proving most difficult. They coded the system directly to the genetic make-up of the ruling dynasty, an unbroken line that stretches back into pre-history. Everyone that has the genetic material needed to open the lock is inside that chamber. From outside all I can do is peruse the database of active coding. It's a short list."

"You can't add to it?"

"No, it is immutable. Created with memory stone from the southern quarries, the best quality. There are no defects or flaws."

"Great. Give me a second."

Kim jogged over to the throne room and chose a position facing Benito, next to Adolf, the captain, and patting him gently on the back. The universal symbol of 'I got this'. The gesture turned out to be less universal than she imagined. He got it a few seconds after growling at her, though, and moved back with heroic control of his disgust. She waved everyone else out too, waiting until it was just her and Ben.

"You know we're going to get in, right? And when we do, it's going to end badly."

"I know no such thing. And it is you for whom things will end. You can still take me up on my offer, you know, to live as a queen on your home planet. It's not such a terrible deal."

"I can't do that."

The targeting system locked at that moment, washing Ben's face with a red light that highlighted the sort of smile on his face from underneath, turning his profile into a horror movie poster, or the face of a child telling scary stories around a campfire. Only this story ended in genuine horror.

Then one of Kevin's earlier remarks percolated up through the darkness clouding her head. Something that had bothered her, but she wasn't sure exactly why. She ran back into the ante-chamber, saying nothing else to Ben, in part because she knew it would annoy him, mostly because she couldn't think of anything else to say. She saved her words for Kevin, who was slapping his terminal with a series of petulant tendrils while fighting a scream.

"Kev. You said it was a short list. The entry codes, a short list, right? Who else is on it other than Benito?"

Kevin stopped what he was doing and moved over to a different terminal, one with a row of pulsating cubes that kept time with an inaudible beat. A few squeezes later, and a list of hieroglyphs scrolled into view over the radiation data. He wasn't paying attention to the names.

"This will be of no use, as the royal line is the only one included in the system, and except for.. Oh."

* * *

NOTHING HAPPENED. THEN A SINGLE, SMALLISH BUTTON on the outer panel, recessed deep into the impenetrable wall, changed colour. It was the only external indicator that her hunch was correct. On the larger screen, Benito was still throwing frantic limbs at an unseen control station to cajole the errant targeting system into hurrying up. It was having none of it, a throwback to the time Kim accidentally forgot to isolate the twelve volt rail when designing the prototype board. Her mistake lead to a small explosion, a large bill for repairs and an even larger delay, which led to yet more cost and embarrassment, especially for the guy who'd taken credit for her solution and was now back-pedalling at an almost impossible rate. After that debacle, any design decisions required approval by consensus. Kim still did all the drawings, ordered the fabrication, maintained contact with the fabricators and so forth, but now the rest of the team could plausibly claim credit for the tricky bits, whilst avoiding blame for any errors. Kim took considerably more care with her work moving forwards, filling her drawings with multiple redundancies and backups of backups, resulting in less optimal solutions that would discharge all the capacitors if it detected too much fluctuation in any of the power rails, or a change in air pressure, of if, like now, it just felt like it.

It would take Ben at least five minutes to reset the system and re-enter the coordinates, keeping him occupied long enough to miss the equivalent change in colour of the door control on his side of the barrier.

He ignored it at first, after all, it was just one loud cracking noise in a whole cacophony of crackling and beeping, but as the air pressure equalised with a satisfying science-fiction whoosh, he looked up in time to catch Kim's eyes as the security door swung open.

She held his gaze for as long as she could, using all the calm she could muster, and hating every single second, but needing to hammer the point home. He'd lost, she'd won, and there was nothing he could say or do that could change the outcome. As her eyeballs dried, and she tried to work out how often she used to blink, and whether now was an appropriate time, Ben flipped a strange mechanical lever and backed away from the controls.

The lights went out. Everywhere.

After around five seconds, the emergency lighting kicked in, bathing everything in a less than satisfactory beige that wasn't unlike the glow of a forty-watt bulb trying to light an entire warehouse. If there hadn't been a stunning atrium atop the audience chamber, allowing the light of all three suns to flood in and fill every crevice, she probably would have struggled to pick Ben out from amongst the equipment. There was, though, and that light rendered his last-ditch hail-Mary of an escape plan moot. It didn't stop him from striking an unconvincing pose behind the stack of copies he'd made of Kim's notes, next to the corpse of whichever tech had failed him most recently.

"You know I can see you, right?"

He actually didn't. She could feel his thoughts again. Kim was expecting some fear, maybe a bit of pragmatic confidence. She didn't expect the utter rage that was consuming him at that moment. As he pulled himself upright again, brushing detritus from his torso with tentacles that had taken on a blueish hue, several other creatures appeared from behind a bulkhead separating the control room from the rest of the beacon. There were fifteen, none of whom looked at

Ben as they filed past, focussing instead on the weaponry being levelled at them by the room full of angry soldiers behind Kim. Their number had grown in the last few minutes, with ordinary citizens now among their ranks, having walked in through the fully open and very much unguarded main gates. The last of Ben's team, a Kevin, addressed him as he moved past.

"On reflection, sire. I don't think I wish to be a part of this team anymore."

The targeting system chose that moment to re-engage with a loud pop.

"I wouldn't recommend it, Ben."

It wasn't a threat. Kim felt a genuine sense that if he moved for the controls, his own citizens would tear him to pieces before he got there. The room was now filled with his citizens, dozens of them, squeezed into the space tight enough to make the emergency lighting necessary, nearly anyway. Kim moved over to the panel, which approximated her original design enough for her to know which blob powered things down, and squelched it with her thumb. All around, the noises stopped, and the lights returned to their normal, much less agitated, state.

"Screw you. You are not better than me, you know. Deep down, you would have done the same, taken whatever you needed to survive."

Kim thought about it for a second before responding.

"You're wrong. I would have done whatever I needed to do for you to survive, and there's a difference. I've defined my entire life by what other people think of me, how they perceive me. What I did never mattered to me, only that everybody else was happy with my end results.

Ben said nothing, but he slumped back against a chair,

making no effort to hold himself up, and that was enough. Kim redirected her attention.

"Kevin, can you patch it now?"

A rustling sound from behind the bulkhead preceded a single tendril carrying a spanner. Then the rest of him followed, along with several more tools and a crease on his face that approximated a raised eyebrow.

"Are these metric? I am unsure as to their designation. In fact, I am unsure what this metric is. Perhaps you can explain?"

"Funny. We don't have a massive amount of time. The beam emitter aboard the citadel is failing, and we need this assembly to ensure our ability to halt further spread here and now. If the radiation reaches.."

"I can do this, Kimberley."

Kevin didn't move right away, instead pausing a little, lightly tapping the end of the spanner against the wall and shuffling his foot-limbs. Kim waited to hear what he had to say.

"When I.. That is.. What I am saying is, when it connects.. You know that.. It's. What I'm saying is.."

"She knows."

Benito had rolled so that he could see the exchange. His chin muffled his voice slightly, but the old authority still carried.

"Once you connect the grid and use it to overlay your proton whatever onto this world, that'll be it, won't it? No more power, and even if there was enough to fire again, the beam thing will destroy the targeting system. She isn't going home. No, she has bigger ideas, right Kim?"

He slumped back into silence, staring out into the throne room. Kim turned to follow his gaze, landing on the throne itself, gleaming and smooth. A giant shimmering golden talisman that was currently unoccupied. A gap opened in the crowd, allowing her clear passage.

"You'll have to kill me first, of course. Then start a new dynasty, forged in my life-fluids. It's the way, and I am ready."

Her desk sat as it always had, disorganised, stained with many coffee rings and a tad too low to suit the chair she was sitting in. A single red line traced across her view screen, running left to right along the exact centre, solid, unbroken, and more than a little aggravating since this was the only remaining functional LCD screen she possessed and that line, drawn on with a kind of indelible ink that stung when touched, was obscuring the line of data she needed to read. She scrolled up a little. The southern hemisphere was looking favourable. Levels were down everywhere. In fact, previously uninhabitable surface regions were rebuilding briskly, with life returning to normal.

Well, as normal as possible, given this was an alien planet.

There was some initial resistance, entirely expected and natural. This planet had seen the rule of a single bloodline for a thousand generations, and a single despotic progenitor for the previous thousand years. This kind of change at the top was always likely to breed brief resistance. It helped that the interim administrator was someone with leadership qualities, someone others already looked up to. It was unfortunate that his name had stuck, but no one got the reference, so it was fine, she guessed.

"Kimberley? Adolf is requesting an update."

The front wall disappeared, replaced by a twenty foot high, high definition representation of an individual Kevin, who was only in the next room and really didn't need to use the intercom system.

"You know I can hear you if you just shout, right? Actually, you know what? Just come in here."

It took a few seconds.

"My liege, you summoned.."

"Knock it off. Have you registered to vote yet? You understand this whole election happens in, like, a handful of months, right? If your name isn't on the official lists, your vote won't count."

"I am still unsure how this democracy concept of yours works, if I am to be completely honest, my lady.. Er, Kimberley."

"Just Kim is fine. It's pretty simple.."

"Oh, no, I understand that a tally of prevailing opinion will select a leader from the proposed pool of candidates. I am just unsure how to be certain their bloodlines are pure and worthy."

"Well. We can't, and that's kind of the point. These candidates want to lead because they believe they can be a positive influence on this world, yes, even Benito, although his single issue platform of swift and deadly retribution against all who turned on him isn't exactly a vote winner.

They'll bring new ideas, fresh perspectives, and, most importantly, you can get rid of them in four years if it later turns out that they're shit at the job."

"I will vote for you, just Kim."

"And that vote would be a waste, since I'm not named on the ballot forms. I'll be voting for Adolf. He's really come into his own since the whole juice-gate thing blew over."

"Then I will also vote for Adolf, as you command.."

"No. That isn't how.. Who's your favourite? On the actual candidate list, who do you believe will be a good leader? Who says things that make sense to you and answers the questions you've been asking yourself?"

"Kevin. I shall vote for Kevin."

"That's the spirit. Kinda. So. What does Adolf need from me?"

"You may ask him yourself, exalted lead.. Kim. He is holding on to a secondary frequency."

With that, the huge view of the next door laboratory phased slightly, becoming a translucent rain of white and gold that passed through the desks and computer equipment, before solidifying into a concrete image of the planet's interim president, who was sitting far too close to the imaging source, filling most of the gigantic screen with a closeup of his right eye.

"Jesus! Could you move back a little?"

He hopped back enough that Kim and Kevin had a clear view of the campaign medal he'd struck in honour of the revolution. There were only four of them. Joseph and Caruthers wore theirs when buried with honours. Kim had hers hanging on a ribbon over the back of her swivel chair. When he spoke, he was still doing the voice.

"How are things progressing?"

Like someone trying to sound British after watching Australian television, he thought it made him sound important and Kim didn't have the heart to tell him otherwise.

"The south is almost completely safe. There is no reason that building can't begin there, but I'd keep it low level for a bit, keep exposure to a minimum for another week. How's things your end?"

"Preparations for our new democracy are complete, and the polling will occur as conceived. I am a little unsure on one.."

"Yes. You can absolutely vote for yourself."

"That is.. Excellent."

"I know, right? So, anyway.. shit."

A purple number had appeared on her LCD a few millimetres below the drawn on red line. It stood out for several reasons, the obvious being that it shone purple in a sea of otherwise nondescript off-white information, but there was more. It was much larger than the surrounding data, showing a spike in energy levels at an impossibly local scale, maybe a quarter mile across, a big spike, like a nuclear explosion big. Another peculiarity was the location. Amid an isolated continent, everybody had assured Kim was not only uninhabited, but was uninhabitable. Maybe it was a mistake? She hit refresh and watched the data recompile.

It wasn't a mistake.

"Listen, while I have you on the line. You asked Benito about the polar quadrant, right? He swore nobody had ever been there?"

"That entire region sits under a gigantic sheet of permanently frozen liquids. It is also beset with noxious gases that no creature can withstand, disintegrating all probes sent in to investigate. Kevin can confirm this."

Kevin nodded his agreement.

Kim refreshed again, hoping the anomaly was temporary and nothing of concern, but the results came back identical. It wasn't the first irregular reading to originate from that region, but until now, each one had self-resolved within a brief period, rarely more than seconds. The scanning equipment was aboard the citadel, and so unaffected by the lingering radiation. It had also passed a battery of tests after each reading, much to Kevins's annoyance. Now here it was again.

There wasn't much point in re-retesting the sensors. They were working fine.

"What do you see, Kimberley?"

"I.. Ah.."

More purple. The abnormalities were pinging up across the ice continent. Ten, now twelve, growing by the minute. The largest energy source, the original, had grown even larger, to where it contained enough energy to power a large city, or maybe something else, something less benevolent.

"Shit. Has anyone asked Ben about this yet?"

"He remains insistent that nothing exists out there. I used a persuasion-proboscis. It is unlikely that his answer was a deliberate falsehood."

"What did I say about torture? Never mind. I think somebody needs to travel there and figure out exactly what the hell is happening. Kevin.."

"I shall prepare for departure.."

On Kim's screen, the purple figures had multiplied further, reaching perhaps a hundred or more. Kim stood and turned to her boss.

"No. Kevin, I need you to take charge here. This is your lab, and almost entirely your work, anyway. You're needed here overseeing the cleanup. I'll head out."

He paused a moment to process the new information, then responded in a strong, confident tone.

"I will arrange for a team to travel with you."

ACKNOWLEDGMENTS

I want to thank my partner, Ross Moynihan, for their unwavering support during the writing of this book. The value of his support, insights, and encouragement cannot be overstated.

I am also thankful to Clare Mackintosh for her amazing writing course and the support of some fantastic test readers.

Special thanks also go to my cats, Wordsworth and Shakespeare, for their patience, understanding, love, and inexplicable need to jump on my keyboard during the long hours spent writing and revising.

Last, I extend my appreciation to all the readers who will embark on this literary journey with me. Your interest and engagement in my work inspire me to continue pursuing my passion for writing. Thank you all for being a part of this endeavour.

Nathan.

Nate Stone is obsessed with stories. Books or films, it doesn't matter. A former burger flipper, physics student, and now author, He loves mixing scientific mysteries with a touch of humour to create stories that make you think. Fascinated by all things, Nate writes novels filled with quirky characters, crazy adventures, and surprises that will keep you hooked.

His personal experience as an autistic person adds a special touch, making his stories resonate with everyone. When he's not busy writing about space adventures or crime, Nate likes to learn new fun facts, watch quiz shows on TV, or just relax with some cheesecake. Nate lives in North Wales with his partner and two cats, Wordsworth and Shakespeare.

Nathan can be found on the following social media.

facebook.com/nathanstoneauthor

instagram.com/nathanstoneauthor

goodreads.com/nathanstoneauthor